Conner Bailey's SHORT STORY PORTFOLIO

TABLE OF CONTENTS

THE LAND OF STORIES

AN AUTHOR'S ODYSSEY

THE LAND OF STORIES

AN AUTHOR'S ODYSSEY

CHRIS COLFER

ILLUSTRATED BY BRANDON DORMAN

LITTLE, BROWN AND COMPANY
NEW YORK BOSTON

Copyright © 2016 by Christopher Colfer
Excerpt from *The Land of Stories: Worlds Collide* copyright © 2017 by Christopher Colfer
Cover and interior art copyright © 2016 by Brandon Dorman
Endpaper illustrations © 2016 by Christopher Colfer
Cover copyright © 2016 by Hachette Book Group, Inc.

Hachette Book Group supports the right to free expression and the value of copyright. The purpose of copyright is to encourage writers and artists to produce the creative works that enrich our culture.

The scanning, uploading, and distribution of this book without permission is a theft of the author's intellectual property. If you would like permission to use material from the book (other than for review purposes), please contact permissions@hbgusa.com. Thank you for your support of the author's rights.

Little, Brown and Company
Hachette Book Group
1290 Avenue of the Americas, New York, NY 10104
Visit us at lb-kids.com

Originally published in hardcover and ebook by Little, Brown and Company in July 2016
First Trade Paperback Edition: June 2017

Little, Brown and Company is a division of Hachette Book Group, Inc.
The Little, Brown name and logo are trademarks of Hachette Book Group, Inc.

The publisher is not responsible for websites (or their content) that are not owned by the publisher.

The Library of Congress has cataloged the hardcover edition as follows:
Names: Colfer, Chris, 1990- author. | Dorman, Brandon, illustrator.
Title: The land of stories : an author's odyssey / Chris Colfer ; illustrated by Brandon Dorman.
Other titles: An author's odyssey
Description: First edition. | New York : Little, Brown and Company, 2016. | Series: The land of stories ; 5 | Summary: "Conner learns that the only place to fight the Masked Man's literary army is inside his own short stories. When the twins and their friends enter worlds crafted from Conner's imagination, the race begins to put an end to the Masked Man's reign of terror."
—Provided by publisher.
Identifiers: LCCN 2016016573| ISBN 9780316383295 (hardcover) |
ISBN 9780316383202 (ebook) | ISBN 9780316383165 (library edition ebook)
Subjects: | CYAC: Characters in literature—Fiction. | Imagination—Fiction. | Twins—Fiction. | Brothers and sisters—Fiction. | Magic—Fiction. | Youths' writings.
Classification: LCC PZ7.C677474 Lahh 2016 | DDC [Fic]—dc23
LC record available at https://lccn.loc.gov/2016016573

ISBNs: 978-0-316-38321-9 (pbk.), 978-0-316-38320-2 (ebook)

Printed in the United States of America

LSC-C

10 9 8

*To Will,
for playing hours of How Do You Spell?, What's
Funnier?, Would a Ten-Year-Old Understand It?,
and other interactive games while I write.
Thanks for being my secret weapon.*

———◆◆×◆◆———

"A WRITER IS A WORLD TRAPPED IN A PERSON."

—VICTOR HUGO

THE FAVORITE STUDENT

Willow Crest Unified School District spared no expense celebrating the retirement of a beloved principal. The community banquet hall was decorated so elegantly, there wasn't a trace of Senior Bingo from the night before. The tables were dressed with lacy tablecloths, floral centerpieces, and battery-operated candles. Each place setting had golden plates and more silverware than the guests knew what to do with.

Teachers, counselors, janitors, lunch ladies, and former students showed up in droves to say good-bye and wish the principal well. The retirement party was one of the classiest gatherings any of them had ever been to. However, as the guest of honor looked around at all the long faces, the occasion seemed more like a funeral than a celebration.

The newly appointed district superintendent tapped his champagne glass with a spoon and the hall became quiet.

"May I have your attention please?" he said into a microphone. "Good evening, everyone, I'm Dr. Brian Mitchell. As you know, we're here to celebrate one of the finest educators Willow Crest Unified School District has ever had the privilege of employing, Mrs. Evelyn Peters."

Her name was followed by a warm round of applause. A bright spotlight hit Mrs. Peters, who was seated at the front of the room beside Dr. Mitchell. She smiled and waved at the guests, but secretly she wished she had never agreed to the gathering. Special attention and compliments from her colleagues always made her uncomfortable, and tonight it was just getting started.

"I've been asked to say a few words about Mrs. Peters, which is very intimidating," Dr. Mitchell said. "It doesn't matter what I say, because rather than taking any praise to heart, I know she'll only be listening to my speech for grammatical errors."

The guests laughed and Mrs. Peters hid a giggle behind her napkin. Anyone who knew her knew it was true.

"It's easy to say someone is good at their job, but I know for a fact that Evelyn Peters is an *incredible* educator," Dr. Mitchell said. "Nearly three decades ago, long before she became a principal, I was in her first sixth-grade class at Willow Crest Elementary School. Prior to meeting her, my childhood had been very difficult. By the time I turned ten, both my parents were in prison and I was bouncing in and out of foster care. When I stepped into Mrs. Peters's classroom I could barely read. Thanks to her, by the end of the year, I was reading Dickens and Melville."

Many of the guests clapped, making Mrs. Peters blush. Most of them had lived or witnessed similar stories.

"We did not get along at first," Dr. Mitchell said. "She pushed me harder than anyone ever had. She gave me extra homework and made me stay after school and read aloud to her. At one point, I was so tired of the special treatment, I threatened to graffiti her house if it didn't stop. The next day she handed me a can of spray paint and a card with her address and said, 'Whatever you write, just make sure it's spelled correctly.'"

The hall erupted with laughter. The guests looked to Mrs. Peters to confirm the story and she nodded coyly.

"Mrs. Peters taught me much more than just how to read," Dr. Mitchell said, and his voice began to break. "She taught me the importance of compassion and patience. She was the only teacher I felt cared about *me* as much as my grades. She got me excited to learn and inspired me to become an educator. We're very sad to see her go, but had she applied for superintendent instead of retiring, we all know I would *never* have been hired."

Mrs. Peters wiped her glasses to distract the guests from

the tears forming in her eyes. Had it not been for this reception, she might never have acknowledged to herself all the differences she had made in so many lives.

"Now, please join me in a toast," Dr. Mitchell said, and raised his glass. "To Evelyn Peters, thank you for inspiring and teaching us all. Willow Crest Unified School District won't be the same without you."

Everyone in the hall raised their glasses to toast Mrs. Peters. When they finished, Mrs. Peters took the microphone and raised her glass back at them.

"Now, please allow me to say a few words," she said. "My late husband was also a teacher, and he gave me the best advice one educator could give to another. So, I would like to pass it along to you in case this is my last chance."

Everyone in the hall sat on the edge of their seats, especially the teachers.

"As teachers, we must not guide our students to become the people *we wish them to be*, but elevate them to become the people *they were meant to be*. Remember, the encouragement we give our students may be the only encouragement they ever receive, so don't use it sparingly. After twenty-five years of teaching grammar school and my brief administration experience, I can assure you my husband was absolutely right. And since that is the best lesson I can teach you, I'll say for the last time, *class dismissed*."

The conclusion of her speech was met with a standing ovation. After a few moments of applause Mrs. Peters urged the guests to sit, but it only made them cheer louder for her.

The lights were dimmed and a screen was lowered. Dr. Mitchell and Mrs. Peters took their seats and watched as group photos of Mrs. Peters's classes were projected, starting with her very first sixth-grade class from almost thirty years before. As the slide show commenced, the former students laughed at their eleven- and twelve-year-old selves and the ridiculous hairstyles and clothes they had sported in earlier decades. Especially noted was how little Mrs. Peters had changed over the years. In every picture the educator's hair, glasses, and floral dresses were exactly the same. It was as if Mrs. Peters were frozen in time while the world changed around her.

The slide show made Mrs. Peters more emotional than anything else that night. It was like watching a family album flash before her eyes. She remembered the name of each face she saw. Most of the students she still knew personally or she knew what they had gone on to become, but there were a few she had lost contact with completely. It was a painful feeling to have been so close to a child at one point, then later to feel as if they had disappeared into thin air.

Mrs. Peters's students were the closest thing to children she had ever had. She hoped they were all happy and healthy, wherever they were. If she was no longer a staple of compassion and guidance in their lives, she hoped they had found someone who was.

"Evelyn?" Dr. Mitchell whispered.

Mrs. Peters still found it strange for a former student to address her by her first name—even if he *was* the superintendent.

"Yes, Dr. Mitchell?" she whispered back.

"Did you ever have a favorite student?" he asked with a grin. "I know we're not *supposed* to have favorites, but is there one child who stands out to you? Besides me, of course."

Mrs. Peters had never thought about such a thing. She had taught over five hundred students in her career and remembered each for different reasons, but selecting a *favorite* had never been a priority.

"I definitely *enjoyed* some more than others, but I could never choose a favorite," she said. "That would require judgment, and I always thought judging a child is like judging an unfinished piece of art. Every child enters a classroom with his or her own set of obstacles to face, whether behavioral or academic. It's a teacher's job to identify those issues and help students overcome them, but never to belittle a student for them."

Dr. Mitchell had never thought of it that way. Even in adulthood, he was still learning a thing or two from Mrs. Peters.

"I may be a superintendent, but I'll always be your student," he said.

"Oh, Dr. Mitchell." Mrs. Peters laughed. "No one ever stops being a student in the classroom of life."

Even though she'd thought not answering was the best answer, Mrs. Peters quickly realized she was mistaken. A picture appeared on the screen of her final sixth-grade class, three years earlier. She scanned the faces of her former students and stopped at a pair of twelve-year-old twins named Alex and Conner Bailey.

Alex's hair was neatly tucked behind a pink headband, and she held a stack of books close to her heart. A large grin filled her face because school was her favorite place in the world. Her brother, on the other hand, was puffy eyed and his mouth hung open. He appeared to have just woken up from a nap and to have had no clue the photo was being taken.

Mrs. Peters laughed because they looked exactly as she remembered them, and the picture reminded her of how much she missed them.

Both of the Bailey twins had unexpectedly transferred schools before Mrs. Peters had a chance to say good-bye. Alex went to live with her grandmother in Vermont halfway through the seventh grade, and then Conner joined her the following year. Even though their mother still lived in town, Mrs. Peters had been assured they were better off with their grandmother.

As far as Mrs. Peters knew, Alex moved away to attend a school for advanced learners. But it was still a mystery as to why Conner had gone to join her.

The year before he moved, Conner had run off during a school trip in Europe with another student, Bree Campbell. The stunt seemed entirely out of character for both students, who had clean records up to that point. Had Conner stayed in Mrs. Peters's school, he would have been punished appropriately, as Bree had been, but Mrs. Peters never thought it warranted a transfer to another school district.

The entire situation was very suspicious and personally upsetting for Mrs. Peters. Conner had just discovered a natural talent for writing and was excelling in school for the first time. Wherever he was now, Mrs. Peters hoped Conner had found someone else to encourage him. To her, there was nothing worse in the world than a student's wasted potential.

The slide show ended and dessert was served in the banquet hall. After a dozen more complimentary speeches from former colleagues and students, the evening finally came to an end.

Mrs. Peters loaded her car with a stack of farewell cards and an armful of bouquets. She was looking forward to a quiet night at home so she could decompress from the long and emotional evening. On her way home, she unintentionally drove past Willow Crest Elementary School. Mrs. Peters slammed on her brakes and parked her car. The school reminded her of one more good-bye she had to make before officially retiring.

Mrs. Peters dug through her large purse to find the key to her old sixth-grade classroom. Luckily the locks hadn't been changed, and she entered room 6B without any trouble. But instead of feeling a wave of nostalgia like she expected, she hardly recognized the dark room.

The current teacher decorated very differently than Mrs. Peters had. The desks were arranged in groups instead of rows. The walls that used to hold shelves of dictionaries and encyclopedias were now lined with computers and tablets. The posters of world-renowned authors and scientists had been replaced with posters of celebrities holding their favorite books—books Mrs. Peters wasn't convinced they had read.

Mrs. Peters felt like an actor stepping onto someone else's stage. She couldn't believe how much a classroom could change in such little time. It was as if she had never taught there at all. The only similarity was the teacher's desk, which was kept in the exact place Mrs. Peters had kept her desk for twenty-five years. The retiree sat in the chair behind it and looked around the classroom bittersweetly.

She hoped the decor wasn't an indication of anything other than the new teacher's taste. She hoped the same morals and values she had taught were still being shared in her absence. She hoped the new technology was enhancing those lessons, and not replacing them with lesser ideology. Most of all, Mrs. Peters hoped the new teacher *cared* about teaching as much as she did.

Before getting depressed about it, Mrs. Peters reminded herself she would have felt worse if there *hadn't* been any change. After all, it was thanks to teachers like her that the current generation was progressing so effortlessly into the future.

And just like all the teachers who had come before her, it was time for Mrs. Peters to pass the torch to her successors. She hadn't expected letting go would be so difficult.

"Good-bye, classroom," Mrs. Peters said. "I'll miss the lessons we taught together, but even more, I'll miss the lessons we learned."

Just as she stood from the desk to leave, a sudden gust of wind circled the classroom. Papers blew off the walls and a vortex formed in the center of the room. A bright flash illuminated the dark classroom like a bolt of lightning and Mrs. Peters dived under the desk for safety.

Peeking out from underneath the desk, Mrs. Peters could see two pairs of feet appear out of thin air. One wore tennis shoes and the other a pair of sparkling slippers.

"Well, this looks a lot different from when we were sixth-graders," said the familiar voice of a young man. "*Aw man*, how come they get computers and we didn't? I would have stayed awake more if we had those."

"Sign of the times," said another familiar voice, that of a young woman. "I'm sure it won't be long before they stop building schools altogether. Every kid will be plugged into a device and taught at home. Can you imagine anything worse?"

"Let's focus on one crisis at a time," the young man said. "You look around the computer desks and I'll look through the file cabinet. My stories have got to be in here somewhere."

The feet split up into different corners of the room. Mrs. Peters knew she had heard those voices many times before, but she couldn't picture the faces they belonged to.

"If they weren't in her old office, what makes you think they'll be in here?" the young woman asked.

"It's the only place we haven't looked," he said. "Teachers are sentimental—maybe she put them in a time capsule or something? I just want to look everywhere before we break into her house."

Mrs. Peters couldn't take the suspense any longer. She slowly got to her feet and peered over the desk. As soon as she identified the newcomers she let out a loud gasp, causing them both to jump.

"Mr. Bailey! Miss Bailey!" she said. The twins had grown so much since the last time Mrs. Peters had seen them, especially Alex. Mrs. Peters couldn't help gawking at the long, beautiful gown she wore. It was the color of the sky and sparkled as she moved, like something out of a fairy tale.

Alex and Conner Bailey were just as stunned to see their former teacher as she was to see them.

"Um...hi, Mrs. Peters!" Alex said with a nervous laugh. "Long time no see!"

"Mrs. Peters?" Conner asked. "What are you doing here so late?"

Mrs. Peters crossed her arms and glared at them over her glasses.

"I was about to ask you the same question," she said. "How did you get inside without a key? Where did all that light and wind come from? Are you in the middle of some sort of prank?"

The twins stared at each other for a moment in silence, but neither knew what to tell her. Without any other ideas, Conner began prancing around the room waving his arms through the air like seaweed.

"Mrs. Peters, this is a dreeeeam!" he sang. "You ate some bad sushi and now you're having a nightmare about your former students! Leave the classroom before we manifest into large school supplies!"

Mrs. Peters scowled at his terrible attempt to fool her, and he quickly dropped his arms to his sides.

"I have a perfectly good grasp over my consciousness, Mr. Bailey," she said. "Now, will one of you explain how you *appeared* in this classroom or do I need to call the police?"

Explaining the situation to someone in the Otherworld should have been an easy task by now, but as the twins stood across from their former teacher in their former classroom, they felt like they were twelve years old again. Mrs. Peters was impossible to lie to, but she would never believe the truth.

"We would, but it's a really long story," Alex said.

"I have a master's degree in English—I *love* long stories," Mrs. Peters said.

The retiree's stern expression suddenly faded from her face. She looked back and forth between the twins, almost in disbelief. It was as if she had figured out the truth all on her own and was having difficulty accepting it.

"Wait a second," Mrs. Peters said. "Does this have anything to do with *the fairy-tale world*?"

The twins' jaws dropped in perfect unison. This was the last thing they expected to come out of her mouth. It was like they were in a film that had suddenly skipped a scene.

"Um . . . *correct*," Conner said. "Well, *that* was easy."

Alex gave Conner a dirty look—certain there was some information he had forgotten to share with her.

"Conner, you told Mrs. Peters about the fairy-tale world?" Alex asked.

"Of course not!" Conner said. "It was probably Mom! She had to explain our transfers somehow!"

When the twins looked back at Mrs. Peters, she was making a face they had never seen her make before. Her eyes were large and glistening and she covered a huge smile with both hands. The retiree looked like an excited little girl.

"Oh my word," Mrs. Peters said. "After all these years, I finally know it was real. . . . I can't tell you how much time I've spent wondering if it was just a dream or a hallucination, but you've appeared just like *she* did . . . and in a dress just like *hers*. . . ."

The twins couldn't have been more confused.

"*What* was real?" Conner asked.

"*Who* are you talking about?" Alex pressed.

"When I was a very little girl, I was sick in the hospital with pneumonia," she said. "Late one night, while the nurses were busy with the other patients, a kind woman wearing a dress just like yours appeared in my room. She brushed my hair and read me stories through the night to make me feel better. I figured she must have been some sort of angel. When she left, I begged her to tell me who she was. The woman told me she was a Fairy Godmother and lived in the fairy-tale world."

The twins couldn't believe their ears. They had known Mrs. Peters for years but never knew she had any knowledge of the fairy-tale world.

"Whoa, *small worlds*," Conner said.

"That woman was our grandmother," Alex said. "She and other fairies used to travel to this world and read fairy tales to children in need. Grandma said the stories always gave children hope."

Mrs. Peters had a seat on the desk and held a hand over her heart.

"Well, she was right," she said. "Once I was healthy, I devoured fairy tales for the rest of my childhood. I even became a teacher so I could share the same stories with others."

"No way!" Conner said. "That's why you made us do those reports on fairy tales when we were your students! This is *meta*!"

"Conner, I hate when you use that word," Alex said.

"I agree with Mr. Bailey—*this is meta*!" Mrs. Peters laughed. "Words can't describe how grateful I am to finally know the truth. All this time, you weren't living in another state; you were living with your grandmother in the fairy-tale dimension! That explains your abrupt transfers, why your mother was so vague about the details—and I'm assuming it has something to do with Mr. Bailey's abandonment of the school's European trip."

"Guilty," Conner said sheepishly. "I'm not a delinquent after all!"

"And your grandmother, is she still around?" Mrs. Peters asked.

She seemed so happy, the twins didn't want to break the news to her.

"Actually, Grandma passed away a little more than a year ago," Alex said.

"Yeah, just after she *slayed a dragon*!" Conner bragged. "But that's another long story that will only lead to longer stories—trust me, our future biographer is going to have his hands full—and right now we don't have time to explain! We're actually here for something really important."

"Oh?" Mrs. Peters said.

"Remember when you saved my short stories in a portfolio—for when I started applying to colleges? Do you know where those are?" he asked.

"You don't have your own copies?" Mrs. Peters asked.

"No, they were handwritten," Conner said. "It was painful enough writing the originals—my hand couldn't take making copies."

"Mr. Bailey, if you're going to be a writer, you need to learn to secure your work—"

"Yeah, I'm learning that the hard way," Conner said. "Look, something terrible has happened in the fairy-tale world, and we need my short stories to save it."

"I'm sure you have a million questions, but like Conner said, we're really crunched for time," Alex added. "If you know where they are, *please* point us in the right direction. A lot of people are depending on us."

From the tone of their voices and the urgency in their eyes, Mrs. Peters could tell they were very serious, so she didn't question them further.

"You're in luck," she said. "I have them with me."

Mrs. Peters retrieved her purse from under the desk and pulled a large binder out of it. She flipped through the binder, and the twins saw it was filled with hundreds of student essays, math tests, book reports, history exams, and artwork.

"Today was my last day before retirement," Mrs. Peters said. "I cleaned out my desk and I found *this*. It's a collection I've kept over the years of the student work that made me the most proud to be an educator. Whenever I had a particularly rough day, I would take a look through this and be inspired all over again."

When she reached the end of the binder, Mrs. Peters unclipped it and handed Conner a stack of papers with messy handwriting.

"Here are your short stories, Mr. Bailey," she said.

The twins sighed with relief. After a long search, they had finally found them! Conner tried taking them out of Mrs. Peters's hand, but she tightened her grip.

"I'll only give you these if you make me a promise," she said.

"He'll do whatever you want!" Alex said desperately.

Conner nodded. "Yeah, what she said!"

Mrs. Peters looked straight into his eyes. "When this troubling chapter of your lives comes to an end, promise me you'll go back to school and continue writing," she said.

Conner was expecting something much worse than that. "Okay, I promise," he said.

"Good," she said. "The world needs writers like you to inspire them, Mr. Bailey. Don't take your talent for granted, and don't let it go to waste."

Mrs. Peters released her grip on the papers, and Conner's short stories were finally in his possession. Alex was thankful it had been an easy exchange—she had been prepared to hex Mrs. Peters with a paralyzing spell if she needed to.

"I'm happy I made your binder," Conner said.

"I never thought I'd say this, Mr. Bailey, but you are the closest thing to a favorite student I'll ever have," she confessed.

"Me?" Conner said. "But . . . but . . . *why?*"

"Yeah, *why?*" Alex said before she could stop herself.

"With all due respect, Miss Bailey, when I'm old and my memory fades I won't remember the students who got the best grades or had the best attendance," Mrs. Peters said. "I'll remember the ones who progressed the most, and your brother has come a long way from taking naps in my class."

"I don't think I progressed any more than anyone else did," Conner said with a shrug.

"That's because no one has the privilege of looking at

themselves through someone else's eyes," Mrs. Peters said. "I watched you struggle after your father died—but you didn't let yourself struggle for long. Rather than wallowing in grief, you developed a strong sense of humor. Soon I was constantly condemning your clown antics in class. The following year, when I became principal, I had a feeling there was a remarkable imagination behind that wit. I had your teacher send me samples of your creative writing and my suspicion was right. You chose to *grow* from tragedy—and it takes a very strong person to do that."

Alex smiled proudly at her brother. Conner's whole face turned bright red—he was as good at taking compliments as Mrs. Peters was.

"Aw shucks," he said. "I guess I'm more sophisticated than I thought."

"You'd be surprised," Mrs. Peters said. "I learned a lot about you from your writing, possibly more than you intended to share. Perhaps as you look through your stories again, you'll learn a thing or two about yourself."

This made Conner a little nervous—how much of himself had he exposed? When he wrote, Conner only worried about telling a good story; he never thought about the fingerprints he left between the lines. He suddenly felt like he was in the shower and had forgotten to lock the bathroom door.

"Thank you, Mrs. Peters," Conner said. "For what it's worth, you've always been my favorite, too. I never would have liked writing if it weren't for you."

Mrs. Peters was so happy she had stumbled upon the Bailey twins tonight. Knowing she helped shape the twins into the wonderful and responsible young adults they'd become was the greatest retirement gift she could have received. She put the binder back into her purse and then glanced up at the clock. It was disheartening to see that the new teacher had obnoxiously decorated the clock to look like the sun.

"I can't believe it's past midnight," Mrs. Peters said. "I'm absolutely exhausted. If you'll both excuse me, I think I'll head—"

With another gust of wind and a flash of light, the Bailey twins disappeared into thin air. It made Mrs. Peters laugh because their quick exit confirmed something she believed with her whole heart.

"Students," she said. "They come and go so quickly."

CHAPTER ONE

THE MASKED EMPIRE

The air was filled with so much smoke, you could barely see the sky. Every time it was cleared by a strong wind, it was quickly replenished from another pillaged town or forest fire. During the day, the sun looked like a weak lantern shining through a brown sheet. At night, seeing a star had become as rare as spotting a shooting star.

The fairy-tale world had faced many troubling times in recent years, but never anything like this. It was the first time in history that *happily ever after* seemed impossible to regain.

Over the course of one night, the Wicked Witch of the West's Winkie army attacked the Charming Kingdom and the Troblin Territory. Her flying monkeys were sent to terrorize the Elf Empire and the Corner Kingdom. The Queen of Hearts marched her card soldiers through the Center Kingdom and then wreaked havoc on the Eastern Kingdom. Captain Hook's band of pirates poisoned the waters of Mermaid Bay, sending the mermaids fleeing deeper into the ocean. Captain Hook's flying ship, the *Jolly Roger*, attacked the Fairy Kingdom, leaving the palace in pieces. Then the captain took the Northern Kingdom by storm.

The soldiers and villagers of every kingdom, who had once banded together to fight off the Grande Armée, were no match for these invaders. Their homes and towns were pillaged and burned to the ground. Their farms and stables were raided, and their livestock and horses were stolen.

All the fairies were presumed dead or in hiding. The kings and queens had lost their thrones, and their homes lay in ruins. The forests were slowly burned one at a time, giving the animals and refugees fewer and fewer places to hide.

The kingdoms and territories of yesterday ceased to exist. All the land in the fairy-tale world had been combined into one large empire ruled by the infamous Masked Man and his newly assembled Literary Army.

The elf, troll, goblin, and human civilians from all over the fairy-tale world were rounded up and marched into the

Northern Kingdom. They were pushed into Swan Lake, just beside the severely damaged Northern Palace. The lake had been dried out by the Literary Army, making it a deep, muddy crater, perfect to hold the civilians prisoner. By the time the lake was filled, the sun had started its descent in the western sky. The Literary soldiers pointed their captives' attention to a large balcony of the palace.

Doors opened and the Masked Man appeared. His entire head was covered in a mask made of rubies and jewels with only two slits for his eyes. His raggedy clothes had been upgraded to a well-tailored suit. He wore a long black cape with a collar that towered sinisterly over his head.

The Masked Man finally looked like the menacing ruler he had always wanted to become.

His entrance was met with a thunderous rumble of booing and hissing, which only escalated when the Queen of Hearts, the Wicked Witch of the West, and Captain Hook joined him on the balcony. The Masked Man held his hands out in front of him, embracing the noise as if it were applause.

"Now, now, now," he said. "Is that how you address your new *emperor*?"

The title was not received well by his imprisoned audience. Many of the civilians had stashed food in their clothing before being forced from their homes, and rather than saving it, they threw it angrily at the Masked Man. The self-appointed emperor was pelted with tomatoes, plums, and heads of lettuce.

The civilians roared with laughter. Even the Wicked Witch of the West cackled at the embarrassing scene. But the Masked Man wouldn't let his first moments as emperor become a mockery.

"SILENCE OR I'LL KILL YOU ALL!" the Masked Man yelled.

The food throwing stopped, and a tense hush fell over the dried-up lake. He had already destroyed their villages and homes; there was no telling how far he'd go to gain respect. A winged monkey brought the Masked Man a rag, and he wiped the food off his clothing.

"From this day forward you will no longer be the *people* of your pathetic kingdoms, but the *property* of this empire," he announced. "Disrespect me again, and I will not show you the same mercy as your weak kings and fragile queens. Anyone who dares to cross me will not only lose their own lives, but will first watch as I take their families' lives as well!"

Children throughout the lake began to cry, and their parents held them tightly. It seemed the darkest days were still ahead.

"I've brought you all here to witness the birth of a new era," the Masked Man preached. "But before we achieve a new future, the ways of the past must be destroyed—and the *leaders* of the past are no exception!"

The Masked Man gestured to a large wooden platform below the balcony, on the lawn between the palace and the dried lake. A very tall man in a long black cloak climbed to the top of the platform and placed a large wooden block in the center.

A dozen flying monkeys pulled a wagon out from behind the palace. It carried all the former kings and queens of the fairy-tale world: Cinderella, King Chance, Sleeping Beauty, King Chase, Snow White, King Chandler, Troll-bella, Empress Elvina, Rapunzel, Sir William, and even the young princesses Hope and Ash. All the royals had their hands tied together and were blindfolded and gagged with strips of white cloth.

The tall man on the platform withdrew a large silver axe from inside his cloak. The civilians began screaming and shouting in horror once they realized the purpose of it—*the Masked Man was going to have the royal families executed*!

Although they couldn't see, the kings and queens knew what was happening by the sound of the terrified crowd. They fought against their restraints, but they didn't budge. The civilians desperately tried to climb out of the dried lake to save their rulers, but they were kicked back into the mud. The card soldiers stood around the lake's perimeter and locked arms, forming a wall to block them.

The Masked Man laughed wildly at all the terror he was causing. Winkie soldiers pulled the royals out of the wagon and pushed them up the steps to the platform, then stood guard around it. The cloaked executioner sharpened his axe as he awaited his cue to begin.

"Start with the men, then the women, then the *children*,"

the Masked Man ordered. *"Your Majesty*, if you would please do the honors..."

The Queen of Hearts stepped to the edge of the balcony. With enlarged eyes and a devious grin, she looked down at the distressed royals like they were a delicious snack.

"OOOOFFFF WITH THEIR HEEEEEAAAAADS!" she roared.

The lake erupted in protest. The women cried desperate pleas for the execution to stop; the men yelled profanities at the Masked Man for being so cruel. The frightened royal families huddled together in a corner of the platform and trembled.

The executioner selected King Chance to be his first kill. He grabbed him by the arm and dragged him to the block. Cinderella and Hope screamed through their gags when they realized he was no longer standing beside them.

The executioner forced Chance into a kneeling position and placed his head on the wooden block. He held the axe above the king's neck and practiced swinging. With each swing, the civilians gasped, fearing it was the fatal blow. Finally, the executioner raised his axe higher into the air than he had raised it before. The pleas and screams from the helpless bystanders multiplied; the royals knew it was only a matter of seconds before the king lost his head.

The executioner brought the axe down—but as he did, he spun his body so it sliced the platform floor instead of the king's neck. Suddenly, the floor caved in, causing the executioner and all the royals to fall through the platform and disappear from sight. It was so unexpected, the panicked crowd went silent—this couldn't have been part of the plan.

"WHAT JUST HAPPENED?" the Masked Man screamed from the balcony. "GET THEM OUT OF THERE!"

Just as the Winkie soldiers went to inspect the platform, *three large horses burst out from inside it*! Porridge, Buckle, and Oats had been under the platform the entire time. They were pulling a carriage with the executioner and all the royals safely aboard. *The platform had been a large trapdoor!*

"NOOOO!" the Masked Man screamed, and leaned over the balcony as far as he could to get a better look.

To his horror, he saw Goldilocks on Porridge and Jack on Buckle! The couple steered the horses and the carriage into the forest beyond the palace, knocking over dozens of Winkie soldiers as they went. *The execution had turned into a rescue mission right before the Masked Man's eyes!*

Goldilocks glanced back at the rescued royals. "Is everyone all right?"

The royals moaned through their gags. Still blindfolded, they had no clue what was going on. The executioner threw off his cloak—*it had been the Tin Woodman all along*!

"Don't fret, Your Majesties!" he said. "This is a rescue!"

The Tin Woodman sliced off the royals' restraints with his axe.

"We're not out of it yet!" Jack said. "Everyone stay low! This is going to be a bumpy ride!"

Meanwhile, the elf, troll, goblin, and human civilians embraced one another and cheered as their leaders got away. The Masked Man was so furious, he was practically breathing fire. The visible skin around his eyes turned so red, it matched the rubies in his mask.

"AFTER THEM! ALL OF YOU!" he ordered the Literary Army. "DON'T LET THEM ESCAPE!"

The rescue party was chased through the forest by droves of Winkies and card soldiers on horseback. The fleet of flying monkeys followed them from the smoky sky. As the royals removed their blindfolds and looked around, an escape didn't seem likely—there was no way their carriage stood a chance against the approaching Literary soldiers. Luckily, Jack and Goldilocks had friends with a few tricks up their sleeves.

The Winkies and card soldiers were gaining speed and moving closer to the carriage. Goldilocks nodded to Jack and he whistled. Suddenly, Sir Grant and Sir Lampton appeared with dozens of their men on horseback. They formed a protective circle around the carriage of royals and knocked the approaching Literary soldiers to the ground.

"Sir Lampton, is that you?" Cinderella said.

"Hello, Your Majesty," he said. "I wish the circumstances were different, but I'm very pleased to see you're alive!"

Sir Grant and Sir Lampton's men weren't alone—they shared their horses with the Lost Boys from Neverland. When they were close enough, Tootles, Nibs, Curly, and the Lost twins jumped off their horses and landed in the carriage with the royals. The Lost Boys pulled slingshots out of their pockets and launched rocks at the Winkies and card soldiers, hitting them in the face and knocking them off their horses.

"This is fun!" Tootles said.

"Let's make it a game!" Curly said.

"Ten points for the big square ones, and five for the gold guys," Nibs decided.

"Deal!" the Lost twins said.

The Lost Boys giggled so hard watching the Winkies and cards fall off their horses that tears streamed down their rosy faces. They hadn't had this much fun since they left Neverland.

Thanks to the Lost Boys and Sir Grant and Sir Lampton's men, the number of Literary soldiers trailing the carriage had significantly lowered. But there were still plenty of Winkies and cards left to be concerned about. Luckily, the rescue party was close to the next phase of their plan.

As they raced farther into the forest, Goldilocks spotted an arrow sticking into the side of a tree—*it was a sign*!

"Jack, I see the arrow!" she said. "We're almost to the Merry Men!"

Porridge, Buckle, and Oats were getting tired and starting to slow down, so Jack was relieved to hear it. He whistled toward the treetops as loudly as he could.

"WAS THAT THE WHISTLE WE'VE BEEN WAITING FOR, OR DO MY EARS DECEIVE ME?" shouted a boisterous voice from the trees.

Jack rolled his eyes and whistled again.

"THERE IT IS AGAIN! OUR TIME HAS COME, MERRY MEN! ATTACK!"

Robin Hood and his Merry Men swung down from the treetops on ropes like monkeys on vines. Little John, Alan-a-Dale, and Will Scarlet slammed into the Winkies and cards. They knocked them to the ground and stole their horses. Robin Hood flipped through the air, landing in the carriage with the royals. He took off his hat and bowed to the queens.

"HAVE NO FEAR, LADIES, FOR THE TRUE HERO HAS ARRIVED!" he said. He winked at them flirtatiously and kissed Rapunzel's hand, which Sir William didn't appreciate.

"Gosh, I really hate that guy," Jack whispered to Goldilocks.

Robin Hood reached for the bow and quiver of arrows fastened to the back of his vest and joined the Lost Boys in shooting Winkies and cards off their horses. After hitting a few, the Prince of Thieves grew cocky and started showing off for the queens, striking ridiculous poses as he fired.

"DON'T BE INTIMIDATED, LOST BOYS," he said, and rubbed Tootles's head. "BATTLE IS MEANT FOR MEN."

Tootles snapped his slingshot against Robin Hood's buttocks, causing him to squeal like an injured swine.

"Tootles, save it for the enemy!" Goldilocks reprimanded.

"Sorry, it slipped!" Tootles said.

By now, the Winkies and card soldiers had all been knocked to the ground or had retreated to the Northern Palace. However, the chase wasn't over yet. Piercing screeches echoed through the forest as the flying monkeys descended upon the rescue party.

Jack whistled again. *"Peter, it's your turn!"* he yelled.

Like a rocket, Peter Pan flew out from underneath the carriage where he had been hiding. It happened so fast, he startled the royal families. The Boy Who Never Grew Up handed two bags of firecrackers to Little John and Alan-a-Dale, and matches to Will Scarlet. The Merry Men tossed the firecrackers to Will Scarlet, and once he lit them, Peter quickly scooped them up. The boy flew above the treetops and threw the firecrackers at the approaching flying monkeys.

Each explosion shocked and discombobulated the flying monkeys, and they fluttered to the ground. Peter and the Merry Men continued their firecracker relay until all the flying monkeys had dropped from the sky.

"Take THAT, you overgrown bats!" Peter chuckled.

Trollbella watched Peter Pan in astonishment. Her heart was beating so fast, if it had wings, she could have joined him in flight.

"It's like I was beheaded and went to heaven!" she said. "He's just like Butterboy—but he *floats* and *sparkles*! *I didn't know a boy so wonderful could exist! Stop it, Trollbella! Pull yourself together! You promised yourself you wouldn't love again until the world was in better condition!*"

Still, the Troblin Queen tried to catch the trails of fairy dust Peter left as he flew beside the carriage.

Finally free from the Masked Man's Literary Army, the royals and their rescuers could all breathe a little easier. Goldilocks and Jack took the reins of their horses and steered them into a sharp left, leading the party straight into the Dwarf Forests.

"Where are we going?" Snow White asked.

"Someplace the Masked Man and his army will never find us," Goldilocks said.

"Now, everyone keep as quiet as possible," Jack instructed. "The less noise we make, the better."

The royals obeyed his instructions. The rescue party spent the rest of the day traveling deeper and deeper into the Dwarf Forests. The kings and queens glanced around nervously at the thick forest, as most of them had never been to these parts before. They kept waiting for something frightening to appear, but the forest that infamously housed the most dangerous creatures and criminals in the fairy-tale world seemed rather empty.

They reached a hilly part of the woods just before nightfall. Goldilocks stopped the procession in front of a large boulder sticking into the hillside. She covered her mouth and made a peculiar shape with her hands.

"Coo-KOO, coo-KOO!" she called.

The birdcall echoed through the forest. The party waited anxiously in silence. A moment later, a faint birdcall came from somewhere beyond the boulder.

"Coo-coo-KA, coo-coo-KA."

The boulder was slowly rolled away by two monstrous black bears, revealing a hidden tunnel in the hillside. The sight of the bears frightened the royals and they held one another closely.

"Don't be scared, they're with us," Goldilocks whispered. *"If anyone has reservations about bears, it's me."*

The carriage moved into the tunnel, and the men on horseback followed. Once the entire rescue party was inside, the bears rolled the boulder back so the entrance was hidden again. The rescue party traveled down the tunnel for several hundred feet and then entered a cavernous mine.

The ground was covered in cart tracks that stretched into more tunnels going deeper into the hillside. Thousands of fireflies covered the stalactites above, illuminating the dark cave like earthy chandeliers. Dozens of sheets and quilts were draped over stalagmites to make several tents.

The royal families were very surprised to see they were among hundreds of other refugees. Families of humans, elves, trolls, and goblins were dispersed throughout the mine. There were also several groups of animals: foxes, wolves, badgers, bears, and birds of every kind. Even *the animals* were taking shelter during this terrible time—which explained why the forest was so empty.

There were a few familiar faces among the hideaways as well. Hagetta and Friar Tuck were cooking a meal together in a large cauldron. The Traveling Tradesman, the old geezer who sold Jack the magic beans that grew the infamous beanstalk, sat against a stalagmite as he counted a collection of chicken feet he kept in a small sack.

Queen Red Riding Hood was in the back of the mine, quietly sitting alone. Her granny and the Little Old Woman from the Shoe Inn sat nearest to her, knitting quilts to make more tents. Slightly, the Lost Boy who had turned into a baby thanks to a youth potion, was taking a nap in a bassinet beside the older women. Blubo, a young flying monkey, was curled up in the bassinet beside him. Thanks to Granny's bad eyesight, she thought he was an extremely furry infant.

Being the pets of high-maintenance women, Clawdius and Lester had become fast friends when they were brought to the mine. The animals also napped together, taking turns using the other as a pillow.

Rook Robins and his father sat in a group with others from their village. Since he had nearly gotten the royals killed a year earlier, seeing them filled Rook with unbearable guilt. He excused himself from his group and took a walk through the tunnels to be alone.

The rescue party's entrance caused quite a commotion. Everyone was so happy to see the royal families were alive that the mine vibrated with emotional cheers. The refugees surrounded the carriage and welcomed their leaders to the only sanctuary left in the fairy-tale world.

"Thank the heavens you're all right!" Hagetta said.

"All our prayers have been answered!" Friar Tuck said.

Jack climbed down from Buckle and then carefully helped Goldilocks off Porridge, an act that became increasingly difficult as Goldilocks's pregnant belly grew every day. It was only a matter of time before they welcomed their child into the world; they only wished a better world awaited it.

Robin Hood and the Merry Men eagerly helped the queens down from the carriage, kissing their hands as they did so, which greatly annoyed their husbands.

"Where are we?" Sleeping Beauty asked.

"We're in an abandoned dwarf mine in the West Hills of the Dwarf Forests," Goldilocks said. "It's not the extravagance you're used to, but we'll be safe here. Very few people know it exists and it's miles from the parts of the woods being burned down."

"We were taking shelter in a small cave in the Northern Mountains, but as you can see, our numbers have grown," Jack said.

"Where are all these people and creatures from?" King Chase asked.

"All over the kingdoms," Goldilocks said. "They're the few who managed to escape the Masked Man's army. Just like you, they've lost everything they had."

The royals were very sympathetic to the people around them, but clearly had hesitations about sharing the mine with the creatures from the forest.

"I assure you, everyone and everything in this mine is safe," Sir Lampton said. "We're all united by the same enemy and must stay so if we want to reclaim our world."

The royal families looked among themselves and nodded.

"You won't find any objection from us," Empress Elvina said on the royals' behalf. "We need to put aside our differences from the past, otherwise there'll be no hope for the future."

Since the elves had a long history of being ostracized by the other kingdoms, the empress's words spoke volumes. They had already lost so much; *unity* was something they couldn't afford to lose next.

"Where are all the fairies?" Rapunzel asked.

"In hiding, hopefully," Goldilocks said.

"Is it true the Fairy Council was turned to stone?" Trollbella asked.

"We don't know," Jack said with a long sigh. "Shortly after the kingdoms were attacked, Alex and Conner went to the Fairy Kingdom to find the council and get help, but they never came back."

Everyone in the mine looked to the ground with worried eyes and a heavy heart. This was the most distressing news of all. Without the Fairy Council or the Bailey twins, how would they ever defeat the Masked Man and his Literary Army? The future looked even bleaker than it had before.

"Alex was right," Cinderella said. "The Fairy Council

should have listened to her. Had they gone after the Masked Man like she requested, none of this would have happened."

"What about Charlie or that monster who took him?" King Chandler asked. "Has anyone tracked down their whereabouts?"

All the refugees turned to Red, but the queen remained silent. She didn't have the strength to relive it.

"Red and the Lost Boys found him at Morina's cottage," Goldilocks said. "The witch has imprisoned him inside a magic mirror. They also found the missing children from the Corner and Charming Kingdoms—they're under some sort of spell that's draining their youth."

With everything else that had happened, the royals had almost forgotten about the missing children.

"Can't we plan a rescue for them, too?" Rapunzel asked.

"The children have been cursed with very dark magic," Hagetta explained. "Moving them from their beds may take their life force away completely."

"But what about Charlie?" King Chandler asked. "How do we get him out of the mirror?"

"We *can't*," Red said weakly. "Once you're imprisoned in a magic mirror, it's nearly impossible to be freed. It takes powerful magic to put someone inside a mirror, but even more powerful magic to take someone out."

"She's right," said Snow White. "My stepmother spent her whole life trying to free the man from her mirror. She was as determined and capable as anyone, and even she needed *the Wishing Spell* to do it."

The Charming brothers didn't want to believe it, but there was no escaping the truth. There wasn't a silver lining in sight—for *any* of their worries.

"They're no longer missing if we know their location," Cinderella said. "We must find comfort where we can, otherwise we'll worry ourselves to death. God willing, the children and Charlie will be among many things we salvage in the months ahead."

"Yes, but how do we begin salvaging anything?" Sir William asked. "Have we ever faced a threat with such disadvantages?"

It seemed every question was only followed with more terrible news, so everyone in the mine went silent. No one wanted to accept defeat, but the little hope surviving in their hearts was dying fast. If something didn't happen soon, the fairy-tale world as they knew it would be gone forever.

The tense silence was broken by the Traveling Tradesman, who had been biting his tongue up to this moment.

"Ah-hum." He coughed.

All the refugees in the mine rolled their eyes at the old geezer. Clearly, he was very unpopular among the survivors. When no one gave him the floor, the old man tried to get their attention again.

"Ah-HUM!" He coughed even louder.

Hagetta was the only one with enough patience to acknowledge him. "Yes, what is it, old man?" she asked.

"May I offer a suggestion?" the Traveling Tradesman asked.

His question was immediately followed by a chorus of loud sighs. Every time the Tradesman opened his mouth he only filled their heads with nonsense. But, to be fair to the old man, Jack raised his hands and silenced the exasperated crowd.

"Unless someone else has a suggestion to share, there's no point in discrediting his," he said.

Red grunted dramatically. "Everyone cover your ears," she said. "I've heard *crazy* is contagious in small quarters."

Despite the rudeness he received from his peers, the Traveling Tradesman went to the center of the mine so everyone could see him, and he offered them his suggestion.

"Perhaps we're all looking at the situation from the wrong perspective," he said. "In times as troubling as these, let's not torture ourselves further with questions we don't have the answers to—*let's ask the rocks!*"

He proposed the idea as if everyone else was supposed to know what he was talking about.

"ASK THE *ROCKS*?" Robin Hood said. "MERRY MEN, I BELIEVE THE STRANGE OLD MAN IS OFF HIS *ROCK*-ER!"

Robin Hood laughed wildly at his own joke, but no one joined him. The Tradesman was frustrated that he had to explain himself.

"Not just *any rocks*!" he said. "In my possession, I

happen to have *precious premonition stones* that are directly connected to *the will of the fates*!"

The wacky old man reached for his stones, but they were missing from his belt. He spun around in circles, looking all over the ground for where he might have dropped them.

"Where on earth are my precious stones?" he demanded. "Has anyone seen them? They were in a skunk-skin sack."

All five of the Lost Boys turned bright red.

"Oops," Tootles said. "We might have used those during the rescue."

"You did WHAT?" the Tradesman yelled. *"Those rocks are thousands of years old! They're meant for predicting the future, not slingshots!"*

"Sorry, we didn't mean to!" Tootles said.

"They didn't look like special rocks to us," Curly said.

"You really shouldn't leave your stones lying around," Nibs said.

"Yeah! There are kids in here!" the Lost twins said.

The Tradesman sat on the ground and wrapped his arms around his head. "Now what am I supposed to use to predict the will of the fates?" he asked.

The Lost Boys checked their pockets.

"Would *marbles* work?" Tootles asked.

The Traveling Tradesman let out a deep, apprehensive sigh. "Very well—hand them over."

Tootles poured a small bag of colorful marbles into the Tradesman's shaky hands. He closed his eyes, rubbed the marbles together, and whispered strange gibberish to them. Finally, he threw them on the ground in front of him and carefully watched them bounce and roll into one another.

"Interesting," he said. "*Very* interesting."

The Tradesman hemmed and hawed as if the marbles were speaking a language only he understood. It was much more of an ordeal than the refugees were expecting. Curiosity got the best of them and they formed a circle around him.

"What are the marbles saying?" Jack asked.

"Don't be ridiculous—*marbles don't speak*! They simply move as the fates command," the Tradesman said. "You see this gray one? Dull, dreary, and stuck in the dirt—*that represents us*! See the blue one and the pink one, moving together in perfect unison away from the gray—*those must represent the twins*! Fear not, the Baileys are alive!"

A few of the refugees cheered—but quickly stopped when they remembered the information was coming from an old geezer talking to marbles.

"But where are they?" Jack asked.

"They're far away from us by now, most likely in the Otherworld—*but wait*!"

All the refugees leaned in a little closer. Crazy or not, this was still the most entertaining thing they had seen in weeks.

"See how the blue and the pink rolled toward the silver, yellow, purple, and red? *Now watch*—the pink and blue are rolling back to the gray with the silver, yellow, purple, and red! *Look, all the marbles have knocked the gray out of the dirt! It's a MIRACLE!*"

The Tradesman leaped to his feet and threw his hands into the air in celebration. The refugees were on pins and needles waiting for the message to be interpreted. Even if the news was not as great as it appeared, the Tradesman's enthusiasm was infectious—they hoped this wasn't the *crazy* that Red was talking about.

"What does it all mean?" Jack asked.

"It means the twins will have to travel to places far, far away, but will return with help and save our world!" the Tradesman said. "But this will happen if, and *only* if…"

"*Yes?*"

"*Worlds collide,*" the Tradesman said with large, energetic eyes.

No one had a clue what the old man was talking about, but they were all so desperate for something positive, they took it as a good sign. Red, on the other hand, was not as enthusiastic.

"All I see is an old man who's lost his marbles," she said.

The other refugees slowly came to their senses, too. Just because this was the closest thing to good news they had received didn't make it credible.

"I agree with the old man," Goldilocks announced. "It doesn't matter what the marbles say or don't say—the Bailey twins have never let us down before. Just because we haven't heard from them yet doesn't mean we should give up on them. We have to have faith they'll return with help."

"But what do we do in the meantime?" Red asked.

"Wait," Goldilocks said. "It's all we can do."

Chapter Two

GROUNDED

Alex and Conner left their sixth-grade classroom and found a neighborhood park where they could rest and form the next phase of their plan. It was an hour or so before sunrise, and the night sky was lightening with every passing minute. Everything was so quiet and peaceful, it was difficult to imagine how chaotic life was back in the fairy-tale world and what awful things their friends might be enduring.

The closer it came to sunrise, the more people drove past the park on their early work commutes. Naturally,

Alex had seen this many times before, but every car she saw gave her a small thrill. It had been a long time since she'd been back to the Otherworld, and it wasn't until this moment that she realized how much she missed it.

"It's nice to see how little things have changed here," Alex said. "The fairy-tale world changes so much, I've never had a moment to catch my breath."

Conner was only half listening. He flipped through the pages of his short stories and separated them into four stacks on the ground.

"Great, they're all here!" he said. " 'Starboardia,' 'Galaxy Queen,' 'The Ziblings,' and 'The Adventures of Blimp Boy'! Those are the stories with characters that can help us! We'll use the potion to travel inside the stories, find the heroes, and then take them back to the fairy-tale world to help us fight our uncle's army."

Alex had only agreed to her brother's plan because their options were so limited. The closer they got to actually going through with it, the more doubtful she became. It was one thing to travel into the books of classic literature, but an entirely different endeavor to go into short stories written by her brother.

"Your stories sound more elaborate than I was expecting," Alex said. "I thought you wrote about our experiences in the fairy-tale world and just changed all the names."

"That's how it started," Conner said. "But after I got the hang of it, I might have exaggerated things a bit and taken some liberties. All good writers do—I think."

"Liberties?" Alex asked fearfully. "Conner, what exactly are we getting ourselves into?"

Conner waved it off like it wasn't a big deal.

"Relax, there's nothing more dangerous than what we've already been through," he said. "'Starboardia' is a pirate adventure, 'Galaxy Queen' is about space exploration, 'The Ziblings' are a group of superheroes, and 'The Adventures of Blimp Boy' follows a young archaeologist. It'll be a piece of cake."

The summaries didn't comfort his sister at all. The twins were lucky they had survived their adventures over the years. If his stories were based on those experiences, Alex wasn't eager to relive any of them—especially if they had been exaggerated by her brother's warped imagination.

"Are you sure this is going to work?" Alex said. "I don't mean to sound like a snob, but maybe we should stick to *published* stories."

"Stop worrying," Conner said. "There are no evil enchantresses, no dragons, no French soldiers, and no literary armies. All my characters are based on people we know and love. They have the same bravery, intelligence, and compassion as our friends—they'll *want* to help us. We'll be in and out before the antagonists even show up."

"What are we going to do with your characters after we bring them out?" Alex asked. "Where are we going to keep them?"

Conner had been so worried about *finding* his stories,

he hadn't thought about what they'd do after they found them.

"Good point," he said. "We need a place they can stay while we recruit the characters from the other stories. We also need someone to keep an eye on them so they don't wander off—someone we trust completely, who won't totally freak out about what we're doing."

The twins thought about the perfect place and the perfect person for the job, but the candidates were few and far between. It had to be someone in the Otherworld who already knew about the fairy-tale world, someone who had seen magic before and wouldn't be alarmed by it. The person had to be responsible enough to supervise several fictional characters and have enough space to host them. Alex and Conner came to the same conclusion at the exact same time. They looked at each other and knew they were thinking the same thing—there was only one person qualified for the task.

"Mom!" the twins said in unison.

The resolution was immediately followed by an avalanche of guilt.

"I can't remember the last time I talked to Mom," Alex said.

"Neither can I," Conner said. "She's probably worried sick."

"We've been so busy trying to save the fairy-tale world, we never had a chance to call home and check in," Alex said.

"We're good people, but *terrible* children," Conner said.

"Regardless of whether she wants to help us or not, we need to visit her so she knows we're alive," Alex said. "Let's just hope she cooperates."

The twins were in complete agreement. Conner gathered his stories, and they headed out of the park. Alex followed her brother but was confused by the direction he was walking in.

"Where are you going?" she asked him.

"Home," he said.

"But home is *that* way."

"No, home *used* to be that way," Conner said. "Mom and I moved in with Bob after they got married, remember?"

Alex's guilt was doubled by another avalanche—she was so out of the loop, she didn't even know where her own family lived anymore. Whenever she thought about her mom and stepdad in the Otherworld, she always imagined them living in the rental house they had moved into when her and Conner's dad passed away. Perhaps the Otherworld had changed more than she thought.

"I'm the worst daughter in the world," she said. "This isn't going to be a fun visit, is it?"

"Nope," Conner said. "Mom's gonna be pretty upset when she sees us, and I won't blame her."

They reached the edge of the park and Conner came to a stop.

"Aren't you forgetting something else?" he said.

"What?" Alex asked.

Conner looked his sister up and down, like it was obvious. "Alex, you're dressed like the Tooth Fairy," he said. "You can't go walking around the suburbs like that."

"Oh," she said. "You're right—one second."

With a quick spin, Alex transformed her sparkling dress and shoes into a T-shirt, jeans, and sneakers.

"I forgot how comfortable Otherworld clothes are," she said.

"You look like *you* again," Conner said. "Now come on, the quicker we do this, the better."

They walked through the neighborhood streets until they found Sycamore Drive. By now the sun had risen and Alex could see all the spacious homes on the street. She was delighted her mom and Bob lived in such a lovely neighborhood. Alex knew which house was theirs before Conner pointed it out because the flower beds were covered with their mom's favorite roses.

"Hopefully they'll be home," Conner said. "They're usually starting a day shift or ending a night shift around this time."

The twins walked up the curved path and knocked on the door. A few moments later, their stepdad answered. Bob was still in his pajamas and on his first cup of coffee. His eyes were puffy, like he had just woken up. The doctor did a double take when he saw Alex and Conner standing behind the door.

"Good morning, Bob," Alex said cheerfully. "Nice to see you again!"

Bob rubbed his eyes and scratched his head. He wasn't convinced he was awake yet.

"Um . . . *hi*," he said. "Well, this is a surprise."

"Is Mom home?" Conner said. "We have to talk to her."

"Yeah, she's upstairs getting ready for work. Boy, she'll be very glad to see you," he said. *"Charlotte, you have visitors!"* he called into the house.

The twins heard a window open above the porch. They looked up and saw Charlotte looking down at them from the second story, already dressed for work in her blue scrubs. Her face had many expressions at once—shock that she was looking at her children, relief that they were all right, joy that they had finally come home—but it settled on anger.

"Hi, Mom," the twins said apologetically.

"INSIDE. NOW," Charlotte said, and slammed the window.

Conner gulped. "We're off to a good start."

Before they knew it, Alex and Conner were seated on the living room sofa and their mother was furiously pacing in front of them. She was so upset, she couldn't form the words to scold them. Bob sat in an armchair beside the twins. He peered cautiously over his coffee, afraid for their safety.

"The new house is really nice," Alex said. "I really like how you decorated—"

"Quiet," Charlotte said. "Do either of you have any idea what you've put me through? I've been so worried, I haven't slept in months!"

"We're really sorry, Mom," Conner said. "We didn't mean to worry—"

"Less talking, more listening," she said. "Do you know what it's like to go to the grocery store and be asked 'How are your children doing?' and have absolutely no clue yourself? Do you know what it's like to tell a school district 'My children have transferred schools' with no proof of a transfer? Do you know what it's like to hear nothing from your children for weeks at a time except 'Sorry we didn't call you back, Mom, we had to fight a dragon,' or 'Got to go, Mom, an army is invading the castle'?"

Charlotte glared at her children as she waited for an answer, but the twins stayed silent. They didn't know if they were allowed to speak or if she was just pausing for dramatic effect.

"For your sake, I hope *your* future children show you more respect and courtesy than *mine* have shown me," Charlotte went on. "Because *not knowing* if your children are dead or alive in another dimension is the worst feeling you could ever have. It's worse than fighting enchantresses, it's worse than slaying dragons, and it's worse than battling armies, *I promise you!*"

Tears came to Charlotte's eyes and she looked away from the twins to wipe them with a tissue. The guilt the twins had felt before was nothing compared to the guilt they felt now. It tightened their stomachs and chests so much, they thought their bodies might implode.

"Mom, we weren't neglecting you on purpose," Alex

said. "We'd like to explain, if you give us a chance. Something really terrible has happened and we need your help—"

"*I don't care what's happened!*" Charlotte said. "There will always be another crisis in the fairy-tale world to tend to! Your family should come first! That's what your father and I raised you to believe, or so I thought."

"You did—and we do," Conner said. "But so many people's lives are in danger—"

"What about *your lives*?" Charlotte asked. "Since you were thirteen years old, you've been so busy saving other people, you've never taken care of yourselves. Do either of you even know what *today* is?"

Alex and Conner looked at each other, but neither knew what she was referring to. They quickly went through a mental list of possible holidays or special occasions that it could be, but both were blanking.

"Is it your and Bob's anniversary?" Conner asked.

Charlotte looked more heartbroken than ever. "No, today's your fifteenth birthday," she said.

The twins were shocked. How could they not have known it was their birthday? Suddenly, everything Charlotte said made perfect sense. They were so occupied with saving other people, they were missing out on their own lives.

Charlotte glanced at her watch and then grabbed her purse and car keys off the rack by the front door.

"I have to go to work," she said. "Both of you are *grounded*."

Conner glanced at Alex. "Wait, can she still do that?" he asked.

"You bet I can!" Charlotte said. "I want both of you to go upstairs to your bedrooms and stay there until I get home."

"Do I even have a bedroom here?" Alex asked.

Charlotte was offended she had to ask. "Of course you do," she said. "When I get back, we're going to go out for a *nice family dinner* to celebrate your birthday."

"Mom, that sounds nice, but we're really pressed for time," Alex said.

"Alexandra Bailey, it's the least you can do for me," Charlotte said. "After we have a *nice family dinner* and discuss *normal family things*, we can talk about what you need help with—but only *after*. Conner, please show your sister to her bedroom."

Charlotte left for work, leaving her children in very uncomfortable silence. They were feeling so many things—guilt, shame, disappointment, anxiety—they didn't know which emotion to settle on.

Bob tried to break the tension, but even he didn't know what to feel.

"So..." Bob said. *"Happy birthday?"*

CHAPTER THREE

THE FALLEN EMPEROR

The civilians were so thankful their kings and queens had escaped execution, they all stood a little taller in the dried-up lake. However, to avoid being the target of the emperor's building frustration, they kept as still and quiet as possible.

Inside the ruins of the Northern Palace, in a large chamber that Queen Snow White and King Chandler once ruled from, the Masked Man paced feverishly in front of his new throne. The large chair had been built from the pieces of all the other thrones of the kingdoms the Literary Army had conquered.

"I don't understand how your idiot soldiers didn't know the platform was rigged!" he yelled. "Why didn't they check it?"

The Wicked Witch of the West, the Queen of Hearts, and Captain Hook stood before the Masked Man. The new emperor had fallen into a daring routine of blaming the literary villains when something didn't go exactly as planned.

"*Our* soldiers?" the Wicked Witch of the West said. "You've been commanding our armies since we arrived! If you wanted them to inspect the platform before the execution, *you* should have ordered it!"

The literary villains had endured about as much as they could stand from the Masked Man. It was thanks to them he was emperor in the first place, but instead of fulfilling his end of their bargains, the Masked Man was bossing them around as if they were his servants. Power had clearly gone to his head, and *that* was far enough.

"I've heard enough about how *we* have failed *you*!" the Queen of Hearts barked. "It's time you coughed up what *you* promised *us*!"

"*You promised me Peter Pan!*" Captain Hook shouted.

"*And you promised me the silver slippers!*" the Wicked Witch of the West hollered.

"*And you promised me HEADS!*" the Queen of Hearts roared.

The Masked Man didn't have an ounce of empathy for the literary villains. Their frustration was nothing compared to the rage boiling inside of him.

"You will get what I promised once the royals have been recaptured and executed," the Masked Man said. "You agreed to make me an emperor, and I won't be a true emperor until all my adversaries have been destroyed!"

Footsteps echoed through the throne room. The Masked Man and the literary villains turned to see Mr. Smee sprinting toward them. The pirate was sweating, wheezing, and shaking—like he had been running from something terrible.

"Excuse me, Your Excellency?" Smee panted.

"This better be important," the Masked Man said.

"It's about the creature in the dungeon, sir," Smee said.

The creature responsible for turning the Fairy Council into stone was kept in the dungeon in the very same cell that once contained the Evil Queen. It was a monster of legendary power, so the Masked Man had ordered all of Captain Hook's pirates to patrol the dungeon and keep an eye on it.

"Yes, what about it?" the Masked Man asked.

Mr. Smee was trembling so much, his knees rattled together. No matter how he put it, he knew the emperor would be furious when he heard the news.

"It escaped!" Smee said. "Somehow it managed to take off its blindfold while it was in its cell! When the pirates went to feed it, they looked it in the eye and were turned into stone!"

Like steam from a teakettle, so much anger built up inside the Masked Man that a thunderous howl erupted from his mouth. He wrapped his hands around Smee's throat and strangled the pirate. The day had turned into an epic disaster, and unfortunately for him, it was about to get much worse.

A horn was blown outside to announce the return of the Literary soldiers who had been sent after the royal families. The Masked Man dropped Smee and bolted outside to the balcony. The Wicked Witch, the Queen of Hearts, and Captain Hook followed him.

From the balcony, the Masked Man could see the Winkies and card soldiers slowly emerging from the forest. They were all battered and bruised; many couldn't even walk without the help of another. They had come back with far fewer horses than they left with. The flying monkeys descended from the skies, but looked just as bad as the Winkies and cards, if not worse. They were so discombobulated that many missed the balcony and smacked into the walls of the palace.

Worst of all, there was no sign of the royal families anywhere. The Masked Man grabbed the closest winged monkey by its vest and shook him violently.

"WHERE ARE THE ROYAL FAMILIES?" he roared.

"They escaped!" the monkey screeched.

"HOW DID THEY GET AWAY? YOU OUTNUMBERED THEM TEN TO ONE!" the Masked Man screamed.

"They had a very strategic plan we weren't prepared for! They had backup waiting in the woods! Men on horses, men in the trees, *they even had a boy who flew*!"

The Masked Man felt like his heart had fallen out of his chest. If it weren't for his mask, they would have seen all the color drain from his face. He prayed he had misheard the winged monkey and that his ears were playing a cruel trick on his mind.

"Did you just say *'they even had a boy who flew'*?" he asked.

The winged monkey nodded. "Yes, sir," it said. "He wore clothes made out of leaves! He flew up from the trees and threw firecrackers at us!"

"PETER PAN!" Captain Hook growled. "You said he'd be trapped inside the book until we retrieved him!"

The Masked Man threw the winged monkey on the floor and clutched his chest. He felt like he was having a heart attack. Every time he thought the situation couldn't get worse, he was proved otherwise.

"No, this isn't possible!" the Masked Man said. "If Peter Pan managed to escape, that would mean my niece and nephew did, too!"

The Masked Man turned to the literary villains, and his fury quickly dissolved into fear. The Queen of Hearts and Captain Hook were more furious than he had ever seen them. With Peter Pan and the royal families out of his reach, the Masked Man wasn't capable of fulfilling his end of their agreements. They had followed him into the fairy-tale world and given him the use of their soldiers and cavalry for nothing.

"Listen, I can still give you what I promised," he said. "I just need more time!"

Captain Hook and the Queen of Hearts slowly moved toward him, backing him into the railing of the balcony.

"LIAR!" the Queen of Hearts roared. "No *royals*, no *HEADS*!"

"And you can't *give* me Peter Pan if you don't *have* Peter Pan!" Captain Hook said through a clenched jaw.

Afraid he was about to be knocked off the balcony, the Masked Man fell to his knees and groveled at the Wicked Witch's feet.

"I can still give you the silver slippers!" he pleaded. "Not all is lost!"

"I won't be fooled by any more of your lies!" the Wicked Witch of the West said. "Your reign ends today!"

The Wicked Witch of the West tapped the floor with her umbrella, and two of her flying monkeys grabbed the Masked Man by the arms. They flew him as high into the sky as they possibly could and dangled him above the forest. The civilians in the dried-up lake alerted one another to the sight, but no one knew what was happening.

"DON'T DO THIS!" the Masked Man cried. "YOU'RE MAKING A MISTAKE! MY NIECE AND NEPHEW WILL DESTROY YOU WITHOUT ME!"

"Our biggest mistake was trusting you!" the Wicked Witch of the West shrieked. She tapped her umbrella again and the flying monkeys dropped the Masked Man.

He plummeted toward the earth, screaming the entire way down, and landed somewhere deep in the forest.

"Look, the emperor has fallen!" The Wicked Witch of the West cackled.

It was obvious to the civilians that the literary villains had just staged a coup. Now that the Masked Man was gone, the civilians wanted to cheer, but the emperor's death didn't mean their troubles were over.

"If we aren't getting what we came for, then what should we do now?" Captain Hook asked. "Return to Neverland, Oz, and Wonderland?"

The literary villains thought it over, but now that they had seen the fairy-tale world with their own eyes, their own worlds weren't that appealing. With the Masked Man gone, they had unlimited power over the strange land, and power is easily addictive when placed in the wrong hands. It seemed the fairy-tale world had much more to offer them than their own worlds did.

"I rather like this world," Captain Hook said. "There are no Lost Boys, mermaids, or Indians to fight. And if Peter Pan is here, there's no reason to return to Neverland."

"There are no White Queens, Mad Hatters, or Cheshire Cats to pester us," the Queen of Hearts said. "Why return to Wonderland when I have plenty of heads to roll right here?"

"There are no wizards, Munchkins, or Good Witches to stand in our way," the Wicked Witch of the West said. "And I have more power here than the silver slippers could have given me in Oz!"

The literary villains shared a menacing smile.

"Let's stay in this world and rule the empire ourselves," the Wicked Witch said. "Perhaps if we work together, we'll achieve even *more* than what the Masked Man promised us."

The villains turned their gaze to the civilians in the dried-up lake.

From the way the three villains glared down from the balcony, the civilians knew the nightmare was far from over. . . .

CHAPTER FOUR

A NICE FAMILY DINNER

The Storybook Grill was a popular place for dinner during the week. By seven o'clock each night, the diner was usually filled with families and teenagers ordering their weight in Goblin Fries and Midnight Milk Shakes. There were always loud and energetic crowds, and tonight was no exception.

However, the group in the booth at the very back did not match the liveliness of the other patrons, so they stuck out like a sore thumb.

Cindy, Lindy, Mindy, and Wendy—four teenage girls

recently reinstated as the Book Huggers—somberly sipped milk shakes and shared a basket of fries. The girls each had a copy of *The Adventures of Sherlock Holmes* by Sir Arthur Conan Doyle in front of them, but none of them seemed very interested in it.

"We should probably talk about the book if we're going to be a book club again," Cindy said.

The other girls nodded, but no one was eager to start. The quartet had recently taken a break from books to focus on other passions—well, *passion*—and started the Conspiracy Club. However, that club only made them more restless than they already were, and they had been advised to take up reading again.

"Did anyone have a favorite passage they'd like to share?" Cindy asked. "Or maybe a favorite character?"

All the Book Huggers were quiet, forcing Cindy to take charge.

"Lindy, let's start with you," she said.

Lindy was awkwardly hunched over her milk shake and staring off into space when Cindy called on her. Wherever her mind was, it wasn't on *Sherlock Holmes*.

"Um . . . I liked the *hound*?" Lindy said.

"*The Hound of the Baskervilles*?" Cindy asked.

Lindy looked uncomfortably from side to side. "Was there more than one?"

"Did you even read the book?" Cindy asked.

Lindy hunched lower than before and shamefully shook her head.

"Did *anyone* read the book this week?" Cindy asked.

The other Book Huggers slumped with embarrassment and shook their heads as well. Cindy let out a long and frustrated sigh.

"We can't revive our book club if we're not going to read books," she said. "But if I'm honest, I didn't read *The Adventures of Sherlock Holmes*, either."

"I started it," Mindy said. "It was just so hard focusing on a fictitious mystery when *the real-life mystery* has never been solved."

The Book Huggers nodded in agreement. No matter how hard they tried to inspire themselves with new interests, new hobbies, and new clubs, or by resurrecting old clubs, the only thing consistently on their minds for the past year was the disappearance of Alex and Conner Bailey.

"You'd think it'd get easier over time, but it doesn't," Lindy said.

"We only started asking questions about Alex because we were bored and had read all the books in the school library," Mindy said. "But every answer only gave us more questions, and the more questions we had, the more infatuated we became."

"I've read books and watched television shows about people with real-life obsessions, but I never thought I'd become one of them," Lindy said. "It's all I think about when I'm awake, and all I dream about when I'm asleep."

Wendy nodded—it was affecting her sleep, too.

"Bree Campbell knows something we don't," Cindy

said. "But until one of us gains telepathic powers—or waterboarding is legalized—I don't think we'll ever get it out of her."

"She's been absent from school for almost two whole weeks!" Mindy said. "I wouldn't be surprised if she's the next one to get 'transferred to Vermont,' as they say."

Life had become exhausting to no end for the Book Huggers. They felt like mice stuck in a maze with no cheese.

"What are we going to do, girls?" Lindy asked the table. "I don't want this to affect the rest of our lives! I want to become a psychologist—not need a psychologist!"

"I'll never be a heart surgeon if I can't focus in medical school!" Mindy said.

"I'll never win my first presidential debate if I can't remember real issues!" Cindy said.

Wendy pointed to the ceiling and made an X with her fingers—implying she would never fulfill her dream of becoming an astronaut.

"It's gone too far, ladies," Cindy said. "This is just like *Nineteen Eighty-Four*, and there's no use fighting Big Brother anymore. We have to pull ourselves together while we still can. For the sake of our sanity and our destinies, we have to forget about the Bailey twins."

The Book Huggers raised their milk shakes and clinked them together. They were ready to turn over a new leaf. The undertaking wouldn't be easy, but it was necessary if they ever wanted to live normal lives again.

Unfortunately, the Book Huggers' noble venture was about to feel like the punch line of a great cosmic joke.

The front door of the Storybook Grill swung open, and the Bailey twins walked in with Charlotte and Bob. Wendy happened to glance up from her milk shake right at that second and was the first to notice Alex and Conner. For the first moments after seeing them, Wendy was certain she was hallucinating. They had *just* been talking about the Bailey twins—it was way too coincidental for them to be in the same diner at exactly the same time.

But the longer they stayed in her sight without disappearing, the more she realized they weren't a mirage—*the real-life Alex and Conner Bailey were right there*! Wendy was paralyzed with shock. The color drained from her face, and she couldn't feel her arms or legs.

"I think we should actually read *The Adventures of Sherlock Holmes*," Cindy said. "Next week, we'll come back to this diner and have a real discussion about it, just like we used to."

"I concur," Mindy said. "But can we do it a week from tomorrow? I'm getting my braces off a week from today."

"Congratulations!" Lindy said. "Will you have to wear a retainer?"

Wendy began humming to get the other Book Huggers' attention, but she was drowned out by the noise of the diner.

"Just for the first six weeks, then only at night after that," Mindy said.

"I was so relieved when I finally had mine taken off," Cindy said. "It felt like handcuffs had been removed from my mouth."

"My dentist said I don't need braces," Lindy said. "It's probably a good thing—I wouldn't have the patience for them."

Wendy couldn't believe they were talking about something so meaningless when something so extraordinary was right in front of them. She managed to regain feeling in one hand and lightly tapped Cindy on the shoulder with it.

"Wendy, are you okay?" Lindy said.

"You look like you're going to be sick," Mindy said.

"Was there something in your Midnight Milk Shake?" Cindy asked.

Desperate for them to see what she was seeing, Wendy used resources she hadn't used since the first grade— *spoken words*!

"Alex . . . Conner . . . over there!" Wendy peeped.

Her voice was high-pitched and squeaky like a baby bird's. The Book Huggers were so shocked to hear her make a noise, it took them a second to realize she had actually used *words out loud* and they had *meaning*. Once the message was interpreted, they jerked their heads in the direction of the door so fast that they pulled muscles in their necks. Once they all saw the Bailey twins with their own eyes, the Book Huggers went as still and pale as Mount Rushmore.

The twins were all eyes as they looked around at the diner's fusion of fairy-tale and 1950s decor. They knew

Cinderella's stepmother and stepsisters had opened a restaurant after moving to the Otherworld, but this was their first time seeing it.

Rosemary was in the middle of taking an order when she saw the Baileys out of the corner of her eye. The waitress abandoned the customers in mid-sentence to greet her old friends.

"Well, look what the cat dragged in!" Rosemary said, and hugged the twins.

"Hi, Rosemary," Conner said. "This place looks great!"

"Are Petunia and your mom around?" Alex asked.

"Mother has the night off and Petunia got another job, working for a veterinarian," Rosemary said. "Good riddance, if you ask me—she was a lousy waitress! I'll be sure to tell them you stopped by! Are you coming for dinner?"

"Yes," Charlotte said. "Table for four, please."

"Right this way," Rosemary said.

The stepsister grabbed four menus and sat them in a booth directly next to the Book Huggers. The girls quickly grabbed their copies of *The Adventures of Sherlock Holmes* and covered their faces with them, but Alex and Conner weren't paying attention. The twins were so amused by all the art and knickknacks throughout the diner, they didn't even notice their former classmates.

"How's Cinderella doing?" Rosemary asked the twins once they were settled in their booth.

"Well, actually—"

Alex was about to tell Rosemary the truth when her mother gave her a stern look. Anything that might get them off the topic of *nice family discussion* wasn't allowed at dinner tonight.

"*Just fine,*" Alex said. "Hope's growing like a weed."

"Wonderful. Please give them my best," Rosemary said. "I hope you enjoy the food. When you're ready to order, just wave me down—oh, we're out of the Beanstalk Salad tonight."

Rosemary went back to the customers while Alex and her family looked over the menu. It referenced so many people and places in the fairy-tale world, it was absolutely aggravating not to talk about the current crisis. The twins hoped their *nice family dinner* would end as soon as possible.

"So kids, what's new?" Charlotte asked. "How are your friends doing?"

She was so calm and casual, Alex and Conner knew she wasn't referring to the truth. They shared a curious look, and it suddenly dawned on them what their mother was doing. Their *nice family dinner* was a chance for Mom to pretend they were a perfectly normal family, living perfectly normal lives. The twins felt like they were in a play they didn't have the script for.

"*Good,*" Conner said. "Um . . . Goldilocks and Jack are expecting their first baby!"

"That's wonderful," Charlotte said. "Do they know if it's a boy or a girl?"

She knew as well as he did that the fairy-tale world didn't have ultrasounds, but he continued playing her game.

"Nope," Conner said. "I guess they're waiting to be surprised."

"Your father and I did the same thing when we had you," Charlotte said. "We weren't sure if we were having two boys or two girls, we just knew there would be two of you. Imagine our surprise when we had one of each—we didn't have to return any of the baby clothes."

Conner found this fascinating. "Really?" he said. "What would you have named us if we were two girls or two boys?"

"The firstborn was going to be an Alex no matter what," Charlotte said. "I've loved that name since I was a little girl—it was the name of my favorite doll. But if Conner had been a girl, his name would have been Sarah."

"What a coincidence! Before Margret passed away, we were planning on having a baby, and if it was a girl, we would have named her Sarah, too," Bob said. "Were Alex and Conner an easy delivery?"

Charlotte let out a long laugh as the memory came to her.

"Giving birth was easy compared to the days that followed," she said. "Their grandmother was so excited to have grandchildren, she visited us every day with someone new from the fairy-tale world. The first day she brought Mother Goose, who almost mistakenly switched Conner's bottle with her flask! Thank goodness I was an overly protective first-time mom and saw it happen! The second day we had the whole Fairy Council in the house. They were lovely, but kept magically upgrading our belongings into nicer things. By the time they left, we didn't even recognize our house!"

The twins had never heard this story before and laughed just as hard as Bob did. They could tell their mom enjoyed telling it as much as they enjoyed hearing it.

"Those were good times," Charlotte said with a bittersweet smile. "I miss them."

These were the moments of *nice family discussion* that Charlotte was so desperate for. The Baileys hadn't had them since the twins' father died. There was no talk of death or turmoil like in their usual conversations; they were just a family laughing and sharing stories with one another.

As much as Alex wanted to continue hearing stories about their parents, not addressing the issues at hand was eating her alive. Conner could feel the impatience boiling inside his sister. He knew it was only a matter of time before she ended their mother's game of pretend.

"Mom, I'm sorry you haven't had more moments to tell us stories like that," Alex said. "You're right, you and Dad raised us to put family first and we haven't for a long time."

"Thank you, Alex," Charlotte said. "That means a lot."

"But," Alex said, "I can't keep pretending everything is okay when we know it's not."

Conner covered his face with his hands. "Oh boy, here we go," he said.

"Alex, I asked you guys not to bring this up—"

"I'm sorry, but I have to," Alex said. "Right now, a lot of people need our help. I know Conner and I have given up a lot, and you've given up a lot by association, but we don't care what we'll have to sacrifice if it saves our friends and all the families like ours. We're *doing the right thing* because *that's* also the kind of son and daughter you and Dad raised. So please—*let us.*"

Charlotte looked at her children differently than she had all day. She wasn't glaring at them with frustration or anger, but with pride. She reached across the table and held their hands with her own.

"I'm sorry," she said. "I guess I've been a little selfish. All I want is for you to have the same experiences every teenager gets to have before this time in your lives is gone, but I forget there's nothing *normal* about you. It doesn't matter what I want—you should be living the lives you were meant for. Forgive me, it was just so difficult losing your father; I hate feeling like I've lost you, too."

"I'm sorry we've made you feel like you lost us," Conner said.

"You're my children, but other people's heroes," Charlotte said. "Any mother would be lucky to be in my shoes, but that doesn't mean they're easy to wear. Sometimes at the end of the day, I just have to pretend you're both asleep in your beds."

Charlotte dabbed the corners of her eyes with her napkin. Alex and Conner couldn't blame their mom for wishing things were different—they did, too. The twins put so much time and effort into ending people's suffering, they didn't realize how much their own mother was hurting. But if their mom was willing, she was about to become more involved in their lives than she was prepared for.

"Now tell me what's going on in the fairy-tale world," Charlotte said. "And how in the world am I going to help you with it?"

Alex and Conner were relieved they could continue discussing their plan. Both opened their mouths to fill her in, but they were at a loss for words. After all, it was a complicated thing to explain. So much of it involved their uncle Lloyd, and they didn't want to overwhelm their mom with news of an evil brother-in-law.

"Long story short, a really terrible man has taken over the fairy-tale world," Conner said. "They call him the Masked Man."

"How'd he take over?" Charlotte asked.

"He stole a potion from Grandma that turns every written work into a portal to the world it describes," Alex said. "He traveled into *Alice's Adventures in Wonderland*, *The Wonderful Wizard of Oz*, and *Peter Pan*. Somehow he recruited the Queen of Hearts, the Wicked Witch of the West, Captain Hook, and all their minions and soldiers into a big Literary Army and attacked all the kingdoms."

"That sounds *terrifying*," Bob said. "Those villains used to give me nightmares when I was a kid."

"They're much worse in real life," Conner said. "Imagine how scary you *thought* they were, now double that image, cover it in butter, and leave it outside for a week—*that's* how frightening they really are!"

"Why can't the Fairy Council do something? Why does it always have to fall on your shoulders?" Charlotte asked.

"The Fairy Council has been turned to stone, and all the soldiers in all the kingdoms are no match for the Literary Army," Alex said. "If we don't find a way to stop them, no one will."

Charlotte hated that so much responsibility had fallen on her children's young shoulders.

"For the record, I am *not* okay with you two fighting these guys," Charlotte said. "But how are you going to stop them?"

Alex nudged Conner. "Tell her *your* plan," she said.

Conner didn't appreciate his sister's unenthusiastic introduction. "We're going to recruit our own army," he said. "We're going to use the same potion to travel into my short stories and bring back my characters."

Charlotte and Bob couldn't believe what they were hearing.

"Oh my gosh!" Charlotte said. "Is that really the only thing you can do?"

"Trust me, I wish I could file a report at the Pentagon," Conner said. "Sometimes you've got to fight fire with fire."

"I still don't see how I fit into all of this," Charlotte said.

The moment had finally come for the twins to tell her. It was such an absurd request, the twins were afraid to ask. If she refused, they weren't sure who could help them.

"We need you to look after Conner's characters as we bring them out of his stories," Alex said.

It was like someone pressed the Pause button on Charlotte and Bob. Without breathing or blinking, they just looked at the twins with open mouths and large eyes. They weren't taking it well.

Conner waved his hand in front of their faces. "Are you still with us?" he asked.

"Sorry," Bob said. "It's just—most parents of fifteen-year-olds only worry about getting asked for money to go to the movies, or driving permits."

Conner sat up excitedly. *"Oh-my-God-Alex-we're-old-enough-for-driving-permits!"* he said in one breath.

"One crisis at time, remember?" Alex said. "So, Mom and Bob, can you help us?"

Bob and Charlotte looked at each other and shrugged.

"If it'll save the fairy-tale world, I won't object," Bob said.

"What *kinds* of characters are going to be in my house?" Charlotte asked. "We just had the carpets cleaned."

"Oh, nothing crazy—*pirates, cyborgs, superheroes, mummies*—the usual fictional suspects," Conner said under his breath. "So, does that mean you guys are in?"

The twins held their breath. Charlotte was hesitant, but it might have been more concerning if she were completely fine with the idea.

"All right," she said. "It'll be an adventure."

The twins were so relieved, they sank a foot into their seats.

"Awesome!" Conner said.

"Fantastic!" Alex said.

Bob and Charlotte glanced down at the Storybook Grill

menus, but it was a very difficult conversation to follow with French fries and hamburgers. They both pushed the menus away.

"You know what, I think I've lost my appetite," Charlotte said. "Maybe we should go home and I'll cook something later."

"I agree," Bob said.

The twins weren't going to argue. They left the Storybook Grill with Bob and Charlotte and headed back home. All of them were completely unaware that their entire conversation had been heard by the patrons in the next booth.

The Book Huggers leaned so far out of their seats to watch them leave that Cindy and Mindy fell onto the floor. The night had consisted of the most important eavesdropping of their lives.

"Girls, did you hear everything I just heard?" Cindy said.

"I'm not sure," Lindy said. "My heart started beating so hard toward the end, I only heard every other word!"

"We've been right all along!" Mindy said. "They never went to Vermont—they were living in another dimension! Did any of us ever think of that?"

Wendy raised a hand—reminding the group it had been one of her suspicions from the very beginning.

"Forget Sherlock Holmes," Cindy said. "We've got our own mystery to follow."

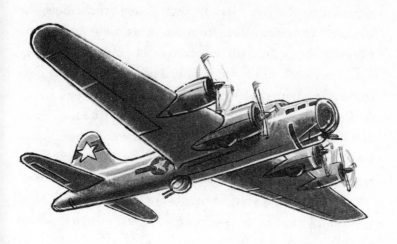

CHAPTER FIVE

CRIES FROM THE CASTLE

Had someone told Bree Campbell two weeks ago that she would soon be flying above another continent on a World War II plane with three distant relatives, she would have laughed. Ironically, that's exactly where Bree was, and she wanted to cry. She had always considered herself a person of good judgment and respectability, but as she bounced around the Boeing B-17 Flying Fortress thirteen thousand feet in the air, somewhere between France and Germany, Bree suddenly felt like the lead character in a cautionary tale.

"Can you believe I haven't flown one of these since the sixties?" Cornelia called from the captain's seat. The old woman's hands clutched the controls, but from the way they jerked her back and forth, it looked like the plane was controlling her more than she was controlling it.

Bree, Wanda, and Frenda were strapped into their seats and holding on for dear life. They had been flying for nine hours straight, and thanks to Cornelia's questionable piloting skills, it had been the bumpiest flight of Bree's life. And from the way things were going, it might be her last.

"Aunt Cornelia, are you sure you don't need a hand up there?" Wanda asked.

"I'm fine, thank you, dear," Cornelia said. "It's just like riding a bike!"

"Yeah, *off a cliff*," Frenda said.

When Bree first met the Sisters Grimm and heard about their lives' work monitoring portals between the Otherworld and the fairy-tale world, she thought they were the most capable group of women she had ever known. However, she was learning the hard way that that capability did not include flying a plane.

"Cornelia, remind me again where you went to piloting school?" Bree asked.

"Well, *technically* I never went to school for it," Cornelia said. "My father was a pilot during the war—this was his plane. He taught me how to fly when I was about your age, Bree. He flew this baby to Germany many times. Thank goodness we're going under different circumstances."

"Your father fought in World War II?" Bree asked. "That must have been difficult with so much family in Germany."

"Most of our family left long before the war," Cornelia said. "Would you like a flying lesson, Bree?"

Bree wasn't convinced Cornelia knew how to fly, let alone give a flying lesson. She looked to Wanda and Frenda, and they motioned for her to go.

"You can't be any worse than her!" Frenda said.

"Learn everything she knows and save us!" Wanda said.

Bree was scared to unbuckle her seat belt, but she quickly unfastened it and dashed to the co-pilot seat beside Cornelia. There was an overwhelming number of buttons, switches, and levers before her.

"I don't think I can do this," Bree said.

"If you can operate that phone of yours so well, this will be a walk in the park," Cornelia said. "Besides, the co-pilot's job is the easiest."

"Wait a second," Bree said. "There should be *two* pilots flying this plane?"

"Traditionally," Cornelia said. "But it always takes two men to do what a woman can do on her own."

Bree would never have gotten on the plane if she'd thought it would lead to this. She was making the trip to save a friend, but who was going to save her?

As soon as she learned Emmerich had been kidnapped, Bree had a strong feeling it wasn't a normal Otherworld abduction. She had no evidence to support the suspicion, but she felt it with every fiber of her being and couldn't shake it no matter how hard she tried. Bree had pestered Frau Himmelsbach for more information about the incident, but Emmerich's mother grew tired of the questions and eventually ignored her calls. Bree had shared her hunch with the Sisters Grimm, and they agreed the circumstances were fishy.

"It is curious he was kidnapped so soon after being in the fairy-tale world," Cornelia said.

"If he was taken by someone from the fairy-tale world, we have tools that can prove it," Wanda told Bree.

"What kind of tools?" Bree asked.

"Cross-dimensional emission-tracking devices," Frenda said. "Whenever someone or something travels between worlds, the portal leaves a radiation-like scent on them. We have machines that can detect it."

"Awesome," Bree said. "All we need now is a way to get to Germany."

Cornelia had been cooped up in their Connecticut home for so long, she was looking for any excuse to get out of the house. She generously offered Bree a ride to Germany on their family plane. Bree was so desperate to find Emmerich, she didn't hesitate to take her up on the offer.

There was only one thing standing in her way: Bree had technically run away from home to find the Sisters Grimm. If she was now going to Europe, she needed a really good excuse so her parents wouldn't call the police. Luckily, Cornelia supplied that as well.

"Is this Little Eddy?" Cornelia had said to Bree's father over the phone. "It's your cousin Cornelia. . . . I know, it *has* been a very long time. . . . Darling, I'm calling to sincerely apologize to you and your wife. You see, Bree recently called me with questions about our family heritage. She was so interested, I invited her to come stay with me so I could tell her more. . . . Well, I *just* found out she never ran it by you. . . . My thoughts *exactly*—inexcusable! I'm sure you were both scared to death. . . . My intention was to send her home immediately, but I unfortunately had a bad fall this morning and injured my hip. . . . No, I'm not in any pain. . . . *Yes*, there is something you can do. . . . Would it be terrible if Bree stayed with me until the end of the week? I'm useless on my own. . . . Just until Wanda gets back into town, then we'll put her on the train home. . . . She's been such help. . . . You bet, absolutely no privileges whatsoever. . . . *Thank you so much, dear!*"

The next thing Bree knew, she and the Sisters Grimm were on their way to a small private airport. However, Bree, Wanda, and Frenda all thought Cornelia had hired a pilot to take them to Germany. They didn't realize Cornelia was planning to *fly the plane herself* until she switched on the propellers and launched them into takeoff.

Now, at just fifteen years old, Bree was sitting next to the old woman, being taught to fly the Boeing B-17 Flying Fortress. If Bree lived long enough to become an old woman herself, she wasn't sure her grandchildren would even believe the story she was currently living.

"Taking off is the easy part," Cornelia instructed. "You simply start the propellers with the blue dial, turn the red gear to Steering Mode to get the plane onto the runway, push down the green lever, and pull up on the controls."

Bree gulped. "Blue dial, red gear, green lever, controls," she repeated.

"Perfect," Cornelia said. "To fly, all you do is pull up on the green lever, turn the red gear to Flight Mode, adjust the altitude with the brown handle, and steer with the controls. Here, *give it a go!*"

Cornelia flipped a switch and the whole plane turned off. They entered a rapid descent toward the earth! Bree watched in panic as the numbers on the altitude monitor dropped hundreds of feet per second. Wanda and Frenda were screaming so loudly, she could barely focus.

"Green lever, red gear, brown handle, controls!" Bree said, mimicking everything Cornelia had just instructed.

The Boeing B-17 Flying Fortress stopped plunging toward the ground and glided smoothly through the clouds. In fact, it was flying much more easily with Bree at the controls.

"You're a natural flier!" Cornelia said. "It's in our DNA."

Bree thought there might be some truth to this. Since the magic in their family's blood came from Mother Goose, she wondered if a few of Mother Goose's flying genes had been transferred, too. There was actually a lot about Cornelia that reminded Bree of Mother Goose. They both had the same twinkle in their eye when they put others in danger.

"How much longer until we're on the ground?" Wanda asked. "*Safely* on the ground!"

"We've already begun our descent," Cornelia said. "We'll land shortly after we pass over Füssen."

Bree recalled that the area didn't have many large cities. "Does Füssen have an airport?" she asked.

"We don't need an airport to land," Cornelia said. "To quote Coco Chanel, 'The world is your runway'!"

"Mother, she was talking about fashion!" Frenda yelled.

"Everyone stop worrying! This baby is built for combat," Cornelia said.

They didn't care what it was built for; landing a plane anywhere but at an airport sounded like a *crash landing* to them! Bree, Wanda, and Frenda tightened their seat belts until there was no slack left. Soon the small Bavarian city of Füssen came into view and Cornelia searched the ground for a smooth surface to land.

"That field should do," she said.

Cornelia jerked the controls and the Boeing B-17 Flying Fortress curved through the air, lowering toward a grassy field below. As the plane turned, Bree caught a glimpse of Neuschwanstein Castle peeking through the hills in the distance. It was as if she were seeing an old friend. The castle was just as majestic as it was the first time she saw it with Conner on Mary's Bridge.

"All right, time for your landing lesson," Cornelia said.

"You start by turning the red gear to Landing Mode, pull up on the green lever, turn the black knob to put down the wheels, and pull up on the controls so we're parallel to the ground."

"Red gear, green lever, black knob, controls—got it," Bree said.

"Splendid," Cornelia said. "Now land us."

Bree, Frenda, and Wanda were horrified. It was like Cornelia had a death wish or something!

"What? But I've never landed a plane before!" Bree said.

The plane was getting closer and closer to the ground—someone had to land it before it was too late! Cornelia looked over her glasses at Bree with total faith in her eyes.

"Sometimes, if we enter situations that scare us with both hands on the wheel, they don't seem as frightening," she said as calmly as ever. "Or in this case, *with both hands on the controls*."

Bree couldn't believe Cornelia was making her do this. She could feel her heart beating in the back of her throat. One wrong move and they would all be dead!

Carefully and quickly, Bree turned the red gear to Landing Mode, pulled up on the green lever, turned the black knob to put the wheels down, and held up the controls to make the plane parallel to the ground.

"We're gonna crash!" Wanda yelled, and vigorously crossed her chest.

"Wanda, you're not Catholic!" Frenda said.

"I know, but we're gonna need all the help we can get!"

The wheels slammed into the grassy field and the plane landed like a rock skipping across a lake. It tore up large strips of earth, as if leaving a long message in Morse code. Finally, the plane decelerated and rolled into a shaky, sudden stop.

"Oh my God," Bree said in disbelief. "I just landed a plane!"

"Mother, how could you let a fifteen-year-old land a plane!" Frenda said.

Cornelia burst into a fit of giggles. "You're all so gullible," she said. "I had the autopilot on the entire time!"

The others didn't find this funny at all.

"You mean, all that was for nothing?" Bree asked with an angry scowl.

"No, no—you did quite well," Cornelia said. "Had the autopilot failed, we would have had a successful landing. My father did the same thing to me on my first flight. The best lessons are learned when it's *sink or swim*, and you're quite the swimmer!"

Once their hearts settled to a normal pace, Bree and the Sisters Grimm locked up the plane and headed for Emmerich's house. Bree thought leaving the plane unattended in a field was a strange thing to do, but Cornelia assured her that planes were very difficult to steal.

Bree led the women through the outskirts of Füssen and into the little village just below Neuschwanstein Castle called Hohenschwangau. Since Cornelia walked with a cane, Bree was worried the journey would be too much for her, but the old woman hobbled along, excited to be on another Sisters Grimm adventure. They walked past all the souvenir shops, restaurants, and inns dedicated to the castle, and found the Himmelsbachs' tiny home on the edge of town.

"There it is," Bree said, and pointed to the front steps. "That's where Conner and I met him."

The sight made Bree feel remarkably nostalgic. It seemed like just yesterday that she and Conner had told Emmerich they were secret agents so he'd take them into the castle after visiting hours. They hadn't been friends for long, but Bree and Emmerich had shared such an incredible once-in-a-lifetime adventure, she couldn't believe there was a time when the little German boy was a stranger. She just hoped they could bring him home, wherever he was.

"Here goes nothing," Bree said. "I hope Frau Himmelsbach is better at answering her door than she is her phone."

They walked up the front steps and rang the doorbell. They waited, but no one answered. Bree rang the doorbell again, holding it down longer. A moment later, Frau Himmelsbach answered the door.

"Kann ich Dir helfen?" she asked.

If Bree hadn't recognized her voice from the phone, she wouldn't have thought it was Emmerich's mother. The woman had brown hair and olive skin, very different from her son's pale skin and rosy complexion. She had puffy eyes and sunken cheeks, like she had been crying and not eating much. She wore a big black robe over a nightgown and probably hadn't changed clothes in days.

The woman wasn't what Bree was expecting, but she definitely looked like the mother of a missing child.

"Frau Himmelsbach, I'm sorry to disturb you," Bree said. "I'm Bree Campbell, your son's friend from the United States."

Emmerich's mother was not happy to see her, and especially not happy to see she had brought friends with her.

"What is wrong with you, child?" the Frau said. "I told you to stop calling me and now you've come to my home?"

"I'm sorry," Bree said. "I know you don't want to talk to me, but I couldn't stay away. These are my cousins, Cornelia, Frenda, and Wanda. We've traveled all this way because we want to help you find your son."

Frau Himmelsbach crossed her arms and shook her head. She wasn't easy to convince.

"You Americans and your egos," she said. "What can you do that the Bavarian police cannot?"

Bree looked to the Sisters Grimm, hoping one of them would have an answer.

"We're private investigators who specialize in child abduction," Cornelia said. "We've brought special equipment along with us that may point us in the direction of whoever took your child."

"The police searched every inch of my home," the Frau said. "They didn't find a single clue."

"With all due respect, ma'am," Wanda said, "the

Bavarian police can't find clues like we can. Please, may we come inside?"

The distressed mother looked back and forth among the women and tried to think of a reason not to let them, but she couldn't.

"Fine," she said. "I apologize, my house is a mess."

Frau Himmelsbach escorted Bree and the Sisters Grimm inside her home. The Frau offered them a seat in the sitting room and Cornelia and Bree happily accepted. From the sofa they could see into Emmerich's bedroom through an open door in the hall. The walls were covered in posters of superheroes. Bree remembered him saying he wanted to visit the United States because that's where all the superheroes lived. The memory made her miss him even more.

"May we have a look around?" Frenda asked.

"As you wish," the Frau said.

Frenda and Wanda went to work right away. They each removed a cross-dimensional emission-tracking device from their purse; the device looked like a long microphone connected to an old radio. They waved the microphone parts around the house and the radio parts beeped as they went.

They searched the sitting room and kitchen, but didn't find anything. The search continued in Emmerich's bedroom, and when they scanned the area by his window, the machines beeped like crazy. Wanda looked to Bree and Cornelia and with one nod she said a thousand words—*someone from the fairy-tale world had definitely been there.* Bree's hunch was right.

"Was Emmerich taken through the window?" Frenda asked.

"Yes," Frau Himmelsbach said, surprised they knew. "The night it happened, Emmerich was sleeping in his bedroom while I was in here reading. I heard a noise, so I checked on him. His window was open and in the distance I saw someone in a black cloak running away with Emmerich over their shoulder."

She broke into tears recalling the terrifying sight and Cornelia offered her a handkerchief.

"I chased them, but they disappeared into the night," the Frau said. "I called the police and they came to the house every day for a week. They never found anything, not even a fingerprint. How did you know he was taken from the window?"

If they were going to tell the Frau the truth, Bree figured it was best to start at the beginning.

"Shortly before Emmerich was taken, he and I made a crazy discovery," Bree said. "We did this thing, like a *blood test*, and it proved he and I are actually *related*. Our blood matches DNA from the Brothers Grimm."

"The Brothers Grimm?" the Frau asked.

"Yes," Bree continued. "Which means Cornelia, Frenda, Wanda, and myself are either related to you or to Emmerich's father."

The Frau was very confused. "I wouldn't know either

way," she said. "Emmerich isn't my biological son—he was adopted."

"*Adopted?*" Bree said in shock. "He never mentioned that."

"That's because I never told him," Frau Himmelsbach said. "He was abandoned when he was a baby. I didn't want him living life thinking he was unwanted."

Everything Bree thought she knew suddenly changed. She quickly abandoned her plan to tell the Frau about the fairy-tale world—clearly she didn't have all the facts straight.

"Where was he found?" Bree asked.

"Neuschwanstein Castle," she said. "My father used to work nights there as a security guard. One night, as he was patrolling the halls, he heard crying. He followed the cries to the Singers' Hall and found Emmerich wrapped up in a blanket in the middle of the floor. Someone must have left him during a tour earlier in the day. It was very strange, because my father swore he had checked the room multiple times earlier that night and never saw the baby."

Bree and the Sisters Grimm were all thinking the same thing: Emmerich wasn't related to the Brothers Grimm after all—*he was from the fairy-tale world*! Someone must have crossed through the portal in the Singers' Hall and left him in the castle!

The Frau's eyes suddenly grew wide and she covered her mouth fearfully.

"Wait a moment," she said. "That reminds me of something I completely forgot! There was a note pinned to his blanket the night he was found. Let me see if I can find it."

Emmerich's mom went down the hall to her bedroom. They heard her searching madly through all her drawers and belongings. A few minutes later, she returned with a piece of parchment. Her hands were shaking, as if she were holding a ransom note. She handed it to Bree, and the Sisters Grimm gathered around her to read the note.

To whoever finds this child, please take him to a loving home that will offer protection. His father is a very dangerous man and the child is not safe with his mother. Should the father learn of his son's existence, the child will be in grave danger.

It appeared that Bree and the Sisters Grimm had helped the Frau uncover a suspect in her son's disappearance—*Emmerich's biological father!*

"It was so many years ago, I forgot the note existed," Frau Himmelsbach confessed. "Even then, I didn't take it seriously. I never thought they would find him."

"Should we take this to the police?" Wanda asked.

"No, we can't!" the Frau exclaimed. "You see, I never *legally* adopted Emmerich. I fell in love with him the minute my father brought him home. At the time, we were very poor. I was afraid he would be taken away if we called the police, so we kept it a secret. If they found out now, I would never see him again."

Bree had so many questions, she could barely see straight. She always loved a good mystery novel, but she never thought her life would turn into one.

"If you're related to him, do you have any idea who Emmerich's parents are?" Frau Himmelsbach asked. "Do you know where they might have taken him?"

"I'm afraid not," Bree said. "But I know someone who might."

CHAPTER SIX

A BEWITCHING OFFER

The Masked Man was awoken by a throbbing headache. He opened his eyes and discovered he was somewhere in the forest, but he had no recollection of how he had gotten there. Even stranger, when he looked around he noticed the ground was above his head and the smoky sky was below his feet.

After further inspection, he realized he was upside down. His cape was caught on a tree branch and he was hanging several feet in the air. As he slowly returned to full consciousness, the Masked Man remembered that flying monkeys had dropped him there. He wasn't sure how long he had been hanging in the tree, but since he was still alive, he assumed his cape must have broken his fall.

He reached toward the branch piercing his cape to set himself free. The motion sent excruciating pain through his entire body and he screamed. The pain was so bad, he couldn't tell where it began or ended. Clearly, he had hit more than one branch on his way down. The Masked Man tugged on his cape and it ripped in half. He fell to the ground and landed on his back with a *thud*.

After a few minutes of lying on the ground, the Masked Man had a better idea of where the pain was coming from. His left arm was definitely broken, one of his right ribs was most likely cracked, and his right ankle was sprained at best. Half his mask had been ripped off by something he collided with during the fall, and bloody scratches covered one side of his face. Still, it was a miracle he had survived.

He moaned as he struggled to his feet. All the blood in his head rushed to the other parts of his body, making him woozy. He removed his damaged cape and ripped his suit jacket into strips to make a sling for his arm.

The physical pain was unbearable, but he was almost thankful for it—it was the only thing distracting him from his mental anguish.

The Masked Man was not a stranger to disappointment, but *losing an empire* was one colossal setback he never saw coming. After a lifetime of meticulous planning, he had finally achieved the power he had craved since childhood.

Only to then have it yanked away like a rug from underneath him.

After such a narrow escape from death, a different man would have abandoned his quest for supremacy, but the Masked Man's need for power was like a disease—and *fulfillment* was the only cure. Like a phoenix, he immediately began calculating his path out of the ashes. Somehow, some way, he would reclaim his power and destroy the literary villains who had taken it from him. But first, he needed to find a path out of the forest.

The Masked Man had no idea what part of the forest he had been dropped in, so he hobbled through the trees in search of an indication. After hours of limping aimlessly through the woods, he only found more and more trees the farther he went. Since the mythological creature had escaped captivity in the Northern Palace dungeon, the Masked Man was as cautious and quiet as possible just in case it was also wandering through the forest.

Eventually he stumbled upon a small clearing with three unusual boulders. They were tall and stuck out from the ground like trees themselves. The Masked Man had a seat against one of the boulders and tightened his makeshift sling. But his rest was short-lived.

A commotion traveled through the woods nearby. The sound became louder and louder as it moved closer and closer. It was a repetitive tremor, like the marching of several pairs of metal boots—*Winkie soldiers were approaching*! The Masked Man assumed the villains must have sent the soldiers to retrieve his body. He was too wounded to outrun them, so he dived into the bushes beside the boulders and was hidden from view.

A few moments later, two rows of a dozen Winkie soldiers entered the clearing, but they weren't alone. The soldiers were escorting the Wicked Witch of the West, the Queen of Hearts, and Captain Hook through the forest. The sight of the literary villains sent a rage through the Masked Man that was so powerful, his injuries were temporarily numbed. There wasn't a word in existence to describe the anger coursing through his veins.

The Wicked Witch of the West, the Queen of Hearts, and Captain Hook paced around the clearing like they were waiting for something to happen. They didn't appear to be looking for the Masked Man, so he wondered what on earth they were doing in the woods.

"Well?" Captain Hook growled. "Where is she?"

"Are we certain we're in the right place?" the Queen of Hearts asked.

The Wicked Witch of the West unrolled a scroll of parchment she held tightly in her hand.

"I'm positive," the Wicked Witch said. "Her instructions say, 'Take the path four miles into the Dwarf Forests and wait for me in the clearing of the three stone trees.' There hasn't been another clearing for miles. This must be it."

As the Masked Man knew all too well, *patience* was not

the villains' forte. The Wicked Witch, the Queen of Hearts, and Captain Hook became more restless by the second.

"Well, *whoever* she is, I don't like her," Captain Hook snarled. "She has some nerve to keep us waiting like this."

"I want to hear what she's offering," the Queen of Hearts said. "But if it isn't appealing, and we've come all this way for nothing, *I say we capture her and—*"

"Cut off her head?" the Wicked Witch asked mockingly. "There are *other ways* to execute someone, you know—most of which are more entertaining and far less messy."

"Like dropping the Masked Man to his death?" Captain Hook said with a nasty grin. "Watching him squirm and scream as he fell was rather fun, wasn't it? If only gravity affected *everyone*—my hook would be covered in Peter Pan's blood by now!"

The Queen of Hearts rolled her eyes. "I'm so sick of hearing that boy's name!" she hollered. "He's a child, Captain! *Let it go!* From the way you obsessively talk about him, I'd say he's taken much more from you than *just your hand!*"

Captain Hook intended to respond with a snippy comment, but the pirate went quiet. He leaned against one of the boulders and placed his hook on his hip, thinking about what the Queen of Hearts had just said.

From the bushes just beside Captain Hook, the Masked Man had a perfect view of a revolver dangling from the captain's belt. He was drawn to the weapon like a moth to a flame. If he got his hands on it, with three quick shots he could terminate the literary villains before the Winkie soldiers knew what was happening!

Carefully, when they were all looking in the opposite direction, the Masked Man reached his good hand toward the captain's waist and unfastened his holster.

It was a painful effort with his cracked rib and it took everything in him not to scream. Slowly, he removed the revolver from the holster with the captain none the wiser.

The Masked Man examined the gun—*it had three bullets*! He had exactly what he needed to shoot the villains! He cocked it and aimed the weapon back and forth at the three of them, indecisive about which one to kill first.

Captain Hook became agitated and started stomping around the clearing.

"I knew it was a trick!" he said in a huff. "We've been fooled! No one is meeting us in the woods today!"

The Queen of Hearts and the Wicked Witch nodded in agreement. But just as they were about to order the soldiers to take them back, they were interrupted by a voice from outside the clearing.

"Haven't you ever heard the phrase 'Good things come to those who wait'?"

The Masked Man lowered the revolver when he heard the voice. It sounded awfully familiar.

The villains and the Winkie soldiers heard footsteps next and quickly turned to see a hooded creature approaching them. The soldiers raised their staffs toward the creature, but with a quick flick of its wrist, their weapons crumbled into dirt. The creature stepped into the clearing and lowered its hood—it was a beautiful woman with horns like a ram's that curved around the sides of her face.

"Morina," the Masked Man whispered to himself. His desire to assassinate the villains was quickly replaced by curiosity. What did *she* want with them?

"Are you the witch they call Morina?" the Wicked Witch of the West asked.

"I am," Morina said. "And you must be the new leaders of this world. It's an honor to make your acquaintance. Defeating the kingdoms of humans and fairies is no easy task—you've achieved what the witches have only dreamed about for centuries."

The villains shared a proud look and stood a little taller.

"Since you're here, I'm assuming you received my letter?" Morina asked.

"It's not every day we receive an invitation delivered by a crow," the Queen of Hearts said. "Now tell us, what is the 'offer of a lifetime' that you wrote about?"

"It requires a lengthy explanation," Morina said. "Please, have a seat."

The witch waved her hand toward the three boulders and they transformed into large stone chairs for the villains to sit on. So far, the witch was very impressive.

"You see, the witches of this world have always had a long and unpleasant history with the people who ruled it," Morina explained. "Before you arrived there were rumors of an impending witch hunt. Those fears were all but confirmed when the Masked Man became emperor. We were certain that once he executed the royal families, it would only be a matter of time before he ordered our extermination. But luckily, that's all changed now that you've taken his place."

"If the Masked Man saw the witches as a threat, why should we view things any differently?" Captain Hook asked.

"Because the three of you are much wiser than your predecessors," Morina said. "Why become enemies when we have a glorious opportunity to become *allies*?"

The villains side-eyed one another. They weren't pleased with where the conversation was going.

"For your sake, I hope you're offering us more than *friendship*," the Queen of Hearts warned.

Morina smiled and her eyes grew wide. They could tell friendship was only the beginning of what she had to offer.

"Of course. I'll cut to the chase," she said. "Recently, I convinced the other witches that the only way we could escape the pending genocide was by leaving this world. We need a place to ourselves where we won't be controlled by fairies or ostracized by humans. So I formed a plan for the witches to invade and conquer another dimension, known as *the Otherworld*."

The villains were instantly intrigued. *"The Otherworld?"* they asked in unison.

"It's a world very similar to this one, but far greater,"

Morina explained. "It has hundreds of countries, thousands of cities, and billions of people. There are structures and machines you could only dream of, and more land and sea than we would ever need. The best part is that this world operates entirely without magic. With no fairies to limit us, we would be unstoppable!"

Her passionate description was hypnotizing. Still, the villains wondered if it was too good to be true.

"How can you prove it exists?" Captain Hook asked.

"Take a look for yourself," Morina said.

The witch's eyes suddenly lit up like the headlights of a car. Morina magically transferred images of the Otherworld into the villains' minds and their eyes glowed as brightly as hers. Visions of London, Paris, Tokyo, and New York City flashed before their eyes. They saw the Eiffel Tower, the Pyramids of Giza, the Great Wall of China, the Golden Gate Bridge, and the Taj Mahal.

The villains had never seen a world so grand and diverse before. The light faded from their eyes, but was replaced by the glow of desire.

"How do we get to the Otherworld?" the Wicked Witch asked.

"The late Fairy Godmother has portals hidden all over the kingdoms," Morina said. "But each one is difficult to open, and the journey takes a toll on anyone who's not a practitioner of white magic."

"Then how do the witches expect to cross over?" the Queen of Hearts asked.

"As luck would have it, the two worlds are scheduled to collide very soon," Morina said. "A *doorway* will open that will bridge the worlds like never before. Once it appears, we can charge into the Otherworld and take it by storm!"

The villains' suspicion grew as much as their interest.

"You seem to have it all figured out," Captain Hook said. "What exactly do the witches want from us?"

A devious smile grew on Morina's face. This was the part she was most excited to tell them.

"The witches don't want anything from you," she said.

"Then why do they want to become *allies*?" Captain Hook asked.

"You misheard me, Captain," Morina said. "The witches don't even know I'm here. I was speaking for *myself* when I proposed an alliance."

The villains shared a look, each more confused than the other. Morina waved a hand over the dirt and a fourth boulder shot up from the ground. She transformed it into a large stone throne, much taller than the villains' chairs, and she had a seat.

"I had every intention of *leading* the witches into the Otherworld," Morina explained. "Sadly, that leadership was stolen from me. Two witches with seniority, the Snow Queen and the Sea Witch, have taken the operation into their own clammy hands. But my frustration has taught me a valuable lesson: *Witches are not like wolves—we don't belong in packs.* Once we cross into the Otherworld, we'll fight one another for dominance until there is only one of us left. So I've begun a new plan for *after* the witches conquer the Otherworld."

The villains shared a smile. Morina's plan was starting to make sense—and they liked where it was going.

"You're going to betray them!" the Wicked Witch said eagerly.

"Precisely," Morina said. "The Snow Queen and the Sea Witch plan to cast a spell on the late Fairy Godmother's granddaughter, a powerful young fairy named Alex. They believe if they curse her strongly enough, they'll be able to turn the girl into a weapon and use her to vanquish the Otherworld. I'm not convinced this will work. I believe there are more traditional ways of invading a new territory."

"You want our army!" the Queen of Hearts said.

Morina clapped her hands excitedly. "Exactly," she said. "I say we let the witches be our pawns. Let them invade the Otherworld and weaken its defenses. Once they've both exhausted all their resources, we'll charge into the Otherworld and steal it from them! We'll destroy Alex, the witches, and whatever is left standing in our way!"

It was the most thrilling and lucrative offer the villains had ever received. They were all fidgeting in their seats at the thought of the conquest. However, they still didn't know if Morina could be trusted.

"How do we know you won't just betray us in the end, too?" Captain Hook asked.

"We've already been deceived once by someone in this world—we won't let it happen again!" the Wicked Witch said.

"Unlike the Masked Man, I don't bite off more than I can chew," Morina said. "We'll divide the Otherworld evenly among us—we'll each have our own territory twice the size of this world. Surely that's more than enough land for each of us. Time is of the essence, so if you're interested, I need to know now. Do we have a deal, or not?"

The villains huddled together to discuss the situation privately, but Morina could tell they had already made up their minds. They were creatures of greed and couldn't refuse.

"We have a deal," Captain Hook said. "But if you disappoint us, we'll end you just like we ended the Masked Man!"

Morina laughed loudly. "You think you *killed* the Masked Man?" she asked.

"Of course we killed him," the Queen of Hearts said. "No man could have survived that fall!"

"Yes, but the Masked Man isn't a man—he's a *roach*," Morina said sharply. "Even if you cut off his head, he'd be back the very second a throne was left unattended. We haven't seen the last of him. But don't worry, I have something that will bring him to his knees should he try to sabotage our plan."

"And what is that?" the Wicked Witch asked.

The villains were curious, but not nearly as curious as

the Masked Man himself. He had very few possessions—what had the witch stolen?

"Not *what*, but *who*," Morina said. "I've kidnapped his *son*, a boy named Emmerich."

"The Masked Man has a child?" Captain Hook asked.

"Not one he knows about," Morina said. "But should he ever cross us, the boy will stop him in his tracks."

The Masked Man was so shocked, he dropped the revolver. He no longer felt any of his injuries or the anger boiling inside him. He forgot all about losing his empire and his desire to kill the villains. All he could feel was adrenaline and his heartbeat. All he could think about was the *son* he never knew he had.

"I should return to the witches before they get suspicious," Morina said.

The witch stood from her stone throne and with a snap of her fingers, the boulders all returned to normal. The villains were buzzing with anticipation. If they could invade the Otherworld today, they wouldn't hesitate.

"When will the invasion take place?" the Queen of Hearts asked. "We want our soldiers to be prepared."

"It won't be long now," Morina said. "When the time is right, we'll strike. I'll be in touch."

The witch covered her horns with her hood and disappeared into the trees. The villains ordered the Winkie soldiers to escort them out of the woods and practically skipped back to the Northern Palace.

The Masked Man was still so astonished, he stayed in the bushes long after the villains were gone. Having a son presented him with a world of new opportunities—opportunities he had never thought possible. If he played his cards right, the Masked Man could regain much more than just his empire—he could salvage *everything* that had been stolen from him....

CHAPTER SEVEN

THE CAPTAIN AND HER CREW

I packed you both a turkey sandwich, chips, yogurt, a banana, two bottles of water, and a cookie," Charlotte said. "There's also a sweatshirt, a flashlight, a Swiss Army knife, a first-aid kit, matches, and a compass."

The twins' mother handed them each a backpack full of the items she'd packed. Alex and Conner appreciated the gesture, but traveling into a fictitious dimension was very different from going on a camping trip.

"Thanks, Mom," Alex said. "You didn't have to do that."

"Yeah, this isn't our first rodeo," Conner said, and looked through his backpack. *"Oh cool, chocolate chip! Thanks!"*

"It's just a few things—I'll feel better knowing you have them," Charlotte said. "So where's your first stop? Any idea how long you'll be gone for?"

Alex turned to Conner, just as curious as their mother. For the first time in their lives, she was leaving all the planning to her brother. She had offered to help a number of times, but Conner was determined to do everything himself. Not insisting was a gamble on Alex's part, but he seemed very confident he had everything taken care of.

"First up is my short story 'Starboardia,'" Conner said excitedly. "It's a pirate adventure set in the Caribbean Sea around the early 1700s. The story's about Captain Auburn Sally and her all-female crew as they search deserted islands for buried treasure."

Charlotte hid her concern behind a smile. "Sounds *progressive*," she said.

"Don't worry—we'll be fine," Conner said. "Auburn Sally is based on Goldilocks. We'll find her ship, tell her the situation, and bring her and her crew back to the house. It'll be easy."

"If you say so," Charlotte said, unconvinced.

"Go get 'em," Bob said, and patted him on the back.

Conner had organized his writing neatly in a binder with tabs separating the short stories. He opened the binder to the first page of "Starboardia" and set it on the living room floor.

"Are you sure there isn't anything we need before we go?" Alex asked one final time. "There's nothing you're overlooking or forgetting about?"

"Trust me. I've got everything under control," he said. "If there's one thing I know inside out, it's my short stories. I've actually been really looking forward to this. I bet my characters will be excited to meet me!"

Traveling into the short stories had been all Conner could think about since he'd first had the idea. Naturally, the circumstances to warrant the trip were terrible, but he still felt like the luckiest author in the world. Who else got to visit the worlds and meet the people that existed only in their imagination? Conner often fantasized about seeing a film or a play based on his writing one day, but *this* would be much better than that. It wouldn't be *someone else's* interpretation or adaptation of his words; everything would be purely as he'd envisioned it.

Conner removed Mother Goose's flask, which contained the Portal Potion, from his back pocket. He poured a couple of drops on the binder and then stored the flask safely in his backpack. The pages illuminated like a powerful spotlight, shining a bright beam of light toward the ceiling.

"Here we go!" Conner said. "Wish us luck!"

"Good luck!" Bob said. "We'll be here when you get back."

"Make good choices!" Charlotte said. "There's also some sunscreen in your bags if it's sunny out!"

Alex and Conner strapped on their backpacks, stepped into the beam of light, and disappeared from the house.

Just like it had when they traveled into *The Wonderful Wizard of Oz*, *Peter Pan*, and *Alice's Adventures in Wonderland*, the Portal Potion first took them into an endless space with nothing but words. Rather than printed text, words were *written* all around them, as if there were hundreds of invisible pencils moving through the air. Each word was in Conner's messy handwriting.

"Awesome!" Conner said. "It's like we've stepped inside my brain!"

"You've got to work on your penmanship," Alex noted.

The handwritten words stretched into shapes, then gained color and texture, and finally transformed into the objects they described. Conner watched in awe as the world of his first short story came to life around him. Alex was excited, too, until she saw the words *ocean waves* stretching below their feet.

"Hey, Conner?" she said. "Should we be worried about—"

Before she could finish her sentence, the twins fell into an ocean that formed under their feet. Strong waves crashed over them, pushing them farther and farther below the water. The water was difficult to swim against, but they kicked their way to the surface and spit out mouthfuls of salty water. Conner saw his binder of short stories floating in the water nearby and retrieved it before the waves carried it away. If he lost the binder, the twins would lose their exit back into the Otherworld.

Alex angrily splashed water in her brother's face. *"Why didn't you say we needed a boat?"* she asked.

"Sorry!" Conner said. "I forgot the first thing I described was the ocean!"

By now the handwritten words had finished forming the world of "Starboardia" around them. They were bobbing up and down in the middle of the Caribbean Sea. The air was so misty, they could barely see each other, let alone any land or ships in the distance. Alex snapped her fingers and a small wooden rowboat appeared in front of them.

The twins climbed aboard and caught their breath. Conner put the binder in his backpack, where it would be safe. If anything happened to it, they would have no way back home.

"Well, *that* was a rough start," Alex said. "What's the *second* thing you described?"

"The *Dolly Llama*," Conner said.

"The Dolly Llama?"

"It's the name of Auburn Sally's ship," he said. "Don't judge me, I thought it was a funny name for a ship. We should see it any minute now."

A towering shadow appeared in the mist—something very large headed their way. The shadow grew larger and darker and details formed as it got closer. Finally, the twins saw that it was a pirate ship sailing straight toward their rowboat with no sign of slowing down. It was going to plow right into them!

"Abandon boat!" Conner yelled.

The twins dived into the water just as the ship smashed into their rowboat, crushing it to pieces. Once again, Alex and Conner were caught under the vicious waves. They swam to the surface and were sloshed around the choppy water as the pirate ship sailed right past them.

"Ahoy!" Conner yelled up at the ship. *"Twins overboard! Help us!"*

A few seconds later, a rope ladder was rolled off the ship, and it landed in the water next to the twins. They grabbed it, climbed up, pulled themselves over the ship's railing, and collapsed onto the lower deck. They were drenched and coughing up seawater.

Alex looked up and saw a large black flag flying above the ship with a llama skull on it.

"This must be the *Dolly Llama*," Alex said. She pointed out the flag to Conner, and a giant smile grew on his face. He leaped to his feet and helped his sister to hers. The flag was proof they were in his short story.

"We made it!" he exclaimed. "Alex, we're in 'Starboardia'!"

His excitement was cut short when they heard footsteps nearby. A dozen female pirates surrounded Alex and Conner, and they didn't look friendly. The pirates pointed their swords and rifles at the twins.

"Well, well, well," said a woman with an eye patch. "Look what we have here."

"What are you two scallywags doing in the middle of the sea?" asked a woman with enormous lips. "Too *young* to be in the navy, too *fair* to be pirates."

Conner almost stepped on a pirate behind him and jumped. Having no legs, the pirate walked on her hands and held a dagger with her teeth.

"My guess is they were *stowaways*!" the legless pirate said. "I'm surprised the sharks didn't find them first!"

Conner couldn't believe his characters were living and breathing before his eyes. The women were just as rough, dirty, and sunburned as he had imagined them. He grinned from ear to ear and jumped up and down.

"I'm so happy to see you guys!" he said.

The pirates tilted their heads at him like confused puppies. No one had ever been *happy* to see them before.

"Guys, it's *me*!" Conner said. "I'm Conner Bailey!"

The pirates raised their eyebrows and scratched their heads—should they know who he was?

"Who?" asked a pirate with a round, flat face.

"Oh, come on." Conner laughed. "I'm the *author*!"

"Author of *what*?" asked a pirate with bare feet.

"Of *this story*," he said. "I created this ocean, I created this ship, and I created all of you. Do you really not recognize me?"

Conner thought for sure it would have clicked by now, but the pirates still stared at him awkwardly, just as perplexed as before.

"He's been marooned for too long—the boy's gone mad," said a pirate with a peg leg, and the other pirates nodded in agreement.

Conner was getting frustrated. "I'm not crazy," he said. "Look, where is Auburn Sally? Let me talk to her. I'm sure she'll straighten this whole thing out. This is my own fault—I should have written you guys to be smarter."

The pirates stopped looking puzzled and began staring daggers at him. Alex covered her face and let out a sigh— this wasn't going to be as easy as her brother thought.

"*Oooooh, Captain*," the pirate with the eye patch called. "There's someone down here who'd like to have a word with you!"

Suddenly, a woman did a backflip off the upper deck and landed directly in front of the twins. She wore a large black hat, a long brown coat, tall boots, and she had a sword and pistol attached to her thick belt. Alex knew this was Auburn Sally from the minute she laid eyes on her. If her acrobatics weren't enough to give it away, the captain looked exactly like Goldilocks. The only difference in their features was the captain's long locks of auburn hair.

"*Sally!*" Conner said like he was seeing an old friend— because, technically, he was. He stepped toward the captain to give her a hug, but Auburn Sally quickly drew her pistol and aimed it at his head.

"Am I supposed to know you, *boy*?" Auburn Sally asked.

Conner was shocked by the treatment he was receiving from his own characters. He had expected a warm and gracious welcome, but instead the heroine of his story was holding a gun to his head. Without him none of them would even exist! He wondered if this was what an underappreciated parent felt like.

He held his hands up and backed away from the pistol. "Okay, time out!" he said. "Everyone just calm down and let me explain! My name is Conner Bailey, and this is my sister, Alex. I know this is hard to believe, but I'm your *creator*! We are living in a short story I wrote for my eighth-grade English class!"

Auburn Sally looked at him with more perplexity than that of all her crew added together. "He's got yellow fever," she said. "Prepare the plank! We need to get him off the ship at once!"

"I'm not sick, either!" Conner said. "Fine! If you don't believe me, I'll prove it!"

He walked around the circle of women, pointing at each pirate.

"That's Winking Wendy, Fish-Lips Lucy, Somersault Sydney, Pancake-Face Patty, Stinky-Feet Phoebe, and that's Peg-Leg Peggy," he said.

"I prefer *Margret*," said the pirate with the peg leg.

"Fine, *Margret*," Conner said, and rolled his eyes. "In the back, that's High-Tide Tabitha, Catfish Kate, Too-Much-Rum Ronda, Big-Booty Bertha, Not-So-Jolly

Joan, and up in the crow's nest, that's Siren Sue. Your captain is Auburn Sally, this ship is called the *Dolly Llama*, and you're all searching the Caribbean for buried treasure!"

Conner crossed his arms confidently and waited for their apologies. The pirates were startled by how much he knew. They all looked at their captain, waiting to see how she would respond.

"There's only one explanation for how a young man we've never met before could possibly know so much," Auburn Sally said. "*He's a warlock!* Tie him and his sister up! We'll burn them at the stake on the next island we find!"

Before they knew it, the twins' backpacks were yanked off and they were pushed against the mainmast. The pirates wrapped ropes around their bodies, binding their torsos to the ship. Conner was so mad, he turned bright red.

"*Let us go or you'll be sorry!*" he yelled. "*Just wait until I get home! I'm going to write a sequel where you all get shipwrecked and have to eat your boots to survive!*"

The pirates laughed at his attempts to scare them. Winking Wendy pulled the ropes even tighter just to spite him.

"*Keep it up, Wendy! We'll see who's laughing when I have a seagull peck out your other eye!*" Conner warned. "Alex, can you believe this?"

"How did you expect them to react?" she asked. "What would you do if a guy showed up out of nowhere and told us we were characters in *his* story?"

"*I would punch him in the face for making everything so damn difficult!*" he said. "Alex, you've got to do something! Zap them with a sleeping spell, turn them into sea horses—*anything!*"

"*No!*" Alex yelled. "I've been asking you for days if you needed any help planning, and you told me you had *everything under control*! Well, so far we almost drowned, we narrowly missed being crushed by a ship, and now we're being captured by *your* pirates! You and I have different definitions of *under control*!"

"Alex, don't be a child!" Conner said.

"Grow up, Conner!" she said. "This is *your* mess—*you* clean it up!"

"Fine, I will!" he yelled. "I don't need you or your stupid magic! I'll find a way out of this myself!"

Although Alex and Conner were tied up right next to each other, they each pretended the other wasn't there and pouted in silence.

A strong ocean breeze began clearing the mist and uncovered the sun. Soon the ship had a breathtaking view of the ocean surrounding it. There was nothing to see but the bright blue Caribbean Sea for miles around them.

Captain Auburn Sally returned to the upper deck and wrapped her hands around the large helm. She looked out at the open water and a radiant smile spread across her face. There was nothing keeping her back and no one to stop her; she was surrounded by an abundance of freedom and possibilities. Conner remembered writing about that expression—it was the expression he always wished the real Goldilocks could have more often.

"Once again, it's a beautiful day to be a pirate," Auburn Sally said to her crew. "Ladies, *lower the sales*!"

The twins looked up, expecting the sails above them to come down and fill with the ocean air. Instead, Siren Sue peeked out of the crow's nest with a treasure chest full of scarves, jewelry, hooks, and weapons. The other pirates gathered below her with hands full of gold coins.

"You heard the captain—time to lower the sales!" Siren Sue announced. "For a limited time, everything is half off! Scarves are two coins, earrings are four coins, necklaces are six coins, and the rifles are eight coins! Get your accessories while the sales are low!"

Siren Sue sold off the items to the pirates below until there was nothing left in her chest. The women ogled their new purchases and showed them off to one another. It absolutely baffled Alex, and when she glanced at Conner, he looked just as confused as she did.

"I don't understand what's happening," he said. "I never wrote *that*."

"Did you mean to write *lower the sails*? Like the *normal sails* on a ship?" Alex asked.

"Oops," Conner said. "I must have spelled it wrong."

To his relief, once the *sales* were over, the pirates lowered the *sails*, too. They were made from cream-colored cloth, the exact color of Porridge's coat. They filled with the ocean breeze, and the *Dolly Llama* sailed into the horizon.

Auburn Sally turned the ship's wheel back and forth as she guided her vessel through the rough waters. She kept a watchful eye on the entire horizon around them. The longer the ship sailed, the more a familiar expression grew on her face—one that the twins had seen Goldilocks wear many times when they'd first met her. The captain seemed a little sad, like she was hoping something would appear in the distance, but it never came.

Conner recognized this face, too, and began to worry.

"Oh no," he said. "We're getting close to the part of the story when the navy shows up."

"How can you tell?" Alex asked.

"From the way Auburn Sally is looking out over the ocean longingly," he said. "The pirates are about to get company."

Like clockwork, Siren Sue climbed down from the crow's nest in a panic.

"Captain!" she shouted. "Look, in the east! A ship from the British Navy is approaching!"

Auburn Sally quickly unfolded a long telescope and scanned the eastern horizon. Alex and Conner squinted and could barely see a small speck moving in the distance. The captain smiled as she spotted the ship—this was what she had been hoping for.

"It looks like Admiral Jacobson has finally caught up with us," Auburn Sally announced to her crew.

"Any orders, Captain?" Winking Wendy asked.

"I'm tired of playing the admiral's game of cat and mouse," the captain said. *"Hoist the sails and prepare for battle!"*

The pirates all saluted her and went to work right away. They loaded the cannons on deck and sharpened their swords. The sails were rolled up and the ship slowed down, allowing the admiral's ship to gain on them. The small speck the twins saw in the distance quickly grew into an enormous ship twice the size of the *Dolly Llama*. Soon they could make out a British flag waving from the tallest mast and the ship's name painted along its side: the *Royal Tantrum*.

While the pirates scurried around the deck preparing for battle, the captain gazed at herself in a compact mirror. Auburn Sally applied lipstick and blush, she brushed her hair to give it extra volume, and she wiped off all the smudges on her clothes. The captain wasn't getting ready for *combat*; she was getting ready for a *date*!

"That's how she prepares for battle?" Alex asked her brother.

Conner nodded bashfully. "Just wait," he said. "In about five minutes it's all going to make perfect sense."

When the *Royal Tantrum* was getting close to the *Dolly Llama*, the pirates dropped the sails and sailed around the navy ship. The twins could see that the *Royal Tantrum*'s lower deck was full of British sailors running amok. They spotted Admiral Jacobson standing on the upper deck.

The admiral was posed regally, with one foot on the railing and a long sword in his hand. He was a very handsome man with broad shoulders and pitch-black hair in a neat ponytail. He wore a blue coat with several gold buttons and badges. The closer the pirate ship sailed around the navy ship, the more familiar he seemed.

"Conner, is it just me, or does the admiral look exactly like *Jack*?" Alex asked.

She glanced between the captain and the admiral. Just like her brother said, it all finally made sense.

"Oooooh," Alex said. "I get it now. Auburn Sally is based on Goldilocks, and the admiral is based on Jack. 'Starboardia' is a love story! That's so sweet!"

Conner grunted like his sister had just insinuated something very crude.

"Excuse me," he said defensively. "'Starboardia' is a *pirate adventure*! It might have *elements* of love, but it is absolutely *not* a love story!"

Alex raised an eyebrow at him. *"Sure,"* she said mockingly.

By now, the *Dolly Llama* was sailing around the *Royal Tantrum* with gusto. The British sailors ran across the deck to watch the pirates circling them. Winking Wendy took the wheel and Auburn Sally went to the railing to see the admiral. She mimicked his pose on the railing of her own ship, and the two commanders locked eyes. If Alex hadn't known there was something between them before, she definitely knew it now.

"Good afternoon, Admiral," Auburn Sally said. "What brings you to this part of the Caribbean today?"

"You're a wanted woman, Auburn Sally," the admiral said.

"You mean, by more than just you?" the captain said playfully. "Honestly, Admiral, you're so persistent, I'm starting to think you have a little crush on me."

The pirates roared with laughter. Even the navy soldiers were amused and covered their mouths to hide their chuckles. The whole scene felt like it should have happened in a high school hallway instead of the Caribbean Sea.

"The entire British Navy is just *smitten* with you, Captain," the admiral said. "They've asked me to personally escort you back to land. Come willingly and I won't sink your ship."

"Admiral, may I remind you I am *literally* sailing circles around you," she said. "It's *your* ship I'm worried about. I'd hate to destroy it and embarrass you in front of all your men. By the way, *nice tights, gentlemen!*"

"So it's going to be the hard way, is it?" Admiral Jacobson said with a grin.

Auburn Sally laughed. "Oh, Admiral," she said, "haven't you learned by now I'm the kind of girl who likes—"

"PLAYING HARD TO GET!" Conner yelled, finishing her sentence.

The captain and her crew quickly turned to him, wondering how on earth he knew exactly what she had been planning to say.

"I told you this is my story," Conner reminded them. "I wrote the cheesy dialogue coming out of your mouths!

Would you quit the innuendos and just get to the battle already?"

Auburn Sally glared at him suspiciously for a moment, then turned to face the admiral again.

"I agree with the warlock," she said. *"Ladies, open fire!"*

As the *Dolly Llama* circled the *Royal Tantrum*, it was like the ships were joined together in a dangerous waltz and the pirates were taking the lead. They lit their cannons and fired them at the navy sailors, blasting large holes in the British ship. The admiral's sailors retaliated, but the pirate ship was much smaller and moving fast, making it a harder target.

The few times the pirates were hit, the entire ship rattled and swayed in the water. But the damage the navy was inflicting was nothing compared to the mark the pirates were leaving. The sailors looked to the admiral for guidance, but he seldom gave them orders. It was almost like he *wanted* to lose.

Cannonballs and chunks of wood flew through the air. Parts of the navy ship were set ablaze and the sky filled with smoke. Conner had written the entire battle, but writing it was nothing like living it. Even though he knew exactly what was going to happen, it was still terrifying to see it come to life.

"This is the most dangerous flirting I've ever seen!" Alex said.

"Don't worry, the pirates win!" Conner said, then

looked up at the captain. "Sally, would you hurry up and tell your pirates to aim for the navy's cannons already? I don't want to get splinters in my eyes!"

The thought had come into the captain's head just a moment before Conner suggested it. "How did you know I was—"

"JUST DO IT!" he yelled.

"Aim for their cannons, girls!" Auburn Sally ordered.

The pirates followed their captain's orders and aimed their cannons at the navy's. They blasted them off the ship, leaving the *Royal Tantrum* virtually defenseless. The pirates cheered and shook their swords at the sailors.

Winking Wendy jerked the wheel, and the *Dolly Llama* slammed into the *Royal Tantrum*, bringing the pirate ship alongside it.

"Now let's take their ship!" Auburn Sally ordered.

The pirates each grabbed a rope and swung aboard the navy ship. The battle continued with hand-to-hand combat on the decks of the *Royal Tantrum*. The sailors were barely trained for sailing and were no match for the pirates attacking them.

Winking Wendy flashed her empty eye socket at the sailors, scaring them and causing them to trip over themselves. Stinky-Feet Phoebe held her bare feet against their noses, and the fumes made the men temporarily lose consciousness. Having no legs made it easy for Somersault Sydney to tumble into the sailors and knock them down like bowling pins. Pancake-Face Patty seemed to enjoy head-butting the men, which explained the odd shape of her skull. Big-Booty Bertha simply turned her backside to any of the sailors charging toward her, and they bounced backward onto the deck.

Some of the pirates weren't as efficient fighters. Siren Sue sang high notes to hurt the sailors' ears. Fish-Lips Lucy irritated them with slobbery kisses. Too-Much-Rum Ronda drunkenly argued with the sailors about religion and politics. Not-So-Jolly Joan simply cried on their shoulders. These pirates offered perfect distractions for Peg-Leg Peggy (or "Margret") to sneak up behind the sailors and trip them with her wooden leg.

On the upper deck, Captain Auburn Sally and Admiral Jacobson walked around each other with their swords raised. They were so lost in each other's eyes that they almost forgot they had to fight to keep up appearances. When the two eventually started dueling, it resembled more of a passionate tango than an actual sword fight.

"This is the most nonviolent violence I've ever witnessed," Alex said.

"I kept it tame in case I had young readers," Conner said.

"That explains why the antagonists are so simple," she noted. "To be honest, I was really worried about what kind of villains your imagination would have come up with. I'm glad they're just men in tights."

"The navy sailors aren't the bad guys in this story," he said. "The bad guys are *way* scarier. They're based on people I've seen in nightmares. But we'll be long gone before they show up . . . *I hope*."

Eventually, the sailors surrendered and the pirates rounded them up in the center of the *Royal Tantrum*'s lower deck. Auburn Sally pushed Admiral Jacobson off the upper deck, and his men caught him. The pirates raised their weapons in celebration—they had won the battle!

"You've lost, Admiral," Auburn Sally said. "The British Navy is going to be so disappointed."

"Sometimes a man fails in order to win," the admiral said with a smirk.

The navy sailors were stripped of their weapons, and their hands were tied behind their backs. The pirates placed a plank between ships and forced the sailors to cross it and board the *Dolly Llama*. Once everyone aboard the *Royal Tantrum* had been taken prisoner, the pirates blasted the navy ship with cannonballs until it sank.

"Put the prisoners in the cells belowdecks," Auburn Sally ordered, and glanced at the twins. "And I mean *all* the prisoners."

The pirates untied the twins and pushed them along with the sailors.

"Oh no," Conner said. "The bad guys are going to show up soon! I've got to convince Auburn Sally I'm the author of this story before they get here!"

"I'm willing to help you if it speeds things up," Alex said with a sigh.

"Well, I'm not willing to accept your help yet," he said. "I told you I can take care of this on my own!"

Conner managed to push past the pirates manhandling him and his sister. He dashed across the deck, but just before he was in reach of Auburn Sally, he was tripped by Somersault Sydney and tackled by Catfish Kate and High-Tide Tabitha.

"Captain, don't lock us up!" he pleaded from underneath the pirates. "I'm warning you! Something really bad is about to happen, but you can avoid it if you just listen to me!"

Auburn Sally laughed at his warning. "Take him away," she said, and turned her back on him.

The pirates forced Conner to his feet and dragged him away, but he wasn't ready to give up.

"I know what you stole from SMOKY-SAILS SAM!" Conner yelled.

The entire ship suddenly froze as if he'd shouted something obscene. Alex could tell that all the pirates and sailors knew who her brother was talking about. Just the mention of the name Smoky-Sails Sam sent a collective chill down their spines.

Auburn Sally turned back to Conner with large, fearful eyes. He continued his warning, desperate for her to listen to him.

"He knows what you stole from him, too—he knows about everything that happened on the island!" Conner said. "Smoky-Sails Sam is looking for you and your crew right now! He's going to see the smoke from this battle and be here before sunrise tomorrow!"

Conner knew that if anything would get through to her this would be it. The captain looked him up and down but didn't say a word.

"Your orders, Captain?" Catfish Kate asked.

Auburn Sally put on a brave face for her crew. "Throw this boy and his sister in the cells with the others," she said. "If he has tall tales to tell, he can share them with the other prisoners."

Auburn Sally turned around and faced the ocean. Conner struggled against the pirates, but it was no use. They were too strong to break free from—that's how he had written them. Conner and Alex were pushed down the steps to the cells belowdecks with the sailors.

"Well, that *totally* worked," Alex said. "Are you sure you don't want my help?"

"Give it a minute," Conner said. "She'll come around—she'll have to."

The captain looked down at the burning wreckage of the *Royal Tantrum*, and her eyes followed the trails of smoke ascending into the sky. Once all the sailors and the twins were belowdecks and there were no pirates around to bear witness, she pulled out a necklace she kept hidden in her shirt. Dangling from a golden chain was a bloodred ruby the size of a human heart.

While she refused to believe everything Conner had said, she couldn't deny that he possessed extraordinary knowledge of her ship and crew. If what he said about Smoky-Sails Sam was even remotely accurate, then the captain's greatest nightmare was about to come true.

CHAPTER EIGHT

THE WRATH OF SMOKY-SAILS SAM

Things were calm belowdecks on the *Dolly Llama*. Alex and Conner shared a small cell, while Admiral Jacobson and his men occupied four larger ones. Everyone was silent, not from the embarrassment of defeat, but from the sheer exhaustion of the battle. In all fairness, the sailors didn't seem disappointed by their loss and sat rather comfortably in the cells. Many were stretched out and gently rocked to sleep by the sway of the ship.

"Don't worry, men," Admiral Jacobson said as he paced

around his cell. "We will find a way off this vessel and bring the pirates to justice! Those criminals may imprison us now, but soon we shall escape and make the British Navy proud!"

The sailors looked around the cells to see whom the Admiral was talking to, because none of them were too worried or eager to change the situation. After months of strenuous labor operating the *Royal Tantrum*, imprisonment was a nice change of pace for them.

"Save it, Admiral," Conner said. "The whole crew knows you've got the hots for Auburn Sally. No one is expecting to escape anytime soon."

The admiral was outraged by his insinuation. "How dare you suggest I *welcomed* the sinking of my ship or *allowed* pirates to capture my men!" he said. "I would never betray Britain with affection for a scoundrel like Captain Auburn Sally!"

Conner sighed and shook his head. "Raise your hand if you knew this was going to happen," he said. "Come on, don't be shy."

He raised his hand and Alex quickly followed. One by one, the sailors raised their hands, too, and the admiral was faced with a rude awakening. Despite his efforts to shield it, the heart on his sleeve was just as visible as the badges of honor on his coat.

"You mean, you've all known the entire time?" he asked.

The sailors nodded in unison with the twins.

"To be honest, Admiral," said the first mate, "I don't

think any of us knew you were trying to *hide it*. We don't hold it against you, though. The whole reason we joined the navy in the first place was to have an adventure, and there's never been a dull moment chasing these dames around the sea."

The admiral wanted to argue further, but the jig was clearly up. Instead of clearing his reputation, he just shrugged and had a seat on the floor.

"Well, I suppose that's a relief, then," Jacobson said.

The admiral lost all desire to form an escape plan. He put his feet up on the metal bars and enjoyed the quiet and calm of the cells with the rest of his crew. Conner, on the other hand, was growing more agitated by the second. His mission to locate and recruit his characters was going to be much more difficult now that he had refused his sister's help.

"So what happens next in this story?" Alex asked with a yawn.

"Auburn Sally is going to invite Admiral Jacobson to dinner in her chambers," Conner said. "They'll admit their affection for each other and then Jacobson will convince his sailors to join Auburn Sally's crew of pirates."

"Nice," Alex said. "And you still think 'Starboardia' isn't a love story?"

Conner grunted. "Okay, fine—*it's a love story*," he said. "You've identified your brother as a big sap. Are you happy now?"

Alex laughed. "I don't know why it's so hard for you to admit it," she said. "Plenty of men write romances."

"I never meant to write a romance," Conner said. "I just thought Jack and Goldilocks had a really cool story. Everyone wants to be a hero, but Jack gave it up to be with the person he loved. He didn't care what people thought of him—Goldilocks was more important to him than his reputation. It takes courage to face a giant, but it takes a true hero to stand up to the world. I guess I wanted to celebrate that by putting it into my own story."

A smile grew on Alex's face as she listened to her brother. He kept his feelings hidden behind an emotional brick wall, but every so often she managed to knock a hole through it and peek inside.

"You're not a sap, but you're definitely a *hopeless romantic*," she said. "I think Mrs. Peters was right. You're going to learn a lot about yourself traveling through these stories."

Conner didn't want to agree with her, but he knew she was right. "Oh brother," he said. "Next thing you know, I'll be collecting porcelain dolls and listening to polka music."

The doors opened and Winking Wendy and Somersault Sydney walked in. They rattled the cell bars with their weapons to disturb their captives, but the tranquil sailors didn't even look up. The pirates unlocked the admiral's cell and pulled him out by the ponytail.

"Ouch!" Jacobson shouted. "What's the meaning of this?"

"The captain wants you to join her for dinner," Winking Wendy said.

The sailors hooted and whistled, making the admiral

blush. Winking Wendy flashed them her empty eye socket and they quickly quieted down. The pirates unlocked the door of the twins' cell next.

"What's going on?" Conner asked.

"Captain wants you two to join her as well," Somersault Sydney said.

Conner wasn't expecting this. Up to this moment, every beat of the story had followed his writing without a hitch. He hoped it meant his warning about Smoky-Sails Sam had caught the captain's attention.

The pirates escorted the twins and the admiral through the *Dolly Llama* to the upper deck. They opened a pair of double doors and pushed the twins and the admiral into the captain's quarters.

Auburn Sally's private chambers were the most elegant part of the ship. The walls were covered in red wallpaper and gold crown molding. A crystal chandelier hung over a long wooden table set for four. The captain looked like she was deep in thought when they arrived. She sat in the back of her chambers at a desk with several maps of the Caribbean spread across it. She was sitting with one foot up and spun a dagger on the desk like a dreidel. Her hat and coat were hung on a rack beside the desk, exposing her full head of long wavy hair.

"Your guests, Captain," Winking Wendy said as she presented the twins and the admiral.

"Thank you," Auburn Sally said. "You may leave us."

Winking Wendy and Somersault Sydney left the chambers, shutting the double doors behind them. Conner had written the next part of the story as a romantic dinner between the captain and the admiral, but obviously things had changed. As soon as they entered, Auburn Sally fixated on him with an inquisitive, unwavering stare.

"Since you seem to know *everything*, I imagine there's no point in pretending the admiral and I are adversaries," she said.

"Nope," Conner said. "You guys are in a complicated long-distance relationship."

"Just for the record," Alex chimed in, "I think it's *very* romantic."

Conner gave his sister a dirty look—she was *never* going to let it go. The admiral glanced between the twins and the captain, waiting for someone to fill him in.

"Will someone explain how this lad knows so much about us?" he asked.

"According to him, we're just characters in a story he's written," Auburn Sally said with amusement. "He believes everything in this world is just a figment of his imagination."

Conner didn't appreciate the disdainful tone in her voice. The admiral looked at him just like everyone else had after hearing the pronouncement.

"Have I done or said anything to *contradict* it?" Conner asked. "Because I'm pretty sure I've been right about *everything* so far."

Auburn Sally glared at him and a challenging look came to her face.

"I have something hidden underneath my shirt," the

captain said. "There are only four people alive who know it exists. Two are in this room, and one is the Queen of England. Guess correctly, and I *might* take you more seriously."

Conner knew exactly what she was referring to and didn't waste a minute to prove it. "You're wearing a necklace called the Heart of the Caribbean," he said. "It's the most prized piece of jewelry in the Western Hemisphere. It was given to Governor Connelly by Queen Anne as a token of her appreciation for governing the small island of Saint Ballena."

The intensity in Auburn Sally's face dissolved and her mouth fell open. She and the admiral were completely dumbfounded. The captain pulled on a gold chain around her neck and lifted a large ruby necklace out of her blouse. The ruby was brighter than the crown molding and the chandelier put together.

Conner pointed at the jewel. "*That's* what you stole from Smoky-Sails Sam," he said. "And you're wrong, by the way. There are *five* people alive who know it exists, seven including my sister and me. A pirate named Killy Billy saw you steal it. He's the one who told Smoky-Sails Sam you have it, and now Sam is on his way to take it back."

Alex was usually really good about filling in the blanks, but the lack of detail was getting frustrating.

"Would you mind sharing with the rest of the class who Smoky-Sails Sam is?" she asked.

Conner hesitated. He knew the story like the back of his hand; it just wasn't a pleasant one to share.

"Smoky-Sails Sam is the most feared pirate in the

Caribbean," he explained. "He's so powerful, the British Navy refuses to go anywhere near him. He has a fleet of five ships and hundreds of pirates. His ships burn rows of torches above their sails, leaving trails of smoke through the sky, so the whole Caribbean knows where they've been and where they're headed. They obliterate any ship they encounter, whether it's a threat or not."

Alex gulped. This was exactly the kind of villain she was afraid her brother would create.

"He sounds *charming*," Alex said. "How did he become so powerful?"

"Smoky-Sails Sam used to be a slave," Conner said. "He was captured from an African village by slave traders and brought to the Caribbean on a slave ship. However, on the way over, he broke the chains that bound him and led the other slaves in a mutiny. They killed the slave traders and took over the ship. Sam became the new captain, the liberated slaves became his crew, and he renamed the ship the *Vengeance*.

"Unfortunately, the power went to Sam's head. His crew wanted to go home, but Sam wanted to continue on and seek more revenge. He sailed the *Vengeance* to the small island of Saint Ballena and ordered his men to raid it. Governor Connelly sent word to the British Navy that they were under attack, but since the island was so small and valueless, the navy abandoned them. The governor and all the men on Saint Ballena were killed and their families were forced to work as servants.

"Since there was no government or authority on Saint Ballena, criminals from all over the Caribbean sailed there and joined Sam. Soon, he had enough men to form a fleet of pirate ships. They terrorized all the colonies nearby, growing stronger and stronger after every target they hit. The liberated slaves from the *Vengeance* wanted nothing to do with it, so they stole a ship from Sam's fleet and headed back to Africa. Sam was so outraged, he sailed after them and sank their ship. The smoky debris from the destruction is how Sam became known as Smoky-Sails Sam, and the whole Caribbean learned of his ruthlessness.

"As time went on, Smoky-Sails Sam had a daughter named Sumire. Governor Connelly's only child, a girl named Christine, was forced to work as her maid. The young women became very close and loved each other like sisters. Sumire helped Christine plan an escape from Saint Ballena. The Heart of the Caribbean was the only object of Governor Connelly's that Smoky-Sails Sam did not destroy, so Christine stole it back before she left. It didn't take long before Smoky-Sails Sam realized it was missing. To save her friend, Sumire took the blame. Rather than showing his only child any mercy, Smoky-Sails Sam made a gruesome example out of her. He cut her throat in front of his entire fleet, further proving his brutality, and no one ever stole from him again.

"Christine escaped from the island and sold the Heart of the Caribbean to a jewel merchant, but then stole it back the following day. The money she had acquired in the sale was enough to buy her own ship and hire a crew. She named the ship the *Dolly Llama*, and became known throughout the Caribbean as—"

"*Auburn Sally!*" Alex said, finishing her brother's sentence.

"Correct," Conner said. "When Jacobson became an admiral, his first assignment was to capture the sailing thief Auburn Sally. It was love at first sight, and they've been chasing each other around the Caribbean ever since. What the captain doesn't know is that Killy Billy told Smoky-Sails Sam that he saw her steal the Heart of the Caribbean. Sam's been following the *Dolly Llama* through the sea, too, and is getting closer by the minute. Since Sally's the only person who's stolen something from him and lived to see another day, he wants to make another gruesome example out of her."

"Conner, that backstory is so dark! Why would you write something so dreadful?" Alex asked.

"I told you, it was based on a nightmare I had," he said. "Besides, it's not like real pirates were any better."

Conner turned to Auburn Sally and Admiral Jacobson with desperation in his eyes. "*Now do you believe I created you?*" he asked.

The captain and the admiral were both astonished by Conner's familiarity with their lives. Whoever he was, wherever he came from, they could no longer deny there was something unique and eerie about him.

"I believe you put pen to paper about all of this, but I'm

still not convinced you *created* this world or the people in it," Auburn Sally said.

Conner had rolled his eyes so many times, his sockets were getting sore. "So you think I *plagiarized* it?" he asked.

"Explorers are quick to claim the places they find, but they don't *create* the land they raise flags on," Auburn Sally said. "Perhaps all writers are nothing more than subconscious explorers, sailing across a sea of other worlds, and you're just the first to discover ours."

Alex was intrigued by the captain's theory. She wondered if every fictional story she had ever read was more of an author's *discovery* than his or her *idea*. Perhaps *imagination* was a *subconscious map* to uncharted worlds of the cosmos. It certainly would explain why her grandmother's Portal Potion was so effective—it didn't *create* the world the text described, but simply provided a doorway into a world that had always been there.

Conner was getting a headache trying to understand it himself. "That sounds really deep and complex, but you're missing the point!" he said. "I'm trying to tell you that Smoky-Sails Sam's fleet is headed here right now! He's planning to kill all of you and take back the Heart of the Caribbean! But if you listen to us, we can help you avoid him!"

"How?" Admiral Jacobson asked.

"By helping my sister and me," Conner explained. "I'm about to make you an offer—it's going to be hard to grasp, so we might want to sit for this."

Auburn Sally, the admiral, and the twins took seats around the long table.

"Do you want me to explain this part?" Alex asked.

"I told you, I got this," Conner said, and cleared his throat. "You know that subconscious sea of other worlds you were just talking about? Well, for all intents and purposes, it exists! There's another world that's in big trouble—one I didn't write about. All our friends live there and a horrible army has invaded it. My sister and I are recruiting people from a bunch of different worlds to help us fight the army. If you come with us and help us defeat them, we'll bring you right back here."

Conner grinned like he was being more than generous. The captain and the admiral exchanged a puzzled look—something didn't add up.

"That's not an offer," Auburn Sally said. "An offer is an *exchange*. Taking us away from our problems, making us fight for you, then bringing us right back to our problems isn't an exchange—it's just more work for us."

"She's got a point," Alex said.

"Okay," Conner said, and quickly thought about something appealing to offer. "Well, if you help us, I'll tell you how you defeat Smoky-Sails Sam."

The captain and the admiral nodded as they considered it. Jacobson whispered something into Auburn Sally's ear, like an attorney speaking with his client.

"So you're telling us we *defeat* Smoky-Sails Sam?" the captain asked. "*Regardless* of whether we help you or not?"

"Duh!" Conner said with a snort. "That's the whole point of this story."

Alex slapped a hand against her forehead. Her brother was oblivious to what Auburn Sally was implying. She appointed herself as *his* attorney and pulled him aside to whisper in his ear.

"Conner, you basically just told them they don't need to help you," she whispered. *"You need to make them an offer they can't refuse."*

"Oh, dang it!" he said. *"I should never have written them to be so cunning. Thanks for the heads-up."*

The twins turned back to the captain and the admiral. Conner let out a low, slow, and menacing chuckle.

"Silly, silly Sally," he said. "What you don't know is that the road to victory is long and tedious. There are dozens of battles, hundreds of casualties, and thousands of miles awaiting you. It takes *years* to learn what I could tell you in a matter of seconds. If you help us, I will give you the *shortcut* to your triumph, and save you a ton of hassle. You'd be sparing your ship from a lot of damage and even saving the lives of a few of your crew."

Auburn Sally and Admiral Jacobson whispered between themselves again. They both knew they would have to face Smoky-Sails Sam eventually; there was no way of getting around it. If Conner could supply them with information on how to do it efficiently, they would have to consider his offer seriously.

They turned to the twins and presented a counteroffer.

"We'll help you if you help us defeat Smoky-Sails Sam *first*," Auburn Sally said.

Conner was about to rip his hair out. He silently vowed never to write another smart character into one of his stories ever again.

"Deal," he said through a clenched jaw.

Conner and Auburn Sally shook hands over the table. Alex wasn't convinced the captain and the admiral were being truthful and pulled her brother aside one final time.

"How do you know they're being honest?" she whispered.

"Because I wrote them to be just as trustworthy as they are calculating," he said. *"And I'll remind them about that shipwreck in the sequel!"*

"Let's discuss the details of our victory over dinner," Auburn Sally said. "I'm famished. Negotiating always gives me an appetite."

It had been hours since their last meal, so the twins were glad to hear it. The captain rang a bell and a few moments later, Fish-Lips Lucy entered the chambers pushing a cart with several covered serving trays. The quarters filled with a delectable aroma and the twins began salivating and their stomachs growled.

"Conner, what did you write for dinner?" Alex asked.

"Tomato soup, mashed potatoes, and rosary chicken," Conner said, and licked his lips.

"Rosary chicken?" she asked. "Did you mean *rotisserie chicken*?"

"Oh no," he said fearfully.

Fish-Lips Lucy uncovered the largest serving tray, and rather than a delicious roasted chicken, she revealed a live chicken wearing a Catholic rosary. The chicken panicked and fluttered amok around the chambers, squawking loudly and shedding feathers wherever she went.

Auburn Sally gave Fish-Lips Lucy a dirty look. "The chicken seems a little *undercooked*," she said.

"Sorry, Captain," Fish-Lips Lucy said. "I knew I was forgetting something."

Suddenly, Siren Sue burst into the chambers, causing everyone to jump and forget all about the chicken. Her eyes were large and she was out of breath, like she had come in a hurry.

"Forgive my intrusion, Captain!" Siren Sue huffed. "I saw smoke rising on the horizon behind the ship! I inspected it and saw a fleet of ships coming this way! Smoky-Sails Sam is following us!"

The captain, the admiral, and the twins stood up so fast, they knocked silverware and plates off the table. Auburn Sally darted to the large windows in the back of her chambers and looked through a telescope beside her desk.

"It's Smoky-Sails Sam, all right," the captain said, and then jerked her head toward Conner. "I thought you said we had until morning."

He racked his brain trying to figure out why they were so early. "It's because I rushed the battle!" he said. "There was smoke in the sky earlier than there should have been! You and the admiral were supposed to exchange a lot more witty banter before the first cannon fired! I accidentally gave Smoky-Sails Sam a head start!"

Auburn Sally put on her hat and coat and immediately went into damage-control mode. "Lucy and Sue, tell the women to drop the sails at once," she ordered. "I want every candle and lantern on this ship extinguished—we'll be harder to follow in darkness. Also, free the sailors from the cells. If they want to survive the night, they'll need to join our crew."

The pirates nodded and ran out of the chambers to inform the others. Auburn Sally hurried out on deck and the twins and Jacobson followed. She wrapped her hands around the *Dolly Llama*'s wheel and looked to Conner.

"Well?" she asked. "What do we need to do to defeat Smoky-Sails Sam?"

"It's not a *what*, it's a *where*," he said. "We need to head *west* immediately, sail through the Parakeet Islands, and pass the Isle of Skulls."

The captain didn't waste a moment asking questions. She spun the wheel so hard to her right, it almost broke off.

"Conner, where are you taking us?" Alex asked.

"Starboardia," he said.

CHAPTER NINE

SAILING CIRCLES AROUND THE BERMUDA TRIANGLE

The pirates scurried across the decks of the *Dolly Llama* like panicked ants. They blew out all the torches, lanterns, and candles until the ship sailed in total darkness. With the moon as their only source of light, they lowered the sails and took full advantage of the night breeze. The sailors were released from the cells belowdecks and put to work loading and positioning the cannons. All it took was the mention of Smoky-Sails Sam's name and the sailors didn't hesitate in joining the *Dolly Llama*'s crew.

Admiral Jacobson stood at the front of the ship with one leg on the bowsprit. He scanned the sea ahead to make sure there was nothing the ship might collide with in the darkness.

"It looks clear," he called up to the captain. "I'll let you know if that changes."

Auburn Sally kept a firm grip on her ship's wheel and a close eye on the approaching fleet of pirates behind them. With every minute, Smoky-Sails Sam was getting closer and closer to the *Dolly Llama*. The captain prayed Conner's shortcut would work and they could finally defeat Sam and his crew.

"You said to sail west to the Parakeet Islands, pass the Isle of Skulls, and then what do we do?" she asked.

"Then we'll sail to the right in a circle for an entire day," he said. "The legend states, if you travel *starboard* for a day in the Bermuda Triangle, it'll take you to Starboardia— hence the name."

"Yes, I know the *legend*," Auburn Sally said. "Every pirate has heard of the myth. Are you sure it's real?"

Conner was getting tired of repeating himself. "Yes, I'm positive," he said. "It's how you guys find it in the end of the story. I'm sure it'll work now, too."

"So, Starboardia is an actual location?" Alex asked.

"Why else would I name this story 'Starboardia'?" her brother said.

Alex shrugged. "I thought it was just a cute name based on pirate lingo," she said. "Is there also a Portworld or Portopia or Portland?"

Conner froze and thought about it for a moment. "No, but that would be a great name for a sequel!" he said. "Hmm... I should write that down."

"Let's stay focused on the original," Alex said. "Is Starboardia a country?"

"Starboardia is an ancient island," Auburn Sally said. "It's believed to be the only surviving land from the Lost City of Atlantis. It's nearly impossible to find because it floats around the Bermuda Triangle like a large ship, and never passes through the same part of the sea twice. They say the debris from all shipwrecks in the Caribbean eventually washes ashore on the island's coast."

"Nice backstory, Conner," Alex said. "How will Starboardia help us defeat Smoky-Sails Sam?"

"Hundreds of years ago, when the Europeans first settled in the Americas, an indigenous tribe was forced off their island by the white men who settled there," Auburn Sally said. "The tribe was outnumbered ten to one, so they had no choice but to vacate and hope they would find another island somewhere else in the Caribbean. They set sail and were caught in the middle of a horrible hurricane. When the storm finally cleared, they saw Starboardia in the distance. The tribe used all the wreckage on the island to build a magnificent fortress. The structure was carefully designed to help the tribe defeat an enemy that outnumbered them ten to one, should they ever be invaded again."

"Oh, I get it now," Alex said. "We're going to use the fortress! How fun!"

"Exactly," Conner said. "Including Sally's pirates and Jacobson's sailors, we have about fifty people on this ship. Smoky-Sails Sam has five ships and about a hundred pirates on each. The fortress should do the trick."

Suddenly, the twins and the captain were startled by loud eruptions coming from above. Everyone aboard the *Dolly Llama* looked up and saw red fireworks exploding in the sky. With each bright burst, the ocean and the ship were briefly illuminated by red light.

"Where are those coming from?" Conner asked.

They turned to the fleet of pirate ships in the distance and saw another set of fireworks being launched from their decks.

"Smoky-Sails Sam," Auburn Sally said as the fireworks exploded overhead. "They're using them to see us in the dark! Clever scum!"

Since all the light on board the *Dolly Llama* had been extinguished, the approaching fleet had lost track of them, and were headed in a slightly different direction. But now with the fireworks illuminating the ship, the fleet repositioned itself and was once again headed straight for the *Dolly Llama*.

"What do we do now?" Conner asked.

"Pray the wind is stronger with us than it is with them," the captain said. "Otherwise, we might not make it to Starboardia."

Conner paced the deck trying to think of a way to put distance between their ship and the fleet. At this point, Alex didn't care how much her brother opposed her help; she wasn't going to let his pride jeopardize their mission. When he was facing the other way, Alex covertly pointed at the sky. Almost instantaneously, thick clouds blew in and covered the stars. The atmosphere became too humid for the fireworks to go off.

Now that the fireworks were taken care of, the *Dolly Llama* needed a boost so the fleet wouldn't catch up. Alex took a deep breath and blew air toward the sails. A strong breeze came out of nowhere and pushed the ship a little faster, causing everyone on board to jolt.

"Captain, it's a miracle!" Siren Sue shouted from the crow's nest. "Clouds are blocking the fireworks and the wind is making us sail faster!"

The pirates and the sailors cheered in celebration. Auburn Sally stared at the sky in awe. Conner was surprised at how quickly the weather had changed in their favor—it was a little *too* convenient.

"Alex, cut it out!" Conner said. "I told you no magic!"

His sister shrugged innocently. "It wasn't me," she said. "Must be some kind of tropical storm."

"Nice try," Conner said. "But tropical storms don't blow clouds in one direction and ships in the other!"

Auburn Sally eyed the sky again and noticed the strange phenomenon he was referring to. "What's going on?" she asked. "*Your sister* is causing this?"

"Yeah," he said. "I forgot to mention she has magic powers—but don't encourage her! This is *my* story and *my* project. I can get us to Starboardia and help you defeat Smoky-Sails Sam on my own."

Conner stomped off the upper deck and joined Admiral Jacobson at the front of the ship. Auburn Sally's imagination had been broadened so much by the twins, *this* wasn't hard to grasp. She sauntered over to Alex and casually leaned on the railing.

"*Men*," she said with a sigh. "They always want to feel like they're in control."

"It's my own fault," Alex said. "He asked for my help earlier and I kind of embarrassed him about it. Now he thinks he has to prove himself to me."

"Rule number one on my ship: No woman is allowed to take orders from a man," Auburn Sally said.

"That's a philosophy I could get behind," Alex said.

"Then as your captain, I order you to leave Smoky-Sails Sam's fleet a few *presents* behind us," the captain said. "If you get my drift."

Alex and Auburn Sally shared a smile—Alex knew exactly what she meant. She turned toward the fleet in the distance and pointed at the water. Several clusters of sharp rocks stuck out of the ocean behind the ship.

"Attagirl," the captain said.

The obstructions and the wind helped the *Dolly Llama* gain distance from Smoky-Sails Sam's fleet. Soon the pirate ships had shrunk so much in the distance behind them, they could barely see the trails of smoke emitting from their sails.

The *Dolly Llama* sailed through the night, and by sunrise the Parakeet Islands appeared on the horizon ahead. Unfortunately, the rising sun gave the fleet of pirate ships a better view of the ocean, and the *Dolly Llama* was spotted again.

The ship entered a narrow channel between the Parakeet Islands, and the crew learned why Conner had named them so. The islands were covered with thousands and thousands of colorful birds. It was a beautiful sight, but the farther the ship sailed through the channel, the louder the birds' squawking became. As if they were competing for the pirates' attention, each bird tried to out sing the next. When the *Dolly Llama* reached the center of the channel, the sound became deafening. The whole ship covered their ears and moaned.

"PUT A SOCK IN IT!" Conner yelled at the birds.

"PUT A SOCK IN IT! PUT A SOCK IN IT!" the parakeets mimicked. "PUT A SOCK IN IT! PUT A SOCK IN IT!"

Alex couldn't stand the noise any longer. She snapped her fingers and birdseed rained on the islands. All the parakeets swooped down from the trees to feed and went silent. Conner shot his sister a look—but one of gratitude.

"Okay, I suppose *some* magic won't hurt," he said. "But nothing crazy—the *Dolly Llama*'s crew has to feel accomplished, too."

A twinkle came into Admiral Jacobson's eye as he watched the birds eat the seeds. "You know, the *red worm* is known to *cleanse* a parakeet's stomach," he said. "Perhaps we could leave a *nasty storm* behind for Sam's fleet?"

The twins made eye contact and mischievous smiles grew across their faces.

"Oh, Conner," Alex said, and clasped her hands together. "Please, please, please let me leave red worms behind!"

"Yeah—you've got to," he said. "It's just too good."

Alex jumped up and down giddily and snapped her fingers again. Small red worms rained down on the islands, too, and the parakeets happily dug in. The admiral and the twins laughed as they imagined the mess the birds would leave on the fleet later that day.

A few hours after exiting the channel, the *Dolly Llama* sailed past the Isle of Skulls. It was a creepy island with a permanent layer of fog hanging in the air. The shore had no beaches and was lined with dark eerie caves. The land was littered with large rocks that had been chiseled to look like large human skulls. Alex could have sworn the heads were following her as the ship passed them.

"Hey, Conner, watch this," Alex said. She cleared her throat and all the skulls started singing an obnoxious song by a boy band the twins knew from the radio.

"Oh baaaaby, please don't play this game,
My heart is so full of shame,
My love cannot be tamed,
I'm a moth and you're the flame,
And even though it's lame,
Remind me of your naaaaame!"

The twins were laughing so hard, their stomachs hurt. The rest of the ship screamed and pointed at the possessed skulls.

"It's the devil's music!" Winking Wendy shouted.

The pirates waved crucifixes at the island and shot the rocks with their rifles. Alex figured the joke had gone far enough. She cleared her throat again and the skulls returned to normal.

Once the Isle of Skulls was far behind the *Dolly Llama*, Conner excitedly ran from the front of the ship to Auburn Sally's side on the upper deck.

"All right, we've passed the Isle of Skulls!" he said. "Time to travel starboard."

"And if we sail in circles to the right all night, we'll find Starboardia?" Auburn Sally asked.

"More like Starboardia will find us," Conner said.

The captain stepped to the side of the wheel and presented it to him. "Would you like to do the honors, *Commander Bailey*?" she asked.

"Oh gosh," he said. "Sure!"

Conner had never even driven a car, so he wasn't going

to turn down the opportunity to steer a pirate ship. He put his hands on the wheel and could have sworn he felt the ship's heartbeat pulsing through it. It was an exhilarating sensation—with just the slightest movement, he had the power to change the ship's course and the crew's destiny. It reminded him of the feeling he had when he wrote, but it was ten times stronger. He was *living* and *breathing* the adventure he had only dreamed about.

Naturally, being chased by a fleet of dangerous pirates took some fun out of steering the ship, but it was thrilling nonetheless. Since they arrived, he had been angry, frustrated, anxious, and scared by different things, but the excitement of being in the world he created never left him. He wished every author got to feel what he was feeling right now.

As the sun started setting, it illuminated the ocean waves around the *Dolly Llama* like golden zebra stripes. Conner turned the wheel as far to the right as it would go and tied it down.

"Starboardia, here we come!" he said.

That night, all the pirates and sailors gathered in Auburn Sally's chambers so Conner could tell them what to expect the next day. It was strange to prepare them for a place he technically had never been before. He could only rely on the images in his head and hope they matched. The Rosary Chicken got cozy on Alex's lap and she stroked her feathers while she listened to her brother.

"Ladies, gentlemen, and chicken," Conner said. "Welcome

to Starboardia 101. I'm assuming by now, whether through eavesdropping or word of mouth, everyone knows why we're headed to Starboardia."

Not-So-Jolly Joan and Too-Much-Rum Ronda raised their hands.

"No one ever tells me anything," Not-So-Jolly Joan said, and burst into tears.

"I was told, but I don't remember," Too-Much-Rum Ronda said, and hiccupped so hard, she fell off her seat.

"No worries, I'll explain," Conner said. "We are outnumbered ten to one by Smoky-Sails Sam's fleet. There is a fortress on Starboardia that was designed for a group in our exact predicament. The fortress is filled with hundreds of booby traps; there are trapdoors, human slingshots, swinging blades, endless mazes, and much more. Once the fortress is activated, the traps will go off every thirty seconds.

"Unless you want to be crushed, cut in half, or fall to your death—listen to this part very carefully. There are safe zones throughout the fortress painted in red. Five seconds before the traps are set off, you will hear a bell—when you hear the bell, find one of those safe zones immediately! I've come up with a motto to help those of us who have difficulty remembering directions. Repeat after me: *In Red, Ain't Dead*."

"In Red, Ain't Dead," the pirates and sailors repeated.

"Very good," Conner said. "Now, once we're on the island and find the fortress, we have to wait until all of Smoky-Sails Sam's men are inside before we can activate it. The fortress sort of works like a clock—a very heavy net of boulders pulls on gears located at the top, which turn and operate all the booby traps. The net is held up by twenty-one ropes and needs all twenty-one ropes to support it. Once one of these ropes is cut, another rope will snap under pressure every thirty seconds, causing the net of boulders to drop a little lower, which pulls on the gears, and activates the booby traps. Does this all make sense?"

The pirates and sailors stared at Conner like he was speaking another language. Even Alex was having a hard time following along.

"Those are just the logistics in case anyone was wondering," Conner said. "There's only one thing you have to remember—*which is?*"

"In Red, Ain't Dead!" the pirates and sailors said in unison. They were very proud of themselves and looked like dogs expecting treats.

"Great," Conner said. "Everybody break a leg tomorrow! Oh—no offense, Somersault Sydney!"

"None taken," the legless pirate said.

As the *Dolly Llama* sailed in large starboard loops around the Bermuda Triangle, the pirates, sailors, and the twins went to bed to rest up for the following day. In the sleeping quarters belowdecks, rows of white hammocks were stacked from floor to ceiling. It was chilly down there, so Alex and Conner were thankful their mother had packed sweatshirts for them.

The hammocks swung with the sway of the ship and

were very relaxing. Soon the pirates and the sailors fell asleep. Their snoring was so loud, the twins were worried the sides of the ship would burst open. Alex glanced down at the hammock below hers to see if Conner was still awake.

"Oh good, you're still up, too," she said.

"I don't think the dead could sleep through this," he said.

"Are you nervous about tomorrow?" she asked.

"A little bit," he said with a long sigh. "I just hope it all works out so the trip here hasn't been for nothing."

Alex could sense the doubt in his voice and she felt a little guilty. Had she been more supportive and encouraging in the beginning, he probably wouldn't be so cynical.

"Everything is going to be fine," Alex said. "You're a really great author, Conner. I keep forgetting to tell you how impressed I am by all of this. Every beat of your story is so well thought out and entertaining. The more it unfolds, the more intrigued I become. I can't wait for you to write your first book—there are millions of little Alexes and Conners around the world who are going to love it."

Conner was touched by his sister's words. It meant a lot coming from her, since he was convinced she had read every book in the world.

"Thanks, Alex," he said. "I would never have met Jack and Goldilocks if it weren't for you—so thanks for supplying all the inspiration."

"But think of everything you came up with all on your

own," she said. "You would have done just fine without me. I wish I had your imagination. What's your secret to making a story so good? Do you have any writing tricks or rituals?"

Conner had never thought about it before. He thought back to the very first time he wrote a story and recalled a tool that had helped him write ever since.

"Whenever I write, I imagine everything in Dad's voice," he said. "I try to describe everything with the same energy and enthusiasm he had when he read stories to us. Sometimes when I miss him the most, writing makes me feel like he's there with me. It's almost like he's telling me the story and I'm just writing it down."

The thought brought tears to their eyes. Alex knew exactly what he meant, because her dad's narrative was ingrained in her mind, too. Whenever they thought about John Bailey, they didn't think about the night they lost him, the funeral that followed, or the days they spent mourning him. They remembered the nights when he'd read them fairy tales by the fireplace in their old house, the animated gestures he'd make while acting out every scene, and the different voices he made for each character. Their father was a storyteller in every sense of the word, and Conner had inherited the same gift.

"Dad would be so proud of you, Conner," Alex said. "He would have loved everything about Starboardia."

"He'd be proud of you, too, Alex," Conner said.

"Other fifteen-year-olds would have given up on saving the fairy-tale world by now."

The twins laughed at the thought of another brother-and-sister duo going to the same extremes. Alex cast a spell so their roommates snored in silence, and the twins let the sway of the ship rock them to sleep, too.

CHAPTER TEN

STARBOARDIA

The following morning, the entire ship was awoken by a loud clanging coming from above deck.

"LAAAAAND HOOOO!" Siren Sue yelled, and rang the bell in the crow's nest.

The pirates, the sailors, and the twins quickly swung out of their hammocks and ran up the steps to the lower deck. They dashed to the bowsprit and joined Auburn Sally and Admiral Jacobson at the front of the ship. The sun had just started rising and slowly shed light on an island directly ahead. It had a beach littered with wooden debris and was covered in a thick forest of tropical trees. The crew could make out the tip of a large fortress towering over the trees in the center of the island.

"That's it!" Conner yelled. "That's Starboardia!"

There wasn't any time to rejoice because the discovery was immediately followed by the thunderous sounds of firing cannons.

"We've got company!" Siren Sue shouted, and pointed to the ocean behind the *Dolly Llama*.

Like a stampede, the twins, the pirates, and the sailors ran across the lower deck, climbed the steps to the upper deck, and crowded the railing at the back of the ship. The five large pirate ships of Smoky-Sails Sam's fleet were so close, they could smell the torches burning above the sails—and the ships were headed right for them.

The ship in the center was the largest and Alex knew it was the *Vengeance* without having to ask. It was the color of charcoal and flew enormous black sails. The *Vengeance*'s sides and bow were covered in metal spikes, making it resemble a large floating cactus. A flag with an image of broken shackles flew proudly at the top of the tallest mast.

All the decks of the five-ship fleet were swarming with pirates eager for a fight. The *Vengeance* fired its cannons at the *Dolly Llama* and cannonballs splashed in the water beside it. Each splash crept closer and closer to the ship.

"We've got to get to the island now!" Conner yelled.

Auburn Sally stood on a barrel and whistled to get her crew's attention. "Everyone gather as many weapons as you can carry and head to the boats," she ordered. "We'll lower ourselves to the water and row to the island."

"They're going to blow the ship apart!" Admiral Jacobson said. "We don't have time to lower the boats! We have to abandon ship now!"

Conner shared a fearful look with his sister and they read each other's mind—a little *more* magic couldn't hurt.

"Everyone follow the captain's orders," Alex said. "I'll keep the pirates busy until we get off the ship."

The crew nodded and split up at once. Alex stood on the railing and faced the oncoming fleet. She twirled her index fingers in the air and two cyclones rose out of the water between the *Dolly Llama* and the *Vengeance*. She pointed at the fleet and the cyclones whizzed toward the pirate ships like bulls released from a pen. The pirates abandoned their vessels and dived into the water. The cyclones crashed into two of the five ships and obliterated them completely.

While Alex stalled the fleet, the crew aboard the *Dolly Llama* unloaded four heavy chests filled with weapons. They stuffed their vests, pants, coats, and boots with as many rifles, swords, and daggers as possible. Conner ran belowdecks and retrieved the twins' backpacks. As he headed back up, he found the Rosary Chicken on the steps behind him.

"Bagawk?" the chicken asked, tilting her head.

"I'm sorry, but battle is no place for a chicken," Conner said. "You need to stay on the ship."

"Bagawk!" she squawked, horribly offended.

"I'm not *calling* you a chicken—you *are* a chicken!" he said. "This is ridiculous! I'm arguing with a typo!"

The Rosary Chicken puffed out her feathers and extended her wings. She had the heart of a turkey, the determination of a duck, and the bravery of a goose. Misspelled or not, she was ready for combat.

"Fine, but you have to stay in my bag," Conner said.

He tucked the Rosary Chicken into his backpack and left the zipper open enough so the chicken could peek her head out. Conner met his sister on the upper deck and handed Alex her backpack. They joined Auburn Sally and Admiral Jacobson in a boat and were lowered into the water. Once the entire crew was off the *Dolly Llama*, they rowed the boats to the shore of Starboardia.

Smoky-Sails Sam's men weren't too far behind. All five hundred pirates swam after the *Dolly Llama*'s crew. There was so much splashing, it looked like a school of hungry sharks was headed for the island.

"Everyone follow me," Conner told the crew. "The fortress is just through these trees!"

Alex, Auburn Sally, Admiral Jacobson, and the crew followed Conner as he raced through the tropical trees. The admiral's first mate gave Somersault Sydney a piggyback ride so she could keep up. Except for a few birds and a couple of large iguanas, the island was mostly deserted. They emerged into a clearing in the center of the island and found the legendary fortress of Starboardia.

"My God," Auburn Sally said.

"Conner." Alex gasped. "It's amazing!"

It was a breathtaking sight and everyone stopped in their tracks to take it in. The fortress was like a large Mayan pyramid constructed entirely out of broken pieces from hundreds of old ships. Everywhere they looked they spotted masts, bowsprits, sails, planks, bows, wheels, rudders, crow's nests, and flags all pieced together to form one massive structure.

It was twelve levels high and looked like a labyrinth of ladders, slides, rope bridges, swings, and tunnels. It was like a gigantic jungle gym, but it definitely wasn't for children. The structure was built on stilts over a shallow lake with sharp rocks that was home to dozens of alligators. The only way inside the pyramid was up a rickety staircase that led to the first level.

The *Dolly Llama*'s crew carefully climbed up the steps and entered the fortress. The inside was hollow and the bottom floor gave a perfect view of the eleven levels above it. Hanging in the very center of the pyramid like a chandelier was a heavy net filled with a dozen large boulders. It hung from a chain connected to a ceiling full of gears, and was secured by twenty-one ropes. Scattered all over the floor were the safe areas outlined in red that Conner had informed them about.

"Well," Alex said as she glanced around the fortress uneasily. "Is it like you were expecting?"

"That and more," Conner said breathlessly. "I feel like I planted a seed and all this grew."

The crew heard the trees rustling outside the pyramid. They walked to the edge of the first level and saw Smoky-Sails Sam's army of five hundred pirates emerge into the clearing. The men were so rugged and filthy, they made Auburn Sally's pirates look like contestants in a beauty pageant. They were soaking wet from their swim, and thanks to the red worms Alex had left on the Parakeet Islands, their raggedy clothes were stained with bird droppings. After a wild-goose chase around the Caribbean, the pirates were ready to take out their aggression on the *Dolly Llama*'s crew.

Most of the pirates were covered in tattoos and had missing limbs, teeth, eyeballs, and ears. Their appendages weren't replaced by traditional hooks and peg legs, but rather by daggers, razors blades, and metal spears.

Smoky-Sails Sam was in the last group of pirates to step into the clearing. He was seven feet tall with a long dreadlock beard. His coat, hat, belt, and boots were all made from black leather. A long sword proportionate to his height and a silver revolver hung from his belt. His appearance was just as intimidating as his reputation.

The pirate known as Killy Billy stood beside him. He had large bulging eyes and greasy hair. He was shirtless and his chest, arms, and back were covered with tattooed tally marks—each strike represented someone he had killed.

Just like the *Dolly Llama* crew had, Smoky-Sails Sam's men stared up at the structure in astonishment, as if they were facing a forgotten Wonder of the World.

"What do we have here," Smoky-Sails Sam said in a deep, raspy voice. "It looks like little Christine Connelly has discovered Starboardia."

"Look: up there!" Killy Billy said. He pointed to the crew on the first level of the fortress. "It's the *thief* and her hags! And they have Admiral Jacobson and his navy dogs with them!"

"Joined forces to finish me off, have you?" Smoky-Sails Sam chuckled. "It's going to take more than an ancient *tree house* to defeat my men."

The *Dolly Llama*'s crew gulped in fear. Auburn Sally put on a brave face and roared with laughter.

"Did you hear that?" the captain asked. "Smoky-Sails Sam thinks he has *men*! It's funny, because I don't see any *men* below us—I only see *swine*."

The pirates roared angrily at the women and men on the pyramid.

"Don't worry, boys," Smoky-Sails Sam said. "We'll put Captain Auburn Sally in her place! Just like everyone who steals from me, *she'll end up at the bottom of the Atlantic*! ATTACK!"

The pirates charged up the staircase and stormed into the fortress. The *Dolly Llama* crew spread out on all levels of the pyramid and Smoky-Sails Sam's men followed them. The clanking of swords echoed through the structure as Auburn Sally's women and Admiral Jacobson's men bravely took on Smoky-Sails Sam's crew.

Once all five hundred pirates were inside the structure,

Auburn Sally pointed her pistol at the ropes supporting the net of boulders and fired. The net descended several feet, pulling on the gears above, and the fortress came to life.

The pyramid worked more like a clock than Conner was anticipating. As the gears were pulled by the net, all twelve levels of the fortress rotated. The even levels turned clockwise, the odd levels turned counterclockwise, and the booby traps were triggered. The first chime went off and the *Dolly Llama* crew quickly found areas marked in red to stand on, crouch under, or hide behind.

Winking Wendy and the navy sailors were fighting Sam's pirates on the first level. They stepped into red circles drawn on the floor and watched as all the pirates around them fell through trapdoors and plunged into the lake below the fortress.

The alligators splashed around happily—the conflict above was going to supply the biggest meal they ever had.

The second level of the pyramid was covered in rope bridges. Sam's pirates chased Fish-Lips Lucy around one side and Pancake-Face Patty around the other, and the women met on a red platform between bridges. When the traps were set off, the bridges snapped like large slingshots and the pirates were launched off the pyramid.

Stinky-Feet Phoebe and Peg-Leg Peggy were dueling pirates in a long wooden tunnel between the third and fourth levels. Five seconds after the first chime went off, the women curled into a cubby outlined in red. A massive stone rolled through the tunnel, knocking Smoky-Sails Sam's men down like bowling pins. It rolled right past the women without leaving a scratch.

On the fifth level, Somersault Sydney and the admiral's first mate were battling eight of Sam's pirates each. They slid under a red platform just as stone blocks from the ceiling fell on top of their attackers. Somersault Sydney barely made it under the platform in time—she would have lost her legs if she hadn't already.

High-Tide Tabitha and Catfish Kate were fighting pirates back to back on a staircase between the sixth and seventh levels. They stayed on the only red step, and the rest of the staircase flattened into a slide. The pirates slid down the slide and into a shoot that dropped them into the lake below.

Big-Booty Bertha had taken a wrong turn on the eighth level and was surrounded by Smoky-Sails Sam's pirates. The floor was tiled and Big-Booty Bertha sighed with relief when she looked down and saw she was standing on the only red tile. Sharp spikes shot up from the floor and pierced through the pirates' feet. They grabbed their injured feet and hopped around in pain. Unfortunately, Big-Booty Bertha's backside was larger than the tile and one of her buttocks was scratched by a spike.

On the ninth level of the pyramid, Siren Sue was running from pirates shooting rifles at her. She dived behind a red door just as an avalanche of logs swept through the level. The pirates were knocked down and rolled off the pyramid with the logs.

Not-So-Jolly Joan and Too-Much-Rum Ronda wandered around the tenth level looking for someplace safe to hide. They weren't paying attention and fell right through a trapdoor and directly into a cage. It wasn't an ideal place to be, but the women figured they were safe enough. Too-Much-Rum Ronda and Not-So-Jolly Joan shared a bottle of rum while they watched their friends battle the pirates around them.

The floor of the eleventh level was covered with unstable floorboards that spun, teetered, or just broke as soon as they were stepped on. Auburn Sally and Admiral Jacobson fought Sam's pirates while keeping their balance on the stable floorboards painted red. To make matters worse, the eleventh level was also subjected to large swinging blades that the captain and the admiral had to avoid. The blades sliced into Sam's pirates and knocked them out of the pyramid.

From the twelfth and top level of the pyramid, Alex and Conner could see the *Dolly Llama* crew fighting the pirates on all the levels below. Conner heard something rattling at the bottom of his backpack and found that the Rosary Chicken had laid a bunch of eggs inside it—the excitement was too much for her.

"Not so brave now, are you?" Conner said.

The Rosary Chicken lowered her head in shame. The

twins threw the eggs at the pirates below, causing them to slip and slide off the structure. They caught the attention of Killy Billy, and the murderous pirate climbed up to the twelfth level, bringing a gang of pirates with him.

"Here, kiddy kiddies," the tattooed pirate called after them. "I've got enough room on my right arm for two more victims!"

"Go take a long walk off a short plank!" Conner yelled back.

Killy Billy and the pirates chased the twins around the top of the fortress. When they reached the south side, the floor crumbled under their feet. The twins spotted red monkey bars above and grabbed them to keep from falling. Unfortunately, Killy Billy and the pirates saw them, too, and hung from them as well. They swung toward the twins and tried to knock them off.

The Rosary Chicken fluttered out of Conner's backpack and began pecking at one of the pirates' fingers until they slipped from the bars. Then she moved on to the next pirate. Soon, Killy Billy was the only pirate left hanging. He kept one hand on the bars and reached for his rifle with the other. Alex gave him a nasty look and all the tally marks tattooed on his body magically turned into ticks. The pests dug into his skin and he screamed. He lost his grip on the bars and fell all the way through the fortress and landed in the lake below. The alligators dived after him, and Killy Billy never resurfaced.

Alex and Conner swung across the bars to solid floor. The Rosary Chicken crawled back into Conner's backpack and boastfully clucked up at him.

"Okay, you've redeemed yourself," Conner said. "Don't get a big head about it. No one likes a cocky chicken."

Every thirty seconds, another chime would ring, another rope would snap, and the *Dolly Llama* crew would find another red zone to shield themselves from the traps of the pyramid. Smoky-Sails Sam's pirates weren't so lucky. His men were dropping like flies around the fortress. Soon, they were reduced to half their original size, then to a quarter, and then the numbers between Smoky-Sails Sam's crew and the *Dolly Llama* crew were even. At this rate, it wouldn't be long before Sam's men were outnumbered.

Smoky-Sails Sam didn't care about his pirates as much as he cared about retribution. He pushed his way through the structure, carefully avoiding the traps, and headed for Auburn Sally.

When eleven of the twenty-one ropes had snapped and the pyramid was halfway through its course, all the traps ceased and the areas in red stopped being safe zones. Instead, the red platforms, cubbies, and tiles started transporting the *Dolly Llama* crew members to different levels throughout the fortress.

Winking Wendy was catapulted from the first level to the third by a spring hidden in the floor. Siren Sue was dropped into a slide on the ninth level that spat her out on the seventh. The platforms High-Tide Tabitha and Catfish

Kate stood on were connected and turned into a lift—High-Tide Tabitha descended into the level below, and her weight sent Catfish Kate into the level above.

Alex and Conner were standing on a red ledge when it suddenly collapsed and dumped them into a small cart. The cart rolled down a hidden track through the pyramid, and the twins felt like they were on a roller coaster. They tripped and pushed all the pirates as they zoomed past them and high-fived the *Dolly Llama* crew as they went.

On the eleventh level, Auburn Sally and Admiral Jacobson ran across a wooden bridge that suddenly dropped two levels down and swung through the air by chain ropes. Like a faulty elevator, every thirty seconds the bridge descended another two levels. The captain and the admiral would hop off the bridge, help their crew fight the remaining pirates, and then ride it down farther.

The element of surprise was exactly what the *Dolly Llama* crew needed to defeat the remaining pirates of Smoky-Sails Sam's fleet. The pirates lost all sense of the whereabouts of the men and women they were fighting, which left them confused and more vulnerable. By now there were fewer than fifty of Sam's pirates left in the fortress. Not wanting to end up in the lake or fall into a trap, the remaining pirates evacuated the fortress and fled into the trees.

The *Dolly Llama* had successfully reduced Smoky-Sails Sam's crew to nothing, but there wasn't cause for celebration yet. Smoky-Sails Sam himself was nowhere to be found.

When the captain and the admiral's bridge dropped to the fifth level, Smoky-Sails Sam appeared out of nowhere and leaped onto the bridge with his sword raised.

Auburn Sally and Admiral Jacobson fought the manic pirate as the bridge swung and spun violently through the air. All three had to keep one hand on the railing so they weren't flung off it.

The *Dolly Llama* crew watched in horror as the bridge descended through the center of the pyramid—but there was nothing anyone could do. The twins' cart reached the first level and slid across the floor. They narrowly missed being crushed as the bridge crashed to the floor beside them.

Smoky-Sails Sam's sword was bent in the crash, so he tossed it aside. The large pirate picked up Auburn Sally by her coat and threw her across the floor. Admiral Jacobson charged him with his sword raised above his head. Smoky-Sails Sam swiftly removed the rifle from his belt and shot the admiral directly in the chest.

"*No!*" Alex screamed.

"*Admiral!*" his first mate yelled.

Jacobson's eyes fluttered shut and he collapsed on the floor. Smoky-Sails Sam turned and aimed his rifle at Auburn Sally. Alex tried to think of something magical to save the captain, but she was so distraught, her mind went blank.

"Any last words, *Christine*?" Smoky-Sails Sam growled.

"Yes," Auburn Sally said. *"In Red, Ain't Dead."*

The final chime rang through the structure. Smoky-Sails Sam looked to the floor and saw he had thrown Auburn Sally directly into an area outlined in red. The last rope snapped, and just as Smoky-Sails Sam glanced upward, the heavy net of boulders fell directly on top of him. The Starboardia fortress had finished the job.

It was so quiet, the *Dolly Llama* crew could hear one another's heartbeats. All eyes were on the slain admiral. Everyone assumed the captain was in shock, because she just stared at Admiral Jacobson's body as if he would get up at any moment.

Tears rolled down Alex's cheeks and she buried her face in her brother's shoulder. "This is so sad," she said. "I can't look."

Conner rubbed his sister's back as he looked around at the devastated men and women throughout the structure. He scrunched his lips to hide a smile—he knew something they didn't.

Admiral Jacobson suddenly sat straight up with a loud gasp that startled everyone in the pyramid. He pulled on a gold chain around his neck and lifted the Heart of the Caribbean out from under his shirt. The bullet had been stopped by the large ruby.

"Ouch," the admiral said as he rubbed his chest. "That still really hurt!"

As far as anyone was concerned, it was a miracle! The

fortress vibrated from the crew's thankful cheers. When Alex saw her brother smiling, she hit him in the chest.

"You knew that was going to happen the whole time, didn't you?" she asked. "You knew the admiral was going to live, and you just stood there and let us think he had been killed! You were playing with our emotions for fun!"

His sister's angry accusation made him laugh so hard, he could barely breathe.

"I'm sorry, but I wanted to see your reaction to the end of the story," Conner confessed. "The fact that you were so invested in the characters and didn't see the surprise coming means I did something right, *right*?"

Alex was so mad at her brother, she turned her back and walked a few steps away from him to calm down. Auburn Sally got to her feet and helped the admiral to his.

"Aren't you glad I gave you my heart?" Auburn Sally asked.

"Both times it saved my life," Admiral Jacobson said.

The captain and the admiral shared a passionate kiss, and the *Dolly Llama* crew whistled and hollered at the lovebirds.

"We did it!" Auburn Sally declared. "We defeated Smoky-Sails Sam and his fleet! His reign of terror in the Caribbean is over!"

The men and women cheered even louder than before. They embraced one another and held up their weapons in victory. Not-So-Jolly Joan and Too-Much-Rum Ronda raised their bottle from inside the cage.

"And since Commander Bailey has so generously and bravely helped us with our enemy, we must return the favor," the admiral added.

The *Dolly Llama* crew went silent and their postures sank. They were hoping to go on a vacation after defeating the most feared pirate on the ocean.

"How do we get there?" Auburn Sally asked. "I hope it's not by sailing in circles to the *left*."

Conner pulled his binder of short stories out of his backpack and set it on the floor. He flipped it open to the glowing pages of "Starboardia," and the beam of light illuminated the fortress.

"It's much easier than that," he said. "We just step through the beam of light and we'll be there in no time."

The pirates and the sailors stared down at the glowing book nervously. Their captain and admiral nodded at them reassuringly, but even they were a little apprehensive. Conner tapped Alex on the shoulder.

"Are you ready to go home, or are you going to stay behind and pout a little longer?" he asked with a sly grin.

It took everything in Alex not to smile back, but after a moment she couldn't resist.

"Okay—I suppose you got me," she said. "You're right, I wouldn't have been so worked up if I didn't care about the characters so much. It's a testament to good writing, and you should be pleased with yourself. I completely forgot we were even in your story. For a few moments there, I truly believed with all my heart that we were living through . . . through . . ."

"What?" Conner asked.

"Well." Alex laughed. *"A pirate adventure."*

Chapter Eleven

CURSES

The Masked Man hobbled through the Dwarf Forests as quickly as his injuries would let him. Anyone traveling through the forests alone had the right to be worried, but with the mythological creature on the loose, the thick trees around him were especially intimidating. He held Captain Hook's revolver tightly in his hand and dashed behind a tree whenever he heard a noise nearby.

He followed a river deep into the forest until it split off into Dead Man's Creek. The Masked Man limped alongside the creek, and by nightfall he reached the site where the Witches' Brew used to stand on the banks of the creek. The tavern was nothing but a pile of ruins now, and a hundred or so witches were spread out around the creek.

The Masked Man hid behind a tree and searched the area for his son. Although he had never seen him before, the Masked Man figured he'd be easy to spot in the crowd of tattered women.

Just like the rest of the world, the witches had been chased out of their homes throughout the kingdoms by the Literary Army. They fled to the forest and formed a camp near their former headquarters, constructing huts from the wreckage of the tavern. The witches sat casually in groups around campfires and cauldrons. They chatted and flipped through spell books as if they were magazines.

Whenever a campfire started dying out, Charcoaline would hawk a flaming loogie into it and the fire would re-ignite. Tarantulene had spun a large web between trees and feasted on bats and owls that got caught in it. Serpentina's long tongue picked the bugs crawling through Arboris's bark skin, which pestered Arboris greatly. Rat Mary glared and hissed at a dozen cats that another witch had brought from home.

At the top of the pile of wreckage, two thrones had been erected. The infamous Sea Witch sat on a seat made of multi-colored coral while she supervised the camp of witches. She stroked her pet cuttlefish, which rested in a bowl of salt water on the arm of her chair. Beside the Sea Witch, the second throne was made entirely of ice that never melted, but the seat was empty.

Morina leaned against a tree at the edge of the camp, keeping her distance from the other witches. She scowled at the women around her with disdain. She couldn't wait to cross into the Otherworld and get rid of them. The horned witch watched the moon like it was a clock, counting down the hours till she would put her plan in motion.

The Masked Man had scanned the whole area for a child and finally spotted a little boy chained to the tree Morina leaned on. The boy looked around the camp of witches with large, terrified eyes like he had awoken to a nightmare. The Masked Man was expecting the child to resemble him, but Emmerich looked nothing like his father. His pale skin, rosy cheeks, and dark hair were all trademarks of his mother.

"He's the spitting image of Bo Peep," the Masked Man whispered to himself.

Unlike a normal father, the Masked Man didn't fill with pride or tenderness upon seeing his son for the first time, but only with the eagerness of a possible opportunity. All he needed was to get Emmerich away from the witches—he just didn't know how or when.

A sudden chill filled the forest air, and all the witches stopped what they were doing and looked toward the north. A wave of frost flowed down Dead Man's Creek and froze the water. They heard bells in the distance, and a moment later the legendary Snow Queen appeared on a white sleigh pulled down the creek by two monstrous polar bears.

Emmerich was so frightened by the bears, he closed his eyes and looked the other way. The sleigh stopped in the center of the camp. Arboris and Serpentina helped the blind Snow Queen down. She used a long icicle like a cane. She held up a white sack and exposed her jagged teeth in a wide smile.

"I've found it!" the Snow Queen announced proudly. "I've found the dust!"

All the witches were rather underwhelmed, but they didn't dare show it on their faces. Morina, on the other hand, couldn't have looked more unimpressed.

"Dust?" Morina asked. "You traveled all the way to the Northern Mountains to bring back *dust*?"

The Snow Queen growled and pointed her cane toward the sound of Morina's voice. "For someone so consumed with the future, you know nothing about the past," she said. "The contents of this bag will ensure our conquest of the Otherworld."

Morina grunted. "By all means, *enlighten* me," she said. "What's in the sack?"

The other witches throughout the camp were curious, too, so they gathered around the Snow Queen.

"Many years ago, before there were witches and before there were fairies, the world was inhabited by angels and demons," the Snow Queen said. "The demons created a magic mirror that transformed the reflection of something pleasant into something foul and grotesque. It made humans look like hideous monsters and landscapes appear as wastelands. The demons got so much pleasure out of torturing the world, they decided to fly the mirror to heaven and torment the angels with it.

"As the demons flew up to heaven, the evil living inside the mirror became so excited, it started to laugh. The closer to heaven they flew, the harder the mirror laughed, until it cracked and vibrated. Just as the demons reached the pearly gates, the mirror was so delighted, it burst into thousands and thousands of pieces that rained onto the earth like *dust*. Most people avoided the dust, but others weren't so lucky. The people that got the dust in their eyes never saw anything pleasurable again, but only the flawed and ugly qualities of everything. Others breathed in the dust and their hearts were filled with hate, anger, and jealousy.

"After centuries of sending blizzards through the kingdoms, I collected the remaining specks," the Snow Queen continued. "My snowflakes cleansed the air and rinsed the land, and brought the dust specks back to me in the North Mountains through evaporation."

The witches were mesmerized by the story, but Morina was still unenthused.

"And what do we need the dust *for*?" she asked.

The Sea Witch crawled down the pile of debris to join the other witches.

"The Snow Queen and I used the dust to curse Ezmia

the Enchantress," the Sea Witch hissed. "Long before she became the dreaded Enchantress, Ezmia was the late Fairy Godmother's apprentice. The favoritism made all the other fairies jealous, and poor Ezmia was often ostracized, heartbroken, and lonely. Many times she would travel deep into the woods away from the fairies and cry. Ezmia always found the same tree and wept into its roots as if it were a friend's shoulder. She cried so much, her tears watered the tree and it grew taller than any other tree in the forest.

"Once this became a routine for Ezmia, the Snow Queen and I covered the tree's roots with the dust of the magic mirror. One day while she was sobbing, she breathed in a piece of it. Immediately, her heartbreak, sorrow, and loneliness were heightened. Her desire to become the next Fairy Godmother and help people was replaced with the desire to seek revenge and inflict pain on those who had wronged her."

Shivers went up the witches' spines as they recalled the Enchantress's terrifying reign over the fairy-tale world.

"We gave Ezmia the steps to create a portal into the Otherworld," the Snow Queen said. "Once she mastered the seven deadly sins, and dominated the past, present, and future of this world, she would have manifested a portal. Our plan was to travel into the Otherworld, unleash the Enchantress, and take it by storm! Unfortunately, she was killed before the portal was complete."

"Well, lucky us," Morina said. "Thanks to *my prediction*, we know a doorway will be formed between worlds, saving us the hassle of building our own portal."

Charcoaline stepped forward and bowed to the Sea Witch and the Snow Queen before she spoke.

"Is your current plan to curse Alex Bailey with the dust and unleash *her* on the Otherworld?" she asked, and then quickly stepped back with the others.

"Correct," the Snow Queen said. "However, we already tried cursing Alex with the dust. It sent her down a destructive path, leading to the obliteration of the Witches' Brew and her departure from the Fairy Council, but it didn't last for long. Alex is the granddaughter of the Fairy Godmother and a child of both worlds—magic is very strong with her— so it's going to take more than one piece."

"How much *dussst* will it take?" Serpentina asked.

"A handful should be enough," the Sea Witch said.

Morina rolled her eyes. "Are you sure your dust hasn't expired?" she asked.

The Sea Witch was getting tired of Morina's disrespectful attitude. She snapped her claws and charged toward Morina, but the Snow Queen held up her cane to stop her.

"See for yourself," the Snow Queen said.

She opened the bag and the witches peered inside it. The dust from the magic mirror looked like silver sand. With her long, frostbitten fingernail, the Snow Queen removed one piece and blew it toward the polar bears. One of the bears breathed it in through its large nostrils, and its eyes turned bright red. For no reason whatsoever, the bear started uncontrollably beating the other bear.

A violent fight broke out between the polar bears, and the

witches quickly backed away from them. The Snow Queen and the Sea Witch cackled at the belligerent beasts. The Snow Queen whistled at the bears, and they sat straight up—resisting the urge to continue fighting.

"I'm still not convinced this will work," Morina said. "Even if Alex becomes as dangerous as the Enchantress and vanquishes the Otherworld for us, what's preventing her from unleashing her fury on us?"

All the other witches nodded—Morina had a valid point.

"Just like you, Morina," the Sea Witch hissed, "the dust has room to be improved. Together, with the magic of all the witches here, we'll cast a spell on the dust so that once it enters Alex's system, we'll be able to control every move she makes."

The Snow Queen pointed her cane at the ground and a large icy cauldron appeared. She poured the bag of dust into the cauldron.

"Ladies, please join us," the Sea Witch said.

The Sea Witch and the Snow Queen held their hands over the cauldron and the dust began to glow. One by one, the other witches throughout the camp raised their hands toward the cauldron as well. With each addition, the light shined brighter and brighter. Morina was the most skeptical and the last witch to join in. Once all the witches were united, a powerful spell was cast. The earsplitting sound of a thousand screams emitted from the dust and echoed through the forest.

"It is done," the Sea Witch said. "Now we must find the girl."

The Snow Queen removed the cloth covering her eyes, and her empty sockets lit up like trains in dark tunnels. She predicted where the young fairy was, and once the answer came to her, the lights faded and she re-wrapped the cloth over her eyes.

"She's already in the Otherworld," the Snow Queen said. "One of us must travel there and make sure she ingests the dust."

The witches looked around at one another, but there were no volunteers. Although Morina hated following any orders but her own, she knew she was the best candidate for the task. Besides, her plan to betray the witches wouldn't succeed unless their plan to conquer the Otherworld succeeded first. If she helped them with this, they'd never suspect a thing.

"I'll go," Morina said.

"*You?*" Rat Mary asked. "I'd trust a *fairy* before I'd trust the likes of you."

"Take a look around you, rodent," Morina said. "I'm the only witch who could possibly blend into a world of humans. Besides, I traveled there when I captured the Masked Man's son—I know the location of a portal and how to use it."

Morina made a good case, and the witches didn't argue any further. They turned to the Sea Witch and the Snow Queen and let the elders decide.

"Very well," the Snow Queen said.

"How long before the doorway opens between worlds?" the Sea Witch asked.

"In a fortnight," Morina said. "I will not have time to return, so I'll meet you on the other side of the doorway. It will open in the forest, in the clearing of the three boulders. It leads to a large city in the Otherworld. I'll travel there now, infect Alex with the dust, and be there when you arrive."

"Do not disappoint us," the Snow Queen said.

The Sea Witch scooped the dust out of the cauldron with her claws and poured it back into the white sack. A little begrudgingly, she handed the sack over to Morina.

"See you all on the other side," Morina said.

The witch covered her horns with her hood and journeyed into the forest away from Dead Man's Creek. She walked with so much determination, she strolled directly past the Masked Man without noticing him.

For the Masked Man's plan of revenge to work, he needed a way into the Otherworld as much as he needed his son. He glanced between Morina and Emmerich, and decided to follow the witch now and come back for the boy later. He trailed after Morina as quietly as possible.

The Sea Witch still had reservations about trusting Morina with the task.

"What if she betrays us?" the Sea Witch asked.

The Snow Queen's blue lips curved into a sinister smile, and a raspy laugh erupted from the back of her throat.

"Morina will *try* to betray us, but she will fail," she said. "Once Alex Bailey is under the dust's spell, nothing will stop her—*nothing*!"

Hearing this scared Emmerich more than anything else had since his kidnapping. He whispered to himself and prayed with all his might that Alex might hear him wherever she was.

"They're coming for you.... They're coming for you...."

CHAPTER TWELVE

MAKING A SPLASH ON SYCAMORE DRIVE

It took the Book Huggers three days to find Conner's current address on Sycamore Drive. In their defense, the Bailey family had moved twice in the past four years and it was difficult tracking them down. After camping outside their previous house, the girls pestered the current residents until they finally gave them the forwarding address.

The four teenagers walked purposefully down Sycamore Drive looking for Bob and Charlotte's house. The

Book Huggers were on a mission to finally expose the Bailey twins once and for all. A bag with tape recorders and a Polaroid camera swung from Mindy's shoulder. Once they gathered enough evidence, their questionable reputation would be cleared and every school administrator, police officer, and representative in their community would owe them a massive apology.

It was a thrilling and nerve-racking endeavor, and their hearts were pounding as they walked down the street. Wendy got a little carried away and dashed from street lamp to street lamp and mailbox to mailbox like a secret agent.

"Wendy, knock it off!" Mindy ordered. "You're going to draw attention to yourself. Everyone act *natural*!"

Their anxiety was so high, the Book Huggers forgot what *natural* looked like. Cindy walked taller than usual and waved at all the neighbors like she was in a parade. Lindy swung her arms and swiveled her head like a cartoon character. Wendy skipped aggressively and broke a sweat.

"Too natural!" Mindy said. "Lindy, I told you to bring your dog! We would have blended in more if we were walking a basset hound."

"But Angela Lansbury has arthritis in her paws," Lindy said. "She has to be dragged around on a skateboard! That would have drawn even more attention!"

"Okay, fine, if we can't move clandestinely, then let's move quickly," she said. "The sooner we get out of the view of the public, the better."

By *the public*, Mindy was referring to an old man

watering his lawn, a pair of kids playing basketball, and an overweight cat napping on a porch. None of the neighbors were paying attention to the Book Huggers, let alone suspicious of them.

"There it is!" Cindy said, and pointed to one of the homes. "That's Conner's house!"

The Book Huggers bumped into one another as if Cindy were pointing out a poisonous snake.

"Remember," Mindy said, "if anyone catches us, we're here for a school project."

Not so *clandestinely*, they tiptoed up the house's driveway and crawled on their hands and knees through the flower bed. They regretted wearing shorts and short sleeves, because the roses' thorns scratched up their arms and legs—but there was no going back now. They slowly sat up and peered through the window.

Inside, the Book Huggers saw Charlotte Gordon vacuuming the living room. The house was spotless, but she was vigorously cleaning anyway, as if the home were covered in invisible dirt only she could see. It had been two and a half days since Charlotte's children traveled into her son's short story, and since she hadn't heard a word from them, cleaning was therapeutic for her overwhelming sense of helplessness.

Conner's binder of short stories was still in the center of the floor in the exact spot he had left it. Charlotte was afraid she might break something if she moved it, so she carefully cleaned around it.

"Honey, why don't you have a seat?" Bob said from the couch.

"Not now, I'm distracting myself from my thoughts," Charlotte said over the vacuum.

Bob got up and pulled the plug, but it didn't stop his wife. She wiped all the surfaces, fluffed all the pillows, and straightened all the couch cushions.

"Stressing isn't going to help anything," he said. "I'm sure they're going to be just fine. It's probably taking longer than they thought to track down Avalon Tammy, or whatever her name was."

"I know," Charlotte said with a sigh. "I wish I was as capable of handling myself as they are of handling themselves. Mothers get trained in how to deliver their children, how to care for and nurture them, how to develop their motor skills and self-esteem—but no one trains you in how to *stop worrying about them*! They say childbirth is the worst part, but it's just the beginning of the pain!"

Charlotte sat on the couch in defeat. Bob sat next to her and put his arm around her.

"I hate to say it, but this is the price you pay for raising two wonderful, intelligent, and responsible young adults," he said.

"I almost wish they weren't so independent," she confessed. "It'd be nice if they needed *their mother* once in a while. Maybe I'd get to see them more often."

The binder suddenly popped open on its own and the beam of light shot straight out of it. A moment later, Conner poked his head out of the beam and had a look around the living room. The sight of Conner's floating head made the eavesdropping Book Huggers flail around the flower bed. They covered one another's mouths so their screams weren't heard.

"Hey guys!" Conner happily greeted his mom and step-dad. "Good news! We found the pirates."

"That's terrific!" Charlotte said. "I was so worried. What took you so long? Was everything all right?"

"Everything went *great*," Conner said with a laugh. "Actually, it couldn't have gone *smoother*. It just took a little longer to track down Auburn Sally than we thought."

"Oh, *Auburn Sally*—that's her name," Bob said. "See, Charlotte, I told you everything was going to be fine."

"Can we bring the pirates into the house now?" Conner asked.

"Just a second," Charlotte said. She retrieved the welcome mat from the porch and set it beside the binder. "Have them wipe their feet on the mat on their way in. I just vacuumed."

Conner nodded and popped back into the world of Starboardia to have a quick word with the *Dolly Llama* crew.

"Remember what I told you guys to say if my mom asks about Starboardia?" he asked.

The pirates and sailors repeated what they had rehearsed. *"It was a piece of cake. Nothing remotely dangerous happened at all,"* they said in unison.

"Perfect," Conner said. "Now, everyone step through

the beam and wipe your feet on the mat—my mom just vacuumed."

The pirates and sailors were puzzled—what was *vacuumed*?

One by one, the *Dolly Llama* crew followed Conner through the beam of light and stepped into the house. Not knowing what to expect, the pirates charged inside with their weapons raised—which nearly gave Charlotte and Bob heart attacks.

"Everybody calm down!" Conner ordered. "You're all safe here!"

The living room filled up very quickly with the characters from "Starboardia." They looked around at all the furniture, decorations, and lighting fixtures in awe. It was the most extraordinary place they had ever been to. The spying Book Huggers had their camera and tape recorders ready, but they were so stunned to see the pirates appear, they dropped their devices and just watched in shock.

"It's like we've stepped into the nineteenth century!" Admiral Jacobson said.

"It's the twenty-first century, actually," Bob said.

"This chamber is so elegant," Winking Wendy said. "Does a royal family live here?"

"No—but thank you," Charlotte said. "It's amazing what a couple of throw pillows and an accent chair will do to a room."

Siren Sue was mesmerized by all the framed photographs on the mantel.

"Commander Bailey, these small portraits of you and your sister are so detailed," she said. "Your face was so round when you were younger."

"That's called a *school picture*," Conner said. "And it was right before a growth spurt."

Peg-Leg Peggy stared up at the ceiling in terror. "What sort of torture device is *that*?" she asked, and pointed her rifle at it.

"That's just a ceiling fan," Conner said. "Relax, it's not going to hurt you."

The pirates and sailors split up to explore the house. They bounced on the mattresses in the bedrooms, turned all the lights on and off, used the toilets to splash water on their faces, and opened and closed the appliances in the kitchen.

"I've found a cupboard that's as cold as winter!" Too-Much-Rum Ronda announced. "And it's full of fruit, vegetables, and colorful liquid!"

"That's the refrigerator, Ronda—stay out of there!" Conner said. "No one touch anything without asking!"

Charlotte and Bob watched nervously as the crew invaded and inspected every corner of their home. They weren't sure which pirate or sailor to follow, because everyone clearly needed supervision.

"Conner, we only have one guest bedroom," Charlotte said. "Where are all your friends supposed to sleep?"

"Don't worry, none of the pirates or sailors are sleeping inside," Conner said.

He said it like it should have been a relief, but it only

concerned his mother more. Charlotte was going to ask him for more details, but she was distracted when Alex suddenly leaned out from the beam of light.

"Hi, Mom—hi, Bob!" she said, then looked to her brother. "Conner, we're ready!"

Alex leaned back and disappeared. Conner went to the window and had a good look at the large pool in their backyard.

"Hey, Bob, how deep is the pool?" he asked.

Bob shrugged. "Ten, maybe twelve feet," he said. "Why do you ask?"

Before Conner could answer, he scooped up the binder and ran into the backyard. The Book Huggers quickly got to their feet and ran to the other side of the property. They peeked between boards and through holes in the fence to see into the backyard. Conner stood at the edge of the pool and aimed the binder's beam of light directly at the water.

"Go for it, Captain!" he said.

Bob and Charlotte joined Conner outside just in time to see the *Dolly Llama* emerge from the binder and land in the pool. Charlotte and Bob screamed and grabbed on to each other. The splash knocked half the water out of the pool and drenched Conner and his parents.

It was too much for the Book Huggers to take. All four girls fainted at once and collapsed in a pile behind the fence.

"Charlotte," Bob said quietly, in shock. *"There's a pirate ship in our pool...."*

"Sorry," Conner said. "The captain was adamant about bringing her ship along. But the good news is that the pirates live in it, so you don't have to worry about them sleeping in the house."

"Right," Charlotte said with large eyes. *"Nothing to worry about."*

Had the *Dolly Llama* been just a tiny bit bigger, it wouldn't have fit in the pool. Auburn Sally and Alex were standing on the upper deck behind the wheel and had a great view of the neighborhood. The Rosary Chicken was perched on the ship's railing beside them.

"So this is the land of Sycamore Drive?" Auburn Sally asked.

"It's just one of many neighborhood streets in the town," Alex said.

"I like it," the captain said. "The cottages in this village are very charming."

Auburn Sally kicked down a gangplank and she, Alex, and the Rosary Chicken climbed down from the *Dolly Llama*. The Rosary Chicken happily waddled onto the grassy yard and pecked at bugs. The twins introduced Auburn Sally to Bob and Charlotte, and the captain gave them each a very firm handshake.

"It's an honor to meet you," Auburn Sally told them. "You have very crafty children."

"Tell me about it," Charlotte said.

"It's never a dull moment," Bob said. "Wait, is that chicken wearing a rosary?"

Now that the twins had successfully escorted the *Dolly Llama* crew into the Otherworld, they immediately began planning their next venture. Conner opened his binder to the second tab, retrieved the Portal Potion from his backpack, and poured three drops on the pages of his next story. Another beam of light appeared and shined into the sky like a spotlight.

"Time for our second stop," Conner said.

"What's your next story about?" Alex asked.

"'Galaxy Queen' is an intergalactic space odyssey," he explained. "It takes place in the year 3000 and follows the queen of a Cyborg civilization as she travels through the universe."

Alex took a deep breath. "It doesn't get easier after 'Starboardia,' does it?"

"Not really," Conner said. "But at least we *learned* a lot from 'Starboardia.'"

"Is there anything I can help with beforehand?" Alex asked. "Think about it."

"There is, actually—we're going to need space suits," he said.

Alex snapped her fingers and their clothes transformed into chic, shiny, and futuristic space suits. Their suits were silver and had round helmets, and there were oxygen tanks attached to their backs.

"These are perfect!" Conner said excitedly.

Charlotte put a hand over her heart. "You both look *so cute*!" she said. "Stay right there—I need a photo of this!"

"Mom, we really don't have time to take a—"

Charlotte gave her son a dirty look that said a thousand words, but most specifically: *There are fifty pirates in my house and a ship in my backyard pool. You WILL take a photo for me whether you like it or not.* Conner didn't say another word, and his mother ran into the house and returned with her camera.

"Stand on the grass so I can get the pirate ship in the background," Charlotte instructed. "That's nice! Now put your arms around each other—smile! This is going on the Christmas card!"

"Mom, this is top secret! You can't put this on a Christmas card!" Conner said.

"Calm down, no one is going to know what you're doing," Charlotte said. "Everyone will just think we took a vacation to a theme park—you know, like *normal families* do. Okay, now just a couple more with my phone!"

Begrudgingly, the twins smiled and posed as their mother took a dozen pictures. Once she was finished, they were permitted to continue their plans. The twins tightened their helmets, turned their oxygen tanks on, and toed up to the binder of short stories.

"Next stop, 'Galaxy Queen'!" Conner said.

Chapter Thirteen

GALAXY QUEEN

The twins stepped into the beam of light and re-entered the world of Conner's handwriting. The words *the universe* stretched around them, and before they knew it, they were floating through an endless galaxy. They were surrounded by thousands and thousands of stars—it was a breathtaking sight, and the twins had never felt so small in their lives.

All gravity disappeared, and the weightlessness gave the twins a falling sensation in the pit of their stomachs that didn't go away. They moved their arms and legs and tried swimming through the emptiness, but there was absolutely nothing to swim against.

Conner barely caught the corner of his binder before it floated out of reach, and tucked it safely into his backpack with the flask of Portal Potion.

In the distance, Alex and Conner could see a large white planet with multi-colored clouds, but they were still thousands of miles away from its atmosphere. The planet looked delicious—like a large piece of candy floating in space.

"What's that?" Alex asked.

"That's Jawbreakeropolous," Conner said. "I had a sweet tooth when I wrote this story."

It was difficult to make out at first, but the twins saw a small light traveling toward the planet. It orbited around Jawbreakeropolous and after the eighth or ninth rotation it shot out a green laser that engulfed the planet. In a matter of seconds, Jawbreakeropolous shrunk and vanished from the universe.

"What just happened?" Alex asked. "Why did the planet disappear?"

"It didn't disappear, it was *uploaded*," Conner explained. "That thing circling Jawbreakeropolous is the *BASK-8*, the Cyborg Queen's spaceship. She travels the galaxy looking for habitable planets in other star systems' Goldilocks zone. When she finds a planet she likes, her spaceship uploads it into its hard drive, and then she takes it back to her home solar system."

"What's a Goldilocks zone?" Alex asked.

"It's the area of every solar system that's *not too hot* and *not too cold* to host life," Conner said. "That's actually what scientists call it—I swear I'm not making it up!"

"Why does the Cyborg Queen need so many planets?"

"The Cyborgs have outgrown their home planet and need more room," he said. "The queen travels with an army aboard her ship in case she runs into any trouble. We need to get aboard the *BASK-8* and convince her to let us borrow her soldiers."

Conner opened the binder and aimed the beam of light in all directions around him, like a busted lighthouse, to get the *BASK-8*'s attention. It must have done the trick, because the spaceship zoomed toward the twins and within a few seconds was hovering just a hundred yards away from them. The *BASK-8* was the shape and size of a cruise ship. It was made from red steel and had wings like a plane. A cluster of satellites and antennas near the top made the spaceship look like it was wearing a crown.

"Whatever happens, just follow my lead," Conner told his sister. "I'm not going to tell them I'm their creator—I learned that lesson in 'Starboardia'—but I think I've got something up my sleeve that will work."

"You're the boss," Alex said.

Large speakers stuck out on both sides of the *BASK-8* and someone aboard spoke to the twins. The voice was very proper and sounded awfully familiar, but Alex couldn't tell who it reminded her of.

"Attention, unidentified life-forms," the voice said. "Please state your name, species, and home star system."

"I'm Conner Bailey and this is Alex," he announced. "We're human beings from the planet Sycamore Drivious of the Willow Crestian system."

"What are you doing in the middle of space?" the voice asked.

"Our spaceship was hijacked by Orphianotics," Conner said. "Would you mind giving us a lift back to our planet?"

Conner was confident the tall tale would grant them admission to the *BASK-8*, and he gave Alex a thumbs-up. She hoped whatever plan he had cooking was going to work. There was silence from the speaker as whoever was on the other end considered the request.

"Any enemy of the Orphianotics is a friend of ours," the voice said. "Please, come aboard."

A large compartment door opened and two steel claws reached out of the *BASK-8* and plucked the twins from space like stuffed animals in an arcade prize machine. They were pulled into a large hangar where several smaller spaceships were kept. The *BASK-8* had artificial gravity, so the twins hit the floor as soon as they entered.

Once the compartment door was shut behind them, a pair of automatic doors on the other side of the hangar opened. A lizard the size of a man walked in with two Cyborgs on either side of him.

The lizard had big yellow eyes and red slimy skin and wore a gray jumpsuit with several buttons. The Cyborgs were half human, half robotic in a variety of combinations. Some were human with robotic arms and legs; others were split evenly down the middle. They all wore red goggles and held guns with barrels that pulsated bright blue light. They also wore vests that monitored their heartbeat and/or remaining battery percentage.

Alex and Conner quickly got to their feet and the Cyborgs raised their weapons toward them. The lizard man cautiously looked the twins up and down.

"Neither Sycamore Drivious nor the Willow Crestian system are registered in the intergalactic database," the lizard man said with the same voice they had heard outside.

"Oh…" Conner said. "That's because we hate solicitors."

The lizard man stepped toward the twins to inspect them further.

"You're awfully young to be traveling through the universe by yourselves," the lizard man said. "Were there more in your crew?"

"We had an android chaperone, but the Orphianotics stole him, too," Conner explained. "Darn those filthy creatures!"

The lizard man nodded to the Cyborgs and they lowered their weapons.

"I'm Commander Newters," the lizard man said. "Welcome to the *BASK-8*. You may remove your helmets—this ship is equipped with oxygen."

The twins unscrewed their helmets and shook Commander Newters's hand.

"Thank you so much for rescuing us," Conner said. "We would have been goners if it weren't for you."

"I'm sorry to hear about your unfortunate encounter with the Orphianotics," Newters said. "The Cyborg Queen has made many exhausting requests to the United Universe Council to ban them from our quadrant of the galaxy, but they won't listen to her."

"What are the Orphianotics?" Alex asked, forgetting to go along with the story her brother was describing. "They stole our ship so quickly, I didn't get a good look at them."

"They're a terrible species," Newters explained. "They destroyed their home planet, and now they travel through the galaxy stealing resources from other star systems."

"But isn't that sort of what the Cyborg Queen does, too?" Alex asked.

"That's *exactly* what the United Universe Council said," Newters said. "Never mind that, we would be happy to escort you to your home planet. The queen loves traveling to new star systems—I'm sure she'd be delighted to see Sycamore Drivious in Willow Crestian."

A loud alarm suddenly went off, startling the twins. The hangar was filled with flashing red lights. Commander Newters and the Cyborgs looked around in panic.

"Oh no!" Newters said. "This is terrible!"

"What's happening—are we under attack?" Alex asked.

"Worse," Newters said. "That alarm means the queen has awoken early from her charging slumber! She's always

in a terrible mood if she doesn't get a full twenty hours. I must get to the Command Bridge before she arrives!"

Newters and the Cyborgs bolted through the automatic doors and the twins ran after them. They ran through the spaceship, passing several hallways full of frantic half-human, half-robotic men and women. The alarm was even louder outside the hangar and was accompanied by a voice that repeated, *"The queen is awake, the queen is awake, the queen is awake."*

They finally reached the Command Bridge in the center of the ship. It was a wide room with a gigantic set of windows that had a view of the galaxy ahead. The walls were covered in screens with information about different parts of the spaceship, the queen's location, and the universe around them. There were dozens of control stations scattered around the Command Bridge like desks in a classroom. Each station was covered in hundreds of blinking buttons, dials, and levers.

In preparation for the Cyborg Queen's arrival, the Cyborg crew throughout the Command Bridge lubricated their joints, tightened their screws, and polished the steel covering their bodies.

"How close is she?" Newters asked the nearest Cyborg.

"She's descending from her chambers now, Commander," the Cyborg said. "The levels of her emotion chip are off the charts—she must be upset about something!"

The Cyborg pointed to the queen's private elevator in the back of the Command Bridge. All the Cyborgs stood at their control stations just as the elevator doors opened. There was a collective hiss as their mechanical bodies compressed into bows. Alex and Conner followed their example and bowed, too.

The Cyborg Queen was more robotic than anyone else aboard the *BASK-8*. She was only humanoid from the chest up, and even that was questionable. Her nose, her chin, and most of her forehead were covered in metal plates. Her left eye was a camera lens, and instead of hair, her head was covered in wires that wove through a beehive of gears like the film in a projector. On the top of her head, above the wires and gears, was a steel crown. The word *QUEEN* blinked on it like the numbers on a digital alarm clock.

The queen had thin metal arms, and her steel body was shaped to look like she was wearing a gown. She had wheels instead of legs and rolled out of the elevator and into the Command Bridge. The twins could tell she was mad because her lens was twitching and a few of her wires snapped and stuck straight up.

"Your Majesty," Commander Newters said with a deep bow. "We weren't expecting you to wake early. Did you have a restful charge?"

"*Someone* left the gravity on in my chambers while I was charging," the Cyborg Queen said sharply. "Not only did it prevent me from a restful charge, but when I awoke, the human side of my face was *puffy*!"

With this, Alex realized why the "Galaxy Queen" was so familiar—she was embarrassed it had taken this long to click. Without a doubt, the Cyborg Queen was based on Red Riding Hood, Commander Newters was based on Froggy, the Orphianotics were based on the orphans Red despised, the *BASK-8* was a clever play on *basket*, and the Cyborg Queen's passion for collecting planets was based on Red's passion for real estate.

"You *didn't*," Alex whispered to her brother.

Conner knew exactly what she was referring to by her smile.

"Yeah, I *did*," he whispered back.

The Cyborg Queen rolled through the Command Bridge and glared at her Cyborg crew, waiting for one of them to step forward.

"Well?" she said. "Someone better claim responsibility or I'll take away battery privileges for the entire ship!"

The smallest Cyborg in the Command Bridge became so nervous, he began short-circuiting. Sparks flew out of his mechanical neck and his head started spinning. He fell to his metal knees and pleaded for forgiveness.

"I'm so sorry, Your Majesty!" the small Cyborg said. *"I was inspecting the artificial gravity generator and forgot to adjust the pressure in your chambers!"*

The Cyborg Queen rolled her human eye and her lens pointed upward.

"Commander Newters, please have this Cyborg re-started before he catches on fire," she ordered. "And have him re-programmed to remember the priorities of his assignments."

"Yes, ma'am," Newters said, and nodded to the Cyborg soldiers. "Take him to the Upgrade Center."

Against the small Cyborg's will, the soldiers escorted him out of the Command Bridge. The Cyborg Queen rolled to the center of the room and the bottom half of her body transformed into a throne. The Cyborg crew took it as a cue to be seated at their control stations.

"Was Jawbreakeropolous uploaded successfully?" the Cyborg Queen asked.

"Yes, Your Majesty," Newters said. "It's been safely added to the hard drive and will be a wonderful addition to your home system.

"Then why are we still in *this* solar system?" the queen asked. "Shouldn't we be at Gumdropida by now?"

"We were en route to the next planet when we answered a distress call," Newters informed her.

"A distress call?" the Cyborg Queen asked. "From whom?"

Newters cleared his throat and gestured for the twins to come stand beside him. Alex and Conner cautiously approached Newters and the Cyborg Queen. Her lens popped several inches out of her head to examine them.

"Who are you?" she asked.

"Hello, Your Electronicness," Conner said. "My name is Conner and this is my sister, Alex. We're human beings from the planet Sycamore Drivious of the Willow Crestian system."

The Cyborg Queen squinted her human eye at them.

"I've never heard of such places," she said. "What are you doing in this part of the galaxy?"

"We were stranded and left for dead after our ship was stolen by Orphianotics," Alex said. "Your commander kindly saved our lives and brought us aboard."

The mention of the Orphianotics' name infuriated the Cyborg Queen. Two exhaust pipes shot out of her shoulders and steam erupted from them.

"I HATE Orphianotics!" she yelled. "I'll admit there are few alien species I can stomach, but the Orphianotics are *extra-terrible extraterrestrials*! I've begged the United Universe Council to do something about it, but they refuse! They had the audacity to tell me collecting planets is no different from the destruction those scoundrels cause! But I don't *steal resources* from other planets, I just move them into a better neighborhood!"

Conner waited for the Cyborg Queen to let off all her steam before he said another word.

"You know, the Orphianotics aren't allowed in our solar system," he said. "They were kicked out eons ago. If you wouldn't mind giving us a ride back to Sycamore Drivious, we'd love to give you a tour of the Willow Crestian system."

"No Orphianotics, you say?" the Cyborg Queen asked. "Perhaps I should move my planets to your system. What type of star does Willow Crestian revolve around? White dwarf? Blue dwarf? Yellow dwarf? Red giant? I like knowing I have at least two hundred billion years left in a new system before making such a big commitment."

Conner wasn't sure how to answer. "It's a *seventh* dwarf," he said. "Yup, seven white dwarves from the Milky Snow White Galaxy combined into one and *boom*—the Willow Crestian system was formed."

The Cyborg Queen nodded as she gave it some thought. She had never heard of stars combining in such a manner, and the impossibility intrigued her.

"I'd like to see this Willow Crestian," she said. "We'd be delighted to give you a lift to your home planet. Unfortunately, there are a few stops we need to make along the way. There are a handful of planets I need to inspect and collect before the Orphianotics get to them. I hope you don't mind waiting."

"No worries," Conner said. "We'd be happy to accompany you!"

"Marvelous," the Cyborg Queen said. "Commander Newters, take us to Gumdropida, please."

"Full speed to Gumdropida!" Newters ordered the crew.

The Cyborgs went to work pressing buttons at their control stations. The *BASK-8* shot through the galaxy at light speed. The powerful jerk almost knocked Alex over and she screamed. The Cyborg Queen gave her a funny look—surely this wasn't her first time experiencing light speed.

"She doesn't get out much," Conner said.

The *BASK-8* whizzed through the stars and then slowed down as it approached the new planet. Gumdropida was bright orange and covered with snowy mountain ranges. The spaceship orbited the planet, and information about Gumdropida loaded on all the screens in the Command Bridge. A detailed hologram of the planet appeared in front of the Cyborg Queen's throne.

"Gumdropida," Newters read from a screen. "It has a diameter of three thousand four hundred seventy-eight miles. Surface temperatures range from negative ninety degrees to positive thirty degrees Fahrenheit. Atmosphere is made of helium. Currently there is no life on the planet, but forty percent of it is habitable for a Cyborg population."

"It would be perfect for that ski resort I've been itching to build," the Cyborg Queen said. "Upload the planet!"

The green laser shot out of *BASK-8* and surrounded Gumdropida. Just like Jawbreakeropolous had, the orange planet shrank and disappeared from the universe. The words *Upload Complete* appeared on all the screens in the Command Bridge.

"The upload was successful, Your Majesty," Newters said.

"Splendid. Please proceed to the next planet," the Cyborg Queen ordered.

The *BASK-8* raced through the galaxy in a different direction and arrived at the next planet. It was green and had white clouds spiraling through its atmosphere. Whatever sweet tooth Conner had when he wrote this story was contagious, and suddenly Alex had a strong craving for candy.

"Mintune," Newters read from the screen. "It has a diameter of fifty-four thousand six hundred thirty-two miles. Surface temperatures range from five degrees to two hundred and three degrees Fahrenheit. Atmosphere is made up of sulfuric gases. The planet is home to an alien species known as Gas Whales, but only five percent is habitable for a Cyborg population."

"*Pass,*" the Cyborg Queen said. "Five percent isn't worth an upload—and I loathe neighbors. Proceed to the next planet."

The queen was served hot oil in a teacup as the *BASK-8* traveled through space to the next planet. However, when the spaceship arrived, they found nothing but a field of crunchy-looking asteroids.

"Oh dear," Newters said. "It appears Granolia was hit by a comet and this is all that remains. Shall we continue ahead, Your Majesty?"

At first the Cyborg Queen slouched with disappointment, but her attitude quickly changed when an exciting idea popped into her head. The twins knew she had had an idea because a flashing lightbulb stuck out of her crown.

"You know, our solar system could use a *belt*," the queen said. "Upload the asteroids and we'll place them between Blousery and Skirturn when we get home."

The Cyborg crew did as they were told and then proceeded to the next stop. The back-to-back light speed was making Alex a little nauseated. The subsequent planet was a russet color and had a rocky surface.

"Nutfugdus," Newters read from the screen. "It has a diameter of two thousand seven hundred seventy-nine miles. Surface temperatures range from fifty degrees to three hundred degrees Fahrenheit. Atmosphere is very thin and made of carbon monoxide. Fifty-six percent of the planet is habitable for Cyborg life. Nutfugdus once hosted an alien species known as the Desert Ferrets, but they're extinct."

"Wonderful!" the Cyborg Queen said. "I love a good dry heat. Upload!"

Once again, the *BASK-8* crew followed their queen's instructions. When the upload was finished, the spaceship zipped across the galaxy to the location of the following planet. Alex pulled her brother aside as it traveled.

"How much longer until we ask the Cyborg Queen to borrow her army?" Alex asked.

"Soon," Conner said. "There's only one more Goldilocks zone left with a planet the queen is going to go nuts over. We're going to help her upload it in exchange for the use of her Cyborg soldiers."

"Did you *intentionally* base a story about a queen who steals things from Goldilocks zones on Red Riding Hood?" Alex asked. "I can't decide if it's brilliant or brutal."

"Oh, I never thought about that," Conner said. "Red is going to kill me if she ever finds out."

The *BASK-8* arrived at the next planet. It was purple with turquoise rings and by far the most beautiful of all the planets they had visited so far. The Cyborg Queen was enchanted by it. Her throne transformed back into a gown and she rolled over to the hologram to take a closer look at the majestic world.

"What's the name of *this* beauty?" she asked.

"Lollipopigust, Your Majesty," Newters read from the monitor. "It has a diameter of three thousand ninety-nine miles. Surface temperatures range from twenty-five degrees to ninety degrees Fahrenheit. Atmosphere is made of pure oxygen, and ninety percent of the planet is habitable for Cyborg life."

"I LOVE it—it's meant to be!" the Cyborg Queen said, and clasped her metal hands together. "Upload it immediately! I'll share Jawbreakeropolous, Gumdropida, and Nutfugdus with the Cyborgs at home, but I want Lollipopigust for myself!"

The green laser engulfed the purple planet. But as Commander Newters read more information about Lollipopigust, a grave expression came over his red face. The commander bolted to a control station and pulled a red lever to abort the mission.

"What are you doing?" the queen demanded.

"Forgive me, Your Majesty, but I just read some troubling information," Newters said. "One thousand years ago, scientists from another planet sent a vial of insects to Lollipopigust to see if it would sustain life. The high oxygen levels in the atmosphere made the insects grow to enormous sizes and now they dominate the planet. If we upload Lollipopigust, it would be like uploading thousands of tiny viruses into our hard drive! The entire ship would crash."

The flashing lightbulb reappeared above the Cyborg Queen's crown. "Can't we send the army to Lollipopigust to terminate the insects?" she asked desperately.

Commander Newters shook his head. "The *BASK-8* has been traveling for so long, it doesn't have enough power to charge the soldiers' battle batteries," he said.

The queen's lightbulb went off again. "Can't they use their solar panels to charge their battle batteries?" she asked.

Commander Newters gulped. "That would only work while the soldiers were on the surface—but most of the insects live in colonies under the ground," he explained.

All the Cyborgs knew their queen wouldn't take the news well, so they dived under their control stations. The Cyborg Queen was so mad, the lightbulb above her crown burst and fiery blasts erupted from her exhaust pipes. Four robot legs wearing boots emerged from her steel gown and stomped the floor. Tears rolled down from her human eye and oil dripped from her lens.

"All I want is every habitable planet within a trillion-mile radius—it's not like I'm asking for *the world*!" the Cyborg Queen lamented. "Everyone put your brains and A.I. chips together! There's got to be something we can do!"

Once the fiery blasts had finished, Conner stepped toward the Cyborg Queen and tapped her on the exhaust pipes. Alex had no clue what her brother was up to.

"Excuse me, Your Mechanicalness, but I might have a solution," he said. "You see, my sister and I just happen to be the children of the best exterminator in the galaxy!"

"*We are?*" Alex said.

"Yes, *we are*!" Conner said, and sent her a dirty look. "*Meteor Magazine* gave our father four and a half nebulas out of five in their review, and the *Alien Voice* gave him three appendages up! Those are the most popular publications in the Willow Crestian system!"

The Cyborg Queen's eye and lens darted between Alex and Conner. Her eyebrows turned into tiny windshield wipers and cleaned the tears off her face.

"So the two of you could exterminate all the insects on the planet for me?" the queen asked hopefully.

"We *could*..." Conner said, lowering his head dramatically. "You've already been so kind to us by offering transportation back to our planet. I hate to ask you for *another* favor in exchange for exterminating the insects, but there is something *else* my sister and I could use your help with."

The Cyborg Queen wanted Lollipopigust so badly, she was willing to strike whatever bargain it took. "That's quite all right, just tell me what you have in mind."

"It's not for us, it's for our friends," Conner explained. "They live on a small planet called Fairytaletopia in the Storybookian Galaxy. Their planet has recently been invaded by a savage race known as the Literarious Villainomous."

"Bless you," Alex said.

Conner ignored his sister. "The Literarious Villainomous are twice as bad as the Orphianotics and ten times more powerful! The worst part is, Fairytaletopia has no way of defending itself."

"That sounds terrible!" the Cyborg Queen said.

"It is," Conner said. "But it's nothing your Cyborg army couldn't help with. If my sister and I exterminate the insects on Lollipopigust, would you lend us your soldiers to help our friends fight the Literarious Villainomous?"

It wasn't every day the Cyborg Queen was asked to lend out her army—however, it wasn't every day she came upon the planet of her dreams, either. She turned to the hologram of Lollipopigust and stroked it with her metal hand.

"Fine," the Cyborg Queen said. "Wipe that planet clean of insects, and I will let you use my Cyborg army to save Fairytaletopia."

Conner shook her metal hand appreciatively. "Thank you so much, Your Engineeredness," he said. "We couldn't be more grateful! Right, Alex?"

"Sure . . . *grateful*," she said unenthusiastically.

"Sure, sure," the Cyborg Queen said. "Commander Newters, please see that the humans from Sycamore Drivious have everything they need for their extermination plan. I'm going to my chambers now to finish my charge. Please see that the gravity is turned *off*, and wake me when the extermination is over."

"Yes, Your Majesty," Newters said with another deep bow.

The Cyborg Queen rolled into her private elevator and ascended through the ship. Alex yanked her brother aside.

"Bugs?" she asked. *"That's* your plan? We're going to kill bugs in exchange for soldiers?"

"Oh, come on," Conner said. "We'll get to travel to another planet and shoot at some overgrown pests! It'll be fun—like we're in a video game!"

Alex shook her head—she couldn't believe she had gone into this situation willingly. There were many times when Alex was convinced she and her brother were from different planets, and this just about proved it.

"Commander Newters," Conner said happily, "lead the way!"

CHAPTER FOURTEEN

UNIVERSAL PESTS

We're going to need two short-range blasters, one Omega GDD, and one Bio-Mat Compass," Conner said. "Oh, and the *2999 Moon Jumper Express* to get us there."

Commander Newters gave him a peculiar look. "You're very well informed as to our armory for someone who's never been aboard this ship before."

As if the *BASK-8*'s arsenal were a vending machine, Newters punched the codes of the devices Conner had requested into a touchscreen and they were brought out on a conveyor belt. The short-range blasters were long and silver with a bright blue light pulsating from the barrels, just like the Cyborg soldiers' guns. The Omega GDD was short and round like a propane tank and had a small keypad at the top. The Bio-Mat Compass looked like a thick silver watch with a holographic arrow.

The commander handed a blaster to each of the twins, and Conner fastened the compass around his wrist. The Omega GDD was heavy, so Alex and Conner carried it together.

"What do the Omega GDD and the Bio-Mat Compass do?" Alex asked.

"The Omega GDD stands for gamma detonation device—it's a very powerful bomb that uses gamma rays to vaporize its targets," Newters explained. "The Bio-Mat Compass detects biological material within a three-hundred-yard radius."

Alex gulped. "I'm sorry I asked," she said.

"To detonate the Omega GDD, type in the code *LRRH215*, wait for confirmation, and then run," Newters said. "The *2999 Moon Jumper Express* is in the spacecraft hangar. I'll show you to it."

The twins followed the commander through the spaceship. The short-range blasters and Omega GDD made Alex uneasy, and she held them away from her body. She was terrified the tiniest bump or tap would set them off and injure someone. Conner, on the other hand, couldn't have been more excited to be holding the weapons from his story.

When he was a kid, he used to spend hours pretending he was fighting evil aliens on a distant planet with the devices now in his hands. He was eager to get to Lollipopigust and live his childhood fantasy.

Conner twirled and pointed the blaster around the halls as they walked through the *BASK-8*. He re-enacted scenes from his favorite action movies and even made the sound effects to go along with it.

"Conner, knock it off!" Alex said. "You're gonna hurt someone with that!"

"Relax, I have the safety on," he said. "Oops—okay, *now* I have the safety on."

The commander and the twins walked through a set of automatic doors and arrived in the hangar. He showed them to a small spacecraft with the words *2999 Moon Jumper Express* engraved along the side of it. The spacecraft was the size of an SUV and looked like a mini version of the *BASK-8*. It was made of red steel and had two wings and a small crown of satellites and antennas. Newters pressed a button on the side of it and the door of the spacecraft slid open. There were two seats inside and compartments to store their weapons, but no sign of steering controls.

"How are we supposed to fly this thing?" Alex asked.

"The *2999 Moon Jumper Express* is controlled from the *BASK-8*," Newters said. "It prevents our spacecraft from being hijacked by Orphianotics—no offense."

Alex was relieved. If her brother had been planning to pilot the *2999 Moon Jumper Express* himself, she wasn't sure they would have made it to Lollipopigust. The twins stored their weapons in the compartments, tightened their helmets, and then strapped themselves into the seats. Newters hesitated before closing the spacecraft door behind them.

"Are you sure you know what you're doing?" he asked like a concerned father.

"One hundred percent," Conner said. "Once you've exterminated one alien insect species, you've exterminated them all. By the way, would you mind holding on to this until I get back?"

Conner handed the commander his backpack.

"It'll be safe with me," Newters said. "Good luck, exterminators. May the cosmos smile upon you."

The commander moved three fingers in a circle through the air and then pointed to his heart. Conner copied the motion exactly and Alex did her best to mimic him, but it was bizarre to her. Newters shut the door of the *2999 Moon Jumper Express* and headed out of the hangar.

"*'May the cosmos smile upon you'?*" Alex laughed. "Is that, like, a 'Galaxy Queen' catchphrase?"

"Do you know how hard it is coming up with an original science-fiction saying?" Conner asked. "Nearly impossible."

Once the commander was safely out of the hangar, the large compartment door opened to space. The gravity disappeared and the twins would have floated out of their seats if they weren't strapped in so securely. The engines of the

2999 Moon Jumper Express roared to life, and the spacecraft flew out of the *BASK-8* hangar and headed toward the planet of Lollipopigust below.

The ride was smooth and serene. The purple planet and its turquoise rings glowed exquisitely. Even though she wasn't thrilled they were en route to exterminate bugs, Alex couldn't deny how amazing it was to be gliding between a massive spaceship and the atmosphere of an alien planet.

"I have to admit, this is pretty cool," she said.

Conner didn't respond. Alex turned to check on him and saw tears glistening in his eyes. He had seen so many things from his imagination come to life, but seeing *an actual planet* was surprisingly emotional.

"Are you okay?" she asked.

"I'm fine," Conner said. "Just allergies."

"In *space*?" She laughed.

"Yeah, I think there might have been a cat in here before us."

Alex just smiled and didn't press it further. "Well, whatever you're reacting to, thanks for sharing it with me. This is an experience I would never have had without you."

The tender moment was interrupted by a loud beeping sound. The twins looked around the spacecraft nervously, afraid something was broken. The beeping was followed by an automated voice.

"*Five...four...three...*" it said.

"Conner, what are they counting *DOOOOWN—*"

The *2999 Moon Jumper Express* blasted toward Lollipopigust with the power of a thousand rockets. The twins were slammed back into their seats by so much force, it felt like invisible elephants were sitting on them. Their teeth rattled and their cheeks rippled. They were moving so fast, they couldn't breathe, let alone speak or scream.

The spacecraft zoomed under the turquoise rings, shot through Lollipopigust's atmosphere, and headed straight for the purple surface. They were moving thousands of miles per second and showed no sign of slowing down. Right when the twins were convinced the spacecraft was going to crash, it suddenly jerked upright and pointed its engines to the ground. The *2999 Moon Jumper Express* made a surprisingly gentle landing on the Lollipopigustian surface.

The spacecraft door opened automatically. "You've arrived at your destination," said the same automated voice. "Enjoy your visit to *Lo-lee-pop-ee-gust*."

Alex's and Conner's hearts were racing so fast, they felt frozen in one perpetual beat. When their bodies finally caught up with their minds, they both let out a long, terrified, and overdue scream.

"Alex, I think I peed a little. . . ." Conner said.

"Me too," she said.

The twins climbed out of their seats and stumbled off the spacecraft. They had a look around the planet's surface as their hearts returned to normal and feeling came back to their arms and legs.

Lollipopigust was covered in rolling purple hills and had a bright pink sky. The planet's turquoise rings arched above them and cast a shadow over the ground. The gravity wasn't as high on the planet as it had been on the *BASK-8*, and the twins felt stronger and lighter in their space suits.

They retrieved the weapons out of the spacecraft's compartments and ventured onto the planet. Conner glanced between the compass and the land around them, but there wasn't a sign of life anywhere.

"What kind of bugs are we looking for?" Alex asked. "Ants? Beetles? Flies?"

"The ones we have to find are called *polycrabs*," Conner told her. "They're a spider, scorpion, and wasp combination."

Just the description of the insects made Alex gasp and choke on the air.

"What the heck is wrong with you, Conner?" she asked. *"How could you even think of something so terrible?"*

"Sorry, it was in one of my nightmares," he said. "I thought it'd make a great alien monster, so I put it in the story. It's not like I *planned* to meet any of the villains in my stories."

"If that's what's crawling around your subconscious, you need *deep* psychological help," Alex said. "What's the plan to exterminate them?"

"It'll be simple," Conner said. "All we have to do is find the entrance to their colony, drop the Omega GDD inside, and then take off!"

Alex shook her head. "You and I both know it's never that easy," she said. "Who would have killed these bugs if we weren't here?"

"The Cyborg Queen would have been so desperate, she would have teamed up with the Orphianotics," Conner explained. "They would have exterminated the polycrabs but would have had to share Lollipopigust afterward."

"Then we make a nice plot twist for her," Alex said. "By the way, I've been meaning to ask, what is Commander Newters's deal? How did he end up working for the Cyborg Queen?"

"She saved his planet from being sucked into a black hole," Conner said. "Newters was so thankful, he devoted his life to working for her. Also, it's helpful to have *someone* aboard the *BASK-8* who's not connected to a battery, in case of a power outage."

The Bio-Mat Compass suddenly lit up and an arrow appeared on its screen.

"Looks like we've got our first catch of the day," Conner said.

The compass guided the twins through the purple hills to the edge of a deep, wide hole the size of an empty swimming pool. The compass pointed to something with biological material at the bottom of it. Alex and Conner held their short-range blasters tightly with their fingers against the triggers and cautiously peered into the hole.

Instead of a polycrab, they found a teal worm the size of

a small dog. It was chubby and had several rolls like a cater-pillar, but was shaped more like a jelly bean than a noodle. It had big black button eyes, no nose, and a wide mouth that was naturally shaped into a smile. The worm merrily rolled around the hole without a care in the world. It laughed and talked to itself like a happy baby.

"That is the cutest thing I've ever seen," Alex said. "What is it?"

"A Blissworm," Conner said. "They're a species of worm that's always happy, regardless of the situation they're in. The Blissworms are one of the few remaining species left on this planet. The polycrabs have hunted all the other bugs."

"What's it doing at the bottom of the hole?" she asked. "Does it live there?"

"No, the polycrabs dig holes to trap prey," Conner said. "The poor little guy must have fallen inside."

The Blissworm certainly didn't look like it had fallen into a trap. It giggled as it somersaulted across the hole. It looked up at the twins and waved with one of its four tiny hands.

"Oh, let's rescue it," Alex said. "It's too adorable to be eaten."

The twins lowered their weapons and slid down the side of the hole. The Blissworm was so excited to have company, it curled around their feet and purred like a kitten. Alex pet-ted the friendly bug. Its body felt like a gummy bear.

"I think it likes us," she said. "Would it survive on earth?"

"You want to take it *home*?" Conner asked.

Alex leaned down and the Blissworm crawled into her arms. It pressed its mouth against the glass of her helmet and gave her a big, slobbery kiss. Alex was filled with a warm fuzzy feeling, and she hugged the Blissworm like it was a long-lost pet.

"You know, maybe we should re-think this extermination thing," she said. "Maybe instead of *killing* all the polycrabs, we could just set traps and release them on another planet. The polycrabs are really no different from this Blissworm—they never asked to come to Lollipopigust. Let's be humane about it."

The Blissworm crawled to the ground and curiously circled the Omega GDD. It stretched its mouth over the top of it and swallowed the bomb whole. Since the detonation device was bigger than the Blissworm, its body stretched around it like a sock over a soda can.

"That worm better cough up our bomb or it's about to have some really bad heartburn," Conner said.

"It must be hungry," Alex said. "What does it usually eat?"

"Space weeds and stuff," Conner said. "Which is really strange, because polycrabs don't eat herbivores—they prey on other predators."

Suddenly, the twins and the Blissworm were eclipsed by a large shadow. Alex and Conner turned around and saw an enormous creature climbing into the hole behind them. It had big red eyes, fangs, two claws, eight legs, and three tails like a scorpion. At the tip of each tail was a long, sharp stinger. The creature's fangs dripped with saliva and it snapped its claws as it approached them.

It was easily the most terrifying thing the twins had ever seen and they both froze. The Blissworm waved at the monster and blew it a kiss.

"And *that's* a polycrab," Conner said.

"It has ten limbs and three tails," Alex noted. "That's thirteen appendages—why would you name it a polycrab? *Poly* means seven."

"Oh," Conner said. "That explains why I failed that geometry quiz."

Alex thought making sense of the creature would somehow make it less scary, but it did the opposite. The more she realized how little her brother knew about the alien insect he had created, the more frightening it became.

"Now I get why the worm was in the hole. It wasn't prey—the polycrab was using it as *bait*!" Conner said.

Alex was afraid to even ask. "Bait for what?"

"Us."

The polycrab vaulted toward the twins with its claws and stingers raised. Alex dived behind her brother and used him as a shield.

"Forget what I said about being humane!" Alex yelled. *"Kill it! Kill it! Kill it NOW!"*

Conner pointed his short-range blaster and shot at the

creature seconds before it tackled them. A bright blue blast hit the polycrab and it exploded into slime and guts. The innards rained down on the twins, and they almost became sick at the sight of it. Alex tried wiping the guts off her helmet, but they only smeared over the glass.

"Next time, I'm going to need a full itinerary *before* we travel into one of your short stories," she said.

"You got it," Conner said.

The Bio-Mat Compass started flickering more than ever before. The arrow spun out of control as something made of biological material approached the hole aboveground.

"We've got to get out of here!" Conner said.

The twins didn't have time to pry the Omega GDD out of the Blissworm, so they each grabbed one of the worm's hands and carried the Blissworm and weapon out of the hole as one. The Blissworm happily swung between them like it was on a trapeze.

Alex and Conner's problems only became worse aboveground. A dozen polycrabs surrounded them and there were even more running in from all directions. The twins set the Blissworm-covered Omega GDD on the ground and stood back to back. They raised their blasters and pointed them at the approaching polycrabs.

"Ready?" Conner said.

"Ready," Alex said.

"It's exterminating time!"

Alex and Conner opened fire on the polycrabs. The purple hillside was consumed in bright blue blasts and pieces of exploding alien insects. The Blissworm swayed and grooved to the sound of battle like it was a song with an electronic beat.

A polycrab in the twins' blind spots knocked them apart with one stroke of its claw. Alex and Conner tumbled onto the ground in different directions. The polycrabs were even harder to shoot at from the ground. The twins had to quickly roll back and forth to avoid being stepped on or stabbed by a polycrab's stinger.

No matter how many they killed, the monstrous insects kept coming. The polycrabs sprayed webs out of their center stingers, and the twins and the Blissworm became entwined in it. Alex and Conner struggled to break free from the sticky restraints, but their arms and blasters were confined against their torsos. The Blissworm rolled onto its back and tried to make snow angels in the web.

The polycrabs scooped up the twins and the Blissworm. But instead of eating them, the polycrabs carried them off into the distance, scurrying over the purple hills like a school of crabs across the sand.

"Now what?" Alex asked. "Where are they taking us?"

"To their colony to feed us to their queen," Conner said.

The Blissworm clapped giddily, as if they were being taken to an amusement park.

"The worm is right—this is actually a good thing," Conner said. "The deeper we get into the colony, the more effective the Omega GDD will be."

The herd of polycrabs arrived at a huge mound that

looked like an anthill the size of a mountain. They crawled into the entrance at the top and then down a long tunnel that snaked deep into the ground. It reminded Alex of the time she and Conner were kidnapped by trolls and goblins and taken to their underground territory.

They entered the largest cavern of the colony. Every inch of it was covered with polycrabs. The insects crawled across the dirt floor and the walls and hung by their tails from the ceiling. The polycrabs snapped their claws, rattled their tails, and hissed in celebration as the twins and the Blissworm were brought inside. The Blissworm waved and pointed at the creatures like it was the front-runner in a polycrab election.

The twins spotted the polycrab queen in the back of the cavern. She was a giant compared to her offspring and shared all their features. The queen also had tall horns protruding out of her head and a pair of wings she wore like a high collar. Under her tails was a thick, long abdomen that curved into a corner of the cavern where she laid eggs. A massive spiderweb hung behind her like a national flag.

Alex noticed the queen bore a slight resemblance to Trollbella. She had a sneaking suspicion the Troll and Goblin Territory was the inspiration behind the polycrab colony.

"Conner, is that supposed to be Trollbella?" Alex asked.

"Of course it is," he said without shame. "She's the biggest pest I know!"

The polycrabs carrying the twins and the Blissworm joined a line of other polycrabs headed for the queen. The creatures each presented the queen with a Lollipopigustian insect they had captured that day. The queen looked each victim over and spit green or yellow mucus on it.

"That's disgusting," Alex muttered to her brother. "What's the purpose of that?"

"The queen is separating the prey," Conner said. "Green mucus means she wants to eat the prey herself, yellow mucus means she wants it to be fed to the larvae, and no mucus . . ."

The twins watched as the queen inspected an alien that resembled a mantis. When no mucus was produced, the alien was dragged to the center of the cavern and the entire colony attacked it. They savagely tore the insect limb from limb as they feasted upon it. It was hard to watch, and the twins looked away.

Conner was the first prey the polycrabs in their party presented to the queen. As she examined him, her large red eyes grew even bigger and saliva dripped from her fangs. It was similar to how Trollbella looked at Conner—she wanted him all to herself. The polycrab queen covered him in green mucus, picked him up with her claw, and tossed him into the web behind her.

Just like a fly caught in a spiderweb, the more Conner struggled to free himself, the more entangled he became.

Alex was presented to the queen next. It was no surprise that the queen wasn't nearly as impressed with her as she was with Conner. She spit yellow mucus all over her and Alex was dragged to the corner of eggs.

The Blissworm was the last in their group to be presented to the queen. The worm was delighted to see her and eagerly reached up like it wanted to hug the gigantic insect. The queen didn't even bother inspecting the worm. With no mucus, the polycrabs dragged the Blissworm to the center of the cavern to eat it themselves.

"Shoot! They'll set off the bomb if they eat it!" Conner said. "Alex, do something!"

Both twins were still wrapped in web from their surface encounter with the polycrabs, but Alex managed to free one of her hands and she snapped her fingers. Suddenly, the polycrab queen tilted her head back and let out a massive sneeze, and the Blissworm was showered in green mucus. When the queen looked down and saw the worm, she didn't realize the green mucus was accidental. She picked it up and tossed it into the web behind her, too.

The Blissworm stuck to the web just a few feet away from Conner. The worm waved at him like they were two friends running into each other at the supermarket. The queen continued separating the other prey her children had brought into the colony.

"Conner, I'm going to cast a spell on our space suits to make them web resistant," Alex said. "Hang on."

She snapped her fingers again and the web covering their bodies melted away, freeing their arms and the short-range blasters that had been compressed against their torsos. Conner hung on to the queen's web like it was a wide rope ladder.

Alex heard snapping and crunching sounds coming from nearby—the polycrab eggs had started hatching. The small larvae poked their heads out of the eggs and looked around for their first meal. As soon as one larva noticed Alex, they all turned their heads to her as if they were connected on the same wavelength.

Alex pointed her gun at the newborns and Conner waved to stop her.

"Don't shoot them!" Conner yelled. "We need to activate the Omega GDD before you cause a scene!"

"Then get to it!" Alex said.

Conner climbed across the web to where the Blissworm hung. He pulled the worm off the web with a *snap* and carried it down to the ground. The Blissworm was very heavy with the bomb inside its body. At first he tried pulling the Omega GDD out through the Blissworm's mouth, but the jolly worm made a game of it and kept its mouth tightly shut.

"You stupid little parasite!" Conner said. *"Just spit it out!"*

He tried squeezing the Omega GDD out of the Blissworm, but it only tickled the worm. The Blissworm kept its mouth shut but Conner felt the laughter building up inside of it.

"So you like being tickled, huh?" Conner said. "I'm gonna *goochie-goochie-goo* that bomb right out of you!"

Conner tickled the Blissworm with both hands. The worm had never been so amused in its whole life, and so much laughter built up inside its body that the Omega GDD looked like it was covered in a teal balloon. Finally, the Blissworm couldn't take the tickling anymore and opened its mouth to laugh. The Omega GDD shot out like a cannonball. Luckily Conner grabbed its handle before it got away.

Meanwhile, in the corner, the larvae started crawling out of their eggs. Once they figured out how to walk, they crawled toward Alex. She kicked them away with her boots, but they were relentless. Each egg hosted several larvae, so the number of newborns coming toward her doubled by the second.

"Hurry up!" she yelled at her brother. *"I'm about to become alien baby food!"*

Conner punched *LRRH215* into the Omega GDD keypad and a red light started to flash.

"The Omega GDD will detonate in thirty seconds," said a calm voice from the device.

"It's set!" Conner announced, and dashed toward his sister.

"Don't forget the Blissworm!" Alex said. *"We can't leave it here!"*

Conner grunted and then dashed back. The Blissworm was waiting with its hands up like a toddler wanting to be lifted, and Conner scooped it up.

The larvae started leaping on Alex—she had no choice but to shoot them. The blasts echoed through the cavern, and all the polycrabs snapped their heads toward her. Conner quickly thought of a distraction to save his sister. He fired his blaster at the corners of the web behind the queen, and it fell on top of her like a net. The polycrab queen hissed and all her children forgot about their newborn siblings and hurried to help her.

Alex and Conner met in the middle of the cavern and ran for the tunnel in the back. The Blissworm waved good-bye to the polycrabs as they passed them. Alex and Conner entered the tunnel and shot at the ceiling behind them as they ran, causing large chunks of dirt to fall and block the passageway so the polycrabs couldn't follow them.

The twins ran as fast as their legs could carry them. The Blissworm held on to Conner's helmet like a jockey clutching the reins of a racehorse. It even slapped Conner's bottom as if that would make him run faster.

"Cut it out!" he said. *"That hurts!"*

They only had a few seconds left before the Omega GDD detonated. They saw light ahead and knew they were almost out of the colony. They heard a thunderous explosion erupt behind them and the whole tunnel vibrated. Alex, Conner, and the Blissworm re-surfaced just in time and rolled down the mound. A powerful gamma ray exploded out of the colony's entrance, vaporizing everything it touched. The purple hills shook and cracked for miles like they had been hit by a powerful earthquake. When the gamma ray dissipated, there was nothing left of the colony but a massive hole in the ground.

With the polycrabs successfully exterminated, Lollipopigust was safe for the *BASK-8* to upload. The twins stayed on the ground as they caught their breath.

"From now on, I'm only writing about bunnies," Conner said, panting.

A spacecraft a teeny bit bigger than the *2999 Moon Jumper Express* descended from the sky and landed near the twins. It was black and its shape was similar to the body of a wolf. *CLAW-DS* was engraved along the side of the spacecraft. Alex and Conner got to their feet as the Cyborg Queen charged out of the *CLAW-DS* followed by Commander Newters and a handful of Cyborg soldiers.

"Well done, exterminators!" the Cyborg Queen said. "We had a bet going on the *BASK-8* that you wouldn't survive—now I owe my crew a week of double battery privileges!"

The twins could tell she was fully charged because she seemed to be in a much better mood than before. The commander shook the twins' hands and gave Conner his backpack.

"Excellent work," Newters said. "I haven't seen the Cyborg Queen so pleased since the time a constellation was named after her!"

The Cyborg Queen clapped her metal hands and a team of short gray aliens with large heads and eyes ran out of the spacecraft. They carried holographic blueprints, laser measuring tapes, and toolboxes that hovered beside them.

"Who are those guys?" Conner asked.

"Once she was certain you would succeed, Her Majesty had the best architects in the galaxy flown out to immediately start construction on the planet," Newters said.

The Cyborg Queen rotated and pointed the gray aliens to different parts of the Lollipopigustian surface.

"I think I'll build the palace right *there* in the eclipse of the rings so it doesn't get hot in the summer," she thought out loud. "And since there's already a gigantic hole in the ground over there—wish someone had warned me that might happen, but oh well—that's where I'll put the gasoline pool."

The Cyborg Queen rolled over to join the commander and the twins.

"Your Magneticness," Conner said, "now that we've exterminated the polycrabs, may my sister and I borrow your Cyborg army to save our friends?"

"A deal is a deal," she said. "You may take us to Fairytaletopia whenever you're ready."

"Wait, *you're* coming with us?" Alex asked.

"Indeed," the Cyborg Queen said. "They're going to start building my new residence as soon as we take the planet to my home system—I'm going to need something to do while it's being constructed. How long is the journey? I must warn you, anything longer than seventy-four seconds makes me irritable."

"We're actually going to make a stop in Sycamore Drivious first, but it won't take long at all," he said. "In fact, I just remembered I have a transportation device right here."

Conner reached into his backpack and pulled out his binder of short stories.

"Lovely," the Cyborg Queen said. She rolled away from the twins and covered her nose. "Friendly word of advice: You might want to change before seeing your friends. You both smell horribly of *bug guts*."

CHAPTER FIFTEEN

THE APPLE MEETS THE TREE

Emmerich wasn't getting much sleep. The witches at Dead Man's Creek stayed up all night like nocturnal animals. They cackled and brewed foul-smelling potions until the sun came up and then rested during the day. Their loud snoring, growling, and mumbling was impossible for Emmerich to sleep through. Like a neglected pet, he wasn't being fed much, either. So he became weaker the longer he stayed there as the witches' prisoner.

He thought his exhaustion was starting to play tricks on

his mind, because one day at sunrise, after all the witches went to bed, he saw a strange man tiptoeing through the camp toward him. He had pale blue eyes and several scratches along the side of his face. He walked with a limp and his left arm was in a sling.

Emmerich had never seen the man before and had no idea what he was doing there. He circled the tree Emmerich was restrained to and quietly untied the chains.

"Who are you?" Emmerich asked.

The man motioned for him to be silent. *"I'm here to rescue you,"* the man whispered.

Once he unwrapped the chains around Emmerich's body, the man offered his good hand and helped the boy to his feet. It was difficult for both of them since the man was injured and Emmerich hadn't been on his feet for a long time.

The man gestured for Emmerich to follow him, and they snuck into the forest, far away from Dead Man's Creek.

"Are you hurt?" the man asked, and inspected the boy front to back.

"No," Emmerich said. "Tired, hungry, and scared—but they didn't harm me."

The man reached into his sling and handed Emmerich an apple. The boy was so hungry, he forgot all politeness and immediately started eating it.

"Make sure you chew your food," the man said with a smile. "Remember what happened to Snow White?"

The Masked Man played the part of a Good Samaritan

very well. With just a few kind gestures, he had the little boy convinced he was a hero.

"Thank you for rescuing me," Emmerich said. "Who are you?"

"You don't know who I am?" the man asked.

Emmerich shook his head. The two had never been face-to-face before, but the Masked Man needed to be certain his reputation hadn't found his son first.

"I'm from the Otherworld," the Masked Man lied. "I've come to rescue you and take you back home."

The little boy was so happy about the prospect of going home, tears came to his eyes and he gave the Masked Man a giant hug. It hurt his broken rib, and the Masked Man pushed Emmerich away.

"I'm sorry," Emmerich said. "I've been away from home for a very long time. My mother must be worried sick about me!"

"Right . . ." the Masked Man said. "Your *mother*."

He paused for a moment to observe his son. The resemblance he shared with Bo Peep was even more striking up close.

"How did you find me?" Emmerich asked.

"Oh," the Masked Man said, thinking on his feet. "Your friends in the Otherworld sent me."

"You mean Conner and Alex?" the boy asked.

The Masked Man was shocked that Emmerich knew the names of his niece and nephew. If he didn't know his own father, how could he possibly know about his cousins?

"Why . . . *yes*," the Masked Man said.

"Are they here?" Emmerich asked.

The little boy looked around the forest excitedly, as if the twins were about to jump out from behind a tree.

"They're in the Otherworld waiting for us," the Masked Man said.

"How do you know the twins?" Emmerich asked.

The Masked Man needed to be careful with the information he shared—especially if Emmerich was friends with the twins. If his plan was going to work, he needed his son's absolute trust.

"Have they ever mentioned their uncle Lloyd?" he asked.

"No," Emmerich said. "I didn't even know they had an uncle."

"Good," the Masked Man said. "I mean—*good for me*. Now I get to introduce myself to you. I'm Lloyd Bailey, Alex and Conner's *favorite* uncle."

Emmerich shook the Masked Man's hand as enthusiastically as if he were meeting a member of his own family.

"It's wonderful to meet you," Emmerich said.

"And you as well," the Masked Man said. "Now, we must hurry out of the woods before the witches realize you're gone. I've just returned from following the witch Morina— she led me to a portal in the Eastern Kingdom that will take us to the Otherworld. We must move very quietly, though; it's a dangerous time to be traveling through this world."

The Masked Man led the way and Emmerich followed.

Even with an injured leg, the Masked Man moved with so much determination that Emmerich had difficulty keeping up with him. Although his head was filled with a hundred more questions, Emmerich followed the man's instructions to stay quiet.

They traveled through the forest for miles without making a sound. Suddenly, a loud crunch came from under the Masked Man's foot. He looked down at the ground and saw he had stepped on a small statue of a bird made from a pale stone. It was an odd thing to find in the middle of the woods.

"Look, there are more!" Emmerich said.

The boy pointed to the treetops above them. The statue under the man's foot was one of many. The branches were covered with hundreds of stone birds—enough to make an entire flock. Each bird looked terrified, as if it had been frozen while fleeing from a predator.

"What strange decorations," Emmerich said.

"These aren't decorations," the Masked Man said. "They've been turned to stone by a terrible monster creeping through the forest. We need to get far away from here as quickly as possible before we're next!"

Emmerich didn't need any further explanation. He and the Masked Man hurried through the woods faster than before. But even with a monster loose in the woods, Emmerich was glad to be away from Dead Man's Creek. Little did the boy know, he would have been better off with the witches than in the Masked Man's care.

CHAPTER SIXTEEN

FULL HOUSE AND
FULL HEARTS

The perseverance of the *Dolly Llama* crew had been put to the test when they entered the Otherworld, but after only one day in the house on Sycamore Drive, the pirates and sailors of "Starboardia" had grown very accustomed to life in the twenty-first century. In fact, they had become a little *too comfortable* for Charlotte's taste. The twins' mother had spent the entire day following pirates and sailors from one room to the next as if she were babysitting fifty toddlers.

Auburn Sally, Admiral Jacobson, Siren Sue, and the navy sailors were spread out in the living room watching television. They shared bowls of popcorn and candy as they watched a program Charlotte didn't recognize.

"What are you watching?" Charlotte asked.

As if it had cast a spell on them, the men and women never looked away from the screen.

"A very wealthy family with very frivolous problems," Auburn Sally said. "It's hard to tell who the parents are, because they *all* act like spoiled children."

"And for whatever reason, we can't stop watching it," Admiral Jacobson said.

Suddenly, they all jumped at the sound of a blender. Charlotte ran into the kitchen to see what the others had gotten into. She found Too-Much-Rum Ronda pouring a red slushy liquid into mugs for herself, Not-So-Jolly Joan, Catfish Kate, and High-Tide Tabitha.

"Can I help you with something, ladies?" Charlotte asked.

"We couldn't be better," Too-Much-Rum Ronda said. "I've recently discovered how to create a marvelous con-coction called a strawberry daiquiri! It's a delicious and cold drink that's so sweet, you can't even taste the rum! It's the nectar of the gods, I tell you! Would you like one?"

"No, thank you," Charlotte said.

Not-So-Jolly Joan, Catfish Kate, and High-Tide Tabitha quickly slurped down their frozen drinks and then held their heads in pain.

"You've poisoned us!" Not-So-Jolly Joan yelled.

"My head is going to explode!" Catfish Kate shouted.

"Quick—put us out of our misery!" High-Tide Tabitha said. She tried to hand Charlotte her rifle.

"Ladies, relax," Charlotte said. "You're having a *brain freeze*—it's what happens when you drink cold beverages too fast. Pace yourselves and it'll go away."

A clump of red slush fell and splattered across the counter. Charlotte looked up and saw the kitchen ceiling was covered with strawberry daiquiri.

"What's all that?" she asked.

"Sorry, that was my first round," Too-Much-Rum Ronda said. "It took me a couple tries before I mastered the pitcher of spinning blades."

Before Charlotte had a chance to clean up the mess, she was distracted by a giant splash that came from the second story. She ran up the stairs and dashed into her and Bob's bathroom.

Winking Wendy and Fish-Lips Lucy were taking a bubble bath in Charlotte's tub fully clothed. Stinky-Feet Phoebe was sitting on the tank of the toilet with her feet in the bowl. She flushed the toilet and sighed with relief as the rushing water gave her a foot massage. All three pirates had clearly gone through Charlotte's things, because they wore green beauty masks and were reading romance novels.

"Hello, Charlotte!" Stinky-Feet Phoebe said. "You blokes certainly know how to live! This is by far my favorite invention of the future."

She patted the side of the toilet happily and flushed it again. Charlotte took a deep breath and slowly let it out. A headache was forming right between her eyes.

"That's not what the toilet is for, Phoebe," Charlotte said.

Stinky-Feet Phoebe was shocked. "Then what *is* its purpose?"

"Human waste," Charlotte said.

The pirate immediately removed her feet from the toilet bowl and wiped them with a hand towel.

"Then what's that bucket in the corner with the pedal that opens the lid?" Fish-Lips Lucy asked.

"That's a trash can," Charlotte said.

Winking Wendy's and Fish-Lips Lucy's faces filled with guilt.

"I wouldn't look inside it if I were you," Winking Wendy said.

Before Charlotte could reprimand the women in her bathroom, she caught sight of something out of the corner of her eye. She stepped into her bedroom and saw that the comforter on her bed had been replaced with a large black flag with the skull of a llama on it. Charlotte rushed to the bedroom window and looked at the pirate ship in the backyard. Big-Booty Bertha was hoisting the lavender bedspread above the *Dolly Llama* like a new flag. The twins' mother hurried downstairs and ran out into the backyard.

"Bertha, that's my comforter!" Charlotte shouted.

"Do you like it?" Big-Booty Bertha asked. "I thought

the ship could use a little color. Don't get me wrong, I like our old flag, but this flag says, *'Yes, we're pirates, but we're also totally in touch with our femininity!'*"

Clink-clink! As soon as Charlotte took her first step to climb aboard the ship, she heard a strange sound coming from the side yard. *Clink-clink!* She inspected the noise and found Pancake-Face Patty playing darts with her nicest silverware.

"Stop that!" Charlotte said, and quickly gathered the utensils. *"This is my great-grandmother's silver! It's a family heirloom!"*

"And fine taste she had," Pancake-Face Patty said. "They're very easy to throw. Your great-grandmother must have been quite a bandit!"

Charlotte could feel her blood pressure rising. She went inside and locked herself in the laundry room before she lost her temper. The racket throughout the house was blocked by the sound of the dryer. It was the first peaceful moment Charlotte had had all day. She was so happy to be helpful to her children, but she hadn't expected that watching the pirates and sailors would be such a chaotic task.

There was a knock on the laundry room door and Charlotte cringed.

"What now?" she asked.

"Charlotte, it's Bob," her husband said. "I just got home. Are you all right?"

Charlotte quickly let him in and shut the door before a pirate followed him inside.

"To be honest, I'm losing my mind a little bit," she confessed. "And these are only the characters from the *first* story! What am I going to do when Alex and Conner get back from 'Galaxy Queen'? The house is too small for all these people!"

"I think we've bitten off more than we can chew," Bob said. "The sailors made a rope net out of my ties, and the Rosary Chicken turned my hamper into a nest. She also laid eggs in all my shoes—I wish I had been warned before I got dressed for work this morning."

"And we *both* have to work tomorrow," Charlotte said. "We can't leave them in the house alone. They'll burn it down by the time we get back."

"It's not like we can call a sitter," he said. "And we certainly can't take them with us to the hospital."

Bob had unintentionally given Charlotte an idea, and her eyes lit up.

"That's it!" she said. "What if we take them to the new wing of the children's hospital? They just finished construction and the inspections don't start until next week. It's empty and spacious—exactly what we need!"

Before Bob could argue with her, the dryer door popped open and Somersault Sydney rolled out of it. The pirate was very warm and dizzy. When her eyes stopped spinning, she looked up at Bob and Charlotte.

"What time is it?" Somersault Sydney asked.

"Almost half past five," Bob said.

"Dang it," Somersault Sydney said. "I was hoping that was a time machine."

A loud *crash* came from the living room. Charlotte and Bob sprinted through the house and found their television on the floor with its screen shattered. Auburn Sally and Admiral Jacobson were helping Siren Sue to her feet beside it.

"What happened?" Charlotte asked.

"The privileged family disappeared and were replaced by a series of merchants," Auburn Sally explained. "First a woman was bewitching us into purchasing a mop of miracles, then a man swallowed a tiny pebble that soothed his aching bones, and then an old woman fell onto the floor and couldn't get up!"

Siren Sue looked down at the floor. "I tried to save her," she said.

Bob and Charlotte looked around their house at all the pirates and sailors and shared a long sigh.

"You're right," Bob said. "We can't let them stay here. We'll take them to the hospital with us. At least we'll be able to check on them while we're working."

"But they're still going to need supervision," Charlotte said.

Conner's binder of short stories was kept safely in the corner of the living room. The cover flipped open and a beam of light illuminated the house. Alex and Conner stepped out of the beam in their newly cleaned space suits with huge smiles on their faces. The Blissworm sat on Alex's shoulder and *oohed* and *aahed* as it saw their house.

"Hey, guys!" Conner said. "Good news—we've recruited the Cyborg army to help us!"

The pirates and sailors cheered, then stopped, sharing the same puzzled expression.

"What's a Cyborg?" Admiral Jacobson asked.

"You'll see," Conner said. "They'll be in the house shortly. The Cyborg Queen was just waiting on a New Planet Construction Permit from the United Universe Council—it's a long story."

The broken television and the messy kitchen caught the twins' attention.

"What happened in here?" Alex asked. "Was there an earthquake?"

"We need to talk," Charlotte said.

Bob and Charlotte pulled the twins into the dining room for a private word.

"The house is getting smaller by the minute," their mother said. "Bob and I were talking, and we think it might be best if we take your characters to the new wing of the children's hospital. There's lots of room there and no one will see them."

"That's a great idea," Conner said. "I was wondering where we'd put a thousand Cyborg soldiers. Good thinking."

"Which brings us to our next concern," Bob said. "We need help taking care of all these characters—your mother and I can only do so much. Is there anyone you know who can help us supervise?"

The Blissworm raised its hand, confident it was the worm for the job. The twins looked to each other and thought of possible candidates.

"We should probably check in with the others in the fairy-tale world," Alex said. "What if we bring Jack and Goldilocks back to help Mom and Bob?"

"Yeah, they're probably worried about us," he said. "We can let everyone else know we've recruited half an army—they might need some good news."

Even though the Blissworm had no idea what the twins were talking about, it nodded along approvingly. It was the first time Bob and Charlotte had noticed the worm on Alex's shoulder, and they both took a step back from it.

"How should we get to the fairy-tale world?" Conner asked. "Grandma's old storybook?"

"Yes, but instead of activating the magic within the storybook, we should use the Portal Potion on it," Alex suggested. "We'll have an easier way of getting back here."

Bob and Charlotte listened to Alex and Conner like they were speaking another language, but if the twins were satisfied with this plan, so were they.

"Where is Grandma's old storybook, anyway?" Conner asked.

"It's on the bookshelf in Alex's room upstairs," Charlotte said.

"Great!" Conner said. "Thanks for being so organized, Mom!"

Alex snapped her fingers and their space suits turned into normal clothes again. She handed Charlotte the Blissworm and the twins ran up the stairs to Alex's room.

Despite its energetic attempt for a hug, Charlotte held the Blissworm away from her body like it was poisonous.

"Charlotte," Bob said in shock, "there's an alien worm in our house."

In her bedroom upstairs, Alex scanned her bookshelf until she found the spine of her grandma's emerald storybook. She pulled it out and read the golden title aloud.

"*The Land of Stories*," Alex said.

"More like *The Land of Troubles*." Conner laughed.

Naturally, the book was nostalgic for the twins, but they didn't have time to walk down memory lane. Conner placed the storybook on the floor, removed the flask from his backpack, and poured three drops of the Portal Potion onto the pages. They lit up as another bright beam of light shined out of the book.

While Conner got the storybook ready, the title of another book on the shelf caught Alex's eye: *King Arthur*. It made her heart sink and her face fall.

"Is something wrong?" Conner asked her.

"Not at all," Alex said. "Go ahead, I'll be right behind you."

Conner stepped into the beam of light and disappeared from the bedroom. Alex pulled her copy of *King Arthur* off the shelf and stared at it. The image on the cover was of an old, weary king seated at the head of a round table. He had bags under his eyes, a long, graying beard, and a mind full of troubles. It made her laugh because the Arthur she knew couldn't have been more different.

Alex wondered what Arthur was doing at that very moment. She wondered if he thought about her as much as she thought about him, if he missed her as much as she missed him, and if he longed to be with her as much as she longed to be with him. Even though it was entirely her choice to leave him in his own world, not a single day went by that she didn't think of him and wonder if she had made the right decision.

Oddly, just holding the book made Alex feel closer to Arthur, as if he were on the other end of an open telephone line. She stuffed the book into her backpack, stepped into the beam of light, and followed her brother into the Land of Stories.

In the world of King Arthur, the once and future king was battling an enchanted scarecrow in the middle of a large open field. The duel would have been a spectacle to any passing observer, but to Arthur it was just another lesson in his training to become the king of England. Merlin and Mother Goose sat in plastic lawn chairs to the side and drank iced tea as they cheered him on.

"That's it, young Arthur!" Merlin said. "Always remember, enemies will come in different shapes, sizes, and materials!"

"Ar-ty! Ar-ty! Ar-ty!" Mother Goose chanted like she was at a football game. "Show that scarecrow who's boss! Kick the hay outta him!"

Arthur was the least enthusiastic of all of them. In fact, he resembled the King Arthur on the cover of Alex's book more than the adventurous young man she remembered. Defeating the scarecrow was an easy challenge, but his heart wasn't in it. Only one thing had been on Arthur's mind for weeks, and he couldn't let it go.

The scarecrow tackled Arthur to the ground. It punched and kicked him with its soft hay hands, but Arthur didn't even try to shield himself. He just lay on the ground and let the enchanted object beat him.

Merlin and Mother Goose did everything they could to encourage him. They magically set off fireworks, they did the wave like a crowd in a stadium, they even danced with pom-poms, but nothing motivated him.

"He's been depressed since Alex left," Merlin said. "Unless we do something to inspire him soon, England will have a very bleak future."

"Let me talk to him," Mother Goose said. "If there's one thing I'm good at, it's convincing young men to do things against their will. Trust me, I had two dates to every school dance, and it wasn't because of my looks."

Merlin shrugged. He was out of ideas himself and willing to try anything. He snapped his fingers and the scarecrow was disenchanted.

"Let's take a break," Merlin told Arthur. "I need to return to the cottage and stir my wormtail ragu so it won't be lumpy for dinner."

The wizard kissed Mother Goose on the cheek and then

headed into the forest to give her and Arthur a moment alone.

"Hey, Arty! Come have a seat next to me," Mother Goose called.

Arthur pushed the scarecrow off his body and sluggishly took Merlin's seat next to her. He kept his eyes on the empty field and let out a deep sigh.

"Why the long face, Arthur?" Mother Goose asked. "You look like I did when the Beatles broke up."

"I'm having a difficult time concentrating on Merlin's lessons," he said. "I don't feel like myself these days."

"Because you miss Alex," she said matter-of-factly.

Arthur's knee-jerk reaction was to deny the accusation, but when he opened his mouth, he couldn't find the words to argue. Instead, he just nodded and sank into his seat. Mother Goose put a comforting hand on his shoulder and smiled sweetly.

"Young love," she said. "It doesn't matter how old you get, you always remember it. You spend five minutes with someone and suddenly you never want to spend a moment apart. They become your sole focus and make you happier, more excited, and more inspired than anything before. They become your armor and give you strength and bravery and make you feel unstoppable. Life doesn't seem so bad now that you have someone to share it with."

Arthur gulped—he couldn't have described it better himself.

"That is, until it *stops*," Mother Goose said. "Then

everything comes to an earth-shattering, heartbreaking, and rude-awakening halt. You feel foolish for ever having been so happy, and embarrassed for letting it show, and the world has never seemed so terrible."

"Sounds familiar," Arthur said.

Mother Goose leaned a little closer to him, and seriousness grew in her eyes.

"Love is wonderful, magical, and beautiful, but it can also be maddening, damaging, and dangerous," she said. "It blinds us more than anything. It makes us selfish, it makes us feel like nothing else matters, and it tricks us into thinking the rest of the world doesn't exist—but it *does* exist. Whether you're on the high or low side of love, the world always moves on."

"So you're saying love is a weakness?" Arthur asked.

"That depends on you," Mother Goose said. "There's a reason we've got hearts *and* brains—we're supposed to listen to them both. A good man follows his heart, but a wise man follows his heart without ignoring his brain. Finding the right balance is one of the hardest parts of life."

"It appears Alex and I are on opposite ends of that scale," Arthur said. "She believes being together would alter my destiny, and I can't imagine a destiny without her."

"Destiny is an awfully big gamble for one relationship," Mother Goose said. "It doesn't matter how strongly you feel about something—even the most stubborn people can change. What if you and Alex grew apart a couple of years down the road? Could you imagine the guilt you'd both feel if you let down the people of England for nothing?"

"But like you said, life is about finding a *balance*," Arthur said. "Surely there's an outcome where we can fulfill our destinies *and* be together? Why does it have to be so black-and-white?"

"Young people from the Otherworld are overly dramatic these days," Mother Goose said. "Every relationship has to be *all-or-nothing*, there's no example of *give-and-take*—I blame television and vampire novels. Alex doesn't want to keep King Arthur from England—so she's keeping King Arthur away from her."

Arthur went quiet and looked at the sky. He thought over and over again about what Mother Goose had just said. An enticing idea came to him and he smiled from ear to ear.

"Then to prove her wrong, I have to prove she won't be depriving England of anything," he said. "If I accomplish everything in the legend she holds me to, Alex will have nothing to put between us!"

Mother Goose was confused. She was trying to convince Arthur to get over Alex and move on with his life, not to get over his life and move on with Alex. She had no idea how her advice could have backfired so easily.

"I suppose you're right," she said. "Heck, Arty, if you founded Camelot, assembled the Knights of the Round Table, located the Holy Grail, and *still* had feelings for Alex after you were done—I'd take you to her myself."

Arthur looked at Mother Goose with deep desperation in his eyes. "You would?" he asked.

"Um . . . *sure*," Mother Goose said. "But I think you're missing my—"

"Then I'd better get back to work!" he said.

Arthur excitedly ran back into the field. She wasn't entirely sure how it had happened, but Mother Goose was pleased to see his spirits change. She snapped her fingers and the scarecrow got to its feet. Arthur fought it with more vigor and purpose than he had ever fought anything before.

Merlin returned to the field and couldn't believe his eyes. He sat beside Mother Goose with an astonished look on his face.

"It's a miracle!" Merlin said. "How did you manage it?"

Mother Goose shrugged. "I have such a way with words, even I'm not sure what I said."

CHAPTER SEVENTEEN

REGROUPING

Alex and Conner stepped through the beam of light and found themselves somewhere near the base of the Northern Mountains in the Northern Kingdom. If it weren't for the range of snowy peaks stretching across the horizon, they wouldn't have recognized the Land of Stories. The smoky sky and the prominent burned smell in the air made them feel like they had stepped into a war zone, not the world of classic fairy tales. But unfortunately, these days they were one and the same.

"This place looks awful," Conner said. "What has Uncle Lloyd done to it?"

"We're not far from the Northern Palace," Alex said. "Let's sneak over and take a look—it might give us some information."

The twins picked up the emerald storybook from the ground next to them and traveled through the woods of the Northern Kingdom, carefully avoiding roads and paths to stay out of sight. Soon the green domes of the Northern Palace came into view above the trees, and the twins crept closer to get a glimpse of it.

If the Northern Palace was any indication, the fairy-tale world was in the worst shape it had ever been in. Snow White's former home was so battered, it was a miracle parts of it were even standing. Captain Hook's flying ship, the *Jolly Roger*, hovered above the palace like a docked hot-air balloon. The grounds were covered with groups of patrolling Winkies and card soldiers.

On the front lawns of the palace, the twins saw villagers constructing three enormous statues: the Wicked Witch of the West, Captain Hook, and the Queen of Hearts. They were watched over by a flock of flying monkeys that pushed and kicked the villagers as they carried supplies past them.

"What have they done to Swan Lake?" Conner exclaimed. "All the villagers from all the kingdoms must be in there!"

"Look up there," Alex said.

She pointed to the palace balcony, where Captain Hook, the Queen of Hearts, and the Wicked Witch of the West watched the villagers build their monuments. The villains were seated on large cushioned chairs and were being served drinks and sweets by Mr. Smee.

"Where's Uncle Lloyd?" Alex asked. "Why isn't he sitting with them or having his own statue constructed?"

"It's weird, isn't it?" Conner said. "Let's get to the cave—the others will know."

Alex held her brother tightly, and with a bright flash she magically transported them to the cave in the mountains. They were expecting to find their friends the Merry Men, the Lost Boys, and soldiers from the Northern and Charming Kingdoms inside, but there wasn't a trace of them anywhere. The cave was completely empty.

"Where did everybody go?" Alex asked. "You don't think they were found and captured, do you?"

Conner looked around the vacant cave, fearing the same thing.

"No, they would have put up a fight," he said. "There's no sign of a struggle anywhere. They must have moved to a different location."

"Maybe they left a clue behind so we'd know where to find them," Alex said.

She and Conner searched the cave, but they didn't even find a footprint that could lead them in the right direction. They stepped out of the cave and looked around at the forest and the mountains surrounding them. Something large emerged from the trees and caught Conner's eye.

"I don't think they left *something* behind—I think they left *someone*," he said.

Conner gestured to the woods ahead, where a chubby unicorn with a broken horn stood.

"Cornelius!" Alex said excitedly.

The twins ran to the unicorn and gave him a huge hug. He was so happy to see them, he neighed eagerly and did an animated dance with his front hooves.

"Cornelius, we're looking for Jack and Goldilocks," Alex said. "Do you know where they and the others went?"

The unicorn nodded his large head up and down.

"Could you take us there?" Conner asked.

The unicorn knelt to the ground and the twins climbed onto his back. His horn glowed like a lantern, and he raced through the forest faster than any normal horse could. Although they zipped past trees at a high speed, the twins could tell how empty the woods were. They didn't see a single living thing in the forest besides each other.

Cornelius took Alex and Conner deep into the Dwarf Forests, to the West Hills. Neither had been to these parts of the woods before, so they didn't know what to expect or what to look for. The unicorn stopped at a large boulder sticking into the hillside.

"Are you sure this is it?" Alex asked.

Cornelius nodded, but even the unicorn was baffled. Jack and Goldilocks had left him near the cave in case the twins returned, knowing his magic horn would guide them to their new location, but they didn't give him any instructions for what to do once they got there.

"It must be some kind of secret entrance," Conner said.

The twins climbed down off Cornelius and inspected the boulder. They knocked on it as if it were a door, but nothing happened. Alex tried using magic to move it aside, but the boulder didn't move.

"There must be a spell keeping it in place," Alex said. "Hagetta must have charmed it to keep intruders out. It must need some sort of password."

"It doesn't need a password, it needs a whistle," said a voice behind the twins.

Alex and Conner turned and saw Rook Robins standing on a hill nearby. Given their history, the twins weren't overjoyed to see him, but it was nice to see a familiar face nonetheless.

"Rook, it's good to see you!" Alex said. "Do you know where we are?"

"We're in the West Hills of the Dwarf Forests," Rook said. "Jack, Goldilocks, and all the others are hiding in an abandoned mine on the other side of that boulder."

"Do you know how to get inside?" Conner asked.

"Only a special birdcall will open it," Rook said. "But I know another way in. There's a tunnel on the other side of the hills—it's how I got out. Follow me!"

Alex and Conner still had reservations about trusting Rook, but they didn't have another choice. The twins and the unicorn followed him over the hills to a small tunnel whose entrance was camouflaged in the hillside. Rook held back cobwebs like a curtain and escorted Alex, Conner, and Cornelius inside.

Rook had to give the unicorn a big push to squeeze him through the narrow entrance. The tunnel was very long and dark, but thanks to Cornelius's glowing horn, they could see where they were going.

"Do you know why they changed locations?" Alex asked Rook.

"The cave became really crowded after Jack and Goldilocks started rescuing refugees," Rook explained. "My village was among the first they saved from the Literary Army. They've been retrieving people when and where they can, but it's been more difficult since the Masked Man rounded up all the citizens and put them in the lake. The royal families were the last to arrive—Jack and Goldilocks barely saved them from being executed."

Knowing the royals were safe felt like a giant weight was being lifted off the twins' shoulders. They sighed with relief and walked a little taller.

"Where is the Masked Man?" Alex asked. "We didn't see him with the villains at the Northern Palace."

"You haven't heard?" Rook asked.

"We haven't been around in a while," Conner said. "What happened?"

"The Masked Man is dead," he said. "The villains took over and had him killed."

The news made Alex and Conner stop in their tracks.

"Well, that's...*something*," Conner said, and shared a look with his sister.

A person they hated and felt so much anger toward was gone, but on the other hand, a family member was dead. The strangest part was not feeling any grief whatsoever for him.

After thinking about it, they realized the loss didn't really change a thing. The face and name they were fighting against may have changed, but their mission was still the same. Hopefully the battle ahead would be easier without him. Perhaps this meant the Literary Army would implode like a circus without a ringleader.

"Everyone is going to be thrilled to see you," Rook said. "How have you been?"

He unintentionally directed the question at Alex, and her brother suddenly felt like a third wheel. As uncomfortable as it made Conner, it was nothing compared to how Alex felt.

"We've been busy," Alex said. "My brother and I are recruiting an army to help us fight the villains."

"I know I'm still earning your trust back, but let me know if I can help," Rook said.

Alex kept trying to incorporate her brother into the conversation to make it less awkward, but Conner wanted nothing to do with it.

"Thank you, but I think we've got it under control," Alex said. "And for the record, we do trust you."

Rook smiled at her, but there was sadness in his eyes. Obviously, he was hoping to regain a lot more than trust. When Alex didn't smile back, the rest of Rook's face matched his eyes. They continued on through the tunnel, walking in a silence that said a thousand words.

The worst part about life in the abandoned mine was the constant waiting. It might have been easier if the refugees had an indication of what they were waiting *for*, but with each passing day, there was no good or bad news to share. They were becoming so restless that *any* information would have been better than none at all.

To pass the time, the refugees formed a little academy within the mine and taught one another different skills. Jack and the Tin Woodman taught the villagers how to sculpt using their axes. Soon, there wasn't a stalagmite in the mine that hadn't been carved into a squirrel, a beanstalk, a tower, or a mermaid.

Robin Hood and the Merry Men gave the queens archery and sword-throwing lessons. The Sherwood natives became a little invasive of the queens' personal space while showing them how to improve their form and received dirty looks from the kings.

Red's granny and the Old Woman from the Shoe Inn kept the kings and soldiers busy with sewing lessons. After a few days, the men had produced their first quilt and proudly hung it on display for the rest of the mine to see it.

"Remember, any man can shape a nation with a crown, but it takes a real man to start a quilt from a thread," Granny said.

Trollbella tried to teach Peter Pan and the Lost Boys to dance, but they weren't enthusiastic students. It didn't matter how many times she went over the steps of her routine, the boys only goofed off and teased one another.

"I don't know how to be more clear with you," Trollbella said. "It's step-touch, step-touch, kick-ball-change, reach to the right, reach to the left, kick-ball-change, shimmy to the front, shimmy to the back, pirouette, and pose! There's no nose-picking, pants-dropping, eye-poking, or tongue-showing in any of my choreography!"

Peter made a funny face at the troll queen behind her back. All the Lost Boys laughed, and she turned around just in time to see it. When Trollbella had first laid eyes on the Boy Who Never Grew Up, she was completely smitten, but the more his true colors showed, the more she disliked him; he was all sparkle and no substance.

The troll queen figured it was time to break the news to him. She looked Peter Pan directly in the eye and caressed his face.

"I had such high hopes for us, but I'm afraid it's not going to work out," Trollbella said.

She covered Peter's mouth to silence his protest, even though he didn't try to argue.

"We simply have different needs," Trollbella explained. "I'm looking for *romantic strolls*—you need a *stroller*. I'm looking for *love* and *lust*—you need a *leash*. I'm looking for a *Butterboy*—you're just a *Buttertoy*. Let's part as friends."

Trollbella sauntered away from Peter Pan and the Lost Boys. The boys exchanged puzzled looks, not sure if that was part of the dance lesson or not.

Goldilocks lay in the corner of the mine using Lester as a pillow and Clawdius as a footstool. The expectant mother was overdue and very eager to deliver the baby. Her backaches and irritability increased every day. Jack had to take all sharp objects away from her so she wouldn't have anything to throw during a mood swing.

Hagetta boiled some herbs in her cauldron and gave the concoction to Goldilocks for the pain. The Traveling Tradesman dangled a triangular stone on a string over her pregnant belly and studied the movement very closely. Red watched the Tradesman like he was a lunatic.

"What are you doing?" Red asked.

"I'm predicting the child's gender," the Traveling Tradesman said. "If the stone swings in a circle, it's a girl. If it moves back and forth, it's a boy."

"And what if it gets ripped out of your hand and thrown across the mine?" Red asked.

"It's all right. I already know it's going to be a boy," Goldilocks said.

"How could you possibly know that?" Red asked.

"Mother's intuition," Goldilocks said. "It's the one perk that comes with the bloating, the back pain, and the unstable emotions."

"A *niece* would be better for me," Red said. "I could dress her up in little dresses, apply blush to her tiny cheeks, and put dainty bows in her hair! I suppose I could do that with a nephew, too, but he might resent me for it later."

Goldilocks rolled her eyes. "Your request has been submitted," she said.

Red grabbed the string of the Tradesman's triangular stone and forced it to swing in a circle above Goldilocks's stomach, as if that would do the trick.

"Have you chosen a name yet?" Hagetta asked.

"Not yet," Goldilocks said. "I want his name to be special, I want it to mean something and inspire him for his whole life."

"You know, *Red* works for both a boy and a girl," Red said. "And *I* happen to be a very special, meaningful, and inspiring person."

Goldilocks cringed at the thought of bringing another Red into the world.

"Absolutely not," she said. "I want it to be original and freeing, like River or Robin or—*Alex and Conner*!"

Red scrunched her nose and crossed her arms. "How are *Alex* or *Conner* original and freeing?"

"*No—Alex and Conner are here!*" Goldilocks yelled. "*Look over there!*"

Goldilocks sat up and pointed to the back of the mine. Everyone went dead silent and turned toward where she was pointing. When they saw Alex and Conner entering with

Rook and Cornelius, the refugees burst into cheers and the mine vibrated with joy. Although it hadn't been too long since they'd seen most of them, the twins felt like they were walking into a reunion. Their friends surrounded them and stood in lines to embrace them. There were so many familiar faces they weren't expecting to see, they didn't know who to say hello to first. Everyone looked more tired, thinner, and paler than before. Living in the mine had worn them down.

"It's so wonderful to see you!" Alex said.

"Goldilocks, you look like you're about to explode!" Conner said.

"From your mouth to God's ears," Goldilocks said.

"Are you guys doing okay?" Alex asked. "Is everyone healthy and unharmed?"

"We're taking it one day at a time," Jack said. "How are you two? Where have you been?"

Alex and Conner shared a smile, knowing their news would excite them.

"We've been in the Otherworld recruiting an army to fight the literary villains," Conner announced.

"That's terrific!" the Tin Woodman said. "What kind of army?"

"An army of *my* characters," Conner said. "We've used the Portal Potion on my short stories from school. So far we've enlisted pirates, sailors, and Cyborgs—I'll explain what those are later."

All the refugees turned to the Traveling Tradesman.

The old geezer crossed his arms, leaned on a stalagmite, and glared at the others with a look that said *I told you so!*

"That's the best news we've heard in ages," Sir Lampton said. "How soon until it's ready for battle?"

"It won't be long," Alex said. "We just have two more stops and the army will be complete."

"DID YOU HEAR THAT, MEN?" Robin Hood asked the Merry Men. "SOON WE SHALL BE OUT OF THE SHADOWS OF SOLITUDE AND UNDER THE SUNLIGHT OF WAR! HOW MARVELOUS!"

Red pushed past the villagers, animals, and other royals to get closer to the twins. "Excuse me, pardon me, a *real friend* coming through," she said. "Alex and Conner, it's so lovely to see you're all right!" She suddenly grabbed them both by the shirt and looked frantically into their eyes. "You've got to get me out of here! There are peasants, animals, and men who talk to marbles! And Charlie isn't here to calm me down!"

The twins gently removed her hands from their clothes and took a step away.

"That's actually why we're here," Conner said. "Our mom and stepdad are watching my characters for us while we recruit others, but they need a hand. We were hoping a few of you could come back with us to help them supervise. There are more characters than they can handle."

"How many people do you need?" Jack asked.

Alex and Conner looked around the mine. Red wasn't the only one who looked desperate for a break. The twins would have a hard time refusing anyone's help.

"The more the merrier," Conner said. "But let's hurry. The people in this world need us."

Alex set the storybook on the ground and opened the cover. The beam of light was the brightest thing many of the refugees had seen in days and they shielded their eyes from it.

Before Conner could even explain where they were going, Red ran into the beam of light and disappeared from the mine. She was followed by Clawdius, Jack and Goldilocks, Robin Hood and the Merry Men, Lester and the Tin Woodman, and Peter Pan and the Lost Boys. Conner had lost count of how many people were traveling into the Otherworld when he felt a tap on his shoulder.

"You've come back for me, Butterboy," Trollbella said. "I don't know why I worried so. You've never let me down before. I know the pain of being away from each other can be overwhelming, so please don't waste your energy with a personal request for me to accompany you—*I'd be delighted to visit the Otherworld*!"

Before Conner could stop her, Trollbella ran into the beam of light with the others.

"Okay, we've definitely got enough help," Conner said. "We should get back and finish recruiting the army. If any of you need us, we'll just be on the other side of this beam."

"We'll stay behind and look after the others," Sir Lampton said.

"Thank you," Alex said. "We'll be back soon with help. Everyone stay safe!"

The twins stepped through the beam of light and returned to the Otherworld. Sir Lampton, Sir Grant, Hagetta, the Traveling Tradesman, Rook, Cornelius, Red's granny, the Old Woman from the Shoe Inn, the royal families, the villagers, and all the animals lowered their heads in a moment of silence. They all collectively said a prayer for the twins' success to continue and for them to be able to form an army to save the fairy-tale world.

Unfortunately for the occupants that remained, their quiet moment was interrupted by another unexpected visitor. Unbeknownst to Alex and Conner, they had been followed through the Dwarf Forests and into the secret tunnel.

The refugees saw something moving in the back of the mine. They heard hissing and rattling coming from a large silhouette.

"What was that?" Sir Grant asked.

The soldiers drew their swords and walked toward the sounds as a pair of bright red eyes glowed from the shadows. All the refugees froze where they stood, but they were frozen by much more than fear. . . .

Chapter Eighteen

SAINT ANDREW'S CHILDREN'S HOSPITAL

It took five trips in each of Charlotte's and Bob's cars to transport the characters from "Starboardia" to Saint Andrew's Children's Hospital. They covered each pirate and sailor in scrubs and medical masks and quickly escorted them through the hospital to the empty commissary in the brand-new wing.

It would have been simpler if the *Dolly Llama* crew weren't such a curious bunch. They pocketed medical supplies as they passed unoccupied countertops, snuck charts off hospital-room doors, and stole pens out of the lapels of unobservant physicians. By the time they reached the commissary, the pirates' pockets were full of scissors, Band-Aids, and medical tape, and a few of them wore bedpans as hats.

The commissary was a wide and colorful room. It had dozens of tables, hundreds of chairs, adjoining bathrooms, and a large, never-been-used kitchen. It was the perfect place for temporarily hosting Conner's characters.

Ironically, the commissary had been decorated with a classic storybook theme. The walls were covered with murals of Alex and Conner's friends, and the support beams had been painted to look like book spines.

Anticipating her children's return from the fairy-tale world, Charlotte had cleared a space in the corner of the commissary and placed the *Land of Stories* book and Conner's binder of short stories on the floor. Once all the characters from "Starboardia" had been successfully escorted inside, the emerald storybook flipped open and the beam of light appeared.

Red ran out of the beam like a bull released from a pen and looked around the commissary. She sighed with relief and stretched her arms out.

"Thank God," she said. "I'm indoors!"

"Hi, Red!" Charlotte said. "Long time no see!"

Without even making eye contact with the twins' mother or the *Dolly Llama* crew, Red ran to the window and yanked the blinds open. Rays of sunlight shined inside and Red blissfully spun in them.

"*Daylight*—I've missed you so much!" Red said, and turned to the others. "No one look at me for at least twenty minutes. I haven't seen the sun in weeks! I'm paler than Snow White with a stomach flu!"

"Good to see you, too, Red," Bob said under his breath.

It wasn't long before the others from the fairy-tale world joined her. Clawdius ran out from the beam behind Red. Unlike his mother, the wolf was very social. He did an excited lap around the commissary and visited with every human he saw.

Jack and Goldilocks stepped out of the beam next and Jack helped his pregnant wife to the closest seat. They were joined shortly afterward by Robin Hood, the Merry Men, Lester, the Tin Woodman, Peter Pan, the Lost Boys, and Trollbella. Just like the characters from "Starboardia" did when they arrived on Sycamore Drive, the characters from the fairy-tale world and classic literature stared in awe at the wondrous new world around them.

"Welcome to Saint Andrew's Children's Hospital!" Charlotte said.

"So this is the Otherworld?" Jack said, and whistled at the sight.

"It's *colorful*," Goldilocks said. She side-eyed the decorations. "They certainly make reading a lifestyle here."

Before Bob and Charlotte began the complicated task of

introducing the new characters to the old characters, Alex and Conner popped out of the beam of light beside them.

"Oh cool, we're already at the hospital!" Conner said, and cleared his throat. "Ladies, gentlemen, chicken, and Blissworm from my stories, allow me to introduce you to the ladies, gentlemen, goose, and wolf from classic literature and fairy tales."

The introduction didn't go as well as the twins had hoped. The characters circled one another like animals meeting in the wild.

"*Pirates!*" Peter shouted at the *Dolly Llama* crew.

"Guys, knock it off!" Alex said. "We're all on the same side here. These people are going to help us defeat the Literary Army."

"Sorry," Peter said. "For whatever reason, I'm always inclined to shout '*Pirates*' whenever I see them—bad habit."

The Rosary Chicken fearfully laid an egg as soon as she saw Clawdius, and he chased after her. The Blissworm didn't want to miss out on the fun, so it jumped aboard the wolf and rode him like a cowboy. Lester thought the Blissworm was the most delicious-looking worm he had ever seen, so he chased after the others, forming a bizarre parade of fictional creatures.

"Rule number one," Conner said. "No one is allowed to eat anyone else!"

The Rosary Chicken clucked with relief. Clawdius and Lester stopped in their tracks and slumped. The Blissworm tugged on Clawdius's collar—Conner didn't say *the fun* had to stop.

It took the fairy-tale characters a few moments to realize that pictures of many of them were painted on the walls throughout the commissary. They walked to their respective murals and stared at the artwork worryingly.

"Look, boys, we're on the wall!" Peter said, and pointed to a mural of them. "Wait a moment. Is this place a church? Are we *gods* in this world?"

"Don't flatter yourself," Conner said. "People just like your story here."

The Tin Woodman found himself in a mural of *The Wonderful Wizard of Oz* but didn't recognize the three others he was traveling with down the yellow brick road.

"Who are the people I'm linking arms with?" the Tin Woodman asked.

"That's Dorothy, the Scarecrow, and the Cowardly Lion," Alex explained. "You would have met them in Oz if we hadn't found you first."

"Did *they* drop a barn on me as well?" the Tin Woodman asked.

"Um . . . I don't remember," Alex lied.

Robin Hood and the Merry Men gathered around the mural of *Robin Hood*. The resemblance between the real Merry Men and the painted Merry Men was striking; however, Robin Hood was depicted very effeminately in the painting. He wore bright green tights and had a short curly bob and no facial hair.

"I DON'T UNDERSTAND," Robin Hood said. "WHAT IS MY MOTHER DOING IN THIS PAINTING?"

Trollbella stared up in awe at a beautiful mural of Cinderella in a ball gown. She smiled from ear to ear and clutched her hands over her heart.

"Oh my Troblin heavens, it looks *just* like me!" she said. "There are some very talented painters in the Otherworld."

Red let out an earsplitting scream when she saw the mural of *Little Red Riding Hood*. The twins looked between the real Red and the painted Red, but they couldn't figure out what was so offensive. All they saw was an adorable girl in a red cape running from the Big Bad Wolf.

"Red, what's the problem?" Alex asked.

"They made me a *brunette*!" Red yelled.

The twins rolled their eyes. Red turned her back to the room and pouted as she continued soaking up the sun.

"That reminds me," Conner said. "I need to go back to 'Galaxy Queen' and get the Cyborgs."

He went to his binder of short stories, flipped it open to "Galaxy Queen," and vanished into the beam of light. As he went, Alex noticed that Goldilocks and Jack were whispering to each other and suspiciously glaring across the room.

"Is everything okay?" Alex asked.

"Alex, are my hormones driving me mad, or do that man and woman look exactly like Jack and me?" Goldilocks asked.

Alex looked at Auburn Sally and Admiral Jacobson on

the other side of the room. They were also whispering to each other and shooting peculiar glances at Jack and Goldilocks. Clearly they were having the exact same conversation.

"A lot of Conner's characters are based on people he knows," Alex said. "But trust me, it could be a lot worse than the captain and the admiral."

As soon as she said this, the Cyborg Queen charged out of the "Galaxy Queen" beam of light. She ignored everyone in the commissary and rolled directly to the windows where Red stood. Two large solar panels came out of her metal shoulders and she pointed them toward the sun.

"*Daylight*, thank goodness," the Cyborg Queen said. "I haven't had a solar charge in weeks!"

The Cyborg Queen stretched her solar panels so far, she took up the whole window.

"Excuse me," Red said. "You're blocking my light."

"Who says it's *your* light to begin with?" the Cyborg Queen said.

Red was appalled by her rudeness, so she left the window and took a seat by Jack and Goldilocks.

"I don't know who or what that woman is, but she's *terrible*," Red said.

Goldilocks fought a smile and leaned close to Alex. "I see what you mean," she said.

Conner and Commander Newters hurried out from the "Galaxy Queen" beam and cleared a large area of the commissary, stacking chairs and tables on top of one another until there was a large open space.

"Conner, what's that for?" Charlotte asked.

"The Cyborgs," he said.

Newters removed a small remote from his belt and pointed it at the beam. Twenty mechanized wagons carrying fifty Cyborg soldiers each rolled out of the beam of light. The Cyborgs were deactivated and were stacked on top of one another like folding chairs. Newters steered the wagons into the cleared area and parked them.

"Is that . . . *humane*?" Bob said with wide eyes.

"Probably not," Newters admitted. "But if we keep them deactivated until battle, we'll save a fortune on our electric bill."

The characters settled into groups throughout the commissary like high school cliques. The people of each dimension had their own sets of tables and cautiously eyed one another from afar.

"Will they be okay?" Charlotte asked.

"They'll warm up to each other," Conner said, and then whistled to get the room's attention. "Everybody listen up! Alex and I have to head into my next story to recruit more characters. Everyone please be nice to one another while we're gone. My mom and Bob are in charge unless they're at work—then Jack and Goldilocks are in charge."

The characters from "Starboardia," "Galaxy Queen," the *Land of Stories*, Sherwood Forest, Neverland, and Oz all nodded respectfully, then quickly returned to watching one another apprehensively. Alex and Conner hugged

Charlotte and Bob and went to the binder of short stories. Conner flipped it open to his next story and poured three drops of the Portal Potion on the pages.

Conner stepped toward the beam of light that appeared, but Alex stopped him before he entered it.

"Hold on a second," she said. "You're supposed to tell me what to expect at the next stop—and don't spare the details this time. If there are bug guts, I want to be prepared."

"The next story is called 'The Ziblings,'" Conner explained. "It's about four kids with superhuman powers. They all lost their parents at an early age and went to live at the same orphanage. One night, an asteroid carrying cosmic radiation hit their orphanage and affected their DNA, giving them phenomenal abilities. They were adopted by a billionaire astrophysicist named Professor Wallet and taken to his laboratory, where he raised them and trained them to become superheroes."

"Professor *Wallet*?" Alex asked.

"Yeah, I lost my wallet the day I wrote it and thought it was a good name," Conner said. "Moving on, we're going to travel to their city and meet them at the scene of a bank robbery. While they're saving the bank, we'll sneak inside the Zibling Mobile, follow them back to their secret laboratory, and ask them to join us."

"Will they cooperate?" she asked.

"The Ziblings are very competitive siblings," Conner

said. "They never pass up a challenge, especially if there's an opportunity to outshine each other."

"Okay," Alex said with a nod. *Zounds zuper.*

"Leave the jokes to me," Conner said.

The twins stepped into the beam of light and disappeared from Saint Andrew's Children's Hospital.

CHAPTER NINETEEN

THE ZIBLINGS

Conner's handwriting wiggled and zoomed through the air as the world of "The Ziblings" was created around him and his sister. The word *highway* stretched beneath their feet, and Alex and Conner were suddenly standing in the middle of a wide country road. Cars and large trucks honked and swerved to avoid them, and they dashed to the side of the highway to avoid getting hit.

Alex and Conner looked up and saw a large city-limits sign above them. The sign read:

BIG CITY, USA
POPULATION 7,654,321

Once the handwritten words finished constructing the new dimension, the twins saw that the highway led to an enormous city a couple of miles in the distance. It had the tallest and leanest skyscrapers Alex had ever seen; the skyline looked more like a bundle of pencils and pens than a row of buildings.

"Big City, USA?" Alex asked. "You couldn't come up with anything more original than that?"

"It was supposed to be a placeholder until I came up with a better name, but Big City, USA, grew on me," Conner said. "Now let's go to the bank before it gets robbed without us."

Alex laughed. "Now, *that's* something I've never heard before," she said.

The twins walked down the road and entered the busy city. The world of the Ziblings was like a highly exaggerated version of the Otherworld. The buildings were more colorful, the streets were cleaner, and the cars were shinier. Even the people were more extravagant. The men were taller and had broader shoulders and wider jaws. The women had impeccable hair, makeup, and clothes. Even the children were cuter and better behaved. It was like the twins had entered a 1950s cartoon.

Alex and Conner zigzagged through the city streets. They walked down Main Street, made a right on Center

Road, and then a left on First Avenue. Alex wasn't sure which city Conner was emulating for "The Ziblings" setting because Big City, USA, had characteristics of every American city she could think of. There were subway stations like in New York City, bridges like in San Francisco, surrounding Great Lakes like in Chicago, and BIG CITY, USA, was written across a hillside like the Hollywood sign.

They eventually found Big City Bank, in the middle of First Avenue. It was a large white building with thick pillars and a massive dome. It reminded Alex of the Capitol Building in Washington, DC. The twins walked up the front steps and went inside.

The bank had marble floors, golden pillars, and wooden counters. There were high ceilings, tall windows, and lots of elaborate lighting structures. A long line of Big City citizens waited patiently to be helped by one of a dozen bank tellers. There were also desks scattered throughout the bank where bankers helped other citizens open new accounts and apply for loans. No one appeared to have been rejected, because all the applicants had big smiles on their faces as they happily shook the bankers' hands.

Conner took his sister to the far end of the bank, near a back door. He got down on the floor, lay facedown, and put his hands over his head.

"Are you doing yoga?" Alex asked.

"No, I'm getting ready," he said. "We're just in time."

"For what?"

"The *robbery*," he said, as if it were obvious. "It should be starting in five . . . four . . . three . . . two . . ."

Five armed robbers stormed into the bank. They wore all black and had mouse ears and whiskers attached to their masks. The robbers fired their guns into the air to get everyone's attention. It was startling even to Alex, and she'd known it was coming.

"Everyone on the ground now!" the largest robber shouted. "Facedown with your hands on your heads! No talking! Don't make me tell you twice!"

The citizens screamed and did what they were told. Alex joined her brother on the floor and copied his pose. The robbers threw big duffel bags on the wooden counters and pointed their guns at the tellers.

"Empty the safe!" the largest robber shouted. "And don't you dare try any funny business or I'll blow you all to the sky!"

The trembling tellers did what the robbers demanded. They opened the gigantic safe in the back of the bank and began filling the duffel bags with stacks of cash and bars of gold.

"What's up with the ears and whiskers on their masks?" Alex whispered to her brother.

"It's part of their gimmick," he said. "These guys are called *the Rat Pack*—they're the most infamous bank robbers in Big City, USA. The tallest one's name is Frank, he's the leader, and then there are his henchmen: Sammy, Dean, Joey, and Peter."

"Just like the Rat Pack from the sixties!" Alex said.

Conner scrunched his forehead. "Dang it!" he said. "I thought I made it up—I must have heard about them from someone."

"You two! I said no talking!" Frank yelled, pointing his gun at the twins.

Alex and Conner went silent. The Rat Pack walked around the bank and patrolled their hostages. They nudged the terrified citizens with their feet and laughed wildly as the hostages cowered and squirmed. After a few minutes of lying uncomfortably on the floor and watching the robbers torment the men and women, Alex was very eager to see the Ziblings come to the rescue. It was taking all her self-control not to transform the Rat Pack into actual rodents.

Conner tapped his sister and gestured to one of the windows. Alex looked up and saw the silhouette of a man wearing a cape. He stood heroically with his hands on his hips. Alex was so excited to see a real superhero that her stomach filled with butterflies, but the feeling quickly subsided. It took a moment for the superhero to enter the bank, not because he was conducting a plan, but because he couldn't open the window.

Finally, with a strong tug, the hero managed to pry it open. He crawled through the small opening, but then he stepped on his cape and slipped off the windowsill. He crashed onto the floor behind a desk with a very loud *thump*. Everyone in the bank heard the crash and jerked their head toward it. The Rat Pack clutched their guns tighter and slowly approached the desk. The hostages waited on pins and needles, hoping it was someone who had come to their rescue.

The superhero jumped out from behind the desk and struck the same heroic pose he had held in the window. After a closer look, Alex was surprised to see he was actually an adorable boy no more than twelve years old. He wore a sky-blue suit and a dark blue mask, with matching gloves, boots, and cape. He had messy dark hair, plump cheeks, and green eyes.

Upon seeing him, the robbers snickered and the hostages lost all hope. Apparently no one had much faith in the hero's capability.

"Don't worry, boys, it's just Bolt." Frank laughed. "The Ziblings have sent the *runt* of the litter!"

Bolt shifted uncomfortably at the blatant disrespect.

"Hello, Rat Pack," the boy said in a tone obviously deeper than his real voice. "I see you've escaped prison and gone right back to your old tricks. I guess you can take the rats out of the garbage, but you can't take the garbage out of the rats!"

"*'But you can't take the garbage out of the rats,'*" Frank mocked him. "You really need to work on your playful jargon if you want to be taken seriously."

"And *you* need to work on following the law," Bolt said. "Good thing there are people like me to put you back in your place!"

Frank turned to his henchmen. *"Get him,"* he said. "But don't waste your bullets—he isn't worth it."

The boy's face turned bright red. "Oh, yes I am!" he argued. "I'm worth all the bullets you got!"

Bolt became angry and his superpowers were activated. His body was covered in static electricity, his messy hair rose above his head, and tiny electric waves buzzed around his fingertips. Bolt somersaulted toward Frank, and with the lightest touch of his index finger, he zapped the robber on the leg.

"Ouch," Frank said. "That *almost* hurt a little."

The boy cartwheeled to Sammy and Dean and shocked them on the arms. He dived to the other side of the bank and zapped Joey on the nose and Peter on the ear. Bolt was very proud of himself, but his efforts did little to wound the Rat Pack. They just looked more irritated than before.

"I changed my mind. *Shoot him,*" Frank instructed.

Bolt flew through the air to avoid the bullet, not with the grace of an eagle or a hawk, but with the clumsiness of a baby bird. His erratic flight pattern made it very difficult for the Rat Pack to aim their guns at him, so they flipped their weapons over and swung them like baseball bats. Frank knocked Bolt out of the air and the not-so-super-hero hit the floor.

"Tie him up," Frank ordered, and eyed the hostages. "And for the rest of you—show's over, *back to work*!"

The Rat Pack tied Bolt to a chair and the tellers continued emptying the vault. Eventually the vault was cleared out entirely and the duffel bags were bulging with cash and gold. The tellers handed the bags back to the Rat Pack and the robbers headed for the door. Bolt tried to free himself from the restraints, but they were too strong.

"This transaction has been a *pleasure*," Frank announced to the bank. "See you next time!"

Suddenly, a thunderous *crash* came from above. Three more superheroes dropped in from the domed ceiling—*the rest of the Ziblings had arrived*!

The oldest Zibling was about sixteen and very athletic. He wore a bright yellow tank top, baggy yellow pants, big sneakers, and a headband. His muscly arms were bare and caught fire as soon as he touched the ground.

The second-oldest Zibling was a fifteen-year-old girl. She wore a pink suit with a built-in miniskirt. She had sandy-blond hair that was braided into two long pigtails. She had complete control over her hair and twirled her braids like the blades of a helicopter until she came to a safe landing.

The third-oldest Zibling wore a dark green suit and a leather jacket. Instead of a mask, he wore very dark sunglasses. His arms transformed into large feathered wings as he glided to the floor, then transformed back once he landed.

All the citizens, tellers, and bankers sighed with relief at the older Ziblings' arrival. The Rat Pack robbers simultaneously gulped and eyed one another nervously. Bolt rolled his eyes at his siblings' splashy entrance—he had been hoping to handle the Rat Pack without them.

"Hello, Frank, Sammy, Dean, Joey, and Peter," the oldest said, acting as the Ziblings' leader. "Have you come out of the sewer for fresh air?"

"Hello, Blaze, Whipney, and Morph," Frank said. "Have you come to save your little brother?"

"I don't need to be saved!" Bolt said. *"Being tied to this chair is part of my plan, which you guys are kind of ruining!"*

The Ziblings ignored their little brother as if he weren't even in the room. They locked eyes with the Rat Pack and never looked away.

"We've come to take you and your boys back to prison, Frank," Blaze said. "You belong in a cage just like all the other rodents."

The Ziblings charged toward the Rat Pack and the robbers ran for the door.

Morph jumped in front of them and transformed into a brick wall. His sunglasses were his only remaining physical trait. He was now blocking the robbers' exit, so they ran for the back door. Whipney whipped her head back and forth and her braids wrapped around Sammy's and Dean's ankles. She raised them into the air and knocked them into each other, and they fell unconscious to the ground.

Joey and Peter aimed their guns at Blaze. He pointed at them and two fiery geysers blasted out of his fingertips. The robbers were set on fire and they dropped to the floor and rolled around to extinguish the flames. Morph transformed into a huge cage and Whipney scooped up Dean, Sammy, Joey, and Peter with her hair and threw the robbers inside it. They had caught all the rats in the pack except for one.

Frank jumped over the wooden counter and ran to the back of the bank. He jumped inside the vault and locked the enormous metal door behind him. Blaze followed him and pressed his palms against the vault door. He heated the vault so much, the door turned bright orange and melted away. Whipney reached into the vault with her hair, pulled Frank out, and tossed him into the cage with the others.

The bank hostages leaped to their feet in celebration. They cheered and applauded their rescuers. Everyone was thrilled the Ziblings had saved another day in Big City, USA—everyone but Bolt.

"You're in so much trouble," Blaze told his little brother.

"Why?" Bolt said. "I had everything under control before you showed up."

"You know the rules," Whipney said. "No crime fighting until your homework is done, and Dad doesn't want you doing it without us!"

"I can take care of myself," Bolt said. "I can do anything you guys can, you just never give me the chance! You never let me prove myself!"

"Prove yourself?" said the cage Morph had turned into. "You can't get out of that chair!"

"How are you supposed to help people if you can't even help yourself?" Whipney said.

Tears came to Bolt's eyes and he looked away from his siblings. It was an expression layered with embarrassment, frustration, self-doubt, and heartache all in one. Alex knew that look. She could have sworn she'd seen it somewhere before.

Suddenly, memories surfaced like a movie playing in her mind. Alex flashed back to when she and Conner were in elementary school.

"Let's go around the room and say what we all want to be when we grow up," their second-grade teacher told the class.

"A doctor!" said a boy.

"A senator!" said a girl.

"A teacher!" Alex remembered saying.

Her brother sat up at his desk, excited to share his answer.

"A fireman!" he said. "I want to help people!"

Even then, Conner wasn't as good a student as Alex was. He had trouble learning to read, how to spell, and how to do math. He was always asking Alex for help with his homework and she became mad that he couldn't keep up with her. So when Conner gave his answer about his plans for the future, Alex was inclined to respond.

"A fireman?" she asked. "How are you supposed to help people if you can't help yourself?"

Everyone in the class laughed. Alex didn't mean any harm by it; she was so young, it just slipped out of her mouth. Even though it had happened almost ten years before, the expression on Conner's face had been engraved in her memory forever. It was exactly how Bolt looked at his siblings now.

Soon, the front steps of the bank were filled with police and reporters. Morph transformed back into his human form and he, Whipney, and Blaze pushed the Rat Pack robbers outside and into the hands of the police. The Ziblings spoke with the reporters about what had happened. They took all the credit and soaked up the attention, leaving Bolt tied to the chair inside.

"Now's a good time to sneak into the Zibling Mobile," Conner whispered to Alex.

The twins exited the Big City Bank through the back door and Alex followed Conner into the alley behind it. The Zibling Mobile was a bright red convertible with rocket engines and a bright yellow *Z* painted on the side. The car was parked out of sight between two dumpsters, but Conner knew exactly where to find it.

He felt around the back tire and pulled a spare key out of a hidden compartment. He opened the trunk and crawled inside it.

"Come on," Conner said, and offered his sister a hand.

Alex hesitated before joining him. Something heavy was weighing on her heart.

"Quick question," she said. "Is this story based on anything that happened in real life? Anything that might have happened between us?"

Conner thought about it, but shook his head.

"Nope, this one is completely made up," he said. "I just loved superheroes when I was a kid. 'The Ziblings' was one of the first stories I ever wrote."

Alex didn't press the issue further; she just nodded and climbed into the trunk with him.

Conner may have forgotten what happened in the second grade, but Alex couldn't shake it. It wasn't just the mean exchange in elementary school that bothered her, though. Alex was worried "The Ziblings" was much closer to home than Conner realized, and that *she* might be the story's villain.

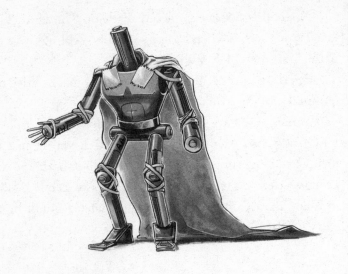

CHAPTER TWENTY

PROFESSOR WALLET'S SECRET LABORATORY

The Zibling Mobile zoomed through the streets of Big City, USA, tossing Alex and Conner around the trunk like clothes in a washing machine. Every turn was sharper than the one before, every acceleration was more forceful, and the vehicle never slowed down or came to a stop. It had only two speeds: *fast* and *faster*.

"Who the heck is driving this thing?" Alex asked.

"Blaze just got his license," Conner said. "He's a little zealous about it."

The Zibling Mobile ran over speed bumps, causing the twins to slam into the top of the trunk.

"I bet his driving puts more people in danger than all the robbers and criminal masterminds combined!" Alex said.

It was pitch-black in the trunk, so the twins had no clue which street or neighborhood the vehicle was cruising through. Conner was able to track their whereabouts to a certain point, but Blaze's reckless diving was so discombobulating, he didn't even know if they were still headed for Professor Wallet's laboratory.

"How much longer are we going to be in this thing?" Alex asked. "I feel like a scrambled egg."

"The laboratory is deep underground just a few miles outside of the city," Conner said. "At the speed Blaze is driving, it shouldn't take much longer."

"And how exactly do we *get* to the laboratory?" Alex asked. "I'm assuming there's more involved than just surface streets."

"They have to go into the Big City Lake, through the sewer, and down an abandoned subway tunnel," Conner said.

"Can their car go underwater?" Alex asked.

"Of course their car doesn't go underwater," Conner said. "It turns into a submarine first."

The twins heard a bunch of mechanisms moving throughout the vehicle as it converted into a submarine. Then they heard a big *splash* outside, and a moment later the trunk began filling with water.

"We must be in the lake," Conner said.

"I thought you said the vehicle turns into a submarine!" Alex said.

"Apparently everything but the trunk," he said. "Gosh, I never thought I'd have to be *that* specific!"

Alex snapped her fingers and the water stopped. The Zibling Mobile moved into the sewer, and the twins gagged and covered their noses with their shirts. There wasn't enough magic in the world to keep out the smell.

The Zibling Mobile converted back into a car, and its tires touched solid ground again. The vehicle rattled and shook as it drove over the tracks of the abandoned subway passage. It was so bumpy, the twins became nauseated. Right before they were about to vomit, the car came to an abrupt stop.

They heard the vehicle's doors open and close as the Ziblings got out.

Conner popped the trunk just a crack, and he and Alex peered out.

"We're here," he whispered. "This is Professor Wallet's secret laboratory."

The underground laboratory was built on a former subway platform. The Zibling Mobile was parked on the subway tracks below it and was only one of many methods of transportation. There was a Zibling Jet, a Zibling Speedboat, Zibling Motorcycles, Zibling Segways, and even a Zibling Carriage with robotic horses.

The laboratory had everything a secret superhero base

could need. There was a wall of televisions with live news feeds from every major city in the world. There were giant computers, microscopes, test tubes, data servers, and generators. In the center of the laboratory was a big red lightbulb that went off whenever a crisis occurred. All the appliances were neatly labeled in case there was any confusion over what the object was.

Not only was Professor Wallet a devoted astrophysicist, he was also a proud father. The laboratory was decorated with photos of his adopted children and tokens of their accomplishments. The Ziblings' very first superhero suits were framed and hung on the walls. There was a lit candle with a plaque that read "Blaze's First Flame." A lock of hair and a pair of mangled scissors were on display and tagged "Whipney's First Haircut." There was a photo of a trash can wearing sunglasses marked "Morph's First Transformation." Another photo, of a toddler sucking on a glowing lightbulb like a binky, was labeled "Bolt's First Spark."

There was also a wall covered with a giant map of Big City, USA. The map was bordered with mug shots of all the criminals the Ziblings had brought to justice. Pieces of yarn stretched from the mug shots to the places on the map where the criminals had been caught.

Each Zibling had a corner of the laboratory filled with personal belongings. Blaze had a collection of hot sauces, matches, and fire extinguishers. Whipney had a vanity full of hair products and industrial-strength brushes and combs. Morph had framed butterflies, moths, beetles, wasps, and shelves of photography books—all inspiration for metamorphosis. Bolt had a desk where he made figurines out of old batteries.

Whipney printed out five mug shots of the Rat Pack and placed them on the wall with the others. Blaze went to the computer and dialed a number on the keypad.

"What are you doing?" Bolt asked.

"I'm calling Dad," Blaze said. "He needs to know you left the laboratory without permission—*again*."

"*Tattletale!*" Bolt said.

A few moments later, Professor Wallet appeared on the computer screen. He was an older man with a gray beard and thick glasses that magnified his blue eyes. He wore a turquoise turtleneck and a white lab coat. The professor held his communication device way too close to his face and the camera was aimed up his nostrils.

"Hello, children," the professor said. "Is this an emergency? I'm just about to step into a meeting with the German chancellor about her new anti-matter research program."

"It's not an emergency, but *someone* snuck out of the laboratory to fight crime on his own again," Blaze said, and nodded at Bolt.

The professor rubbed his eyes under his glasses. "Oh, Bolt," he said disappointedly. "What am I going to do with you?"

"It's not fair!" Bolt said. "Blaze, Whipney, and Morph

were allowed to fight crime on their own when they were my age!"

"Young man, we've been over this a hundred times," Professor Wallet said. "Your abilities haven't reached their full potential yet. The radiation from the asteroid reacted differently with each of your DNA, meaning your powers will peak at a different time than your siblings'. Remember, not all flowers bloom in the spring."

"What if I'm more like a Venus flytrap than a flower?" Bolt argued. "Maybe my powers are just waiting for an opportunity to show up!"

"Science doesn't work that way," the professor said. "I don't make the rules to upset you—I make them to protect you. You're grounded until I get back home."

Bolt grunted and stomped his feet. He sulked over to his corner of the laboratory, zapping Blaze on the ear as he went, and then pouted at his desk.

"I'm being summoned into the chancellor's office," the professor said. "I'll call you tonight when I get to my hotel room."

"Tell the chancellor we said hello," Morph said.

"And tell her I love the new highlights!" Whipney said.

The professor looked confused. "Of the anti-matter program?" he asked.

Whipney sighed. "No, Dad, in her *hair*," she said.

"Oh, of course," the professor said. "I will pass along the message. Good-bye, children."

The professor hung up and disappeared from the computer screen. The Ziblings went to their respective corners to decompress. Blaze drank a bottle of hot sauce like it was water and did push-ups. Whipney's hair unbraided and brushed itself while she flipped through a magazine. Morph looked at a photography book and practiced transforming into the objects he saw. Bolt played with his battery figurines and tied a tissue around one to give it a cape.

Conner quietly closed the trunk of the car to have a private word with his sister.

"Here's my plan," Conner said. "We're going to get out and tell them we're reporters from the *Otherworld Times*, a syndicated school newspaper that runs in twenty-five states. We'll say we're looking to do a personal-interest piece on the bravest, strongest, and smartest superhero in the country. And to prove which one of them deserves the title, we'll take them to the fairy-tale world, where whoever defeats the most soldiers in the Literary Army will be the winner. What do you think?"

Alex definitely saw some flaws in her brother's plan, but she kept them to herself. She was still consumed by guilt from her realization at the bank. She never wanted to discourage her brother again.

"Brilliant!" she said. "That's a great idea—no, it's an *amazing* idea! Gosh, all your ideas are so wonderful. I don't know how you do it."

Even though the trunk was dark, Conner gave his sister a funny look. Something was up. Alex was never *that* supportive. He worried she might have hit her head in the car ride over.

"Alex, are you feeling okay?" he asked.

Before she could answer, the red lightbulb in the center of the laboratory started flashing and a loud siren went off. The Ziblings jumped to their feet like protective canines and ran to the wall of televisions. They scanned the screens and saw a frantic reporter on the French news. Blaze turned up the volume and pressed a button so the reporter's words were translated into English.

"Paris is under attack," the reporter said from the newsroom. *"The mad scientist and criminal mastermind known as the Snake Lord, notorious for his interactions with the Ziblings in Big City, USA, has taken over the Eiffel Tower!"*

The news program played footage of the Snake Lord from earlier that day. He was a tall, muscular middle-aged man with a villainous scowl. His eyes were yellow with narrow pupils like a reptile. He wore a large helmet shaped like the head of a king cobra and a long purple cape. The Snake Lord licked his lips and exposed a forked tongue.

"That slithering son of a gun!" Blaze said.

The Snake Lord was accompanied by two sidekicks, a man and a woman—but neither appeared to be entirely human. They had scaly green skin, large nostrils, and reptilian eyes. The man had an orange Mohawk and a collar like a frilled lizard. The woman had red horns and long nails like the claws of a raptor.

"*Collared Joe* and *Lizzy Liza* are with him!" Whipney said, and raised a lock of hair at the screen.

"He's got more friends than that," Morph said. "Look!"

The three criminals were followed by a long procession of thousands and thousands of serpents. There were boa constrictors, pythons, anacondas, and even tiny garden snakes. The serpents were colorful and moved behind the Snake Lord like a slithering rainbow.

The news showed footage of the Snake Lord and his scaly accomplices storming the base of the Eiffel Tower. They knocked down security guards in their way, and hundreds of tourists ran for their lives. The snakes formed a circle around the Eiffel Tower and didn't let any of the Parisian police pass.

The camera zoomed in on a device the Snake Lord was carrying that looked like a mini-satellite.

"The Snake Lord has the *Reptilalizer*!" Bolt said in horror.

"At this time, the Snake Lord hasn't made any demands and isn't holding any civilians hostage," the reporter said. *"It is a complete mystery as to why he has come to Paris and what he wants with the Eiffel Tower."*

The Ziblings shared fearful looks with one another.

"It isn't a mystery to us!" Blaze said. "We've got to get to Paris and stop him! *Ziblings to the jet!*"

The four superheroes ran straight to the Zibling Jet parked on the subway track.

Conner was more upset by the news than any of the superheroes were. "This is *terrible*," Conner said.

"Hold the phone," Alex said. "The Snake Lord? The Reptilalizer? You never mentioned any of that before we left."

"That's because I forgot how short this story is. It moves much faster than the other ones," he said. "The Snake Lord is the Ziblings' arch-nemesis. He was a scientist who used to work with Professor Wallet. A failed experiment turned him and his research assistants into partial reptiles. When Professor Wallet couldn't reverse the effects, the Snake Lord became evil. He invented a helmet that gave him control over all reptiles. The Reptilalizer is his newest invention, and it turns mammals into reptiles. It has to be activated from the tallest point in a city—that's why he's at the Eiffel Tower!"

"So once he activates it, he'll turn everyone in Paris into a reptile and be able to control them!" Alex said as she figured it out. "That's intense!"

The Ziblings climbed aboard the jet and strapped themselves into the seats, but Blaze blocked Bolt from entering.

"What do you think you're doing?" Blaze asked.

"I'm going to Paris to fight the Snake Lord with you guys," Bolt said.

"No you're not," Blaze said. "You heard Dad—you're grounded."

"Oh, come on," Bolt argued. "The Snake Lord is the

toughest bad guy we've ever fought! You're going to need help!"

"Exactly. Which is why you need to stay in the laboratory," Blaze said. "We'll have our hands full saving the people of Paris—we won't be able to watch you. If you come with us, you'll just be a burden."

Bolt's posture sank almost an entire foot. He had never been called a *burden* before.

"But...but...but I'm a *superhero*," Bolt said with a quivering lip.

Blaze sighed. "No you're not," he said. "You're just a kid with tricks."

Blaze closed the jet's door right in front of Bolt's face and joined Whipney and Morph in the cockpit. The engines roared and the Zibling Jet rocketed down the abandoned subway, heading for Paris.

Bolt waited until his brothers and sister were gone and then burst into tears. He went to his corner of the laboratory and cried at his desk. Once it was out of his system, he tried to make himself feel better by playing with his homemade figurines. He picked up the one with the tissue cape and moved it through the air like it was flying.

"Here he comes now to save the day!" Bolt said, pretending he was a news reporter. "It's the world's favorite Zibling—it's *Bolt*!"

Fantasizing about being a real superhero only made him feel worse. Bolt crumpled up the figurine until it was nothing but a pile of used batteries. He rested his head on his desk and continued crying.

"We need a new plan to recruit the Ziblings," Conner whispered to Alex. "Any ideas? Alex?"

He turned to his sister and saw that the sad little super-hero had brought Alex to tears. In fact, she looked sadder than Bolt did.

"Alex, are you okay?" he asked.

"Conner, I'm so sorry." She sniffled.

"Sorry for what?" Conner asked.

"Sorry if I ever made you feel like *that*," Alex cried. "I know you don't remember, but there was a time I treated you exactly like the Ziblings are treating Bolt—and just like them, I had no idea how much I was hurting you. This story is much more personal than you think. It's about *us*."

"Alex, I think you're over-reacting," he said.

"You just don't see it," Alex said. "Since we were kids, people have always compared us to each other. Everyone always shamed you for not getting good grades like me, for not being as mature as me, or for not being as organized as me. But no one ever made *me* feel bad for not being more like *you*—I had no idea what it was like. But now that I'm watching Bolt, I see how painful it must have been."

At first Conner thought his sister was crazy. There was no way a silly story he wrote could have been *that* meaning-ful. But the more she explained, the more sense it made. Alex had always been capable of so many things, she was like a superhero in his mind, a superhero he could never live up to.

"I apologize if I ever made you feel bad about yourself or made you feel left behind," Alex said. "You've always been so supportive of me, and I should have returned the favor more often. You're so gifted and deserve a lot more champions than just Mrs. Peters. I'm sorry it took a trip into your stories for me to see that."

Conner had no idea what to say. He looked around at the world of the Ziblings as if he were seeing his own story for the first time.

CHAPTER TWENTY-ONE

CITY OF LIGHTNING

*T*he Ziblings have arrived in Paris! I repeat, the *Ziblings have arrived in Paris!"* the French reporter announced. *"Parisians can take a deep breath! It looks like help is here!"*

The twins were still sitting in the trunk of the Zibling Mobile. Conner was trying to come up with a new plan to recruit the superheroes, but all he could think about was his sister's analysis of his story. Was there really more to the Ziblings than he realized?

"So what happens next?" Alex asked.

"The Snake Lord captures the Ziblings at the Eiffel Tower," Conner said. "When Professor Wallet returns to the laboratory, he gives Bolt a pep talk that boosts his confidence. Bolt goes to Paris to save his brothers and sister, and when he faces the Snake Lord, the rest of his powers kick in and he saves the day."

"Oh, Professor Wallet must be based on Mrs. Peters!" Alex said. "She's the person who gave you the confidence to write—and it activated the rest of *your* abilities!"

"Stop analyzing and focus," Conner said. "Professor Wallet doesn't get back to the laboratory for a week. *We* need to boost Bolt's confidence or we'll be stuck here for a couple days."

"Can't you and I just go to Paris and save the Ziblings ourselves?" Alex asked.

"No. The Ziblings are too divided right now," Conner explained. "We need them working as a team if we want them to help us fight the Literary Army. When Bolt saves them, he restores their bond as a family."

"Got it," Alex said. "So how do we make him confident enough to go?"

Conner scratched his head as he thought about it. He peeked out of the trunk and saw that Bolt was still pouting at his desk.

"He wants nothing more than to be a superhero," Conner said. "So let's make him *feel* like a superhero. We'll still pretend we're student reporters from the *Otherworld Times*, but we'll say we're doing a story all about him."

Alex nodded. "Let's look the part," she said.

She snapped her fingers and a notepad and pen appeared in Conner's hands. Alex snapped again and a camera appeared hanging around her neck. The twins quietly crawled out of the Zibling Mobile, tiptoed across the subway tracks, and climbed onto the platform. Conner knocked on the wall of mug shots like it was a door.

"Excuse me?" he called into the laboratory. "Is this Professor Wallet's secret underground laboratory?"

The voice startled Bolt and he jumped up from his desk. He had never seen strangers in the laboratory before. He eyed the twins suspiciously and made fists with his hands.

"What are you doing in here?" he asked.

"Oh my goodness!" Conner said. "It's the incredible Bolt himself! We must be in the right place!"

"Oh my gosh, I can't believe we're seeing him in person!" Alex said.

The twins acted starstruck. They giddily jumped up and down like they were meeting their idol. Their enthusiasm made Bolt stand a little taller.

"Who are you?" he asked. "How did you find the laboratory?"

"I'm Conner and this is my photographer, Alex," Conner said. "We're from the *Otherworld Times*. Professor Wallet didn't tell you we were coming?"

"No," Bolt said. "What's the *Otherworld Times*?"

"It's a syndicated school newspaper that's printed in over twenty-five states nationwide," Conner explained.

"We're here to do a human-interest piece on you. We asked our readers who their favorite Zibling was, and over seventy percent of those polled said it was you. Congratulations!"

Bolt couldn't believe it. His eyes grew wide and his mouth dropped open. He had never been anyone's favorite *anything* before.

"Me?" he said in shock. "But . . . but . . . but *why*?"

Conner hadn't thought this part of his plan through yet. He looked to Alex for help.

"Because you're the Zibling our readers identify with," she said. "They think it's very brave of you to fight criminals much bigger and older than you. You inspire young kids around the country to go after their own dreams— despite their size or age!"

Bolt held a hand over the lightning bolt on his chest. He had never been so honored in his life.

"I never thought I was so *inspirational*," he said.

"Would you mind if we interviewed you and took some pictures?" Conner asked.

"Would I *mind*?" Bolt asked. "Please—I insist!"

The superhero checked his reflection in the computer screen and straightened his hair. He pulled up two chairs for him and Conner to sit in while they chatted. Conner scanned his blank notepad as if it were full of questions. Alex walked around them and took photos while they spoke.

"Now, tell us, what's it like being a superhero?" Conner asked.

Bolt hesitated to answer. Truthfully, he had never felt more *unlike* a superhero than today. But he didn't want to disappoint the readers of the *Otherworld Times*, so he gave the answers he thought they'd want to hear.

"It's the best job in the whole world!" Bolt said. "The asteroid hitting our orphanage was the best thing that ever happened to me."

Conner scribbled down notes so quickly, he wasn't even writing real words.

"What's your favorite part about being a hero?" Conner asked.

"Oh, that's easy," Bolt said. "Helping people! I love seeing the relief in their eyes after they're rescued from a burning building, or a runaway train, or a sinking ship. Actually, I've never saved anyone myself, but I've been with my brothers and sister when they have."

The thought made Bolt a little sad and he sank in his chair. Conner quickly changed the subject to keep his spirits up.

"Our readers love watching you fly," he said. "Do you have any special techniques that get you off the ground?"

"Actually, I'm still working on the whole *flying thing*," Bolt said, like it was a secret. "Hopefully I'll get better at it one day. Never go so high you're afraid to look down: That's my motto."

"Words to live by," Conner said. "And what about all that electricity you produce? Where does it come from?"

"According to my dad, my body generates a lot of

friction, which pulls the electricity out of the environment around me," Bolt said. "Right now I can light up a fourteen-watt battery all by myself, but I'm hoping to get to a sixty-watt by the end of the year."

"That's *very* impressive!" Conner said. "It makes perfect sense why our readers said they'd prefer having *your* powers over any of your siblings'."

"*Really?*" Bolt asked. "That's crazy because most of the time I wish I could switch! I think it would be so cool to create fire like Blaze, or turn into stuff like Morph, or use my hair for chores like Whipney."

The more Conner buttered him up, the happier he became. With every picture Alex took, Bolt had a bigger and bigger smile. So far, their plan seemed to be working.

"Nice. This is all such great stuff," Conner said. "What would you say to someone who wanted to be a superhero as amazing as you?"

It took Bolt a few moments to respond. He had never thought anyone would want to be a superhero like *him*. He wanted to give his followers an answer from his heart.

"I suppose it would be to never give up," he said. "Courage is what makes a superhero super!"

Suddenly, the red lightbulb in the center of the laboratory lit up and the crisis alarm sounded again. The twins and Bolt turned to the television and saw that the situation in Paris had become much worse.

"*Breaking news,*" the panicked reporter said. "*The Snake Lord has captured the Ziblings! I repeat, the Snake*

Lord has captured the Ziblings! Something has gone wrong in their attempt to save the city. There is still no information at this time of what the Snake Lord is doing at the Eiffel Tower or what he is now planning to do with the Ziblings."

The news played live footage from a helicopter circling the Eiffel Tower. Blaze, Whipney, and Morph were wrapped around the base of the tower's antenna by a large anaconda. They were so close together, Blaze couldn't use his powers without burning his brother and sister. It was so tight between them that Morph couldn't transform into anything. A rattlesnake was covering Whipney's head like a turban, constricting her hair.

The Snake Lord was standing on a small platform at the very top of the Eiffel Tower's antenna. Screw by screw, he attached the Reptilalizer to the antenna and connected it to the tower's power. He operated unwaveringly and never looked up from the device.

Bolt was horrified to see that his family had been captured. Even though they'd known it was coming, Alex and Conner pretended to be just as surprised as him.

"This is awful!" he said. "The Snake Lord is going to turn everyone in Paris into a reptile!"

"Good thing there's still *one* Zibling left who can save them," Alex said.

The boy shook his head and paced back and forth. He couldn't fathom facing such a threat without the help of his brothers and sister.

"I can't defeat the Snake Lord on my own!" Bolt said.

"My powers haven't reached their full potential yet! I'm no match for him."

"Sure you are," Conner said. "You're the *Otherworld Times'* favorite superhero!"

"No I'm not!" Bolt exclaimed. "Your readers got it wrong. I'm not even a real superhero. My own family said it! I'm just a boy with tricks! The Snake Lord is going to win, and there's nothing I can do about it!"

Bolt went to his corner of the laboratory and sat at his desk. Alex and Conner exchanged worried glances. They had built up his ego only to watch it collapse like a building under demolition.

"I don't think we can convince him," Conner said to his sister. "To be honest, I'm not sure I would go to Paris if I were in his shoes."

"But you *were* in his shoes once," Alex said. "Bolt is you. He represents the little boy inside you who used to doubt himself. You have to be *his* Mrs. Peters—tell him exactly what you would have wanted to hear."

It was unsettling how Alex understood Conner's characters better than he did, but that's how he knew she was right. He let out a deep sigh and walked over to Bolt.

"For what it's worth, I know how you feel," Conner told him. "I used to doubt myself a lot. When people told me I wasn't good enough, I believed them. It's hard not to when you're young."

"Tell me about it," Bolt said. "Does it get better when you're older?"

"It did for me," Conner said.

"How?" Bolt asked.

"Someone else believed in me," Conner said. "All it took was one person's approval and suddenly I believed in myself, too. It gave me a shield to block out all the doubt and negativity. It made me realize I was just as capable and deserving as the people I compared myself to. But you know what? I was wrong."

"You were?" Bolt asked.

"Totally," Conner said. "I didn't *need* someone else. I had confidence in myself, deep down inside, the whole time. Approval is just a shortcut to self-worth, but sometimes we have to find things out on our own. Sometimes if we want something bad enough, we have to inspire ourselves to get it. Sometimes we have to be our own superhero."

Out of everything Conner said, he could tell this resonated with the boy the most. If he wanted to help people, maybe he had to start with himself.

"But what if I fail?" Bolt asked. "What if the Snake Lord wins and I don't save anyone? Then I'll *never* be a superhero."

"A very wise man once told me that 'courage is what makes a superhero super,'" Conner said. "He never said anything about succeeding."

Bolt looked down at the pile of used batteries on his desk. If the batteries had feelings, he imagined they'd feel the same way he did: useless, crumpled, and empty. But if he could glue junk together and turn it into a hero, he knew he could make a hero out of himself, too. Bolt stood up from his desk and looked Conner in the eye.

"Let's go to Paris," he said. "I've got a family and a city to save."

"Attaboy!" Conner said. He patted Bolt on the back. The contact shocked Conner's hand and he yelped. "Sorry, I forgot who I was talking to."

"How am I supposed to get to Paris in time?" Bolt asked. "My brothers and sister took the jet."

"Luckily for you, Alex and I happen to have a teleportation device," Conner said. "It'll get us there in a matter of seconds."

Alex did a double take. "We *do*?" she asked.

"Yes—*you do*," Conner mouthed at his sister. *"We'll use your magic."*

"Oh, right." Alex played along. "I completely forgot about the *teleportation device*. I have it right here in my hand—it's small and invisible. Boy, it sure is easy to misplace."

Bolt was impressed. "My dad doesn't even have one of those," he said. "How did two school journalists get one?"

"Our school has a great science department," Conner said. "More on that later. Do you want to get to Paris or not?"

Alex put her arms around Bolt and Conner and they formed a group hug. She had never magically transported between locations in one of her brother's stories before. She hoped it would work like it did in the fairy-tale world. Alex closed her eyes and visualized the Ziblings tied to the Eiffel Tower's antenna by the anaconda and also remembered how desperately she and Conner needed the superheroes to defeat the Literary Army.

"Activating the teleportation device," she said. "Here goes nothing."

With a bright flash, the twins and Bolt disappeared from Professor Wallet's secret laboratory. The first thing they felt was a cool night breeze. They looked around and saw lush rectangular lawns, fountains, and a winding river. There were gorgeous buildings for miles around with tall windows, domes, columns, steeples, and French flags. Every building was lit up like the entire city was in the middle of a photo shoot.

"We're definitely in Paris," Alex said. "But I don't see the Eiffel Tower anywhere."

"That's because we're *in* the Eiffel Tower," Conner said. "Check it out!"

After further inspection, she realized they were hundreds of feet in the air. Alex had transported them directly onto the roof of the lower observation deck. The rest of the structure towered above them like the skeleton of a steel giant. It was so tall, the twins got vertigo just looking at it. Despite the circumstances, the Eiffel Tower was a breathtakingly beautiful sight.

On the ground below, they saw the Snake Lord's circle of serpents keeping the Parisian police at bay. Beyond the police were thousands of French citizens observing the scene. A dozen news helicopters flew in the air around the Eiffel Tower and they shined their spotlights on Bolt and the twins as soon as they arrived.

It was a blessing they did, because the spotlights illuminated Collared Joe and Lizzy Liza sneaking up behind them.

"Bolt, look out!" Conner yelled.

Collared Joe leaped toward Bolt and knocked him to the floor. Lizzy Liza stood on her hands and kicked the twins. Alex and Conner rolled across the roof and over the edge. Conner grabbed on to the ledge with one hand and his sister with the other. They swung from the roof like rock climbers without a harness. The observers below gasped and screamed.

As they climbed back over the ledge, Collared Joe and Lizzy Liza started circling Bolt as he got to his feet. Collared Joe puffed his frilled neck out like an umbrella around his head. Lizzy Liza scraped her claws across the roof and hissed at the boy. They were like predators surrounding their prey.

"What a treat," Collared Joe said. "All four Ziblings in one day! The Snake Lord will be thrilled!"

"I say we keep the little one between us," Lizzy Liza said. "I could use a *Znack*, if you know what I mean."

The overgrown reptiles cocked their heads and laughed. At that moment Alex noticed something on the roof behind Bolt that had the potential to help him, and she hoped he'd get the same idea when he saw it.

"Bolt—behind you!" Alex yelled.

Bolt turned around and saw the bucket of water she was referring to. He ran to it and kicked it over. The water spilled across the roof as Collared Joe and Lizzy Liza charged after him. Bolt put both hands down and sent electric waves through the spill. The evil sidekicks' feet and legs were electrocuted. They hopped around the roof like it was covered in broken glass. They tripped on each other and then fell over the edge of the observation deck and never returned.

The twins crawled back onto the roof and Bolt helped them to their feet.

"Smart thinking, guys," Conner said.

"My dad always says, 'Science is a superpower in itself,'" Bolt said.

With Collared Joe and Lizzy Liza gone, the Snake Lord was the only person preventing them from saving the city. The twins and the youngest Zibling went to the edge of the roof and looked up at the Eiffel Tower's highest observation deck.

"We've got to get up there," Alex said.

"No, it's too dangerous," Bolt said. "You both need to stay here. This is between me and the Snake Lord."

Alex opened her mouth to argue, but Conner gave her a look to keep quiet. As he had explained before, for the Ziblings to reunite, Bolt had to face the Snake Lord alone.

"Good luck, Bolt," Alex said.

"We believe in you," Conner said.

Bolt gave them a nervous salute. He flew into the air and

ascended the Eiffel Tower, gliding from steel beam to steel beam like a flying squirrel jumping from branch to branch. Eventually, he made it all the way to the roof of the highest observation deck, where he saw the other Ziblings at the base of the antenna. Blaze, Whipney, and Morph were shocked and upset to see their little brother.

"Bolt, what the heck are you doing here?" Blaze asked.

"I'm here to save you and the city," Bolt said.

"No, get out of here while you still can!" Whipney said. "You can't face the Snake Lord alone!"

"You need to get Dad!" Morph said. "You can't help us—you aren't strong enough!"

"It doesn't take *strength* to be a superhero," Bolt said. "It just takes *courage*."

Just like Conner, Bolt pretended he had a shield protecting him from all the doubt and belittlement his siblings were sending him. He flew over them to the antenna's ladder and climbed up to the platform where the Snake Lord stood.

The Snake Lord had reached the final step of the Reptilalizer's installation, and a pleased grin stretched across his face. It would only be a matter of time before everyone in Paris was transformed into a reptile, and he would have total control over the world's most cosmopolitan city.

The Snake Lord was distracted by movement coming from beneath his feet. He looked down just as the youngest Zibling was pulling himself onto the platform. The Snake Lord kicked Bolt hard in the chest and he slipped down the ladder.

It knocked the wind out of Bolt, but as soon as he caught his breath, he climbed back up. When he reached the platform, the Snake Lord kicked him down again. But no matter how many times the Snake Lord kicked Bolt down the ladder, the boy was never going to give up. Even if he was kicked down a hundred more times, Bolt was going to do whatever it took to keep the Snake Lord from activating the Reptilalizer.

On the boy's fifth trip up the ladder, the Snake Lord stared down at him pityingly. Bolt's determination amused him. Instead of kicking him down again, the Snake Lord grabbed Bolt by the lightning logo on his suit and looked the boy closely in the eye.

"You're a brave little hero, I'll give you that," the Snake Lord said. "But there's a thin line between *bravery* and *stupidity*—and I'm afraid you just crossed it."

"And there's a thin line between *bad breath* and *halitosis*," Bolt said. "I'm afraid you crossed *that* a while ago."

The remark angered the Snake Lord to no end, so rather than putting Bolt with his siblings, he threw the boy off the antenna. The youngest Zibling plummeted toward the ground, falling so fast he couldn't fly.

"Bolt!" the Ziblings yelled as they watched helplessly.

He fell past Alex and Conner on the lower observation deck and landed somewhere among the trees below the Eiffel Tower. It was over before the twins even knew what was happening. They looked at each other in total shock.

"This is all my fault," Conner cried. "I pushed him too

far. I made him face the Snake Lord when he wasn't ready! *I killed him!* Now the Ziblings will never be united!"

Conner was so ashamed of himself, he buried his face in Alex's shoulder. She felt just as responsible and couldn't find the words to comfort him.

"*You murderer!*" Blaze yelled at the Snake Lord.

"*How could you do that to a child?*" Whipney screamed.

"*He was just a boy!*" Morph shouted.

The Ziblings struggled against the anaconda binding them, but the large snake only tightened its squeeze. The Snake Lord finished the final phase of the Reptilalizer's installation and laughed uproariously to himself.

"The Reptilalizer is complete!" he announced. "Not only have you lost a brother, but once I activate my invention, you'll be the first people in Paris to turn into reptiles! And with no Ziblings left, no one will ever stop me! Soon the whole world will be in my control!"

The Snake Lord flipped the switch on the Reptilalizer and the machine came to life. A thick green gas spewed from the antenna and traveled down the Eiffel Tower like a looming fog. But just before it reached the Ziblings below, the Eiffel Tower's power unexpectedly went out. The Reptilalizer shut off and the green gas dissipated in the night breeze.

"*What in the name of Kaa?*" the Snake Lord said, and desperately tried to re-start his machine.

As the twins mourned the loss of Bolt, a strange phenomenon occurred in the city around them. Not only did the Eiffel Tower lose its power, but all the buildings in a ten-block radius blacked out, too. It was like the Reptilalizer had blown Paris's fuse.

"Wait a second," Alex said. "Didn't Bolt say his power comes from absorbing the electricity around him?"

"Yeah, when he was alive," Conner said. "But he's dead—isn't he?"

Suddenly, the twins' hair rose above their heads and their bodies were tickled by a strong wave of friction. They looked down to the trees where Bolt had landed. The trees were buzzing and emitted a glowing bright white light.

Bolt launched from the trees like a missile: He was alive and more powerful than ever. Strong electric waves charged out of his body like he was a human plasma ball. His body was producing so much friction that the air hummed around him. His hair stood straight up above his head and his eyes glowed with energy. Bolt had never looked so confident or capable in his life.

"It worked!" Conner said. *"Bolt's reached his full potential!"*

"Go, Bolt!" Alex yelled.

Conner couldn't have been more proud of the little superhero. Watching Bolt flourish made him feel like a part of him had succeeded and beaten the odds, too. The twins hugged in celebration.

Bolt soared back to the antenna of the Eiffel Tower. He pointed a finger at the anaconda and rattlesnake restraining his siblings and zapped the reptiles with electricity. The snakes curled into balls and fell to the ground. The Ziblings couldn't believe their eyes. It took them a moment to realize that their rescuer was their brother.

"Bolt?" Blaze said.

"You're alive!" Whipney said.

"And POWERFUL!" Morph said.

The youngest Zibling could have gloated, he could have made his brothers and sister feel as lousy as they had made him feel, but none of that was as important as saving the city.

"I have two friends on the roof of the lower observation deck," Bolt said. "Get them to safety and I'll take care of the Snake Lord."

The Ziblings didn't argue with their brother. Blaze jumped off the tower, and fiery blasts erupted from his feet like he was standing on a jetpack. Whipney swung down the Eiffel Tower beam by beam, as if her hair were the long arms of an orangutan. Morph turned into a huge paper airplane with sunglasses and glided down to the lower observation deck to retrieve the twins.

"Hop on!" Morph told them.

Alex and Conner climbed aboard the paper airplane, and the Ziblings escorted them to the rectangular lawns below. Once they were safely on the ground, the twins and Ziblings all looked up at the Eiffel Tower and anxiously watched as Bolt went head-to-head with the Snake Lord.

At the top of the antenna, the Snake Lord was fidgeting

with the wires and gears of the Reptilalizer, but nothing he adjusted made the device regenerate. Bolt landed on the platform behind him with so much force, the entire structure rattled. He raised both hands toward the Reptilalizer and fired it with electricity until it exploded.

If looks could kill, the Snake Lord would have murdered Bolt with his hateful glare.

"You think *you're* powerful?" he asked. "You have no idea what power is!"

The eyes on the Snake Lord's helmet started to glow. As if they were connected by a wireless frequency, he sent instructions to the serpents guarding the base of the Eiffel Tower. The snakes joined their bodies together and formed one monstrous beast. Thousands of snakes made up of hundreds of species were now slithering in perfect synchronicity. The gigantic reptile coiled up the Eiffel Tower toward the antenna to join its master and attack Bolt.

The observing twins, the Ziblings, the police, and the Parisian citizens all screamed. They had never seen such a gargantuan creature take form. Bolt only laughed at the approaching giant. In the Snake Lord's ruthless quest for power, the mad scientist had forgotten one basic scientific fact.

"Science 101," Bolt said. "Nothing helps electricity move faster than metal, and you just sent your entire entourage into a steel structure."

The Snake Lord's yellow reptilian eyes widened and his pupils shrank into narrow slits. He had made a grave mistake. Bolt looked toward the sky above the antenna and sent a wave of friction into the clouds, causing a mighty bolt of lightning to descend and strike the Eiffel Tower.

The lightning illuminated the tower and it shone more brightly than it ever had in history. Every lightbulb on the tower burst, covering it in tiny explosions. The electricity coursing through the structure electrocuted the Snake Lord and his scaly accomplices until there was nothing left of them but burned dust.

When the lightning had finished, a thunderous roar erupted throughout Paris. The Ziblings, the twins, the police, and all the witnessing Parisians cheered and applauded the little superhero. Bolt flew down to the rectangular lawn and joined the twins.

"Way to go!" Conner said. "I'd hug you, but I'm definitely not touching you after all that!"

"We knew you could do it!" Alex said.

Blaze, Whipney, and Morph sheepishly stepped toward Bolt. They hung their heads shamefully, feeling so guilty they couldn't even look their brother in the eye.

"Bolt, we're so sorry," Blaze said.

"Thank you for saving our lives," Whipney said.

"We should have believed in you," Morph said.

Bolt stared blankly at his brothers and sister, not knowing what to say to them. A sly grin appeared on his face. It felt so good to finally *prove himself* that he didn't care about *proving them wrong*.

"It's okay," he said. "All that matters is that I believed in myself. And I'll definitely find ways for you to make it up to me."

The Ziblings went to speak with the French police and press. Blaze, Whipney, and Morph gave all the credit for saving the city to their little brother. The reporters crowded around him and praised him for his efforts. The Parisians chanted Bolt's name, and Blaze and Morph lifted their brother onto their shoulders so the people could get a better look at him.

Bolt had never smiled so big in his whole life—he was finally a *real* superhero.

"That's so sweet," Alex said. "This is such a great story, Conner."

"Thank you," he said. "You know, I've been thinking a lot about what you said in the trunk of the Zibling Mobile. You were right. 'The Ziblings' is definitely about us."

Alex took a deep breath. "I told you," she said. "And just to reiterate, I want to apologize for anything I might have—"

"But you were wrong about one thing," Conner interrupted. "Blaze, Whipney, and Morph aren't based on you. Alex, you might not realize it, but *you* were the first person to encourage me to write. *You're* my Professor Wallet, not Mrs. Peters."

"Me?" Alex said. "But . . . but . . . *Mrs. Peters*—"

"Mrs. Peters also tried getting me to finish my homework and study for tests, but that never happened," Conner said. "I don't remember the second grade, but I do remember the seventh. Just before we went into the fairy-tale world to fight the Enchantress, I showed you my stories for the first time. You liked them, you said they were special, and *you* gave me the confidence to keep writing. It was *your* approval that inspired me—*you* were my champion."

Alex was more relieved than words could describe. Thinking she had somehow harmed him in the past was the worst feeling in the world. She hugged her brother, squeezing him so tight that he could barely breathe.

Professor Wallet appeared in the crowd of Parisians and pushed his way through the people toward his children. He was so out of breath and sweaty, he looked like he had run all the way from Germany.

"Dad!" Bolt said when he saw him.

"I'm sorry I didn't get here sooner," the professor said. "The chancellor let me borrow her plane. I've been watching the whole thing unfold on the news!"

"I'm sorry I broke the rules again," Bolt said. "I know I was grounded and shouldn't have left the laboratory, but the others were in danger, and I didn't want the Snake Lord to win, so I—"

Professor Wallet silenced his son with a hug. The embrace was slightly electrifying, but the professor didn't care.

"We can talk about the logistics at a different time," Professor Wallet said. "But right now, I couldn't be more proud to be your father. It took a lot of bravery for you to save all these people—bravery you must have found on your own.

Paris is known as the City of Light, but after tonight, I believe it'll be remembered as the City of *Lightning*."

It was a touching display, and many of the observers teared up. The reporters tried sticking their microphones closer to the father and son, but the Ziblings pushed them back to give Bolt and the professor some privacy.

"It wasn't all thanks to me," Bolt said. "If it weren't for my new friends, I would never have had the confidence to come here. They taught me how to believe in myself. I couldn't have done it without them."

Bolt led the professor to the rectangular lawn in front of the Eiffel Tower and introduced him to the twins.

"Conner and Alex, meet my dad, Professor Wallet," he said.

"It's a pleasure," the professor said, and shook their hands. "Thank you for giving my son the inspiration he needed to save his brothers and sister. If there is anything we can do to return the favor, please don't hesitate to ask."

Alex and Conner exchanged quick smiles.

"As a matter of fact," Conner said. "We *could* use your help with something. . . ."

Chapter Twenty-Two

A CASTLE OF QUESTIONS

After a long and exhausting journey across the fairy-tale world, Emmerich and the Masked Man arrived in the woods of the Eastern Kingdom. They had only stopped to rest once since leaving the Dwarf Forests, and Emmerich was so tired that he was falling asleep as they walked.

"We're almost there," the Masked Man said. "Keep up, boy."

The closer they got to the portal, the more cross the Masked Man became. Emmerich was starting to realize he wasn't as nice a person as he had first thought. The longer Emmerich accompanied the twins' uncle, the louder a voice in the back of his mind urged him not to trust the man.

They entered an area of the forest that Emmerich recognized. It was the part of the woods he had entered with Conner and Bree on his first trip to the fairy-tale world. He would never forget seeing the Grande Armée soldiers raining down on the trees after they arrived.

"This is it," the Masked Man said. "This is where I saw Morina activate the portal. Now all I need is the magic panpipe. Let me think, which tree did the witch stash it in?"

The twins' uncle searched all the trees in the area. He stuck his hand in every hole, crack, and bird nest in every tree trunk. Finally, he found the instrument in the back of a squirrel's nest.

"Aha!" the Masked Man said with delight. "I found it. Now I just need to play the right tune and the portal will open."

The Masked Man played a series of melodies on the panpipe. He waited a few moments after each one, but none of the notes did the trick. Even when he was certain he had remembered the correct tune, a portal to the Otherworld did not appear.

"Blast that damn witch!" the Masked Man said. "Why isn't it working?"

"Is it the right panpipe?" Emmerich asked.

"Of course it is," he said. "Morina stole it from the

fairies. I watched her open the portal just a few days ago. For whatever reason, it won't cooperate with me."

Emmerich thought back to when Conner played the panpipe and opened the portal in Neuschwanstein Castle. He remembered there was something very specific the instrument needed in order to work.

"It needs to be played by a person of magic blood," Emmerich said. "That must be why it isn't working. My friend Bree thinks she and I might have magic in our blood. Would you like me to give it a try?"

The magic in the Masked Man's blood had been taken away a long time ago, so it made sense that the portal wasn't opening for him. However, if his son was able to do the trick, not only would it grant them entrance to the Otherworld, it would also prove the Masked Man's plan would work. He glanced down at his son, trying to conceal the eagerness in his eyes.

"Be my guest," he said, and handed his son the panpipe.

Emmerich licked his lips, held the instrument to his mouth, and blew the eight notes he remembered Conner playing at the castle. Almost instantaneously, a bright light appeared out of thin air among the trees. The light grew bigger and bigger, and it started to spin, sucking all the leaves on the forest floor inside it like a wormhole.

Emmerich smiled. He had activated the portal all by himself! This confirmed Bree's theory that there was magic in his blood. More than ever, Emmerich couldn't wait to get home so he could tell her.

Unbeknownst to him, the Masked Man had other plans for the boy. He stared at the portal as it grew, mesmerized by its spinning light. He placed his hand on the back of Emmerich's neck and pushed his son toward it.

"Good boy," he said softly. "*Very* good boy . . ."

Bree and the Sisters Grimm had spent the entire week in Germany searching for clues to Emmerich's disappearance. Just as they expected, nothing in the Bavarian countryside revealed where the boy was or who had taken him. There was only one place that might give them more insight, and unfortunately, it wasn't an easy location to get to.

After days of trading voice mail, Cornelia finally got through to the groundskeeper of Neuschwanstein Castle. She told the man she and her family were private investigators from the United States and needed access to the castle. The groundskeeper wouldn't hear a word of it until Cornelia mentioned it was regarding Emmerich Himmelsbach. By now all of Bavaria had heard of the missing boy, and the groundskeeper was inclined to help her.

Late one night, once all the tour guides and tourists had left and the janitors had finished their shifts, the groundskeeper snuck Cornelia, Wanda, Frenda, and Bree inside the castle.

"You have one hour," the groundskeeper said. "I can't give you any more time than that or I might lose my job."

"We really appreciate this," Cornelia said.

"Would you mind showing us around to the lower levels of the castle?" Wanda asked.

The groundskeeper escorted Wanda and Frenda to the stories below, giving Cornelia and Bree a chance to thoroughly inspect the Singers' Hall without supervision. Bree looked around at all the instruments, the pillars, the chandeliers, and the mural of the enchanted forest: She couldn't believe it had been more than a year since she and the boys were there.

"That's where the portal is," Bree said, and nodded to the mural.

Cornelia removed a cross-dimensional emission-tracking device from her purse and waved it around the painting. The device beeped with gusto.

"If I didn't know that before, I would now," Cornelia said. "The detection rates are off the charts. This portal was activated recently—*very* recently."

"I knew it. Emmerich isn't in this world," Bree said. "Whoever kidnapped him took him back to the fairy-tale world."

Bree sat on the floor and sighed. Cornelia kneeled next to her and put the tracking device aside.

"Sadly, I think we've done all we can do," she said. "We should think about heading back to the States tomorrow morning."

Bree would have stayed in Germany for months if she

could. She felt like she was abandoning Emmerich by leaving, but Cornelia was right. There was no point in staying if there was nothing they could do.

"Have you contacted the Bailey twins and told them about Emmerich yet?" Cornelia asked.

"I tried calling Conner as soon as I found out Emmerich was taken," Bree said. "At the time, his mom didn't even know where he and his sister were. I bet they're still somewhere in the fairy-tale world."

"Then perhaps Conner will find Emmerich," Cornelia said. "The three of you were brought together by chance—we need to have faith it'll happen again."

Bree nodded. "Let's go," she said. "I don't want to waste any more of anyone's time."

Just as she got to her feet, the tracking device began a beeping frenzy: Something otherworldly was headed their way. A bright light appeared in front of the mural and became brighter and brighter. It grew bigger and bigger, swirling like a vortex.

"My word!" Cornelia gasped. "What's happening?"

"It's the portal!" Bree said. "Someone must have activated it from the fairy-tale world!"

Instead of pulling them in like it had before, the portal blew powerful gusts of air into the room, knocking all the furniture and instruments to the floor. Bree and Cornelia held on to each other so they weren't knocked off their feet. Leaves from the fairy-tale world blew inside the hall, and

Bree could make out the silhouettes of two people stepping through the portal. It was so bright she couldn't tell who they were.

Finally, the portal closed and the swirling vortex disappeared.

"Bree?" said a familiar voice with a German accent.

As soon as her eyes adjusted, Bree saw Emmerich running toward her. She couldn't believe it—all her prayers had been answered! She embraced her friend and twirled him around in a circle.

"Emmerich!" Bree cried thankfully. "We've been looking all over for you!"

"I was kidnapped by witches!" Emmerich said. "They held me prisoner at their camp in the woods until this man rescued me!"

Emmerich gestured to the Masked Man behind him. Even though Bree was overjoyed to see her friend, there was something very peculiar about the man with Emmerich. He seemed familiar, but Bree couldn't think of who he reminded her of.

"Thank you for saving my friend," Bree said. "Who are you?"

"He's Alex and Conner's uncle Lloyd!" Emmerich exclaimed. "They sent him to find me and bring me home!"

"You know my niece and nephew, too?" the Masked Man asked. "Well, it's certainly a *small world*."

From the sarcastic tone in his voice, he was anything but thrilled by the connection.

"We go to the same school," Bree said. "I didn't even know they had an uncle."

"We aren't close," the Masked Man said.

Emmerich was so happy to be back home in Germany, he hugged Cornelia before being introduced.

"I'm Emmerich," he said. "Who are you?"

"My name is Cornelia Grimm," she said. "It's so wonderful to see you're alive and well!"

"Cornelia is my cousin," Bree said. "When I heard you were missing, she brought me here in her very own plane and helped me look for you. She's part of a secret group of women called *the Sisters Grimm*—they're descendants of the Brothers Grimm and they know all about the fairy-tale world."

Emmerich's eyes grew wide and he jumped up and down.

"Bree, that reminds me of something I have to tell you!" he said. "I activated the portal from the fairy-tale world all by myself! You were right—there's magic in our blood! That must mean that you, Cornelia, and I are all related!"

"Actually, Emmerich," Bree said, "we found out some information while we were visiting with your mom. It turns out you're not related to the Brothers Grimm like I thought, you're from the—"

Her train of thought was interrupted when Cornelia suddenly screamed. Bree and Emmerich looked up and saw that the Masked Man was pointing a revolver at them.

"What are you doing, Lloyd?" Emmerich asked.

The Masked Man ignored him. He stepped toward Cornelia and aimed the gun at her. The old woman raised her hands in the air.

"Did the girl say you have a *plane*?" he asked.

"Well...yes," Cornelia said. "I do."

The Masked Man jerked his head and gun toward Bree next.

"And you go to school with my niece and nephew," he said. "Do you know where they live and how to get there?"

Bree was scared speechless. *"I...I...I..."* she mumbled.

"JUST ANSWER THE QUESTION!" the Masked Man yelled.

"Yes!" Bree said.

Emmerich was petrified. He regretted not trusting his instincts in the woods. Clearly, the man wasn't who he said he was.

"You're not Alex and Conner's uncle, are you?" he asked.

"Yes, I most certainly *am*," the Masked Man said. "Actually, I'm a lot more than what you realize, but we'll have plenty of time for that later. The four of us are going on a little trip to the twins' house—*right now*!"

"But Alex and Conner aren't there," Bree peeped. "They're in the fairy-tale world!"

The Masked Man chuckled. "Stupid girl," he said. "I never said I was looking for *the twins*."

CHAPTER TWENTY-THREE

FAMILIAR STRANGERS

In the commissary, the Blissworm was standing on a table entertaining all the pirates and sailors from "Starboardia." The space worm theatrically re-enacted the twins' encounter with the polycrabs on Lollipopigust. It used sound effects, large gestures, and impersonations to tell the exciting tale. Although it never articulated any words, the *Dolly Llama* crew seemed to understand everything the worm was saying. They *oohed* and *aahed* at the descriptive story; some even covered their eyes like they were watching a scary movie.

"You're telling us that Alex and Conner found you in a hole the polycrabs dug to capture prey?" Winking Wendy asked.

"Then you were all captured and taken to the polycrabs' colony deep underground?" Siren Sue asked.

"And after Conner rescued you from the queen poly-crab's web, he detonated a massive bomb that vaporized the whole species?" Stinky-Feet Phoebe asked.

The Blissworm nodded happily. They were a very attentive audience. All the pirates and sailors were astonished by the story. The *Dolly Llama* crew had never heard such an adventurous tale, and *they* were *pirates*.

The commissary was still segregated. The characters from the fairy-tale world glared at the characters from Conner's short stories from their table across the room. They were also astonished, not by the events in the story, but that the *Dolly Llama* crew understood what the worm was saying.

"How do they know what it's talking about?" Jack whispered to Goldilocks.

"They're all from Conner's imagination," Goldilocks said. "They must share some kind of language."

Red casually slid into the seat across the table from Jack and Goldilocks. Her eyebrows were raised and she pursed her lips tightly to keep from smiling: She obviously had a secret she was dying to share. Red leaned over the table so only Jack and Goldilocks could hear her.

"Have you noticed how *familiar* all these strangers are?" Red whispered.

Jack and Goldilocks stared at her blankly. Was she just now realizing that?

"Can't say I have," Jack said. "Have you, Goldie?"

"Familiar?" Goldilocks said. "Whatever do you mean?"

Red was so eager to talk about it, she didn't realize they were being sarcastic. Her eyes enlarged like her theory was scandalous.

"All the characters on *that* side of this odd ballroom are from Conner's short stories, right?" Red said. "But I'm not convinced they're entirely from his imagination. I think many of the people in this room are *based* on people he knows—people like *us*."

Red swiped the table like she was laying out a winning hand of cards. Jack and Goldilocks both sighed. Sometimes Red was so naïve, it was impressive.

"I think you're onto something, Red," Jack said.

"Nothing gets by you," Goldilocks said.

Red was so pleased with herself, she shimmied her shoulders. Captain Auburn Sally walked by their table and Red waved her down.

"Excuse me, lady with the big hat!" Red called. "Come sit with us!"

Red patted the seat next to her. The captain looked around the room to make sure Red wasn't speaking to someone else, and then sat down next to the queen, with no clue of her intentions.

"It's rather silly for us to share such close quarters and not get to know each other," Red said. "Allow me to introduce myself. I'm Queen Red Riding Hood. These are my subjects Jack and Goldilocks."

Jack and Goldilocks glanced at each other. *Subjects?*

"It's nice to meet you," Auburn Sally said. "I'm Captain Auburn Sally of the *Dolly Llama*."

"Tell me everything," Red said. "Where are you from, what do you do for a living, what are your hobbies, et cetera, et cetera?"

"Well, like I said, I'm the captain of a ship," Auburn Sally said. "We're the only all-female vessel in the Caribbean, but one of the most feared in the sea. We spend our days sailing across the ocean, looking for buried treasure. Occasionally we'll meet other women like ourselves, on the run from their pasts, and we invite them to join our crew."

Red was so charmed by the captain, she gently placed her hands over Auburn Sally's. The queen smiled like they were long-lost sisters who had finally been reunited.

"You must be *me*," Red said.

Auburn Sally was confused. She understood what Red was insinuating, but the queen didn't seem to notice that *Goldilocks* could have been the captain's identical twin.

"Are you sure?" the captain asked. "No offense, but I would have guessed someone *else* was inspired by you."

The captain gestured to the Cyborg Queen in the corner

of the commissary. She was sitting in throne mode as Commander Newters tightened the wires around the gears on top of her head.

"Don't be so humble," Red said. "I'm certain you're me. The similarities are uncanny! Both of our names start with colors, we're both very powerful and accomplished women, and we're both very flamboyant dressers. My style is more *privileged and pampered* but the *dirty-and-daring* look works well on you."

Auburn Sally looked to Jack and Goldilocks for help.

"Just play along or it'll never stop," Goldilocks whispered to the captain. "I think you're right, Red. Auburn Sally is definitely based on you."

"You're practically the same person," Jack said, and nodded over-dramatically.

Red happily turned to the crew of the *Dolly Llama*. She now saw the pirates from a completely different perspective.

"Pardon me for a moment," she said. "I'm going to introduce myself to *our* crew—oh, what fun this has turned into!"

The queen skipped to the table of pirates and sailors and introduced herself. Auburn Sally stared at Red like the queen had just escaped from an asylum.

"She's not sailing with a full set of sails, is she?" the captain asked.

Across the commissary, the twins' mother was happy to see the characters finally warming up to one another. Charlotte took the intermingling as a sign that she was succeeding as a glorified babysitter. Things had gotten significantly easier now that they were in the hospital. There was plenty of room for all the characters, no one was breaking Charlotte's possessions, and everyone was getting along for the most part. There was only one thing missing to make it an enjoyable experience: Alex and Conner. Spending several hours a day with her son's characters made Charlotte miss Conner more than ever. He had never shared his stories with his mom, so it was nice for her to see them come to life piece by piece.

Charlotte heard a familiar jingle and turned toward the door of the commissary. It swung open and her heart sank into the pit of her stomach—*they had company*!

Dr. Sharon Jackson, a clinical psychologist at Saint Andrew's Children's Hospital, stepped into the commissary with an elderly couple. Sharon was an African American woman with curly black hair who wore several bracelets around each of her wrists that jangled as she walked.

"And *this* is the new storybook commissary," Dr. Jackson told the couple as she escorted them inside.

The psychologist was floored to see that it was filled with so many strange people. The elderly couple cleaned the lenses of their glasses to make sure their eyes weren't deceiving them. All the characters in the room froze and went dead silent—*they had been caught*!

"Hi, Sharon," Charlotte said. "What brings you to the new commissary?"

"Charlotte, meet Mr. and Mrs. Carmichael," Dr. Jackson

said. "They're two of the donors who paid for the construction of the new wing. I was just giving them a tour of the facility. *Who are all these people?*"

Charlotte's options were limited. Telling her co-worker the truth was out of the question, and there were very few lies that could explain why so many costumed adults were gathered there. Coming up with something that wouldn't get her and Bob into trouble with the hospital was nearly impossible.

"They're *performers*," Charlotte said. "Bob and I wanted to surprise the patients and the staff with a little entertainment."

The characters were impressed by how convincing Charlotte's lie was, especially one that had been thought of on the spot. Dr. Jackson and the Carmichaels were touched by Charlotte and Bob's generosity.

"Oh, how wonderful!" Mrs. Carmichael said. "They remind me of the circus! When is the performance? We'd love to see it."

"Tomorrow night," Charlotte fibbed again. "In the multi-purpose room, at eight o'clock."

"It'll be a late night for us, but we'll be there!" Mr. Carmichael said.

"That is so kind of you, Charlotte," Dr. Jackson said. "What show are they performing? Is it something I know?"

Charlotte eyed the characters for assistance, but none of them were helpful. They watched the twins' mother like she was a show herself.

"They're still figuring it out," she said. "That's why everyone is dressed so differently. They're going to rehearse all the shows in their repertoire for me so I can select one that will be best for the children."

"We'll be looking forward to it!" Dr. Jackson said. "May I spread the word, or are you still keeping it under wraps?"

Charlotte laughed. "I guess the cat is out of the bag now," she said. "Feel free to let everyone know."

"Sounds terrific!" Dr. Jackson said. "The kids are going to love it! We'll let you get back to rehearsals."

Dr. Jackson escorted the Carmichaels out of the commissary. Charlotte faced the characters in a panic. Her face turned bright red, and she was thinking only in swear words.

"Looks like we're putting on a show," she said. "Anyone have an idea of what we should do?"

"William Shakyfruit has a collection of hysterical plays, but I don't think we can pull one of them off by tomorrow night," Red said.

"Anyone *else* have a suggestion?" Charlotte asked.

Trollbella was the only character to step forward. She went to the center of the room, looked up at the fluorescent lighting, and spread her arms out like she was having a religious experience.

"My time has come," she said in a trance. "Finally, life has presented me with an opportunity to show my purpose. At last, I have an outlet to combine all my talents for something that matters."

"You mean, besides being a queen?" Goldilocks asked.

"Governing is just a side gig," Trollbella said. "My true calling has always been the performing arts. I have the perfect performance for our predicament. It's the greatest story ever told."

"'Little Red Riding Hood'?" Red asked.

"'THE PRINCE OF THIEVES'?" Robin Hood asked.

"'Peter Pan'?" Peter asked.

Trollbella raised a finger to silence them. "No," she said. "'The Life and Times of Queen Trollbella'!"

The troll queen flicked her hands through the air and mimed falling confetti. The other characters slumped— each thought *their* story was a much better choice.

"We need to start at once!" Trollbella said. "I'll write, direct, and narrate the performance myself, as nobody knows Trollbella like Trollbella. I'll need the pirates to build the sets and the Cyborgs to adjust the overhanging fireless torches."

"Those are called *lights*," the Cyborg Queen said.

"Now for casting," Trollbella said. "The Merry Men will be my goblins, the Lost Boys will be my trolls, handsome Jack will be my Butterboy, beautiful Red will play the title character, and fat Goldilocks will be the creature that keeps us apart."

"I'm pregnant," Goldilocks said.

Trollbella winked at her. *"Of course you are."*

"Can I have a bigger role?" Peter Pan asked.

"I have the perfect part for you," Trollbella said. "No one can portray the highs and lows of life like a boy who can fly! You will symbolize my heart and personify the joy, the conflict, and the agony I've experienced in my very short life."

"Wicked!" Peter Pan said.

Trollbella took charge of the room like a mad conductor, and her eyes widened with power.

"This will be the best surprise performance in the history of Saint Andrew's Children's Hospital!" Trollbella declared. "The audience is going to be so invigorated, so inspired, so dumbfounded—it's a good thing medical professionals will be standing by!"

The characters throughout the commissary were a little frightened by the troll queen. None of them had given her the authority to direct the performance, but none of them were going to take it away from her, either.

"Don't just sit there like porcelain porcupines—*let's get to work*!" Trollbella ordered.

Right away, the characters split into the groups she had assigned. Trollbella walked around the commissary and met with each cluster privately to discuss her vision in greater detail.

As they deliberated over the performance, the binder of short stories flipped open and the twins stepped out of the beam of light with Professor Wallet, Blaze, Whipney, Morph, and Bolt. The Zibling characters looked around the commissary in wonder. The other characters were so busy planning the performance, they didn't even look up at the superheroes.

"Welcome to the Otherworld," Alex told the Ziblings.

"Wow!" Bolt said. "A whole other dimension! This is so cool!"

"There's no science to prove this is possible, but I've always said there is too much world for just one planet," Professor Wallet said.

Conner whistled to get the room's attention. "Hey, everybody," he said. "These are our friends the Ziblings—they're superheroes and have agreed to help us fight the Literary Army."

"Can one of you sew?" Trollbella asked.

"I can transform into a sewing machine," Morph said.

"That'll do," Trollbella said. "You'll be in charge of costumes."

The troll queen grabbed Morph's hand and pulled him into her group of set designers.

"Costumes for what?" Alex asked.

"We were caught by one of my co-workers," Charlotte told the twins. "I didn't know what to say, so I told her the characters were performers. The good news is she believed it. The bad news is we have to put together a show for tomorrow night."

"Oh, *Butter-in-law*," Trollbella sang to Charlotte. "Is there a place we can get materials, or can we use the tablecloths and the wood from the walls?"

"Yikes," Alex said. "I'd better get them some supplies before Trollbella tears this place apart."

"I could probably travel into the next story alone if you want to stay here and help," Conner said.

"Are you sure you won't need a hand?" Alex asked.

"Positive," Conner said.

Alex didn't want to desert her brother, but she knew he'd be fine on his own. Charlotte was glad Alex was sitting the next one out because it presented a wonderful opportunity—one she had been hoping for.

"Conner, I have today and tomorrow off," Charlotte said. "Maybe I could join you in the next one? I would love to travel into one of your stories and see everything you've created."

Having his mom tag along seemed like the worst idea in the world. It was like she wanted to walk him to his classroom when dropping him off at school. He forced himself to smile so he didn't hurt her feelings.

"Oh . . . *great*," he said through his teeth.

Charlotte could tell her son wasn't thrilled by the idea. "Only if I won't be a burden," she said sadly. "I would hate to interfere. I'm just as happy to stay here and continue watching the characters."

He couldn't tell if she was *intentionally* making him feel guilty or not, but the effect was strong. Obviously it was something Charlotte really wanted to do, and Conner didn't have the heart to tell her no.

"It'll be totally fine," he said. "I'd *love* to have you there."

Charlotte clapped cheerfully. "What's the next story about?" she asked.

"It's called 'The Adventures of Blimp Boy,'" Conner explained. "It's about a young archaeologist in the 1930s who travels across the world on a giant blimp. He searches through ruins and finds precious artifacts before they're stolen by tomb raiders, and then donates them to museums."

"How exciting!" Charlotte said. "Is there anything special we need to do while we're there?"

"We have to find a magical talisman in an ancient pyramid," Conner said. "Whoever possesses the talisman is granted control over a legion of mummified soldiers. Once we bring the mummies here, we'll finally be finished recruiting the army we need to face the literary villains."

"I can't wait!" his mom said. "Let me just find my purse. Alex, if you see Bob, tell him I briefly stepped into another dimension with your brother."

Charlotte searched the commissary for her bag. Alex gazed at Conner with her deepest sympathies.

"Good luck," she said.

Conner sighed and shook his head. "What could be better than an afternoon of *mummies and Mom*?"

CHAPTER TWENTY-FOUR

THE ADVENTURES
OF BLIMP BOY

Conner poured the Portal Potion on his next story, and he and his mom stepped through the beam of light. Charlotte marveled at the world of hand-written words waiting on the other side. She laughed and gasped as her son's handwriting whirled around them.

"Conner, this is incredible!" she said. "Where are all the characters?"

"Mom, we're not in the story yet," he said. "This is just

the area that creates the story around us—it's like the Portal Potion's lobby. 'The Adventures of Blimp Boy' starts in India. You'll know we're there when you see a jungle."

"How fun!" Charlotte said. "I've never been to a jungle before."

She watched in wonder as the words *jungle trees*, *temple ruins*, and *screeching monkeys* stretched and filled the empty space around them. Word by word, a tropical Indian wilderness was created before their eyes. There were thousands of thick trees with large, drooping leaves and vines. It was very warm and so humid that their clothes stuck to their bodies. Playful monkeys growled and shrieked as they climbed through the tree branches above. Over the treetops, Conner and Charlotte could see the spiraling towers of an ancient temple in the distance.

"This is it," Conner told his mom.

Charlotte dug through her purse and pulled out a bottle of lotion. She rubbed it on her face and arms and then handed it to her son.

"What's that?" Conner asked.

"It's insect repellent with SPF," Charlotte said. "I don't want us getting sunburned or bitten while we're in the jungle."

Conner could already tell this was going to be a long trip. He rubbed the repellent on his skin and handed it back to his mom. Charlotte walked around the jungle like she was inspecting a house for sale.

"Well, it's *nice*," she said. "There are lots of plants and interesting animals to watch, but that heat really gets to you, doesn't it?"

"Don't worry, we won't be here very long," Conner said. "The lead character should be running by any minute now."

They heard a rustling in the jungle as someone ran toward them from the temple. A few moments later, a fourteen-year-old boy appeared. He came to a halt when he saw Conner and Charlotte. They were the last things he had expected to see in the jungle.

The boy wore an aviator hat with goggles and flaps over his ears, a fitted brown leather jacket, khaki pants, and tall boots. His face was bright red and he panted from running. He held a golden relic shaped like a human hand tightly under his arm. The boy looked like he could have been Conner's little brother.

"Who are you?" he asked them.

Charlotte shook his hand excitedly. "Hi there," she said. "I'm Conner's mom, Charlotte. It's very nice to meet you!"

The boy stared at her strangely: Was he supposed to know her son? Conner sighed and slapped his palm against his forehead.

"Mom, he doesn't know who we are yet," he whispered to her. *"We have to act like this is the first time we're meeting him."*

"My apologies," Charlotte whispered back. *"I'll let you do all the talking."*

Conner turned toward the boy and tried to smooth things over.

"Forgive my mom," Conner said. "She's a little delirious. We got separated from our tour guide and have been lost in the jungle for days! It's so good to see another human being. What's your name?"

"I'm Beau Rogers," the boy said.

A series of thunderous growls came from the jungle behind him. Beau glanced back and gulped nervously. Although they couldn't see what was coming, they could hear a group of animals rushing through the trees toward them.

"We're all about to become *lunch* if we don't get out of here," Beau said. "Follow me if you value your life!"

Beau sprinted into the trees and gestured for Conner and Charlotte to come with him. Conner ran after him, but when he turned around he saw his mom hadn't moved. She was standing in the same spot, stretching her feet and legs.

"Mom! We've got to go!" Conner yelled.

"I know, I heard him," she said. "But I'll really regret it if I don't stretch before running. You'll know what I'm talking about when you get to be my age. Okay, now I'm ready."

Another roar sounded through the jungle. Conner and Charlotte could see that the commotion was coming from a pack of tigers running straight toward them. Charlotte screamed and ran after Beau faster than Conner had ever seen her move before. He followed but could barely keep up with her.

"I never knew you ran so fast!" Conner said.

"I ran track in college," Charlotte said. "Those are *real tigers* chasing us! What are *real tigers* doing in your story?"

"What were you expecting? Puppets?" Conner asked.

"I guess I was expecting everything to be more innocent, like a school project!" she yelled. "I didn't think I'd be running for my life!"

Conner and Charlotte caught up with Beau, but as they gained distance, the tigers did, too. They got closer by the second, and it wasn't long before they were close enough to swipe at them. Whenever a tiger got too close, Charlotte smacked it in the nose with her purse.

To add to their troubles, Beau was leading Conner and Charlotte right to the edge of a cliff. The tigers started slowing down, assuming their prey had nowhere to go. Beau didn't seem discouraged at all by the cliff, though; in fact, it made him run even faster.

"We're almost there!" Beau said.

"Almost *where*?" Charlotte said. "We're trapped between *death* and *death*!"

"Mom, Beau knows what he's doing!" Conner said. "When we get to the cliff we have to jump!"

"WHAT?" Charlotte yelled.

"You have to trust me or you'll be cat food!" Conner said.

Charlotte ignored every instinct to slow down and continued running with the boys.

Right when they reached the cliff, a massive blimp rose above the edge like a sunrise. The blimp was bright white like an oval cloud, and a long silver gondola with several round windows stretched under its belly. An old woman aboard the blimp slid its wide door open just in the nick of time, and Beau, Conner, and Charlotte jumped over the cliff and landed inside. They collapsed on the blimp's floor and stayed in a dog pile until they caught their breath.

The tigers on the ground dropped their jaws in unison. They had never seen their lunch float away in a giant balloon before.

"Time to diet, you overgrown felines!" the old woman yelled at the tigers below, and she slammed the door shut with gusto.

The old woman wore pearls, high heels, and a fur coat, with goggles and an aviator hat just like Beau's. She had a familiar raspy voice and saucy attitude. It only took Charlotte a couple of seconds to realize the old woman was based on Mother Goose.

"That was closer than the run-in I had with Bonnie and Clyde," the old woman said. "I see you picked up some friends, Beau."

"I wasn't expecting the temple to be filled with tigers!" Beau said. "Why are ancient ruins always filled with giant predators? Just once I'd like to walk into a tomb and find a flock of sheep."

"I wasn't talking about the cats," the old woman said.

"Oh, obviously," Beau said. "Aunt Emgee, this is Conner and his mother, Charlotte. I found them in the jungle right after I left the temple. Apparently they got separated from their tour guide and have been lost in the jungle for a couple of days."

Emgee eyed Conner and Charlotte over her goggles. "You look awfully cleaned-up for being lost in the jungle," she said.

"My mom's really into personal hygiene," Conner said.

"I'm a nurse," Charlotte said with a shrug.

Emgee was pleased to hear it. "I always love meeting a fellow working woman," she said. "Welcome aboard the *Charlie Chaplin*!"

The old woman helped Beau, Conner, and Charlotte to their feet and shook their hands.

"Did you name the blimp after the actor?" Charlotte asked.

"Actually, he named himself after the blimp," Beau said. "He's Emgee's ex-boyfriend."

Emgee twirled her pearls and blushed. "Oh, no, he was just a *fling*," she said. "Poor kid fell madly in love with me, but I was too old for him and had already vowed not to date any more actors. Speaking of ancient history, did you get the relic, Beau?"

Her grand-nephew held up the golden hand. "Presenting the fourth and final Golden Hand of Shiva!" he said happily.

"Way to go, kiddo!" Emgee said. "You've collected them all! The Delhi Museum will be ecstatic!"

Beau placed the golden hand on a shelf with three

identical relics. Conner and Charlotte looked around the blimp with wide eyes. There were shelves and cases filled with artifacts, statues, tools, coins, and jewelry from ancient ruins around the world. All the walls in the *Charlie Chaplin* were covered in maps of various places with pins indicating where Beau and Emgee had traveled.

Conner knew where each and every artifact came from and the different adventures Beau had had collecting them. The only one he didn't recognize was a small doll made of rope. Beau slapped his hand as he reached for it.

"Don't touch that—*it's cursed*," Beau warned him.

Conner nodded. He remembered it now. Charlotte looked around the blimp at all of Beau and Emgee's belongings. She couldn't believe her son had created a world with such unique details and original characters.

"You've collected all of these?" Charlotte asked.

"Not *us*—it's all *him*," Emgee said, and patted her grand-nephew on the back. "Beau is the youngest archaeologist in the world. He earned his doctorate when he was just twelve years old!"

"It was actually my second," Beau clarified. "I got my first doctorate in political science when I was ten, but that was before I realized archaeology was my passion."

"That's extraordinary," Charlotte said. "I'm sure your parents are very proud!"

Beau lowered his head sadly. "Actually, my parents died when I was five," he said. "My mom was a flapper and my dad was a musician. They were performing at an underground nightclub when the building above it collapsed from all the barrels of gin the owner was hiding in the attic."

"*Prohibition.*" Emgee groaned. "It took away so much joy from so many people. I've been caring for the little rascal ever since. I've supported him through every step of his archaeology ambitions. A lot of my friends thought I was crazy when I sold my brownstone and bought a blimp to travel the world, but if you ask me, it was a great investment. Everyone's crazy about *planes* these days, but I think blimps will be the transportation of the future."

"We've had some good times aboard the *Charlie Chaplin*," Beau said. "We've gone on so many adventures, seen so many astonishing places, and met so many interesting people. Speaking of which, where are you guys headed? Is there a place we could drop you off at?"

With just a look, Conner reminded his mom to let him do all the talking.

"The rest of our group headed to Egypt," he said. "You wouldn't by chance be headed in that direction, would you?"

Emgee was so tickled by the coincidence, she slapped her knee.

"You're in luck!" Emgee said. "We're headed to the Ancient Pyramid of Anesthesia right now! Beau's got his heart set on a mythical talisman."

Charlotte was confused. "*Anesthesia?*" she whispered to her son.

"I heard you and Bob talking about it once and thought it sounded like an ancient pyramid," Conner whispered back. "Tell us more about this talisman. It sounds super-neat!"

Beau was more than excited to talk about it. He retrieved a rolled-up map from a stack in the corner and spread it over the table in the center of the gondola. The map was of southeast Egypt and showed a giant pyramid located near the Nile a few miles south of Cairo. Beau yanked an illustration of a talisman off the wall and placed it on top of the map. The talisman was a gold medal with several Egyptian hieroglyphics carved into it.

"The Lost Talisman of Pharaoh Eczema," Beau said theatrically. "According to legend, the pharaoh was so beloved by his people, they presented him with a golden talisman. Unfortunately, the token of appreciation made the gods jealous. When the pharaoh grew old and became ill, he was afraid the gods would punish him unfairly in the Underworld. So at the time of Eczema's death, one thousand of his most devoted soldiers were killed, mummified, and buried with him in the pyramid so he wouldn't enter the Underworld alone. The gods were furious and denied the soldiers entrance to the Underworld, forcing them to roam the pyramid as the undead. Since they can't protect the pharaoh in the Underworld, the soldiers devotedly protect his remains in the pyramid."

"Wow," Charlotte said, and glanced at Conner. "That's unsettling."

"But wait, there's more!" Beau said. "The legend also states that Pharaoh Eczema's soul bestowed mythical powers on the talisman. Whoever wears it has complete control over the mummified soldiers in his pyramid. The pharaoh was buried with the talisman in a golden chamber deep in the Pyramid of Anesthesia. The chamber is surrounded by a maze, and the pharaoh's casket is patrolled by his most treasured and loyal guardian."

"Conner, that sounds *just* like the talisman you wanted to collect," Charlotte said. "Is it the same or is there more than one?"

The horrified gaze Conner sent his mother was the exact expression Beau sent him. Once again, Conner slapped his palm against his forehead, and Charlotte knew she had made a mistake by sharing their plan.

"*You're* after the talisman, too?" Beau asked.

"Um...kind of," Conner said. "I happen to dabble in archaeology as well. My mom and I are planning to find the talisman and donate it to...um...the Not-So-Natural History Museum in Cairo."

"Well, you can forget about it!" Beau yelled. "The talisman is mine! It's one of the reasons I went into archaeology! Emgee, open the door—let's kick these tomb raiders off the *Charlie Chaplin*! I should never have saved you in the jungle!"

"Easy, Beau," Emgee said. "Technically the talisman doesn't belong to either of you. It belongs to Pharaoh Itchy, or whatever his name is. Seems only fair to get you both to the pyramid and let you duke it out the old-fashioned way."

Beau nodded. "You're right, Aunt Emgee," he said. "We'll fight to the death!"

Emgee sighed. "No, Beau," she said. "I meant you'll have to *race* for it."

"That seems reasonable," Charlotte said. "We can even set a starting mark so it's completely fair."

Conner quickly pulled his mother aside. "Mom, stop agreeing! You know I need the talisman to recruit the mummies into our army!"

"If my son is going to become a warlord, he's going to come by it honestly! Besides, I am not letting you go inside that pyramid alone now that I know it's filled with zombie mummies!" Charlotte snapped. "How much longer until we reach the Pyramid of Anesthesia?"

"It'll take all night, but we'll get there by morning," Emgee said.

"Then it's settled," Charlotte said. "Tomorrow you can both go into the pyramid together, and whoever finds the talisman first can keep it."

Neither of the boys was happy about having to race for the talisman. Conner never pictured a scenario where the hero of his story would turn into his competition. He had created the Pyramid of Anesthesia, so hopefully it wouldn't be too hard to navigate it, but he had also written Beau to be the best archaeologist in the world. It wasn't going to be an easy race.

Emgee shifted the gears of the *Charlie Chaplin*, and the blimp sailed into the western sky.

"Anesthesia or bust!" the old woman said.

After a long evening of reminiscing, Emgee convinced Charlotte and Conner she had single-handedly put the *roaring* in the Roaring Twenties. While she sipped from a jug of homemade potato gin, she told them all about her five failed marriages, her many connections to organized crime, and her early days of performing on a burlesque circuit.

Even though Beau had found a reason to resent their guests, Emgee loved having an audience besides her grand-nephew.

Beau spent the whole evening looking over his map of the pyramid and the illustration of the talisman. He only glanced up to glare spitefully at his new opponent. Conner became so tired of the hateful looks, he moved his seat so his back faced the archaeologist.

At night, Emgee pulled out some guest cots and set them up for Charlotte and Conner to sleep on. She tied down the gears of the *Charlie Chaplin* so it would continue floating west while they slept, and then she and Beau retired to their rooms in the back of the gondola.

Spending the night on a blimp was anything but restful. The sudden bursts of elevation and unexpected turbulence made it very difficult for Conner and his mom to stay asleep. However, Charlotte was kept awake by much more than the bumpy ride. Something had been eating at her since she learned about Beau's parents, something she was desperate to get out.

"Conner, are you awake?" she asked.

"I haven't been able to sleep since that sudden dip over Persia," he said.

"Well, I just wanted to tell you how proud I am of you, honey," Charlotte said. "I'm really amazed by everything you've created, not just in 'The Adventures of Blimp Boy' but in all of your stories. Why have you never shared them with me before now?"

"I guess I just never wanted to bother you," he said. "I first started writing shortly after Dad died. You were always so busy with work and taking care of us, I never wanted to put one more thing on your plate."

Unknowingly, Conner had just answered a difficult question she had been meaning to ask him.

"I suppose that's why there aren't any mothers in your stories," Charlotte said. "Your writing represents so many facets of your life, and I spent so much time away from you, I can't expect any representation of me in your writing. You know, I think one of the reasons I'm so afraid you and your sister are missing out on your lives is because *I've* missed out on so much of your lives. I'm sorry there have been so many times you felt like you didn't have a mom. It's never the kind of mom I wanted to be—life just had other plans."

This was as heartbreaking for him to hear as it was for Charlotte to confess. "The Ziblings" was the first story that made Conner realize just how meaningful each character in his writing could be; he never thought the *lack* of a character could be so symbolic, too. But even though there were no mothers in his stories, it didn't mean Charlotte was missing from them. She didn't see the stories like Conner did.

"Mom, you've got it all wrong," Conner said. "You're in my stories a bunch, you just don't realize it. Auburn Sally is based on more people than just Goldilocks. There's a reason I made her hair the same color as yours. After Dad died, you sailed through all the hard times so bravely; it reminded me of a pirate sailing through a storm. You were the real inspiration behind 'Starboardia.' Jack and Goldilocks just helped me add some layers to it."

"Really?" Charlotte asked. "You're not just saying that?"

"You'd know if I was lying to you—you always do," Conner said. "That's not all, though! Every day when you went to work and took back-to-back shifts just so we could get by, I always thought you must have had superpowers to get through it. That's why I made Bolt's superhero suit the same color as your nursing scrubs. You might have been gone a lot, but you were still a superhero to me and Alex."

Charlotte was moved to tears. She leaned over Conner's cot and kissed him on the cheek.

"I love you so much, sweetheart," she said. "And from now on, I want to be the very first person you share your stories with."

"The next one'll go straight off the presses and into your hands," he said. "I promise."

Charlotte's heart gave a sigh of relief. Knowing she wasn't missing from her son's imagination felt like a weight had been lifted off her chest. And Conner rarely got to reassure his mom about anything, so he was happy he could put her mind at ease. They both finally drifted off to sleep as the blimp drifted over Arabia.

The following morning, Conner and Charlotte awoke as the sun rose and shined through the *Charlie Chaplin*'s round windows. It felt even hotter than it had in the jungle in India. When Conner looked out the window, he saw they were floating above an endless sandy desert. He could barely see the tip of a triangle peeking out on the horizon.

"The Pyramid of Anesthesia!" Conner shouted. "We're almost there!"

His excited declarations woke up Emgee and Beau. They hurried out of their rooms dressed in pajamas and joined Conner at the window. Emgee couldn't see until she strapped on her goggles and used them like prescription glasses.

"That's the pyramid, all right!" she said. "Personally, I would have built my own pyramid closer to a beach, but to each their own."

Less than an hour later, Emgee was piloting the *Charlie Chaplin* toward the sandy earth beside the pyramid. The landing alone was enough evidence for why blimps never became the transportation of the future as Emgee had predicted. The bottom of the gondola bumped across the sand over a dozen times before the blimp came to a stop. Each contact made the whole gondola rattle, and things toppled overboard.

Once they landed, the boys got ready for the race to the talisman. Beau fastened the straps of his aviator hat, laced his boots, and zipped up his leather jacket. Conner tied his sneakers, applied sunblock, and put his backpack over his shoulders. Conner tried offering Beau a friendly handshake before they started, but Beau wouldn't even look at him.

Outside the blimp, Emgee drew a line in the sand and made Conner and Beau stand behind it. The old woman raised a revolver in the air, careful not to aim it at the *Charlie Chaplin*.

"I want a good, clean race," Emgee said. "No cheating, no sabotage, and no swearing! May the best archaeologist win!"

"Good luck, honey!" Charlotte said. "Please watch where you're going—pyramids are dark and dusty."

Emgee fired the revolver and Beau and Conner charged toward the Pyramid of Anesthesia. The thick sand was almost impossible to run in. But even wearing tall boots and a leather jacket in the desert heat, Beau was much faster than Conner. Once Beau was in front of Conner, he purposely kicked the sand backward, aiming for Conner's eyes.

"Hey!" Conner said. "That's cheating!"

"Eat my dust!" Beau said.

The boys reached the base of the Pyramid of Anesthesia. Beau immediately ran up the north side like the pyramid was a wide stone staircase. Conner knew the entrance was on the south side of the pyramid, so he ran around it. Beau noticed Conner going in a different direction, so he followed him from higher ground. They arrived at the entrance on the south side of the pyramid at the same time.

"How did you know where the entrance was?" Beau asked him.

"Because I made it," Conner said truthfully in a sarcastic tone, so Beau was none the wiser.

The young archaeologist kicked the entrance open and a gust of sandy air almost knocked the boys down the pyramid. The entrance led to a long, dark, and dusty hall. The walls were hung with a row of unlit torches and were engraved with hieroglyphics from floor to ceiling. Cobwebs draped across the hall like torn curtains. Clearly there hadn't been another person in the pyramid for thousands of years.

Beau took a torch off the wall and pulled a matchbox out of his pocket. He struck a match using the zipper of his jacket and lit the torch. Conner removed the flashlight from his backpack and hit it against the wall until the batteries worked. The boys ran down the hall, venturing farther into the pyramid.

The hall was just the beginning of a multi-dimensional maze that zigzagged through the pyramid. As soon as the maze split into different directions, Beau purposefully chose the path opposite from Conner, hoping it would get him to the pharaoh's chamber faster. Conner just rolled his eyes and took the route he knew would get him there quickly.

After a mile of winding narrow passages, steep staircases, and sharp turns, Conner stepped into an enormous room at the very bottom of the pyramid. The walls were covered with layers and layers of tombs like novels stacked on a giant's bookshelf. The crypts contained the mummified corpses of the pharaoh's soldiers. The room marked the halfway point of the pyramid's maze, which continued on the other side.

Beau entered the room several moments after Conner. He was red-faced and winded. Obviously the archaeologist was having a rougher time navigating the maze than Conner was. Beau looked around in astonishment. He had never seen so many tombs in one place.

"What is *this*?" Beau asked.

"This is the pharaoh's army," Conner said.

Beau saw where the maze continued on the other side and dashed toward it, hoping to get a head start on Conner.

"No, Beau! Wait!" Conner yelled after him.

"Nice try, but I'm not falling for—"

Beau suddenly tripped on a rope that was so thin he couldn't see it. The rope snapped, and two enormous metal gongs fell from the ceiling and crashed to the floor on either side of him. The noise was deafening and the boys covered their ears before it damaged their eardrums.

"That's loud enough to wake the dead!" Beau said.

"That's the whole point!" Conner said.

All the crypts began shaking at once. One by one, the lids were pushed off and the pharaoh's mummified soldiers slowly crawled out of their tombs. They moaned and groaned in agony and crept toward Conner and Beau.

"Mummies!" Beau yelled. *"So the legend is true! It's all true!"*

Beau and Conner continued into the second half of the maze and the mummies chased after them. Once again, Beau took an alternative route from Conner on purpose.

Conner knew the second part of the maze even better than he knew the first. He had no hesitation whatsoever as he snaked through hall after hall, climbing higher and higher into the pyramid. Each level he reached became smaller and smaller the closer he got to the top of the pyramid. Soon he came to a pair of golden double doors with the hieroglyph of a phoenix carved into them.

"I did it!" Conner said proudly. "I made it to the pharaoh's chamber!"

His victory was cut short by a blood-chilling scream coming from the maze behind him. It was followed by a clamor of monstrous wails and growls. It sounded like the mummies had caught up with Beau.

"Help!" Beau screamed. *"Help me!"*

Conner was conflicted about what to do next. He was only a few short steps away from retrieving the talisman, the only thing he needed to complete his army and save his friends in the fairy-tale world. For a split second, Conner thought Beau deserved to be attacked by mummies for the way he had acted. However, Conner knew his mom would be upset if only one of them came back alive. So to avoid a potential guilt trip (and because it was the right thing to do), Conner turned around and went to save the archaeologist.

"Stupid conscience," Conner mumbled to himself. "It never knows when to quit."

He followed the screams through the maze as he carefully took note of the route to get back to the pharaoh's chamber. Conner found Beau in a corner of the maze surrounded by eight mummies. He was on the floor, and the mummies were viciously hitting and kicking him.

"Hey!" Conner said. "Toilet-paper heads! Over here!"

The mummies turned to Conner and crept toward him. He shined his flashlight directly in their eyes, temporarily blinding them. The mummies scattered like roaches, and Conner helped Beau to his feet.

"You saved my life!" Beau said in shock.

"I *gave* you life," Conner said under his breath.

"I wasn't expecting you to come back for me, especially after how I treated you," Beau said. "Thank you!"

"You can thank me later," Conner said. "I found the pharaoh's chambers. Follow me! There are a lot more mummies where these guys came from!"

Conner quickly retraced his steps through the maze to the highest point in the pyramid where the pharaoh's chamber was located. Beau was amazed by how effortlessly he was moving through the pyramid. Finally, the boys arrived at the golden doors with the phoenix, and Conner grabbed the handles to push them open.

"Wait," Beau said. "Remember, the pharaoh's chamber is patrolled by his most treasured and loyal guardian. It might take both of us to defeat it."

Conner let out a light laugh. "Yeah..." he said. "I wouldn't worry about that if I were you."

He pushed open the doors and the boys stepped into Pharaoh Eczema's chamber. Unlike the rest of the pyramid, the chamber was spotless. The walls were made of pure gold and the pharaoh's colorful casket rested on a platform in the center of the room. They knew they were at the top of the pyramid because the high ceiling rose to a peak above them. There was a small opening in the ceiling that allowed a ray of sunlight to shine directly on the casket.

Beau eyed the chamber nervously: Something was missing. "Where's the pharaoh's most treasured and loyal guardian?" he asked.

The boys heard high-pitched barking. Peeking around the casket on the floor was a small mummified dog.

Although it barked at Conner and Beau, it was clearly more frightened of them than they were of it.

"It's a *dog*?" Beau asked.

"I don't know anything more treasured and loyal than someone's dog," Conner said.

Conner held out his hand, and the dog slowly approached it and sniffed around it. There was something familiar about Conner, and the mummified dog became excited when he sensed it. He happily ran around Conner's feet and rolled on his back, allowing him to rub the wraps covering his belly.

"Good boy, Bones," Conner called. "Who's a nice three-thousand-year-old pup, huh?"

"You know the dog's name?" Beau asked him suspiciously.

"Um...yeah," Conner said. "I must have read it somewhere."

They heard stomping echo through the maze outside the chamber. Conner and Beau turned and saw hundreds and hundreds of mummies creeping toward them.

"We've got to get to the talisman!" Conner said. "Those mummies are about to take out millenniums' worth of pent-up aggression on us!"

The boys hustled to the casket and tried sliding the lid off. It was incredibly heavy and they had to use all their strength. Just as the mummies entered the chamber, Conner and Beau knocked the lid over and saw the golden talisman around the neck of the mummified pharaoh. It grossed him out to touch a dead body, but Conner pulled the talisman off the corpse and put it over his own neck.

"Knock it off!" Conner yelled at the approaching mummies.

Now that Conner had complete control over them, all the mummified soldiers froze and attentively put their hands at their sides. Beau looked at the talisman around Conner's neck and became very depressed. The young archaeologist had spent most of his life dreaming about the day he'd find it, only to see it in someone else's possession. He looked so pathetic, Conner couldn't help feeling sorry for him.

"Look, I only need the talisman for a little while," he said. "I'm going to use the mummies to help out some friends. When I'm done, you can have it."

Beau was overjoyed to hear this. "Really?" he asked.

"Totally," Conner said. "Besides, it won't be worth much where I'm from."

The archaeologist squinted at Conner. He had been trying to figure out how Conner knew so much about the pyramid and had finally come to the only probable conclusion he could think of.

"You're Pharaoh Eczema reincarnated, aren't you?" Beau asked. "That's how you knew where the entrance was, how you moved so quickly through the maze, and how you knew the name of his dog."

"It's way more complicated than that," Conner said. "I'm not sure you'd even believe me."

"Try me," Beau said. "I'm an archaeologist—I *live* for complication."

Conner sighed. After their race through the pyramid, he was too tired to come up with any more lies.

"Okay, fine," Conner said with a shrug. "But before I explain, let me ask you this: How familiar are you with classic fairy tales?"

Chapter Twenty-Five

"THE LIFE AND TIMES OF QUEEN TROLLBELLA"

Written and Directed by Trollbella

D r. Sharon Jackson had been the resident clinical psychologist at Saint Andrew's Children's Hospital for over two decades, and today she was facing the most difficult patients of her career. Four stubborn teenage girls sat across from her with their arms folded. They each wore the same hospital gown and the same defiant expression. Unbeknownst to the girls, their worried parents were watching them through the mirror on the wall.

"Hello, ladies," Dr. Jackson said. "My name is Dr. Sharon Jackson and I'm a psychologist here at Saint Andrew's. I've been asked to have a word with you. How are you all feeling today?"

"Don't answer any of her questions," Mindy told her fellow Book Huggers. "The less we say, the less they can use against us."

"I promise you, we are only trying to take care of you," Dr. Jackson said. "Do you remember why you were brought to the hospital?"

Cindy tilted her head in suspicion. "Were we *brought* to the hospital or were we *sent* to the hospital?" she asked.

"Well, you were *brought* to the hospital by an ambulance," Dr. Jackson said. "And it was *sent* here because all four of you were found unconscious on a sidewalk. Does that answer your question?"

The Book Huggers shared a look—their newest suspicion had been all but confirmed.

"Do *you* work for *them*?" Lindy asked.

"For who?" Dr. Jackson asked.

"The people who don't want us knowing what we know," Mindy said.

"*What* do you know?" Dr. Jackson asked. "And *who* doesn't want you knowing it?"

The Book Huggers could tell that the psychologist was

genuinely confused. Perhaps she wasn't as informed as they thought.

"Maybe it's best if we don't tell you," Lindy said. "They might lock you up next!"

"We've been here for three days—but they can't keep us in here forever!" Cindy said.

"We know our rights!" Mindy said.

Wendy leaped out of her seat and went to the door. She yanked on the handle with all her might, but the door didn't budge.

"Ms. Takahashi, if you'd like to leave, just *push* the door open," Dr. Jackson said. "No one is keeping you here against your will."

Wendy turned the door handle and pushed it open easily. She blushed and took her seat.

"Prisoners or not, we know that someone very high up doesn't want us spreading *the facts*," Cindy said. "That's the real reason we're here!"

"I'm glad you brought that up," Dr. Jackson said. "I think it would do us all some good if we go over the facts together and take a break from suspicions."

Dr. Jackson went down a list on her notepad, hoping it would comfort the girls if she put things into perspective.

"You were found unconscious—that's a fact," the psychologist listed. "Just like any young person found in your condition, you were brought to this hospital to be examined—that's also a fact. When you regained consciousness, you told the doctors that you had seen 'pirates appear out of thin air,' and that you had overheard a discussion about 'recruiting armies of fictional characters' and a 'threatened fairy-tale world.' "

"Yeah," Mindy said. "Because we *did!*"

"Why do you think we fainted in the first place?" Cindy asked.

"That aside, usually when patients awake from a trauma and describe such eccentric events, I'm asked to have a word with them to make sure there isn't any psychological damage," Dr. Jackson explained. "This is all standard procedure, and I assure you that no one *high up* has any control over you."

The Book Huggers slumped in their chairs. Given the circumstances, perhaps the psychologist had been brought in for legitimate reasons. Maybe it wasn't part of a big conspiracy against them like they thought.

"We're just so tired of being told we're wrong when we know we're right," Mindy said.

"It's very unlikely four different people would have the exact same hallucination at once," Cindy said.

"But no one will listen to us," Lindy said. "Every time we try to tell someone what we've uncovered, they either hang up, point to the door, or threaten restraining orders."

The Book Huggers were getting worked up. Dr. Jackson raised her hands to calm them down.

"Ladies, it's *my job* to listen," Dr. Jackson said. "Tell me what you saw, what you heard, and what you're worried about. I'll be honest about what I believe is real or exaggerated, but I'll also be open-minded."

The Book Huggers eyed one another apprehensively. Dr. Jackson was the first person to have shown interest willingly. She took vigorous notes as the teenagers explained the cause of their paranoia.

"It started in junior high," Mindy said. "Alex and Conner Bailey disappeared without a trace, and no one could give us a good reason why. We wanted to know the truth, but the more answers we looked for, the more questions we found."

"It seemed like there was something our school, our city, and possibly the government were keeping from us," Cindy said. "Finally, after a year of searching, we saw the twins in a restaurant called the Storybook Grill four days ago!"

"We heard them talking about 'recruiting armies of fictional characters' to save a 'fairy-tale world,'" Lindy said. "It confirmed all our suspicions that something much deeper was going on! That's when we snuck to their house, peered through the window, and saw the pirates and their ship appear out of thin air!"

To their surprise, Dr. Jackson was *relieved* to hear this. She set her notes aside and a big smile came to her face. She even gave a thumbs-up to the mirror, which the Book Huggers thought was very odd.

"Ladies, I have good news for you," the psychologist said. "I believe every word you just said."

The Book Huggers were shocked. They had never

heard those words come out of someone's mouth before. For a second, they thought Dr. Jackson—not the pirates at the twins' house—might be a hallucination.

"You believe us?" Cindy asked.

"Absolutely," Dr. Jackson said. "You aren't experiencing delusions or hallucinations—you're suffering from a simple *misunderstanding*. You see, the twins' mother and stepfather work at this hospital. As a surprise, they hired a group of entertainers to perform for the patients in a show. The pirates you saw at their house are just performers and the ship was probably a set piece."

"A set piece?" Lindy asked. *"But it appeared out of thin air!"*

"Haven't you ever seen a magician or a Broadway show?" Dr. Jackson said. "That's what good set pieces do—it's all part of an illusion."

The Book Huggers shook their heads and covered their ears. They didn't want to believe what the psychologist was telling them—it was all too simple!

"No!" Mindy said. "That can't be it! There has to be more to the story than that!"

"I understand your confusion," Dr. Jackson said. "I met the performers yesterday. Their costumes were so colorful and elaborate, had Mrs. Gordon not explained to me who they were, I might have been just as puzzled as you."

"But that doesn't explain the conversation we heard over dinner!" Cindy said. "Why would they say things like 'recruiting armies' to save 'a threatened fairy-tale world'? Those aren't words normal people use to describe a show!"

"I imagine they were using code words to keep the performance a secret," Dr. Jackson proposed. "I'm sure it took them a very long time to put it together, and they were being extra-cautious. This is a small town—people talk, and clearly people listen."

The Book Huggers had put so much time and effort into tracking down and exposing the Baileys—it couldn't have all been for a *performance*! They were intelligent girls; they should have spotted a misunderstanding from a mile away.

The teenagers rocked in their seats, trying to think of where they went wrong. Dr. Jackson glanced up at the clock.

"Actually, the performance is tonight," she said. "But if it's *that* unsettling to you, I would recommend sitting it out. Now that we know you aren't suffering any psychological damage, I recommend you all go home and get a good night's rest. Doctor's orders."

Once the psychologist prescribed the troubled Book Huggers some sleep, she escorted the girls back to their parents and headed to the hospital's multi-purpose room.

Thanks to the characters' hard work, Trollbella's thorough direction, and a little touch of Alex's magic, they had put together a performance for Saint Andrew's Children's Hospital in just under a day. The quality of it was questionable, but it was a performance nonetheless. The tedious and frantic task had created a much-needed union among the characters and taught them to work together—which was necessary if they planned on joining forces to defeat the Literary Army.

The pirates of the *Dolly Llama* and the Tin Woodman constructed a large stage with red velvet curtains at the far end of the multi-purpose room. The sailors set up the chairs and made sure every patient, their families, and all the hospital employees had a seat.

Cyborg soldiers were hung from the ceiling and their illuminated body parts were pointed toward the stage like lights. The Cyborg Queen herself converted into a large spotlight and was operated by Commander Newters. Instead of using the hospital's electricity, all the Cyborgs were hooked up to Bolt, who functioned like a human generator.

The other Ziblings were working behind the scenes. After Morph had assisted with costumes by turning into a sewing machine, the shape-shifter transformed into the set. Since Whipney had the most dexterity, she was put in charge of props. Blaze was assigned special effects, but it was the easiest job in the entire show since there was only one, at the very end.

Trollbella insisted the performance have programs so the audience would have something tangible to take away. Bob helped her design the exact flyer she had in mind, and one was laid on every seat. The programs read:

At around fifteen minutes to eight o'clock, the multi-purpose room began filling up with an eager audience. Doctors, nurses, and other hospital staff escorted the patients and their families to their seats. Some children were rolled in on wheelchairs or transported in their hospital beds. Although the children weren't feeling their best, they looked around the room keenly, curious about what was waiting for them on the other side of the curtain.

Alex and Bob were sitting together in the front row. Alex couldn't sit still and nervously shook her legs and bit her nails.

"Are you worried about the show?" Bob asked.

"Not the show," she said. "I'm worried about Conner and Mom. I was expecting them to be back by now."

Bob laughed. "You look just like your mother when she's worried about you and your brother," he said.

"Now that I know how it feels, I'm never going to keep her waiting again," Alex said. "I hope they're all right. It's not that I don't trust them, or that I think they need *me*, it's just... just..."

Alex couldn't think of the words to describe the feeling.

"You just *love* them, Alex," Bob said. "It's as simple as that."

To Alex's relief, just a few minutes before the performance started, Conner and Charlotte hurried into the multi-purpose room and found her and Bob at the front. They had come straight from "The Adventures of Blimp Boy" and Conner hadn't even had a chance to take off his backpack.

"Well?" Alex asked. "How did it go? Did you find the talisman?"

Conner and Charlotte exchanged a smile. Conner pulled the talisman out from under his shirt and showed his sister.

"Let's just say there's a blimp parked in the field next

to the hospital and there's a thousand mummified soldiers and one mummified dog in the commissary," Conner said.

"So it's done!" Alex said. "We've recruited all the soldiers we need to take on the Literary Army!"

The twins were so thankful the recruitment was finally over. They couldn't have done it without the help of their mom and stepdad, so they pulled Bob and Charlotte into a tight family hug. It may not have been the family vacation their mom was looking for, but the twins and their parents had accomplished something extraordinary together.

Bob noticed a foul scent lingering around Conner and Charlotte.

"What's that smell?" he asked.

"Mummies," Charlotte said. "I sprayed each of them with perfume and disinfectant, but *decay* isn't an easy odor to take off."

"Should we tell the others before or after the performance?" Conner asked.

"Let's wait," Alex said. "If they pull off the performance, we'll have two miracles to celebrate."

"Is it any good?" Conner asked.

Alex hesitated to answer. "Let's just say it probably won't be your *favorite* show," she said. "Trollbella took some *liberties*."

The lights dimmed and all the audience members sat in their seats. The Cyborgs illuminated the stage, and Commander Newters aimed the Cyborg Queen's spotlight at the center of the curtain. Trollbella stepped through the curtain and waved to the crowd. All the children gasped—they had never seen such a lifelike troll before. The troll queen went to the microphone stand and greeted the audience.

"Good evening, big room of small people," Trollbella said. "Welcome to tonight's performance. As you probably know, I am Queen Trollbella of the Troblin Kingdom. If you don't know, please ask the person beside you to slap you. I am known for many things in my kingdom: beauty, intelligence, charisma, elegance, *passion*—but I'm best known for bringing my nation together. Thanks to my brilliant leadership, what was once a territory of greedy trolls and obnoxious goblins is now a kingdom of respectable and sophisticated Troblins. Tonight you will see that transformation before your symmetrical human eyes in 'The Life and Times of Queen Trollbella'!"

Conner was already annoyed and it was just the introduction. The audience sat on the edge of their seats—they were loving it. Trollbella dragged the microphone stand to the side of the stage and snapped at Commander Newters to keep the spotlight on her.

The curtains opened to reveal a dismal set depicting the Troll and Goblin Territory. The Merry Men and the Lost Boys ran onstage in ridiculous costumes. The men were dressed in green and wore goblin ears over their own. The boys wore brown and headbands with horns. All of them looked very uncomfortable.

"We are the goblins!" the Merry Men announced.

"We are the trolls!" the Lost Boys said.

"The kingdoms of man have forced us to live with the trolls," the Merry Men said.

"The kingdom of fairies has forced us to live underground with the goblins," the Lost Boys said.

"None of us are pleased," they said together.

"OH THE AGONY!" Robin Hood said. *"SORRY, THAT WASN'T IN THE SCRIPT. I JUST THOUGHT THE SCENE COULD USE A LITTLE PIZZAZZ."*

The Merry Men and the Lost Boys were terrible performers. Many of them stood motionless with dead eyes and said their lines like robots. Others put way too much effort into their characters and pranced around the stage. Some of them were terrified to be in front of an audience; others enjoyed it too much. Despite their problematic stage presence, they were entertaining to watch. The children in the audience laughed at everything they said.

"WHY DON'T WE PUT ASIDE OUR DIFFERENCES AND FORM OUR OWN NATION?" Robin Hood said.

"Robin, you're skipping lines!" Tootles said.

"APOLOGIES!" Robin Hood said. "I AM THE GOBLIN KING AND I HATE TROLLS!"

"And I am the Troll King and I hate goblins," Tootles said. "How can we live together underground? *Now say it!*"

"WHY DON'T WE PUT ASIDE OUR DIFFERENCES AND FORM OUR OWN NATION?" Robin Hood asked.

"That is a good idea!" Tootles said. "We will form the Troll and Goblin Territory, start our own society, and prove we are not savage creatures!"

"Hooray," the men and boys said with very little enthusiasm.

Trollbella cleared her throat to get the audience's attention. "The trolls and goblins lived harmoniously in the underground territory for many years, until tragedy struck!" she narrated.

All the performers froze on the stage. They waited for something to happen, but nothing did.

"I said *until tragedy struck!*" Trollbella repeated. *"Braid girl, that's your cue!"*

"Sorry, I was texting!" Whipney called from backstage.

Using her hair, Whipney lowered onto the stage two pillows painted to look like rocks. The "rocks" gently touched both Robin Hood and Tootles on the head. The actors fell to the floor and acted out dramatic death scenes. Tootles's performance was much simpler than Robin Hood's, who convulsed around the stage for almost five minutes before he lay still.

"GOOD-BYE, CRUEL WORLD!" Robin Hood shouted. *"THAT WASN'T IN THE SCRIPT, EITHER! I BELIEVE IT'S CALLED AN ABBY LID!"*

Trollbella shot him a dirty look and then turned to the audience.

"Sometimes rocks fall and you die—that's just life," Trollbella said into the microphone. "With the Troll King and the Goblin King both gone, the territory needed a new ruler!"

Red suddenly rose from a trapdoor in the center of the stage. She was dressed similar to Trollbella, with horns and a brown dress. All the performers sang like an angelic chorus as she entered, but none of them could find the right note or harmonize.

"I am the Troll King's only daughter, Trollbella," Red said. "I will be your new queen and guide you to prosperity! And . . . and . . . *what's the rest of my line?*"

"My heart is so full!" Trollbella whispered.

"Yes, that's it," Red said. "And my heart is so full, I can't imagine needing anything else but the affection and gratitude of my people!"

Peter Pan suddenly flew across the stage wearing a large cardboard heart. It was completely unexpected, by both the audience and the other performers. The children pointed him out to one another, wondering how the boy was able to fly.

"Not yet, Peter!" Trollbella snipped, and continued the narration. "Although she thought her heart was full, the young queen soon realized something was missing. There was a void in her life that the trolls and goblins couldn't fill."

Jack stepped onstage dressed in jeans, sneakers, and a T-shirt.

"I'm the handsome Butterboy," Jack announced. "I'm the queen's soul mate. I just don't know it yet because I'm emotionally immature. *Sorry, Conner.*"

Conner was so embarrassed, he sank into his seat and covered his face with his backpack. Trollbella was sporting a wide grin—this was her favorite part of the show. Red struck a theatrical pose with her hands over her heart.

"Be still my heart, for I am in love!" Red announced.

"Now, Peter!" Trollbella whispered.

Peter soared out from backstage and flew in circles over the audience. The children laughed and clapped—they reached up and tried to touch him. Conner was irritated by how much they were enjoying the show.

"Hello, Butterboy!" Red said to Jack. "Would you like to be my king and rule the trolls and goblins with me? Oh, how happy we will be together!"

"Oh boy, that sounds wonderful!" Jack said. "How lucky I am to be loved by such a beautiful and brilliant troll queen. I will never find someone like her ever again—nope, not once, no how, no way, not going to happen! I want to be with Trollbella for all eternity!"

"I never said that!" Conner shouted from his seat. "She's making this up!"

Trollbella glared down at him from the stage. *"If you get to tell stories, so do I!"*

Jack and Red ran toward each other in slow motion across the stage. Suddenly, the lights began flickering melodramatically. Goldilocks stomped onto the stage dressed as a large yellow toad with big warts and a purple beanie. Of all the performers, she looked the least excited to be there.

"I am the terrible Bree Monster," Goldilocks announced. "My mission in life is to rid others of happiness. I must keep Butterboy away from Queen Trollbella so their powerful love does not inspire others. I will bewitch Butterboy with a curse so he thinks he has feelings for me, when in reality, I'm so hideous I can't be loved by anyone."

"Oh, come on!" Conner said. "This is just ludicrous!"

The audience booed as Goldilocks dragged Jack off the stage. Red lowered her head and pretended to cry.

"After Butterboy was taken from her, Trollbella became very sad," Trollbella narrated. "But luckily, the troll queen was so commonsensical, she bounced back quickly. She used her misfortune to create something positive!"

"If I can't have my Butterboy, I'll put all my energy into being queen!" Red said with a big smile. "I'll help the trolls and goblins improve their image by combining them into *the Troblins*! We'll turn our territory into a brand-new kingdom so the world will see how much we've changed!"

"The troll queen made the world a much better place for the trolls and goblins," Trollbella said. "Although it broke her heart to be away from Butterboy, the distance taught the queen a valuable lesson and a secret to success: When you can't have what you want, make the most out of what you have!"

A big sign hanging above the stage suddenly caught on fire. It burned THE END and the curtains closed.

Conner was thankful the show was over. "Well, that was probably the worst piece of theater in the history of—"

He was interrupted by thunderous applause coming from behind him. Conner turned around and saw every patient in the hospital clapping ecstatically and smiling from ear to ear. Trollbella's show might have been stupid and silly, but it was exactly what the audience needed. It gave the patients of Saint Andrew's Children's Hospital a night off from their troubles and an evening of mindless fun.

When the curtains opened again, Trollbella and her company reappeared and took a bow. The audience cheered loudly and the patients who could stand gave them a standing ovation. The performers could feel the patients' gratitude in the applause and they bowed again and again until the clapping stopped.

After the show, the characters came down off the stage and mingled with the audience. They took pictures, signed autographs, and did everything they could to make the patients feel special. The doctors and nurses appreciated how the performers "stayed in character" while visiting with the children, never suspecting the actors were actually who they claimed to be.

Dr. Jackson and Mr. and Mrs. Carmichael found Bob and Charlotte in the crowd and shook their hands.

"Thank you for such a *unique* performance," Mrs. Carmichael said.

"It wasn't Shakespeare," said Mr. Carmichael. "But on the bright side, *it wasn't Shakespeare*."

"I've never seen so many smiling faces in this hospital,"

Dr. Jackson said. "It was so kind of you to treat the children to a night of fun."

"It was our pleasure," Charlotte said. "It's amazing what a story can do."

It was getting late, and the doctors and nurses escorted the patients out of the multi-purpose room and back to their own rooms. Tootles was a little confused about where to go and wandered off with the other children. Luckily the twins spotted him before he went too far.

"I'll get him," Alex told Conner. "Actually, it's probably best if I do a lap around the hospital to make sure he isn't the only one who's wandered off. You should share your good news with the others!"

Alex followed Tootles out of the multi-purpose room. Conner waited until everyone had left but his parents, the characters from "Starboardia," "Galaxy Queen," and "The Ziblings," and his friends from the fairy-tale world. He stood on a chair and whistled to get the group's attention.

"Congratulations on a good show, everyone," Conner said. "Trollbella put together a really *creative* and *totally fictional* show. You should all be very proud of yourselves!"

"Fiction is a matter of opinion, Butterboy," Trollbella said, and winked at him.

Conner ignored her. "Now, I have some great news to share!" he said. "My mom and I went into my last story and recruited one thousand mummified soldiers into our army! We finally have enough people to face the literary villains and take back the fairy-tale world!"

The characters erupted into cheers and applause of their own. Their spirits were already high from the performance, but the news sent their spirits soaring. Jack, Goldilocks, and Red shared a celebratory hug.

"That's fantastic!" Red said. "I was getting so tired of that commissary!"

"Good job, my friend," Jack said, and patted Conner on the back.

"Well done, Conner," Goldilocks said. "We couldn't have done it without YOOOOOUU!"

Her words turned into a scream, and the room went silent. The color drained from her face and her mouth dropped open. Goldilocks looked to Jack and grabbed his hand.

"Goldie?" Jack asked. "What is it?"

"Jack, my water just broke," Goldilocks said. *"I'm going into labor!"*

All the characters glanced at one another in panic. This was such an anticipated moment, but no one was prepared for it. They were characters from children's stories—none of *them* knew how to deliver a baby!

"Quick! We need scissors, boiling water, and recycled paper!" Red shouted. "Or is that for papier-mâché?"

Trollbella covered her eyes. *"Keep it inside while I'm in the room!"* she said. *"I don't want to see a baby come out of you!"*

"CALL THE MIDWIFE AND WET NURSE!"

Robin Hood yelled. "BUT DON'T TELL THEM I SENT YOU!"

"Everyone calm down," Charlotte said. "I'm a nurse—I know what to do. Bob, make some calls and see if there's an ob-gyn close by. I'll take her to the operating room in the new wing of the hospital and get her prepped."

"Got it," Bob said.

"Isn't Bob a doctor?" Red asked. "Can't he help?"

"He's not that kind of doctor," Conner said.

"There are different *kinds* of doctors in the Other-world?" Red asked. "That just seems unnecessarily complicated to me."

Bob immediately got on his phone and Charlotte quickly retrieved a wheelchair. They were in a room filled with cutthroat pirates, advanced Cyborgs, and daring superheroes—but Charlotte was the one taking the situation by the horns. It was fun for Conner to watch his characters gawking at his mom. Just like he told her on the blimp, she was the true hero.

Charlotte gently sat Goldilocks in the wheelchair and pushed her down the hall. Jack held Goldilocks's hand as they traveled and Red followed them.

"You guys stay here!" Conner told his characters. "When Alex gets back, tell her where we are!"

"Good luck!" all the characters said together.

Conner ran down the hall and caught up with the others.

"Goldilocks, how's the pain?" Charlotte asked.

"Not terrible, actually," Goldilocks said. "The contractions aren't nearly as bad as I was expecting—NEVER MIND, THEY'RE BAD! THEY'RE REALLY, REALLY BAD!"

"Ouch, my hand!" Jack cried.

"Thank goodness you're in a children's hospital, Goldie!" Red said. "I can't imagine a better place in the world to have a baby! Good timing!"

"Red, babies aren't born in children's hospitals," Conner said. "They're usually delivered at standard hospitals."

"That makes absolutely no sense!" Red said. "This world is so backward!"

They traveled through Saint Andrew's to the operating room in the new wing of the hospital. Conner ran ahead and held the doors for the others to enter. When they went into the operating room, there were three people waiting inside—two of whom were the last people Conner was expecting to see.

"Bree? Emmerich?" he said in shock. "What are you doing here?"

His friends were standing with an old woman no one recognized. Conner could instantly tell that Bree and Emmerich weren't their normal selves. They both looked pale, exhausted, and frightened.

"Conner!" Bree said frantically. "I didn't know you would be here, too!"

"Bree, what are you guys doing here?" Conner asked. "Is something wrong?"

Bree burst into tears. "I'm so sorry," she cried. "I didn't want to bring him, but I had no choice."

The doors slammed shut and locked behind them. Conner, Charlotte, Jack, Goldilocks, and Red turned around and saw the Masked Man behind them. He had a crazed look in his eye and he raised a revolver toward them.

Tonight's surprises were just getting started.

Chapter Twenty-Six

ALEX ALONE

Alex found Tootles before he wandered into the Saint Andrew's ICU and escorted him back to the multi-purpose room. Alex completed a quick round of the hospital, and the Lost Boy appeared to be the only character who had strayed from the group.

Right before Alex rejoined the others in the multi-purpose room, she saw something out of the corner of her eye: A woman with horns was entering the women's restroom down the hall. Alex could have sworn Trollbella was with the others when she left, but she decided to inspect the bathroom just to be sure. Who else would have horns in a hospital?

Alex searched the women's restroom, but didn't find the troll queen anywhere.

"Trollbella?" Alex asked. "Was that you?"

Morina suddenly lunged out of a bathroom stall and blew a handful of magic dust directly into Alex's face. Alex was so startled she gasped, breathing the dust deeply into her lungs. She coughed like she was choking on poisonous gas, and her eyes watered like she had been hit with pepper spray.

"What...what have you done to me?" she cried.

"I've enhanced you," Morina said with a wicked smile.

Alex collapsed on the floor and tried to recuperate, but she couldn't catch her breath or stop crying. The witch stared down at Alex, like a vulture waiting for its prey to die.

"That's it," Morina said. "Let it sink in, let it course through your veins, let it *consume* you...."

The coughing and tears eventually subsided, but the irritation was replaced by even harsher symptoms. Alex was filled with more anger than she had ever felt in her entire life. She tried to fight the magic manipulating her emotions, but the struggle only infuriated her even more. Why was her life a constant battle? Why did she have to fight so hard? Why did *she* always have to save so many others?

To comfort herself, Alex thought of the people she

loved, but the dust wouldn't let Alex *feel* love. As visions of her friends and family flashed before her eyes, the spell convinced her that they all secretly hated her and wished she would disappear. She thought her brother resented her, that her mother was ashamed of her, that her grandmother had died disappointed in her, and that her father had died just as an excuse to abandon her.

Alex grabbed the sink and pulled herself to her feet. She looked into the mirror but didn't see her own reflection. Alex only saw the face of a complete failure. The dust altered not only her perception of the world, but also how she viewed herself. She saw a girl who didn't deserve affection, who was unworthy of success, and who was incapable of anything but making mistakes.

She wasn't going to save her friends, she wasn't going to defeat the Literary Army, and she wasn't going to save the fairy-tale world. It would fall apart like everything else in her life, and Alex had only herself to blame.

"Do you feel the anger boiling inside of you?" Morina asked. "Let it grow, let it shape you, let it blind you. . . . Let it *become* you."

The bathroom walls and floor started to shake and the lights flickered. Alex's eyes began to glow, and her hair rose above her head like flames in slow motion. She disappeared from her body and the magic dust transformed her into someone else entirely. . . .

CHAPTER TWENTY-SEVEN

CEMETERY OF THE UNDEAD

Conner was so stunned to see the Masked Man in the hospital, he lost his train of thought. He didn't stop to wonder what Bree and Emmerich were doing with the Masked Man, how they'd got there, or who the older woman with them was. All he could think about was getting his friends and his mom away from such a dangerous man.

"They said you were dead," Conner said.

"I've lived to seize another day," the Masked Man said. "Sorry to disappoint you."

Charlotte looked at the Masked Man like she was seeing a ghost. Despite his injuries and tattered clothes, he was the spitting image of her late husband. Alex and Conner had tried so carefully to keep his existence a secret from their mother, but the disturbing reality was right in front of her face.

"Mom, this man isn't Dad," Conner said. "It's his younger brother, Lloyd. He's a criminal from the fairy-tale world, don't believe a word he—"

"I know who he is, Conner," Charlotte said. "Your father told me all about him before you were born. I'm sorry you know about him. Your father never wanted you to find out you were related to such a horrible person."

"You're not the only person he's related to, Conner," Bree said. "Emmerich is the Masked Man's son—he's the child the Masked Man had with Bo Peep!"

The information was so unexpected, Conner felt like he had been slapped. He remembered the story Hagetta had told him and his sister about hiding Bo Peep's child from his father, but that was long before they discovered who the Masked Man really was. Conner had forgotten all about the child until this moment.

"I guess that makes us cousins," Emmerich said.

"This has turned into quite the family affair," the Masked Man said. "But I'm afraid it won't be remembered as a *pleasant* reunion."

"What do you want from us?" Conner said.

The Masked Man grunted. "*Teenagers,*" he sneered.

"You always think both worlds revolve around you. To be frank, dear nephew, you're quite useless to me."

"Then what do you want with Alex?" Conner asked.

"He's not here for your sister, either," Bree said. "He's come to the hospital to take your mom!"

"Me?" Charlotte said. "What could you possibly want with me?"

"I'm in need of an Otherworld nurse," the Masked Man said. "You see, the medical knowledge of the fairy-tale world isn't as advanced as it is here, and I'm in the market for a complicated procedure."

Goldilocks moaned as another contraction began.

"This woman is about to have a baby," Charlotte said. "Please, we need to get her to a doctor immediately."

"What a coincidence—I'm going to need a lift out of the hospital," the Masked Man said. "I thought I'd have to give the old woman here a bullet wound to do it, but the mother-to-be is even more convenient."

"You won't lay a finger on her!" Jack yelled.

Jack charged toward him, but the Masked Man fired his gun into the air and Jack froze.

"That was my only warning," the Masked Man said. "I will not *waste* another bullet—that goes for all of you."

Their captor was growing visibly impatient. His most recent scheme was so close to fruition, he could almost taste it. He paced around the room and gave his hostages more insight into what he had in store.

"This is what's going to happen," the Masked Man said.

"Charlotte is going to collect from this room whatever she needs to perform a *blood transfusion*. Then she, Emmerich, and myself are going to escort Goldilocks downstairs to the emergency room. We're going to tell the paramedics Goldilocks needs to be transferred to another medical facility, and as they load her into the ambulance, we're going to steal it. Then we're going to drive far away, where Charlotte will transfer my son's blood into my own veins, until there isn't a drop left in the boy."

His plan was so barbaric, it took Conner a moment to understand the reasoning behind it.

"If Emmerich is your son, that means there's magic in his blood," Conner thought aloud. "You want his blood to regain your powers. You're so obsessed with power, you're willing to kill your own son!"

"I'm willing to kill more if I have to," the Masked Man warned.

"I'm not draining your son's blood!" Charlotte said.

The Masked Man pointed his gun at Conner. "I'll find ways of convincing you," he said.

The tense silence was broken by another painful cry as Goldilocks's contractions increased.

"It's okay, Charlotte," Emmerich said. "I'm not scared— I'd rather he hurts me than anyone else. I'm sure it'll just feel like I'm falling asleep."

Charlotte would have sacrificed herself before harming a child, but Emmerich had given the nurse an idea. The Masked Man nudged her toward the supply cabinet and she collected syringes, gauze, bags, surgical tape, and other equipment. Charlotte put everything she needed for a blood transfusion into a large bag—and pocketed a little something extra.

"Now everyone else lie on the floor," the Masked Man ordered. "Emmerich, take those ACE bandages out of the cupboard and tie their hands and feet together. Make sure the knots are tight—I'll be checking before we leave."

With no alternative options in sight, Conner, Jack, Cornelia, Red, and Bree did as the Masked Man demanded. Emmerich tied their hands tightly behind their backs and their feet together. The Masked Man inspected his son's knots to make sure they'd last. Once he was satisfied, he tucked the revolver under his sling—making a point to show his hostages it was hidden but easily accessible if he needed it.

"Now let's go," he said.

Charlotte wheeled Goldilocks out of the room with the bag of supplies, and they headed for the emergency room. The Masked Man pushed Emmerich out the door, and they followed the women. The others left in the operating room struggled against the bandages with all their might, but they wouldn't budge.

"We have to do something!" Jack said desperately. "Goldilocks is about to give birth! Who knows what that madman might do to her!"

"Help us!" Cornelia yelled. *"Help us!"*

"Let me try," Red said. "No offense, but I'm an attractive young blonde—someone's more likely to answer me! HELP US! HELP US!"

"Guys, we're the only people in an empty hospital wing!" Conner said. "No one can hear us!"

"We have to stop him!" Bree said. "He's going to kill Emmerich if we don't!"

"You see, this is why I'm not close to my own relatives!" Red said. "Families are nuts! They give you life, then you're lucky if you survive them!"

Red's rant inadvertently reminded Conner of something in his bag—something they could use!

"Survival!" Conner said happily. "That's it!"

Charlotte had packed Swiss Army knives in the twins' backpacks before they left for "Starboardia." Thankfully, the Masked Man hadn't instructed Conner to take his backpack off before he was tied up. If he could just reach the knife inside it, he might be able to cut himself free.

Conner rolled onto his back and with his tied hands painfully reached up to the backpack's front pouch. Just when it felt like he was about to break his arms, he pried the zipper open with his fingertips.

"Bree, see if you can find the Swiss Army knife in my bag," Conner said.

They shuffled around the floor until they were back to back and Bree was able to remove the small knife from his backpack.

"I got it," Bree said, and unfolded it. "Stay still—I'm going to cut the bandages around your wrists."

She sawed the small blade against Conner's bandages until she cut through them. Once Conner's hands were free he removed the bandages around his feet and sliced them off the others. They helped one another to their feet and ran out of the operating room, but Cornelia stayed behind.

"Cornelia, are you coming?" Bree asked.

"I can't keep up," Cornelia said. "Go! Get to them before it's too late! I'll call Wanda and Frenda and let them know where we are!"

"Cornelia, go to the multi-purpose room," Conner said. "Find my sister and tell her what's happened—her name is Alex and she looks like me."

"I will," the old woman said. "Now hurry!"

Conner, Bree, Jack, and Red ran through the hospital as fast as they could. They followed the signs to the emergency room, pushed past the people waiting in the lobby, and ran out to the driveway where the ambulances were parked.

They arrived just in time to see two paramedics loading Goldilocks into the back of an ambulance. As soon as they shut the doors behind her, the ambulance screeched down the driveway, and the paramedics watched helplessly as the vehicle was stolen in plain sight. They ran inside the hospital to call the police. As the ambulance passed Conner and the others, they saw the Masked Man at the wheel and Charlotte and Emmerich sitting in the front beside him.

The driveway curved around the hospital like a horseshoe. If Conner ran straight ahead, he might be able to stop the ambulance—but with *what*? What did he have that could stop a speeding vehicle? As soon as he thought of the question, the answer hit him like a bolt of lightning hitting the Eiffel Tower.

"They're getting away!" Bree yelled.

"Oh no they're not!" Conner said. He ran across the driveway and retrieved the binder of short stories from his backpack. He flipped it open to the very last page and dived in front of the ambulance. Just before the vehicle ran him over, the beam of light hit the ambulance and it disappeared into his short story.

Jack and Red sighed with relief—they couldn't believe Conner had pulled it off. Bree had no clue what had just happened, but she was amazed by what she saw.

"Come on!" Conner said. "Follow me!"

With no time to lose, Conner jumped into the beam of light and his friends followed him inside.

Since he had opened the binder to the very last page, Conner was certain he had sent the ambulance into "The Adventures of Blimp Boy." He expected to see an Egyptian desert and the Pyramid of Anesthesia, but Conner didn't recognize the world around him at all. In fact, he had never seen the strange environment they had landed in, not even in his imagination.

They were standing on a tall knoll surrounded by rolling hills of dark soil. A full moon peeked through dark clouds above them, and a misty fog hung in the air. In the distance they saw a tall wrought-iron fence along the perimeter of an enormous and eerie cemetery. The fence guarded a sea of gothic tombstones, and through the fog beyond the graves, they could make out a forest of stone mausoleums.

The tombstones were so old they were cracked and covered in mildew and their engravings were virtually illegible. They were decorated in crucifixes and macabre statues of angels and the grim reaper. Even though the fog distorted the view, the cemetery seemed as endless as the deserts of Egypt. There wasn't a sign of life anywhere; there were no trees, grass, or flowers, only tombs for miles and miles around.

"Conner, were you in a bad mood when you wrote this story?" Red said.

"This isn't my story," Conner said. "I never wrote about anything like this."

Suddenly, they saw something moving across the graveyard. A red fox was prancing among the tombstones. The animal batted its eyes and twirled its tail flirtatiously, almost as if it were trying to lure them into the cemetery. Bree recognized the fox and rubbed her eyes to make sure she wasn't seeing things.

"Conner, where was that beam of light supposed to take us?" Bree asked.

"It should have transported us into one of my short stories," he explained. "We've been using a potion to travel into my writing, but I have no clue where it's taken us."

Bree gulped nervously. "I do," she said. "This is *my* short story—we're in 'Cemetery of the Undead'! I wrote it in the eighth grade!"

Conner tried to make sense of the situation. How could they be in one of Bree's stories?

"I got my stories from Mrs. Peters," Conner said. "She must have mixed your writing with mine when she gave them to me! It's been in the back of my binder the whole time! I didn't have a divider between them, so the Portal Potion must have seeped through my writing and into yours."

Traveling into his own stories had been a jarring experience for Conner, but at least he knew where he was going. He couldn't imagine how Bree felt after accidentally stumbling into a world from her imagination with no prior warning.

"Look over there!" Jack said, and pointed.

They saw tire tracks and followed them into the cemetery. The ambulance had crashed into the fence just beside a wide-open gate. They checked the vehicle, but it was empty. A moan came from somewhere in the graveyard and they ran toward it.

"Goldie!" Jack shouted. *"We're coming!"*

They found Goldilocks on the ground a few hundred feet inside the graveyard. She was leaning against a tombstone, with beads of sweat covering her forehead, and she was breathing deeply. Jack knelt beside her and held her hand.

"The Masked Man..." She panted. "I couldn't keep up, so they left me here.... He took Emmerich and Charlotte somewhere over there.... I didn't see which one they went inside...."

Goldilocks pointed to the mausoleums, but there were hundreds of them. Finding Emmerich and Charlotte among them would be like finding a needle in a haystack.

"Let's get you back to the hospital," Jack said. He tried to get Goldilocks to stand, but she wouldn't move.

"My contractions are too close together," Goldilocks said. "I can't stand! This baby is being born right here!"

Jack and the others exchanged fearful looks— Goldilocks needed help.

"You guys stay with Goldie," Conner told them. "I'm going to find Emmerich and my mom. As soon as I get them away from the Masked Man, I'll send my mom here to help."

"I'm coming with you," Bree said.

"You can't, it's too dangerous," Conner said.

"Conner, I know you're used to being the hero of your own stories, but this is mine," Bree said. "I know this cemetery like the back of my hand. Besides, we only have twenty minutes until midnight—we have to get everyone out of here before then!"

"What happens at midnight?" Red asked.

Bree looked frightened. "The characters come out," she said.

"What's wrong with you writers?" Red yelled. "If you wrote instruction manuals, we wouldn't have this problem!"

Goldilocks moaned again and squeezed Jack's hand. They didn't have much time before the baby arrived. Conner and Bree ran into the cemetery and searched through the mausoleums one by one.

The Masked Man had taken Emmerich and Charlotte deep into the cemetery and forced them inside a mausoleum with stained glass windows and a statue of a fallen angel on the roof. He and his son sat on the casket inside as Charlotte prepared the equipment for the blood transfusion. The Masked Man kept a watchful eye on the nurse and a steady grip on his revolver as she worked.

To keep up appearances, Charlotte drew blood from Emmerich and let it fill a small bag. Emmerich watched the blood drain from his body as if it were sand pouring out of his personal hourglass.

"If you see my mom, please tell her I love her." The little boy sniffled.

"You can tell her yourself—I promise," Charlotte whispered, and winked at the young boy.

Next, the nurse prepared the Masked Man's IV. She made it as unpleasant for him as possible. She forcefully straightened his broken arm and stuck him with the dullest needle she had.

"Easy!" he barked.

Charlotte pulled a small vial out of her pocket and filled a syringe with its clear liquid. She started injecting the solution into the Masked Man's IV but he became suspicious and stopped her.

"What is that?" the Masked Man snarled.

"It's just saline," Charlotte said. "It's to prevent infection."

"I don't want you putting anything inside my veins except the child's blood."

"I can't put his blood into your system until the area is sterilized," Charlotte said. "If you don't want me to do my job correctly, then there was no point in leaving the fairy-tale world."

The Masked Man glared at her, held his revolver a little tighter, and allowed her to proceed. Charlotte injected the solution into his arm and watched him closely. The Masked Man suddenly felt very tired. His eyelids became heavy and the small mausoleum started spinning around him—*he had been tricked*! Charlotte hadn't injected him with *saline* but with a *sedative*!

"YOU WENCH!" the Masked Man yelled, and raised his revolver.

Charlotte twisted his broken arm and the Masked Man shrieked in agony. He dropped the gun and scrambled to the floor to retrieve it. Charlotte threw the IV pole at the stained glass window and it shattered. She and Emmerich quickly crawled through it just as the Masked Man got his gun. He shot at them, but the sedative made him a lousy shot and he missed. The bullet ricocheted off the mausoleum's stone wall and hit the side of his right leg. He screamed in pain.

Conner and Bree were searching the mausoleums nearby when they heard the sounds of broken glass, gunfire, and screaming.

"Mom!" Conner gasped.

"Emmerich!" Bree said.

They ran toward the sounds, praying nothing had happened to either of them. A dark and foggy graveyard was scary by itself, but knowing a dangerous man was lurking nearby with a gun made Conner and Bree feel like they were in a real-life horror movie. They jumped at every statue they saw, afraid it was the Masked Man looming through the fog. Luckily, they ran into Charlotte first.

"Mom!" Conner said. "Thank God you're okay! Where's Emmerich?"

Charlotte's eyes darted around the cemetery. "He was right beside me a moment ago," she said. "We escaped from your uncle but got separated in the fog."

Another scream echoed through the cemetery, but this time it was coming from Goldilocks.

"Mom, you have to go and help her," Conner said. "Bree and I will find Emmerich."

From the look in her eyes, Conner knew leaving him and Bree alone was the last thing his mother wanted to do.

"We'll be fine," Conner said. "Right now, Goldilocks needs you!"

Charlotte was torn between her obligations as a mother and her duties as a nurse. But she had to remind herself she wasn't the mother of a normal child—she knew Conner was more than capable of taking care of himself. He had proven it time and time again.

"I love you, sweetheart," Charlotte said. "Be safe."

She hugged her son and kissed him on the cheek. Then Charlotte followed Goldilocks's moans to the front of the graveyard and prepared to deliver the child.

Conner and Bree hurried in the opposite direction, looking for their friend.

"Emmerich!" Bree whispered. *"Where are you?"*

They found Emmerich crouching behind a tombstone. He was trembling and looking around with large, frightened eyes. The fog was the thickest in this part of the cemetery, and he hadn't been able to tell who Bree and Conner were until they were just a few feet away from him.

"There you are!" Bree said.

"Conner! Bree!" Emmerich cried with relief. "Where's Charlotte?"

"She went back to help Goldilocks," Conner said. "Come on, let's get you out of here."

"NOT SO FAST!" shouted a voice behind them.

Conner and Bree slowly turned around and saw the Masked Man creeping toward them. He was in the worst shape of his life: His limp was much worse now that he had a sprained ankle *and* a bullet wound on the same leg. His clothes were covered in blood, and the sedative had made the bags under his eyes droopier than usual. He was fighting the medication off with all his remaining strength.

"The boy is coming with me!" the Masked Man yelled.

Conner stood between his uncle and Emmerich.

"No one is going anywhere with you!" he said.

"Stupid boy!" the Masked Man said. "Get out of my way or I'll shoot!"

"Go ahead!" Conner said. "You'll never be satisfied no matter how many people you kill and no matter how powerful you become! And if I can't stop you, my sister will! Good luck facing her once she finds out you killed me!"

The Masked Man ignored Conner and pointed his gun at his nephew's head. *"Give my regards to your father."*

Just as he was about to press his finger against the trigger, they were all startled by a loud scraping sound. The lids of three stone caskets nearby were pushed open, and the corpses inside suddenly stood up from their graves.

"What's going on?" Conner whispered to Bree.

She glanced down at her watch. "It's midnight," she said. "All the bodies in the cemetery come back to life for a few minutes every night to stretch their legs and visit with each other. It's supposed to be a morbid representation of what break time is like in a public high school!"

All three corpses were women, and although in Bree's story they were less decomposed than they would have been in real life, each had obviously been dead for a long while. Their skin was so pale, it was a shade of blue, there were dark circles under their eyes, and parts of their bones stuck out from their skin.

The women wore very specific clothing from different eras in history. The first woman wore early-fifteenth-century armor, and her skin was partially burned. The second woman wore a dress with wide sleeves, a necklace with the letter *B*, and a headband with a long veil. The third woman wore an enormous ball gown and lots of jewelry and had a towering white wig. The two women in dresses also had stitches around their necks, as if their heads had been detached from their bodies and then sewn back on.

"Who are they?" Conner asked. "Why do they look so familiar?"

"This area of the cemetery is called 'Wronged Women Row,'" Bree said. "These are the women I thought had unfair deaths in history. That's Joan of Arc, Anne Boleyn, and Marie-Antoinette."

The historical figures stretched and yawned as they came back to life. It was like they were waking from a long nap rather than coming back from the dead.

"I just adore our nightly stretches," Joan of Arc said. "Don't you, Anne?"

"It certainly gives us something to *live* for." Anne Boleyn giggled.

"You know what I always say," Marie-Antoinette said. "Death is what you make of it. Just like everything else, it's all in the *execution*!"

The corpses laughed wildly among themselves. Apparently nothing tickled them more than jokes about their mortality. The women turned to a fourth casket in their row whose occupant hadn't risen yet.

"It looks like Bo is sleeping in again," Joan of Arc said.

"She'd better wake up and stretch, otherwise she'll be very stiff tomorrow," Anne Boleyn said.

"Oh, Bo, darling?" Marie-Antoinette called to the casket. "It's midnight, dear! Come out and join us!"

The lid on the casket slid open and a fourth corpse stood up in her grave. She wore a dainty dress and a bonnet and held a staff. She must have been the most recently departed, because she was far less decomposed than the other corpses were.

"Sorry, girls, I was counting sheep," the woman said. "It helps me pass the time between stretches."

"What's your count up to now?" Joan of Arc asked.

"Twenty-eight million, nine hundred and seventy-four thousand, eight hundred and sixty-three," the woman said.

Conner recognized the woman immediately. It caught him completely off guard because he thought he'd never see her again—even in a fictional story.

"That's Bo Peep!" Conner whispered to Bree. "You put *her* in 'Cemetery of the Undead'?"

"This must be my second draft," Bree said. "I was upset by how Bo Peep died, so I added her to the story."

As strange as it was to see their deceased acquaintance, it was nothing compared to how Emmerich felt at the sight of his birth mother. He had hundreds of questions he wanted to ask, but he was too afraid to speak.

Seeing her corpse come to life made the Masked Man feel like he had stepped into a nightmare. He couldn't tell if she was really there or if she was just a hallucination brought on by the sedative.

"Bo Peep?" he asked in shock.

All the undead women turned to the sound of his voice. It was the first time they realized their row had visitors.

Bo Peep was enraged to see him. *"Lloyd!"* she yelled.

The other corpses gasped.

"Is this the man you were telling us about, Bo?" Joan of Arc asked.

"Yes, he is," Bo Peep said. "He's the one who *used* me, who *tricked* me, and who *broke my heart*! He's the whole reason I'm in this cemetery! I'd still be alive if it weren't for him!"

"And look—he's not alone," Anne Boleyn pointed out. "There are three young people with him."

"I know them, too," Bo Peep said. "What are the three of you doing with a man like *him*?"

"I promise, it's not by choice!" Conner said. "He's holding us hostage!"

Hearing this angered Bo Peep to no end. She stepped out of her casket and charged toward the Masked Man. He had never been so terrified in his entire life. He aimed his revolver at her, but it didn't stop her from approaching him.

"Don't come any closer or I'll shoot!" he warned her.

"You can't hurt me anymore," Bo Peep said.

She reached toward him with her cold dead hands, and the Masked Man shot at her—using the third and final bullet in the revolver. Bo Peep looked down at the bullet hole in her torso, but it only infuriated her even more.

"Kill me once, shame on you. Kill me twice, shame on *me*!" she said.

"Get away!" the Masked Man said. "I'm warning you!"

"Your threats are as empty as your soul!" Bo Peep said.

The Masked Man hobbled away from her as quickly as his injured leg would allow. He wasn't paying attention to where he was going, though, and fell right into an empty grave with an unmarked tombstone. He tried to climb out of it, but dozens of decaying hands suddenly stuck up from the dirt below and grabbed hold of him. They pulled on his legs, his arms, and his clothes and pulled him into the ground with them.

"UNHAND ME AT ONCE, YOU DEMONS!" the Masked Man yelled.

He screamed and tried to free himself, but there were too many for him to fight. The more he struggled, the more hands appeared. Even after he was completely underground, his screaming could still be heard aboveground, but the sound of his voice became fainter and fainter as he was pulled deeper and deeper into the earth.

When the noise had finally disappeared completely, an engraving appeared on the tombstone: HERE LIES LLOYD BAILEY—BELOVED BY NONE.

As much as Conner hated the Masked Man, it was still a terrifying thing to witness. He wondered if his uncle was really gone for good, but when he turned to Bree, he saw she looked just as frazzled as he did. Bree's story of the undead had taken on a life of its own.

"Well, that's all the excitement I can handle for one night," Joan of Arc said.

"Time to go back to sleep," Anne Boleyn said with a yawn.

"See you tomorrow night, girls," Marie-Antoinette said. "Same time, same place—for all eternity."

The women lay back down in their graves. They pulled the lids over their caskets, tucking themselves in for a good night's rest. Bo Peep wandered back to her casket, but Bree stopped her before she stepped inside it.

"Bo?" Bree said. "I'm not sure this is the right thing to do, but if I were you I would want to know. It's so difficult to say—I guess I'll just spit it out: Emmerich is your son."

Bo Peep stared at the young boy in bewilderment. If she still had a pulse, it would have been racing. If she still needed to breathe, she would have been breathless.

"You're my *son*?" she asked.

"Yes," Emmerich said.

"Hagetta said she would find you a good home. Did she?"

"She did," he said. "I have a mother—an adoptive mother, who loves me very much."

"That's good to hear," Bo Peep said. "Knowing that, I might finally be able to rest instead of counting sheep."

Emmerich eyed Lloyd's grave. "Is my father ever coming back?" he said.

"Not from where he's going," Bo Peep said. "He'll never harm you or anyone else ever again."

Bo Peep removed a small necklace from around her neck and placed it in her son's hand. Bree and Emmerich remembered her showing it to them while they traveled down the secret path with the royals the year before. It had a thin chain and a small stone heart with a crack across it.

"Here, something to remember me by," Bo Peep said. "You seem like a kind child. I'm sorry I didn't raise you myself, but you were better off with your adoptive mother. I was too young and foolish to be a mother. You didn't deserve to inherit my mistakes."

"I understand," he said.

"Good night, Emmerich," she said. "I hope we see each other in our dreams."

Bo Peep lay back in her casket and pulled the lid over her body. Bree put her arm around Emmerich as he watched her go. Once she was gone, he looked down at the necklace and held it tightly in his hand.

"Speaking of mothers," Conner said, "we should probably find my mom and the others."

Conner, Bree, and Emmerich hurried to the front of the cemetery to regroup with their friends. The closer they got, the louder and clearer the others' voices became.

"*Push, Goldilocks!*" they heard Charlotte shout. "*Push! Push! Push!*"

"*ERRRRRRRR!*" Goldilocks grunted.

"*You can do it, Goldie!*" Jack encouraged his wife. "*You're almost there!*"

"*I can see the head!*" Charlotte declared. "*Just one more push!*"

"OH MY GOD, WHAT IS THAT?" Red screamed loudest of all. "I AM NEVER HAVING CHILDREN!"

Soon the sounds of a crying infant echoed through the cemetery. By the time Conner, Bree, and Emmerich found the others, Goldilocks and Jack were the proud parents of a healthy and beautiful baby boy. There wasn't a dry eye in the bunch.

Charlotte cleaned the baby off and wrapped him in towels she found in the ambulance. He had his mother's golden curls, his father's strong chin, and his aunt Red's doe-eyed expression.

"Jack, we're parents," Goldilocks said tearfully. "We have a son!"

"We're an official family," Jack said affectionately.

"We did it!" Red said, and burst into happy tears. *"I only wish Charlie was here to see it!"*

Although she had had nothing to do with creating the child, she hugged Jack and Goldilocks as if she were a new parent, too.

"What are you going to name him?" Conner asked.

"Hero," Goldilocks said confidently. "That way, it won't matter where he's from, what he becomes, or who his parents are—he'll always be the hero of his own story."

CHAPTER TWENTY-EIGHT

A SITUATION

As soon as they stepped through the beam of light and returned to the Otherworld, Charlotte and Jack took Goldilocks and Hero to the Saint Andrew's emergency room to be examined by a doctor. Conner, Bree, Emmerich, and Red went straight to the multi-purpose room to tell the others what had happened in the "Cemetery of the Undead" and to share the good news of Jack and Goldilocks's son.

Conner figured Cornelia must have spread the word about the Masked Man, because everyone in the multi-purpose room had a long, somber face and seemed worried sick. Even the Blissworm's smile wasn't as pronounced as it usually was. Bree and Emmerich were a little overwhelmed by all the people they didn't know but could have sworn they recognized.

"Conner!" Bob shouted. "Are you all right? Where's your mother?"

"Everything is fine, we're all safe," Conner said. "Mom is in the emergency room with Jack and Goldilocks. They have a son and they named him Hero! They're just getting checked out to make sure everything is okay."

"And what about that horrible man?" Cornelia asked.

"The Masked Man is gone," Conner said. "And this time, he's not coming back."

The news wasn't as comforting as Conner thought it would be. In fact, the expressions of the characters around the room didn't change. They didn't even seem excited about the new baby.

"Guys, what's wrong?" he asked. "You all look like someone died."

The characters parted and Conner realized they were gathered around the Tin Woodman. He sat in a chair beside Blubo, the small flying monkey. The monkey was distraught and his eyes were puffy from crying.

"Blubo?" Conner asked. "What are you doing here? Why aren't you in the fairy-tale world with the others?"

"We wanted to share the good news about completing our army with the others back in the mine," the Tin

Woodman said. "We traveled through the emerald story-book but when we arrived, they were all gone. *Everyone in the mine had been turned into stone!* Blubo was the only one who wasn't affected."

Conner shook his head as if he were trying to clear out the words he didn't want to hear.

"What?" he said. "You mean the royal families, the animals, the citizens, Hagetta, the Tradesman—"

"THEY WERE ALL STATUES!" Robin Hood said. "STILL AS ROCK AND PALE AS BONE."

"Oh no. *Granny.*" Red gasped. "What happened to them?"

"Right after you left the mine, we were attacked by a horrible monster." Blubo sniffled. "I was so afraid, I hid and covered my eyes. I never even got a good look at it."

Conner had an idea of what had happened. "The creature that turned the Fairy Council into stone must have found a way into the mine," he said.

He walked in a circle around the room, wondering what to do next. Apparently he had left one crisis only to stumble into another. He looked for his sister but didn't see her.

"Has anyone seen Alex?" Conner asked.

"She hasn't been here since I arrived," Cornelia said.

"I'll check to see if she's in the bathroom," Red said.

Red left the room and sprinted down the hall. As soon as she opened the door of the women's restroom she let out a bloodcurdling scream.

"Conner!" Red yelled. *"Come quick! You need to see this right away!"*

He was already headed toward her before she finished the sentence. As Conner dashed down the hall, all the characters followed him. Whatever Red had found was so bad, she hadn't even needed to step inside the bathroom to see it. The queen just held the door open and stared inside in total shock.

Conner arrived at her side and peered into the bathroom—but there wasn't a bathroom to see. He saw the night sky and other buildings outside. He looked up and saw into an empty office above; he looked down and saw into a deserted basement below. There was drywall, sparking electrical wires, and broken water faucets—it looked like an explosion had gone off.

Even though there was no evidence that Alex had caused it or that she had even been present for it, Conner knew in the pit of his stomach that it had something to do with his sister.

"Alex . . ." Conner said. *"What's happened to you?"*

President of the United States Katherine Walker was sitting in the Oval Office of the West Wing with two foreign ambassadors.

"Gentlemen," President Walker said, "I understand it's difficult for the prime minister and the sultan to agree on a location, but I'm not going to sit here day after day while innocent people are suffering because of their negligence. If we can't find a way to resolve this matter in the next forty-eight hours, I will put troops on the ground."

The meeting had been a major priority on the president's schedule and was booked weeks in advance. As far as she was concerned, no other matter was more important, and her entire afternoon had been cleared for the discussion. So it was surprising when the door of the Oval Office swung open and her Chief of Staff interrupted.

"Madam President," the Chief of Staff said. "I'm sorry for the interruption, but you're needed in the Situation Room immediately."

"What's wrong?" President Walker asked.

"It's best if you see it for yourself," the Chief of Staff said. "There's a *situation* in New York City."

"Terrorism?"

"No, ma'am," he said with difficulty. "Our most educated analysis, with all means of science and technology in mind, is that it's *magic....*"

ACKNOWLEDGMENTS

I'd like to thank Rob Weisbach, Alla Plotkin, Rachel Karten, Derek Kroeger, Heather Manzutto, Marcus Colen, Jerry Maybrook, and the amazing Brandon Dorman. Also, I couldn't have written this book without the support of Alvina Ling, Bethany Strout, Melanie Chang, Nikki Garcia, Megan Tingley, Andrew Smith, Kristin Dulaney, Svetlana Keselman, and everyone at Little, Brown. And, of course, all my friends and family! Thanks for being mine!

TURN THE PAGE FOR A SNEAK PEEK OF THE EPIC
CONCLUSION TO THE LAND OF STORIES SERIES!

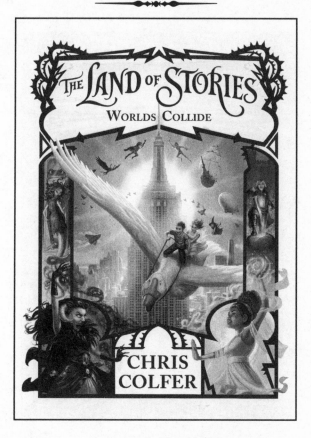

AVAILABLE JULY 2017

CHAPTER ONE

DISTRESS CALL FROM THE PUBLIC LIBRARY

It was just a typical afternoon at the main branch of the New York Public Library. The marble halls of the world-famous structure echoed with the footsteps of obnoxious tourists, restless college students, and noisy groups of elementary school students on field trips. Tour guides shared little-known facts about the library's expansive history and refrained from rolling their eyes at questions about the movies that had been filmed there. Librarians gave directions to the renowned reading rooms on the upper floors and reminded the guests that library books weren't allowed in the bathrooms.

There was absolutely nothing to suggest that anything strange or peculiar might occur later that evening, but strange and peculiar events rarely give any warning before they happen.

Security guard Rudy Lewis began his four PM to midnight shift by patrolling the library's entrance on Fifth Avenue. He yelled at teenagers for climbing the iconic lion statues that flanked the library's sprawling front steps. He kindly asked the homeless people sleeping beside the fountains to continue their naps at the shelter down the street, and once they obliged, he went *back* to the statues to yell at a new gang of teenagers for climbing them. Once the library closed and was cleared out, Rudy spent the rest of his shift patrolling the library's interior.

For hours and hours Rudy walked up and down the vacant halls of the four-level structure, inspecting its various forums, galleries, studies, and stairwells. Five minutes before the end of his shift, he was positive there wasn't another soul in the library and was eager to hand his duties off to the next security guard. But as he made his final inspection of the third floor, Rudy discovered he was mistaken.

At the end of a long, dark hallway, the security guard found a young woman standing alone. She wore a sparkling white dress and had strawberry-blonde hair, and her head was bowed as if she had fallen asleep standing up. At first, the sight of the woman startled Rudy. He had walked past this part of the library a dozen times and hadn't seen anyone before now. It was like the young woman had appeared out of thin air.

"Excuse me," he said. "What are you doing?"

The young woman didn't respond.

"Hey, I'm talking to you," Rudy said.

The angry security guard shined his flashlight on the young woman to get her attention, but she didn't move. Once she was illuminated, Rudy could see that she was trembling and her skin was as pale as a ghost. For a split second, he worried that she *was* a ghost. His coworkers had always warned him that the library was haunted, but until now, he had no reason to believe them.

"The library's closed." Rudy's voice cracked as he spoke. "Unless you're an employee, you're trespassing on city property."

Still, the young woman never looked up or said a word. Her silence was making Rudy paranoid. The longer he stood in her presence, the creepier the young woman became. The fate of every security guard in every horror film flashed before Rudy's eyes, but he mustered the courage to approach the strange woman.

"I'm gonna call the police if you don't say something!"

Suddenly, the young woman gasped and jerked her head up, causing Rudy to jump. She frantically looked around in a panic as if waking from a bad dream.

"*Where am I?*" she panted.

"You're at the library," Rudy said, but it only confused her more.

"The library? *Which* library?"

"The New York Public Library at Fifth Avenue and East Forty-First Street," Rudy said.

"Oh no," the young woman cried. "You have to get out of here! Something terrible is about to happen!"

"What are you talking about? How did you even get in here?"

"I don't know what she has planned, but you've got to go before she makes me hurt you!" she pleaded. *"Please, you have to listen to me! I can't control it!"*

Tears spilled out of her blue eyes and rolled down her face.

"Who are you talking about?" Rudy asked. "No one is in here but me and you."

"The witch who cursed me! She put me under some kind of spell that makes me do things—awful things!"

"Lady, you're clearly on a lot of drugs," Rudy said. "I'm taking you outside and calling the cops."

"You have to get my brother! He's the only one who can help! His name is Conner Bailey—he should be at Saint Andrew's Children's Hospital in Willow Crest—"

"Yeah, yeah, yeah," Rudy said and grabbed her arm. "This city is full of places that help people like you, but you can't stay here."

The security guard tried to escort her to the exit, but the young woman wouldn't budge. He pulled on her arm with all his might, but she stayed exactly where she was, as if she was glued to the floor.

"It's too late!" the young woman said. "The spell—I feel it coming! *Please, you have to run!*"

To the security guard's horror, the young woman's eyes rolled back and began to glow. Her hair rose above her head and floated in the air like a slow flickering fire. In all his years in security, Rudy had never seen anything like this before.

"What the heck is happening to you?"

The young woman placed a palm on his chest, and a bright blast erupted from her hand, knocking him all the way down the hall. As Rudy lay on the floor, his whole body tingled as if he had just been electrocuted. His vision was blurry and fading fast. With all his remaining strength, and the few moments of consciousness he had left, Rudy reached for his radio and held it against his mouth.

"Police…" he wheezed. *"We need police at the library…NOW!"*

Within minutes, Fifth Avenue was illuminated in red and blue lights as two police cars sped toward the New York Public Library. A policeman emerged from the first vehicle and a policewoman from the second. The officers hurried up the front steps with their guns raised.

"I just got the call. What's the situation?" the police-woman asked.

"We don't know," said the policeman. "A distress call came from somewhere inside the library. Approach with caution."

"Oh my God." The policewoman gasped. *"Look!"*

The officer pointed to the library's entrance as the large doors slowly opened on their own. A moment later the young woman in the white dress levitated through the doorway and landed at the top of the library's front steps. Even in New York City, the police weren't accustomed to seeing someone with glowing eyes and floating hair fly out of a building. Once the initial shock faded, the officers knelt behind a lion statue and aimed their weapons at her.

"Hands up!" the policeman ordered.

The young woman didn't follow his instructions. Instead, she pointed at the statues and two powerful bolts of lightning struck the lions. The police dove to the ground to avoid getting hit.

"What was that?" the policeman asked.

"Lightning!" said the policewoman. "But I don't understand. There aren't any clouds in the sky!"

Once the officers helped each other to their feet, they jerked their heads toward a strange cracking noise coming from the statues. They watched in astonishment as the stone lions stood from their perches, leaped into the air, and landed on the steps in front of the young woman, blocking the officers from coming any closer. The statues roared so loudly they set off all the car alarms within the city block.

"Holy crap," the policeman said. *"The statues are alive! How is this possible?"*

The policewoman clicked the radio on her shoulder.

"Officer Sanchez to Dispatch," she said. "The library is under attack, I repeat, the library is under attack! We need all available units to join us immediately!"

"Copy, Officer Sanchez," a voice responded over the radio. "All available units have been notified. Are you able to identify who or what is behind the attack?"

Still in disbelief, the policewoman hesitated to respond.

"It's *magic*," she said breathlessly. *"The library is being attacked by magic!"*

Acknowledgments

I'd like to thank my mom, my stepdad, Goldie, Jack, Red, Froggy, M.G., and especially Mrs. Peters. Also, a big thank you to my sister, Alex. I wouldn't have survived these stories without you!

Rosary Chicken

Bolt

Bones

The Dolly L!

Isle of
Skulls

Lollipopigust

Polycrab

Blissworm

Eiffel Tower

In Memory of John E. Holing, Capt. US Army

In 1968, America was a wounded nation. The wounds were moral ones...
— Thurston Clarke

SAIGON – Jan. 30 **North Vietnam Launches Tet Offensive**

MAI LAI – Mar. 16 **Vietnamese Say G.I.'s Massacred Civilians**

MEMPHIS – Apr. 4 **Martin Luther King Slain by Sniper**

LOS ANGELES – Jun. 5 **Bobby Kennedy Gunned Down**

WASHINGTON – Nov. 5 **Richard Nixon Elected President**

1

        Sparks from the campfire mixed with stars that salted the night sky. The burning sticks of dead sagebrush and greasewood blazed in the middle of a flat, scrubby playa in a lonesome corner of southeast Oregon. I sat cross-legged and shirtless as close to the flames as I could take. Sweat poured down my face and my heart beat as feverishly as a drum solo.

A coal-black bird circled overhead, its knowing head cocked, its yellow eyes piercing. I had tried to flee it by speeding into the night on my motorcycle, but the bird found me. Just as it had the first time I saw it when I was crawling through elephant grass, my M16 clutched in one hand, my lieutenant's wrist in the other as I dragged him to safety. We were the only two in our squad that had made it, but the bird was giving away our position with its telltale circling, its incessant cawing. *Let him go*, it screeched. *He's already dead. Save yourself.* I would've fired off a clip to silence the maddening harpy if not for the enemy soldiers hunting us.

The bird had been right. I was trying to save a corpse. When we reached the LZ and were loaded into the bay of a Huey and the medic pronounced the lieutenant KIA before jabbing me with a morphine syrette, I thought it would be the last I'd ever see of the raven-like creature. Afterward, when I was released from the field hospital in Qui Nhon with my wounds stitched up, I told myself it was a phantasm born in the fog of war, but then it began reappearing wherever I went, from the back alleys of Saigon where I couldn't get my fill of pipes stuffed with opium to dull the discovery that glory was a myth told by generals and valor couldn't salve all wounds, to a locked ward at a veterans hospital. Now it had followed me all the way to the middle of nowhere.

I did what a rehab nurse did when she tried to calm me during detox, reminding me the bird was nothing more than a product of trauma and stress. She would play a new Beatles song on her 8-track tape recorder, coaxing me to sing along about a blackbird with broken wings learning to fly. I kept at it, not sure if I was really singing aloud or only thinking the lyrics. A pair of headlights stabbed the horizon and aimed straight at me. I sang even louder. The headlights grew closer and the ebony bird circled higher and flew into the light of the dark black night. A pickup rolled to a stop on the other side of the campfire. The door opened and closed.

"You Nicholas Drake?" a gruff voice called.

"It's Nick, but most people call me by my last name," I said.

"Okay, Drake it is. What are you doing way out here, roasting hot dogs?"

"Myself, mostly."

"You know who I am?"

The man stepped closer. He wore a small brim Stetson and the glow of the flames turned the shiny star on his breast orange as well as the buckle on a wide leather belt that held a holstered .45.

"I saw you when I first got to town. You're the sheriff. I forget your name."

"Deputy Warbler. I used to be the sheriff, but that's a long story."

"Am I breaking a law?"

"Nope."

"Is there something you want?"

"I didn't drive all the way out here for a snipe hunt."

"How did you find me?"

The lawman had a bulldog's build. He held his meaty palms toward the fire as if warming them.

"Son, Harney County may be the largest in Oregon, and Lord knows with only seven thousand souls living in it, it's also one of the least populated. But if a man wants to hide, he'd be a helluva lot better off doing so in Portland. There's not a person in No Mountain or living on a ranch for a hundred miles that couldn't tell me exactly when you left and which direction you headed."

He allowed himself a chuckle. "The Lord also knows there's been a few husbands and wives not married to each other around here who thought no one would notice them either."

I peeked at the sky, but the bird was nowhere to be seen. When I reached for my shirt, the deputy watched my movements carefully, but didn't go for his gun. I mopped my face and chest before pulling it on.

"Mind if I ask you a question?" he said.

"You're the law."

"You on drugs? Your doctor at Walter Reed sent me a note after you moved here. I'll tell you what I told him. I'm no probation officer. But I do want to know what I'm dealing with late at night in the back of beyond facing a man who must have serious sand to earn a chest full of medals but some serious short circuits to trade a hero's hardware for a week of dope."

"It was only a couple of medals and I only got a couple of days' worth for them."

"Well, I'm glad to see you're honest, though I expect nothing less in a man. But you didn't answer me. You using right now?"

"It's why I'm sitting here sweating. I'm trying awfully hard not to."

He studied me and then ambled around the fire and plopped down. He stuck his legs straight out, careful not to let the soles of his cowboy boots get too close to the flames.

"Me? It's Iwo Jima I still carry. I was 4th Marines. War of attrition is what the historians call it now, but hand to hand is what it was. One stretch, five days and nights straight, we're crawling inside their tunnels and caves clearing them out. It was an honest-to-god horror show, us using nothing more than our KA-BARS for fear of ricochets and them with those long blades." He paused. "Anybody doesn't catch a dose of shell shock in war wasn't there. Plain and simple. You a fellow leatherneck?"

"Army. 1st Cavalry."

"A scout, huh? I suppose that's why the brass cut you some slack and sent you out here." He paused. "What's the battle you keep fighting, son?"

I stared into the fire. Scene after scene flashed as if someone was clicking slides on a Kodak Carousel. I could hear the bullets whine, feel the thump of artillery, shrink from the heat of the napalm. I never spoke of it in rehab no matter how hard they tried to get me to, and I wasn't about to start now with a stranger, especially a lawman wearing a gun.

"All of them, I suppose."

"I hear you. The whole damn shooting match."

We sat for a while, the silence broken by the crackle and hiss of the now dying fire. Finally, the deputy who was once a sheriff pushed himself up.

"Listen, I came looking for you to ask for some help. Some big shot lives up in Salem, I hear he's a friend of the governor, well, his daughter ran off. There's a lot of that going around these days. He got hold of her diary and believes she hooked up with some swami type. You know, religious from somewhere else. There's one moved into the old Crossed Bars Ranch. It's a bit north of No Mountain. He's got some followers living with him. You seen them? They wear orange robes and bang tambourines. Stick out around here like balls on a steer."

"I don't go north much. My work is south at the Malheur and Hart Antelope Refuges."

I didn't see any point in adding that the caseworker who got me the job as a ranger with the US Fish & Wildlife Service warned me it was my last chance. One screw up, one lapse back on the needle, and I'd be committed to a state hospital if I was lucky, sent to a federal pen if I wasn't. I figured the deputy already knew that.

"Well, there's only seven of us in the sheriff's department for the entire county and most are stationed in Burns. I'm it for all of down here, and I'm half-retired as it is." He patted his hip. "Got between a wife holding a gun and a husband trying to take a branding iron to her. Domestics. Give me a bank robbery any day."

"I don't see how I could be much help," I said.

"You're the only other man in these parts wears a uniform."

"There's a fish and duck on my badge. I make sure hunters have licenses and ranchers keep their stock out of restricted areas."

"Uniform is a uniform. That's all anyone ever sees. Trust me. I need a show of force."

"I thought you said they were religious?"

"Don't you watch the news? There are monks in Vietnam pouring gas on themselves and striking a match to protest the war over there, nuns over here carrying peace signs and chucking rocks at cops. It's like the whole world got turned upside down this past year. Assassinations, riots, you name it."

He sighed heavily. "These folks up at Crossed Bars have been acting cagey ever since they moved in a few months ago. I want to go there first thing in the morning, talk to the head swami about this little gal, and if she's there, take her in. She's underage. All you got to do is stand there and look official."

I took my time buttoning my shirt while I searched for an excuse to say no. I couldn't find one. "Okay, Deputy Warbler. I'll help you."

"All right. I'll owe you one. And you can call me Pudge. Everyone does except the folks I lock up and the ones got something to hide." He paused. "Any chance you could cut that hair and shave before we go?"

~

PUDGE WARBLER'S pickup had four-wheel drive and beefed-up suspension that helped smooth the ride across the playa and down the two-lane blacktop that led back to the blink-and-you'll-miss-it town of No Mountain. I'd tried to decline when he offered to give me a ride, but he'd insisted. He explained he wasn't about to risk wasting my offer to help him to a cow that might wander onto the road.

"A two-wheeler is no match for a ton of beef," he said.

Even though it was June, the deputy kept a heavy plank in the back of his truck for loading and offloading snowmobiles, as a matter of course. I'd ridden my motorcycle up it and into the bed where I tied the bike down.

"You don't see many of that type around," he said as he steered one-handed. "It's English, right?"

"Yes, a Triumph Trophy."

"The kind Steve McQueen rides in *The Great Escape*? I love that movie."

"Same model, but most call it a Desert Sled now because it's won a lot of races."

"You do that, race?"

"No."

"But you drive fast, I bet. There's plenty of salt flats to do that around here, but don't let me catch you speeding on the blacktop."

"You won't."

He chuckled. "Meaning you'd outrun me. I imagine you would. Getting parts can't be too easy. You work on it yourself?"

"It's a hobby I picked up as a kid."

"Which was where? Not here in Oregon, right?"

There wasn't much to see in the halo of the headlights. The landscape was desert chaparral and the lights from distant ranch houses were no brighter than the lightning bugs I'd seen while walking night patrol along the Mekong. His questions sounded innocent enough, but I knew they were as intentional as the ones I'd asked rice farmers when tracking the enemy or a VA shrink had asked me.

"My folks moved around a lot," I said.

"Let me guess. Your old man was a lifer. Which branch?"

"Whichever one he hadn't pissed off last."

Pudge laughed and smacked the steering wheel. "Mine? He thought the world ended at the fence line. Eight hundred acres and he knew every damn tumbleweed on the place. Called his cows by their first names. First time somebody brought sheep into Harney County, he lost his voice for a month from all the cussing. He sounded like a lonely bullfrog til the day he died."

I asked him why he thought the girl might be here. "She could be anywhere," I said.

"That's true, but her daddy's rich. The rich are rich because they have power but no patience. As far as I know, they're checking every church and religious outfit in the state, but there was something in the child's diary made him think she'd come our way. He called the governor, the governor called the attorney general, and so on down-the-line. My boss told me it needed being done yesterday. Did I tell you I used to be the sheriff?"

"You said it was a long story."

"I suppose I got time now. When that wife plugged me, it was right before the election. Buster Burton was a deputy over in Klamath County and moved to Harney to run against me. He's a real up and comer. His campaign posters called him Bust'em Burton. Someone gave the *Burns Herald* a photograph of me on a stretcher right after I got shot. I'm pretty sure Bust'em was behind it. The front page showing me laid out like a dressed elk was all she wrote. I'd been reelected sheriff four times before that. I joined right out of WW Two as a deputy."

"Are you going to run again?"

Pudge shook his head. "Truth is, Bust'em did me a favor. It wasn't til I was voted out of office and went back being a deputy I admitted to myself the top job's mostly politics and paper work. I'm good with living on the ranch I grew up on instead of in a clapboard box up in Burns. And, no, I don't know all the tumble-weeds and I don't call the cows George and Martha either."

After a few minutes, the lawman said, "Speaking of, that's my place up there on the right. I'll drop you off at yours and double back."

"You don't need to do that. Pull in and I'll drive myself home."

"You sure you sweated out all the bad stuff? I don't want you heading right back out and racing hell-bent for leather again. There's a gully or two would swallow you up whole."

"I gave you my word."

"I like that in a man, but I expect nothing less. Okay then, I'll pick you up at first light."

"I'll meet you there."

"Best we go in my rig. It's got the star on the door and the Christmas lights on the roof. You show up on your motorcycle or in your pickup with the bugs and bunny sticker, and we'll be doing more answering than asking."

He turned onto a gravel drive that crossed over a metal cattle guard and led to a ranch house bookended by a barn and corral.

"Home on the range," he said.

The front door swung open. A young woman stepped onto the porch and eyed us. She had long hair pulled into a pony tail and wore jeans.

"You certainly put in your eight," she said.

"No rest for the righteous," he replied.

She glanced at me and then back at him. "Who's your friend, Pudge, and what have you boys been up to?"

"A little bit of stargazing, a little bit of story swapping." He turned to me. "Meet my daughter Gemma. Gemma, meet Nick Drake. He's new in town."

"Evening," she said.

"Hello," I said.

"You two got something in common," Pudge said.

"And what would that be?" Gemma asked.

"Animals. Drake gets paid to look after the wild ones." He winked at me. "And Gemma is the best big animal vet ever graduated from Oregon State. Why, she's castrated more bulls—"

Gemma rolled her eyes. "I'm sure he gets the message. November has leftovers waiting for you in the oven."

"She does, does she." Pudge turned to me. "You hungry?"

"Thanks anyway, but I better get going."

I hopped into the bed of the deputy's pickup, unfastened the ties that bound the bike, and coasted it backward down the plank.

"At first light," Pudge called as he climbed the porch steps. "I'll bring the coffee."

Gemma hesitated before following him inside. "Pudge asked you to help find that girl, didn't he?"

"Does your father usually tell you about his work?"

She jutted her chin. "Always."

I couldn't think of anything to say to that, so I pulled on my goggles.

"I've been to Crossed Bars since the new owners took over," she said.

"They have a sick cow or something?"

"I moonlight for the Department of Ag checking to make sure cattle brought into the county have all their vaccinations. The Crossed Bars herd was sold off before the auction and now there's new stock there. The paper work checked out, but the people I met, well, there's something strange about them."

"Because they dress different and pray to a different god?"

"Because they act like they have something to hide," she said sharply.

Gemma was about my age and sure didn't have her father's build, but she did appear to have inherited his bluntness. "Did you tell your dad that?"

"Of course. He needs to know what he's walking into."

"So, why tell me?"

"Because there's been a lot of talk about you since you arrived in town."

"I thought you didn't know who I am."

"I don't."

"Fair enough. Anything in particular you want to ask?"

"I don't care what you did before you got here, but I do care if Pudge can't rely on you being quick on your feet."

"Are you asking me to look out for him?"

Gemma snorted. "Other way around, hot shot. Most people in Harney County still consider him the real sheriff. Don't let his name fool you. Pudge carries the extra weight so people will underestimate him. Plenty have paid for that mistake. If he doesn't like what he finds out there, well, his bite can be a lot worse than his bark. You don't want to get between him and who he's going to sink his teeth into."

"It wouldn't be the first time."

I kick started the Triumph, revved the engine, and roared off. If the black bird was following, I didn't stop to look for it.

Home on the outskirts of No Mountain was an abandoned lineman's shack once used by the Oregon and Northwestern Railroad, a fifty-mile line built in the 1920s to haul lumber to Burns from a mill near the Malheur Refuge. It wasn't much, just one room with a kitchen in an alcove, but it was better than a muddy foxhole in a jungle or a windowless hospital room with a door that could only be unlocked from the outside. The shack had a sagging front porch furnished with a single ladder-back chair. I was sitting on it when Pudge Warbler arrived in the morning.

The sun came up as we drove north. A thermos of coffee rode on the bench seat between us. That and a brown paper bag filled with Indian fry bread dusted with powdered sugar.

"Try one," the deputy said. "It's still warm. November got up before dawn to bake them."

"Is she your wife?"

"No, mine's been gone for some time. Cancer. November moved in to look after Gemma when my wife died and I was off sheriffing. November's people have been living in this part of the world for thousands of years. Ask her something she doesn't agree with, and you better be prepared to hear a lot of Paiute words and not many of them polite. She's not without opinion on everything and anything."

"I take it your daughter still lives with you."

Pudge sighed. "On and off and only when she needs to."

"What else do you know about the man who bought the Crossed Bars Ranch?"

"Not a whole lot. He moved here from San Francisco, but he's from someplace foreign. India or over there somewhere."

Pudge went on to explain that the ranch occupied three thousand acres of rangeland. Neighboring ranchers had tendered bids for it, but they didn't come close to matching a mystery buyer's all cash offer made over the telephone. After the sale closed, a caravan of cars led by a brand new 1968 Rolls Royce Silver Cloud pulled up to the main ranch house. A little man with a flowing gray beard and a sheepskin skullcap popped out. He bowed, placed his palms on the ground, and kissed the dirt.

"I guarantee you there's plenty of old timers living here with their mouths still open after seeing that," the deputy said.

We reached a pair of upright timbers supporting two equally thick crossed timbers that marked the entranceway to the ranch. Garlands of orange marigolds and strings of Tibetan prayer flags hung from them. The quarter-mile drive was lined with wooden plaques, some painted with rainbows, others with scribble.

"Wonder what that stuff is?" Pudge asked.

"It's Sanskrit. The mother of all languages in India. It's ancient and used mostly for religious writings."

"Like I said, balls on a steer. Can you read it?"

"I recognize some of it."

"From when you were in 'Nam?"

I nodded, but didn't explain how I'd gotten an up close and personal look.

A tall, hairless man wearing a saffron robe greeted us. He was joined by a woman cloaked in an identical garment. She had wildflowers braided into her long dark hair.

"*Namaste*," the man said. He steepled his hands under his chin and bowed. "I am Brother Michael and this is Sister Star. Welcome to our ashram."

"I'm Sheriff Warbler and he's Ranger Drake."

I didn't blink when he used his old title. I was sure it wasn't a slip of the tongue.

"How can we be of service, Sheriff?"

"I need to talk to the man in charge."

"We are pleased to speak with you."

"No, I need to talk to your boss."

Brother Michael smiled. "There are no bosses at an ashram, only enlightenment."

"The swami. The little fella with the beard. He's the leader, you're the flock, right?"

If the man was offended, he didn't show it. "You mean Vasudeva."

"That his name?"

"The enlightened one is not accepting visitors at present. He is in temple."

"Church, huh? How long is he gonna be praying?"

"Meditating. It could be hours. It could be days. One does not question the divine."

Pudge's back stiffened. "Well, you can bet the ranch I'm gonna question somebody."

"I can see your aura," Sister Star said in a strangely hushed voice. "It glows with determination."

"Don't know about any aura, Sister, but if by determined you mean I won't take no for an answer, you got that straight."

The woman's lips fashioned into a fixed smile, but her eyes narrowed.

"Why not tell us that which you seek?" Brother Michael said. "It could be a better use of your energy."

The deputy rubbed his jaw. "Okay, Brother Mike, it's like this. I got reason to believe a girl by the name of Kathryn Jenkins might be here. Kathy is what her folks call her. She's a minor. I need to check on her."

"I know of no one here by that name, but many in our ashram have been given spiritual ones or taken totemic names. Can you describe her?"

"I can do you one better. I got a picture sent over on the facsimile machine last night."

The deputy extracted a shiny square of paper from the breast pocket of his tan uniform and unfolded it. Brother Michael looked at the streaky black and white image, and then showed it to Sister Star.

"I do not recall having seen this person," he said. "But we receive many travelers on the path to enlightenment wishing to meet Vasudeva. His reputation as a holy man is passed from seeker to seeker."

"What about you, Sister?"

The woman closed her eyes. When they opened, the pupils were glazed. "There was a seeker who passed through earlier that bears some resemblance, but I cannot see her name."

"Was she alone or traveling with someone?" Pudge asked.

"I cannot see that. Seekers come alone or in groups. Some arrive by car, others on foot."

"Kathy doesn't drive. She's seventeen, but her folks didn't want her to get a license until she got older. I don't see her walking all the way here from Salem. That's where she's from. So, if it was her, she must've taken the bus or gotten a ride from a friend. You say she left? When was that?"

Sister Star closed her eyes again. She spoke without opening them. "All I can see is she is no longer here."

Pudge turned to Brother Michael. "That doesn't bother you, an underage girl showing up without her folks and then taking off?"

"We do not know for certain it was her," Brother Michael answered smoothly. "But even if it was, how were we to know her age? We do not ask for identification when travelers arrive. We provide sustenance to those who are hungry and a place in the field to sleep if they are weary. If someone wishes to join our ashram, then they must accept our beliefs and abide by our tenets. Ours is a simple life, monkish some might say. We rise early, we tend to our spiritual needs, and then we tend to our garden and animals."

"I see you're raising cattle, sheep, and chickens," I said. "You're not vegetarians?"

Brother Michael flinched at the sound of my voice as if he'd forgotten I was standing there. "Vasudeva teaches us all living creatures are sacred, but some in this world are put here to sustain others as they travel the path to enlightenment."

"Meaning you're neither Buddhist, Hindu, Jainist, or Taoist."

Brother Michael raised his hairless eyebrows. "I see you are knowledgeable about Eastern religions. That is unusual to find in this part of the world. May I ask how you came to learn of them?"

Pudge cut off the question. "Sounds to me the swami enjoys a T-bone like a lot of people. Nothing wrong with that. Now, if you and the sister don't recollect talking to this girl who may or may not be Kathy Jenkins, then maybe there's someone here who does. We're gonna need to talk to everyone."

"Certainly." Brother Michael clasped his hands together and formed a steeple again. "But first, may I please see a warrant authorizing such a search?"

"Who said anything about a search or needing a warrant?"

"This is private property, and we enjoy the same rights as any citizen. A warrant is a requirement of the law before you can conduct a search. Since you possess no actual evidence that Kathryn Jenkins may or may not have been here, then you do not have probable cause. Without probable cause, there can be no basis for a warrant. I can only presume you do not have one."

Pudge's jaw tightened. "You some kind of lawyer, Brother Mike? Maybe got experience defending lawbreakers?"

"I was an attorney-at-law in my former life, but then I met Vasudeva and learned of the true path to enlightenment."

"Well, I'll enlighten you about the two ways we can go here. One, you invite us in to talk to anyone who might know if the girl was Kathy Jenkins. Two? I go get a warrant."

Pudge hitched his belt. "But you ought to know, I've been sheriff of Harney County a long time. I know every judge from traffic court to superior court. I'll have that piece of paper here before a whisker can sprout on your head. And when I get it, I won't stop at asking questions. I'll turn over every bed, pull down every book on the shelf, and check every straw in the hayloft looking for that little gal. If I still don't find her, then I'll take you and the swami to jail. Trust me, it ain't divine."

Brother Michael showed no expression. "Please understand, Vasudeva's presence makes this a holy site. We have suffered sacrilege before and that has made us more guarded than we would wish. You are welcome to speak with anyone here. All I ask is that you allow Sister Star and me to escort you. We are an observant people and must ensure that none of our sacred tenets are desecrated." He gave a slight bow and swept his arm toward the cluster of buildings behind him.

"Lead the way," Pudge said.

Sister Star tried to loop her arm through mine as we walked toward the main house, but I shrugged away. I didn't like being touched by anyone.

"You are troubled," she whispered. "I see it in your eyes. You

have caused great pain and experienced great pain yourself. You
seek absolution. Vasudeva can show you the way to achieve
inner peace."

I didn't reply.

The interior of the house was scrubbed clean and smelled of
cinnamon, clove, and nutmeg.

"Natural disinfectants and useful for controlling pestilence,"
Brother Michael explained. "All of the buildings on the ashram
were infested when we arrived and required cleaning as well as
sanctifying."

The kitchen was spotless. A pair of enormous soup pots
were simmering on a stove. Towers of ceramic plates and
wooden bowls were stacked on open shelves. Loaves of bread lay
in straw baskets. Two women were chopping vegetables. They
wore white aprons and matching bandanas covered their hair.
Their robes were much drabber than Brother Michael's and
Sister Star's. When Pudge showed them the facsimile, they said
they didn't remember seeing the girl.

The answer was the same from every person Brother
Michael introduced us to, from the women making beds in the
bunkhouse to the men repairing siding on the buildings. Kathy
Jenkins, if it was her, seemed to have come and gone without
leaving any impression at all.

"That makes sixteen people we've talked to," Pudge said.
"How many did you say live here?"

"There are twenty-one members of our ashram," Brother
Michael said. "We are hosting no pilgrims at present. If we were,
you would find them camped in the field. As you can see, it
is empty."

"So, there's five we still need to talk to," Pudge said. "Where
are they?"

"Two are repairing a fence in the far pasture and another

pair went to Burns to buy supplies. They left shortly after morning mantras."

"And the swami makes five."

"Yes. As I said, he is at temple."

"That the barn over there?"

The double doors were closed, and the windows blackened by dark cloth hanging on the inside.

"Yes," Brother Michael said. "It was sanctified by Vasudeva himself."

"Excuse us while Drake and I have a little chat," Pudge said.

We moved out of earshot. "I don't see much point trying to force a meeting with the swami," the lawman said. "The Brother's apt to make it his line in the sand. I doubt we'd learn anything anyway. Everyone gets instant amnesia as soon as we're introduced."

"Why not tell the Brother and Sister you've seen all you need to and then go to Burns and find the pair that went shopping and talk to them alone?" I said.

"I like the way you think, son, but since I don't trust them, that means they probably don't trust me either. There's nothing to stop them from picking up the phone as soon as we leave and calling stores trying to locate their people to tell them to keep mum. But I can radio Bust'em and he can send one of the other deputies to find them while you and me keep everyone down here busy. I'll make up some excuse, so I can call him."

Pudge told Brother Michael and Sister Star it seemed we were on a wild goose chase, but since we were there, we might as well talk to the two working on the fence. Brother Michael led us across the field. Just as we passed a garden planted with pole beans and tomatoes, Pudge started hobbling.

"It's my damn gout. I must've forgotten to take my pills this morning. They're back in the truck. You all go ahead. I'll catch up."

He didn't wait for an answer and limped off. I asked Brother Michael and Sister Star if they practiced Maharishi transcendental meditation.

"The technique taught by the esteemed Yogi is one of many forms," the hairless man replied. "Vasudeva has established his own methods which we follow. Do you meditate?"

"I suffered an injury a while back and there was a nurse who made meditation part of my rehab. She said it was good for blood flow. She was also big into yoga."

"That was very progressive of her. Most practitioners of Western medicine have been conditioned by the pharmaceutical industry to rely solely on expensive drug therapies to fight disease and address pain. Did you find meditation helped your healing?"

"I ended up going with something else."

"Vasudeva can introduce you to a power far greater than can be achieved through the corporeal," Sister Star said. "The divine one's mantras will take you to a place of peace and joy where there is no pain."

I didn't ask her if it was like heroin. There wasn't any pain or any nightmares as long as you kept shooting or smoking it, but stop and it was as if every bad memory descended upon you like the Furies hungry for vengeance.

We reached a downed section of fence. Two men were repairing it. Both wore Jesus sandals and had stripped down to T-shirts. Their thin cotton pants were like the black pajamas worn by Vietcong. The deputy rejoined us and passed around the facsimile. The older of the pair glanced at it and shook his head. The second man was barely in his twenties. His hair was more red than blond, and his body lean and muscular. He seemed unable to take his eyes off the picture of the missing girl.

"Recognize her?" Pudge said. When he didn't answer, the deputy asked him again. "Did you see her here? Talk to her?"

"No, I don't remember her," the young man finally said. "Sorry."

"All right. By the way, I didn't catch your name."

"It's Damian."

"And your last name?"

"We are all one family at the ashram and Vasudeva is our divine father," Brother Michael said before Damian could answer. "We have no need for last names."

Damian handed the photograph back. When he did, the tip of a tattooed dagger poked beneath the sleeve of his T-shirt. I didn't need to see the full tattoo to know what it looked like. It was a grunt's helmet perched on a dagger's hilt with a python entwined around the blade. The design had been a favorite among cherries on their first leave to Saigon. The shills working in front of the parlors on Tu Do Street told them it had magical powers that would keep them alive.

It didn't work for too many.

It was an hour drive from the lineman's shack to the Hart Mountain National Antelope Refuge. The narrow highway got little traffic as it skirted farms and passed through flat stretches of high desert where the early morning sun sent bits of mica in the soil sparkling and the silvery leaves of the sagebrush shimmering. Wisps of horsetail clouds whisked a sky as blue as a sapphire, and I welcomed the wide openness after years spent in thick jungles and months in a locked ward.

I was driving a radio-equipped four-wheel-drive Ford pickup I'd been issued along with a badge and uniform by the district office supervisor in Portland. The rig came with a warning. "You break it, you buy it," he said. "Same goes for the 12 gauge shotgun and scope-mounted Winchester .30-30."

The long guns were cradled in the rack on the rear window. They were standard issue for all wildlife rangers. So was a Smith & Wesson .357 magnum revolver. The sidearm weighed over two pounds and was powerful enough to stop a grizzly bear, but since the supervisor told me grizzlies disappeared from Oregon long ago, I left it in the glove box. Still, lessons learned in combat died hard, and I kept the big six-shooter loaded.

The road transitioned abruptly from asphalt to gravel to dirt after I left the two-lane. There were still wide swaths of the 400-square-mile sanctuary I'd yet to patrol. The northern section required the most attention. A study area was recently declared off limits to cattle grazing, but the restricted zone remained unfenced. My job included informing ranchers about it and kicking out trespassing cows.

Ranch houses near the refuge were far and few between. I made a point of stopping whenever I passed one to explain the rules about the new cow-free zone. A rusty piece of sheet metal with a crescent moon cut out of the middle hung between two posts at a fork in the road. It marked the entrance to a ranch I'd never visited. A potholed road led me a quarter mile to a ramshackle house no bigger than a single wide trailer. A shoeless mule as swaybacked as the roof barely looked up from a patch of weeds it was nibbling.

I honked the horn and stood by the side of my pickup. A thin man wearing a gray flat brim cowboy hat with a rounded crown and an eagle feather stuck in the band walked around from behind the house.

"Help you?" he said.

"I'm Nick Drake. I'm the new Fish and Wildlife ranger."

He pulled a red bandanna from his hip pocket and wiped his hands. "Joe Moon," he said.

Moon looked to be in his late thirties, early forties and had skin that was either brown by heritage or days spent working in the sun. I glanced around his property. The wood in the split-rail fence around the corral was as gray as his hat and appeared so dry it would crumble upon touch. No trees shaded the house or barn. Dust devils twisted in pastures that no longer sprouted alfalfa.

"Have you lived here long?" I asked.

"Born and raised. As was my pa and his before him. Ranch's been in the family a long time. It's all we got and ever will."

The house appeared so modest, the out buildings and pastures so dried out, I couldn't imagine the place had been able to sustain multiple generations.

"Have you heard about the section of the refuge that's been set aside for wildlife only? It's to protect them from coming into contact with cattle-borne viruses," I said.

"Nope."

I handed him a pamphlet. "This explains the what, where, and why. I have a topographic map in the truck that shows the boundary in more detail and can show it to you."

He handed the pamphlet back. "Don't matter. I don't graze there. I only got twenty-five head."

The surrounding fields were so bare, I couldn't imagine they could produce enough grass to feed even five cows.

"Don't you have irrigation?"

An oblong shadow cast by his hat swung back and forth on the dirt as he shook his head. "Used to, but the well run dry."

"Maybe it will rain soon," I said.

"Maybe. But we gone through long years without before. That's ranching."

I could feel the resignation in his voice. "It was nice to meet you, Joe. I'm on my way to the refuge now. If you have any questions about the restricted area, let me know."

"Can I ask a favor?"

"Sure, what is it?"

"I got a couple letters need mailing. Mail man don't come out here. It'd save gas money now that they're charging thirty-seven cents a gallon."

"Sure, I'll drop them off at the post office for you."

"Much obliged."

He went inside and brought out a couple of envelopes. They

were already stamped and the addresses were handwritten in childlike block letters. I tucked them behind the driver's side visor with the ends sticking out so I wouldn't forget them. I looked in the rearview mirror as I drove away. Joe Moon hadn't moved despite the dust kicked up by my tires. It was as if he was rooted in place and the ranch wouldn't let him go even if he wanted to leave.

The refuge was ten miles to the west and the new restricted zone a few miles past that. I shifted into compound low and climbed to the top of a hill. The vantage point provided a view of the surrounding hills and valley below. I started scanning with binoculars. A bighorn ram was leading four ewes across a distant slope. A golden eagle pursued a scrambling jack rabbit. A herd of pronghorns grazed on clumps of native bunchgrass.

The district supervisor had given me another piece of advice. "The Hart Refuge is misnamed," he said. "Has been since the get go when it was established thirty years ago. Those are pronghorns down there, not antelope. Antelope live in Africa, not Oregon. An entirely different species altogether, but don't try explaining that to anyone. Makes them ornery, especially the hunters."

I kept my binoculars trained on the herd to see if any showed signs of bluetongue. The virus struck sheep and cattle but was on the rise in the wild. The faces of stricken animals turned blue from choking on swollen tongues. I'd spotted one my first week on the job. Putting it down was hard, not because I questioned what was best for the animal, but because I hadn't fired a weapon since Vietnam. I broke out in a cold sweat when I snugged the Winchester against my shoulder and sighted through the scope. Pulling the trigger took all my will. The echo of the shot sent me scrambling for cover.

A large dust devil swirled to my right. Several cows were plodding nose to tail. I got in the truck and headed down to intercept them, threading my way between boulders and gulches. The pronghorns bounded away when I reached the valley. The cows were nowhere in sight. I drove in widening circles until I picked up their trail and followed it to the entrance of a gully. It was narrow, and so I got out to follow on foot. I grabbed the 12 gauge and carried it at port arms. Rattlesnakes nested in gullies and were big, fast, and aggressive.

I looked ahead and then left and then right and then up and down and even behind me. It was another habit I'd acquired from walking point in-country. *Always rotate. Always anticipate. Never be late.* The gully's floor turned cobbled, but I could still pick out the signs of cows. There was a dislodged rock here, a trace of a hoofprint in the sand between stones there. The walls showed fresh scrapes from cattle squeezing through bottlenecks.

The sun beat down. Perspiration beaded and rivulets ran down my chest and back. My tan uniform turned into green fatigues and was soon yoked with sweat. The shotgun took on the weight of an M16. The gully became the banks of the Perfume River on the outskirts of Hue and I could sense the squad strung out behind me. Somehow I'd missed the signs. Machine guns opened up and hundreds of black-clad guerrillas rushed from behind the green walls. Everything blurred: firing while running backward, stopping to grab a buddy, making it back to the garrison. I was reliving a month of nonstop combat in seconds where the days were distinguished only by the sun that rose bloodred every morning and set bloodred every night. It was the same color as the wounds our bullets made in the enemy and those the enemy made in us. When we finally beat back the offensive, two hundred in our regiment were KIA.

A screech snapped me back and an ominous shadow started circling on the ground. *Over here*, shrieked the bird as black as night. *Over here.*

I told myself the flashback of the Tet Offensive surely had

triggered it. I took a deep breath to begin humming The Beatles tune, but choked on what I tasted. I covered my mouth and sucked air through my nose. The smell was stronger than the taste. It was a smell I smelled every day I was in-country. A smell I could smell no matter how much opium I smoked or how much heroin I cooked in a bent spoon. I looked skyward and watched the bird straighten its obsidian wings and glide over the length of the gully before being swallowed by the glare of the sun.

I didn't have to walk very far. She was naked and laying on her back in a makeshift sarcophagus carved in an undercut in the wall of the gully. An animal had found the open side. It might have been a weasel, maybe a fox. I couldn't tell what kind for sure from the small bites taken out of the side of her arm, her torso, her leg.

Deputy Warbler parked alongside my truck. He wore an expression that reminded me of my company commander. His jaw was set as if made of iron and his spine bolted to a steel rod. He'd cinched his belt in a notch and unsnapped the strap over the top of his holstered .45.

"I called it in right after you radioed me," Pudge said. "Had to straighten out jurisdiction. Hart is in Lake County. Their sheriff is stationed down in Lakeview. He said since this section of the refuge is closer to Burns, it'd be easier for us to handle the investigation."

He rubbed his jaw. "Truth is, I don't think he wants anything to do with a murder involving the daughter of a rich man who's a friend of the governor. There's bound to be blowback. I told you being sheriff can be more politics than policing."

"Are you the only one coming?" I asked.

"Lord no. Bust'em is on his way along with the rest of the Harney County deputies. He's sure to bring the coroner with him too. He may have even called in the state troopers, though I hope not because that will alert the *Burns Herald,* and then we'll have a goat rodeo for sure. You didn't touch her did you?"

"There was nothing I could do for her. See for yourself."

I led him to her. He didn't go straight to the body, but stood from twenty feet away and took in the entire scene. Then he took a few steps closer and took it in again. Twice more he did that until he was within arm's length.

"That son of a bitch is gonna pay. Whoever he is, wherever he is, he's gonna pay. She's someone's little girl, their baby daughter. And look at what he's done to her."

I didn't say anything. There was nothing to say. I'd seen plenty of dead before. Men. Women. Children. The old and the young. Some had been soldiers. Some had been rice farmers. I'd seen them in the field. I still saw them in my dreams. It may have happened during war, but I wasn't the only soldier trained, encouraged, and commended for killing who struggled with whether it was morally right or wrong. The wards at Walter Reed were filled with them. So were the back alleys of American cities, the redwood forests, and the locked and curtained bedrooms of suburban homes.

"I'm not gonna touch her, not get any closer," Pudge said. "The coroner needs to see it as it is and then us lawmen will take it from there."

"Are you going to wait for them?"

"Hell no. We're gonna scour this damn place. Walk it and note anything we find that the good Lord didn't put here. Whoever brought her here walked in and walked out. He didn't do it without leaving something behind. A cigarette butt. A boot print. Dried blood on a rock. We're gonna find it, and we're gonna find him."

"There aren't any tracks coming in. I've walked it back and forth. If there was something, I would've seen it."

"What makes you so sure you didn't miss something?"

I could've said because I spent three years tracking the enemy and MIAs across paddies and through jungles, but I didn't. "You want to retrace your steps, go right ahead. I'll go this way and see where it leads."

He pushed back the small brim Stetson and glared. After a few moments, he said, "Let's go together. Four eyes are better than none."

We set off, walking slowly and carefully, shoulder to shoulder, searching the ground and the gully's walls. I tried not to think about how the girl's parents would react when they got the call no one ever wants to get, and no one ever wants to make.

The ground became even sandier and any footprints that may have been there were erased by the hoofprints of shuffling cows. The gouge in the Earth's skin ran for a quarter of a mile and spilled onto a playa that was mostly sand and rock. Lizards sunbathed on some. Quail skittered in what little brush there was. The beat of a sage grouse drumming his chest sounded in the distance.

"I don't see your cows anywhere," Pudge said.

"There's a lake a few miles to the west. They probably headed there in search of water."

"Well, if the killer came in from this side, he either rode or drove. It's a long way from the highway, and he sure as hell didn't parachute."

We retraced our steps. When we reached the body, a horn honked.

"That'll be Bust'em wanting an escort so he doesn't scuff his new boots," Pudge said. "You stay here, I'll go fetch him."

I looked at the makeshift tomb. Whoever put her in it had surely killed her here or at least nearby; it was too far to carry someone. And why here? There were plenty of places where he could've hidden a body, but he chose here. What made it so special? And why did he leave one side of the tomb open? If he'd closed it with loose rocks, it would've gone undetected forever.

Pudge led in four men. Three wore uniforms like his, and the fourth had on a blue blazer and carried a leather bag. One of the uniformed men had a carefully groomed moustache and wore aviator sunglasses. He approached me.

"I'm Sheriff Burton. I'll need a full statement from you, but we can do that later. Right now, I need you to step aside. This is sheriff's business, and I can't allow untrained personnel contaminating the scene."

Pudge groaned. "Ah, hell, Bust'em. You'd still be back in Burns shuffling budget papers if it wasn't for Drake here. Let him stay. He can spot a horsefly on an antelope's ass from a mile away."

The coroner took off his blazer and replaced it with a white lab coat. He dabbed Mentholatum beneath his nostrils and pulled on pair of thick latex gloves, the kind used by dishwashers.

"First off, we'll need photographs from all angles," he said. "Is your team ready?"

Sheriff Burton gestured to one of his deputies who was holding a tape measure and a thick piece of white chalk. He ran the tape on the outside of the earthen tomb and marked feet and inches on the walls.

The coroner motioned to another deputy who was holding a 35mm camera. "Photograph everything."

The deputy snapped wide shots and then changed lenses and started in on the close-ups. He stood, he knelt, he even got down on his stomach and shot from ground level as if it were some kind of fashion shoot. Twice he stopped to change rolls of film.

I told Pudge I was going back to my truck to take a look at a topographical map. "Maybe I can narrow down access roads and trails to the playa on the other side of the gully."

"I was about to order you to go do that," Sheriff Burton said hastily.

I unfolded the map on the pickup's hood. Only a couple of dirt roads were marked, but they belied the truth. I'd seen plenty of four-wheel-drive tracks and illegal campsites littered with beer cans and broken bottles. Most had been made by hunters, others by ranchers rounding up their cattle.

A familiar *thwap-thwap-thwap* split the desert's silence. The sweats came pouring back. All my senses went on full alert. I looked for a place to take up position. I looked for the enemy. I looked up at the sky. It wasn't an inbound Huey Cobra attack chopper coming toward me but a red and white civilian version of the same Bell model, right down to the bubble cockpit. The pilot hovered overhead and then started setting it down on a clearing next to the parked trucks.

The racket brought Sheriff Burton and Deputy Warbler hurrying from the gully. "What in the Sam Hill?" the older lawman shouted.

Two men jumped out of the chopper. They crouched to stay beneath the murderous blades and duck walked toward us.

The whine of the helicopter's engine didn't drown out the sound of the sheriff gulping. "It's Aubrey Jenkins."

"You got to be shitting me," Pudge said. "You called the father and told him we found his dead little girl out here?"

Aubrey Jenkins wore a tailored hunting jacket with a leather recoil patch on the right shoulder and matching leather patches on the elbows. His pants were pressed twill and his boots handmade in London.

"Mr. Jenkins, what an unexpected surprise," Sheriff Burton stammered.

Jenkins's gray eyes were as resolute as a glacier grinding through miles of rock. "Show me," he demanded.

The sheriff blocked his advance. "Please, sir, allow us to do our job. I promise you we are handling this with the utmost care."

Jenkins focused on the entrance to the gully. "That is my daughter in there."

"Please, Mr. Jenkins," he tried again.

The second man from the helicopter pressed forward. He wore a gray suit and dark tie. "Sheriff Burton is it? I'm Richard Travers with the governor's office. No one respects law enforcement more than Governor Lane. After all, he did serve as attorney general for eight years, and no one wants to interfere with your investigation. He asked me to communicate to you his deepest personal concern in this matter. I can assure you the governor won't forget how you extended Mr. Jenkins every courtesy in providing what any father in this tragic circumstance would ask." He paused and then switched tone. "I'm sure you get my meaning."

The sheriff licked his moustache as he did a quick political calculation.

Pudge didn't wait for him to respond. "We don't know what we got in there yet, but we do know we all want the same thing. And that's to make sure no one steps in cow flop and tracks it in there so some ACLU lawyer type can use it to keep a killer from getting his due." He mimicked Travers's pause. "I'm sure you get my meaning."

The father's head swiveled to bring his eyes to bear on the deputy. "You are the one who found her? You saw her?"

"I have."

"Did she suffer?" Jenkins's voice didn't crack when he asked it, and that's what struck me—the iciness to it, the sheer control over what must be the worst imaginable.

"She looks asleep. As peaceful as a little lamb napping in a soft green meadow," Pudge said.

The quiver in Jenkins's grimace was fleeting. "I need to see her. If someone will not take me this instant, I will take myself."

Travers hissed at Sheriff Burton. "Make it happen or come next election—"

The sound of someone tripping grabbed our attention. It was the coroner. He reached down to rub his shin. "Damn," he swore. When he looked up, he beckoned to Sheriff Burton, who scurried right over.

The sun was moving toward late afternoon and our shadows grew longer. The blades of the chopper were twirling in a slow wind down. I closed my eyes and could hear pings of metal on metal as the Huey that carried me and my dead lieutenant from the LZ took incoming rounds. I could feel the drunken pitch and yaw as the pilot juked the stick to keep the chopper airborne when the red flash of a shoulder-launched missile whooshed by. I could hear the *chuck-chuck-chuck* of the .50 caliber as the machine gunner sprayed the ground and the clang of brass as the empty cartridges hit the deck like teeth spit from a boxer.

The sheriff ushered over the coroner. "We have some news. Doc is going to tell you what he told me."

"Yes, well, uh, while I obviously can't make any pronouncement of the exact cause or time of death yet, I can say without equivocation that the deceased has been *in situ* for approximately two weeks. The dryness of the climate has had a preservation effect of sorts. The victim is a Caucasian female with brown hair between twenty to twenty-five years of age."

Aubrey Jenkins jolted. "Are you saying it is not my Kathy?"

"I cannot ascertain the identity of the victim, but given what I've been told about your daughter, there is no way it could be," the coroner said. "The deceased's age precludes it."

Jenkins's nod was dismissive. He turned to Sheriff Burton. "My daughter is still missing. I expect no resource to be spared finding her. Alive."

He turned on the heels of his custom boots and strode back toward the helicopter.

Richard Travers made a hissing sound again as he leaned into the sheriff. "Mr. Jenkins and Governor Lane are as close as brothers. You don't want to disappoint either of them. Is that clear enough for you?"

He didn't wait for an answer as he raced after Jenkins and climbed into the bubble cockpit. The chopper's engine revved up to takeoff speed, and both the main and tail rotors became blurs as they spun faster and faster.

~

PUDGE and I watched the convoy of vehicles leave. Sheriff Burton rode in the lead truck, the coroner in the second, and a black vinyl body bag encasing the body of the unidentified girl in the third.

"They're driving ten miles an hour without another car in sight until they hit the blacktop, but they got their lights and sirens on." Pudge shook his head. "That's Bust'em for you. All hat, no cattle, right down to the pearl handle on his service weapon."

I'd helped the deputies carry the body bag from the undercut in the gully, humming "Blackbird" to myself to keep from thinking about the eighteen-year-old private from Louisiana I'd slung over my shoulder after the teen caught a round in the face on his very first patrol and the mother cradling a baby engulfed in flames that I'd rushed out of a burning hut in Quang Ngai Province. As I watched the retreating emergency vehicle lights add red to a sky already painted by the setting sun, I hoped the dead girl would be the last body I'd ever have to carry. Something told me it wouldn't.

"We might as well join the parade," Pudge said. "Dark's on its way, so there's nothing more we can do here."

"You go ahead," I said. "I still got those cows to track down. I'm going to drive over to the lake and see if that's where they went. If I'm lucky, they'll have passed through the refuge by now and I can call it a day."

His eyes narrowed. "You're not gonna go all shell shock seeing that dead girl now and go looking for dope, are you?"

"One thing about living in a place where animals outnumber people is there's not enough business for pushers."

"Fair enough. I'll take your map home and think on the most likely routes this bad guy could have taken. I'm betting most of my day is gonna be spent in Burns listening to Bust'em lay out his big plan for finding little Kathy Jenkins now that the governor's man ripped him a new one. Why don't you come over to my place around this time tomorrow evening, so we can talk about what's what on the map. I'll ask November to set a place at the table for you."

We drove away. As we rounded the hill, Pudge steered toward the road that would take him back to No Mountain and I turned west. I kept it in four-wheel drive as I bounced through a roadless patch. My plan was to intercept a dirt road just beyond the refuge's boundary that connected to the lake.

The off-road route took me along the northern edge of the playa. The truck's headlights picked up the frantic flights of bats feeding on insects. Somewhere in the distance came the *yip-yip-yip* of coyotes. A great horned owl flew silently alongside the open window, the big bird's rounded feathers muffling any sound. I knew it was going to be a rough night for some poor creature.

The ground became rockier and the ditches carved by runoff closer together. As I navigated some of the deeper cuts, I wondered if maybe I'd miscalculated the whereabouts of the lake road, but then the silhouette of a ridgeline rose ahead. Poker Jim Ridge. The lake was on the other side, so that meant the dirt road to it must still lay to the north. I turned to intersect it. The headlights picked up a faint track as wide as a pickup. I braked and shined the door-mounted spotlight on it. It wasn't the start of a track, but the dead end of one. I followed its length with the spotlight until darkness swallowed the beam. I grabbed a flashlight and the 12 gauge and stepped out to take a closer look.

The dead end showed no sign of fresh tire tracks. Bushes destined to become tumbleweeds had taken root. I started walking, keeping a circle of light on the ground. The track entered a deep thicket of junipers. Their trunks were sclerotic, and the limbs intertwined with their neighbor's in a skeleton's embrace. I kept going. The forest started to thin, the trees growing farther away as the track widened. It was a turnaround. The soil was soft and revealed tire marks. A dusting of juniper needles and berries covered them in spots. I picked up a twig and sniffed. The pungent odor of juniper was fresh. I felt the needles. They were still supple. I squeezed a berry. It squished easily.

I shined the light farther up the track. A purplish spot gleamed a few yards away. I touched it and brought my fingertips to my nose. Motor oil. A noise stopped me cold. It came from somewhere in the thicket of trees. I cocked my head. I heard it again. It was deep, eerie, like the bass guitar on a Creedence Clearwater tune. I doused the light and stood still. There it was again. Deeper, more eerie. I raised the shotgun, clamped the still dark flashlight beneath the gun's fore-end, and slipped my finger through the trigger guard.

Again the noise sounded. Higher pitched this time, fluttering. I inched forward until I left the track and entered the thicket. Again the noise. I thumbed the switch on the flashlight and touched but didn't squeeze the trigger. A pair of yellow eyes glowed back. A bobcat bared its teeth. All of its weight was back on its powerful hind legs. I shouted. It hissed and sprung sideways. It was gone in a flash of white fur.

The water hole between me and the bobcat was only a few inches deep, no doubt fed by an underground spring. I crouched and cupped a handful of water. It tasted of minerals, but was not heavily alkaline like most in the high desert. I shined the light around to see if the wild feline had really left. There was no sign of it, but to my right, a horse length from the water's edge, lay a lumpy pile. I didn't need to smell or taste it to know what it was.

Road apples.

The windshield magnified the sun. The rays woke me. I'd spent the night in the front seat parked alongside the shore of Bluejoint Lake. I didn't need binoculars to locate the wayward cows. They were grazing down by the water. Pigs were said to be a lot smarter, but this herd was smart enough to take themselves out of the refuge. They also took me out of my jurisdiction.

Bluejoint was the northernmost lake in a chain that ran along the Warner Valley. It could go dry for long stretches, but it had enough water in it now to support rafts of ducks in the middle and shorebirds wading in the shallows. My approach barely earned a raised head from the cows, much less a moo. I traced the brand on the haunch of the closest. The letter *H* was positioned atop a curved bar. The others bore the same brand. I tore a page from my logbook and made a rubbing and then drove off in search of coffee.

Plush was the name of the nearest town, but there was nothing swanky about the wooden storefronts along the main street. I took a seat in the only café. When the waitress brought a menu, I waved it off.

"Coffee black, please, and whatever you bring for breakfast I'll like."

She wore her hair piled in a lopsided beehive and had on three shades of eyeliner. "Well aren't you the politest. And cute too."

I placed the rubbing on the table and looked around. Men dressed in snap button shirts who didn't bother to take off their cowboy hats while they ate occupied the other tables. I nodded hello but didn't earn a single return. The waitress brought a pot of coffee and a thick brown porcelain mug.

"Don't mind them. We don't get many out-of-towners, especially this early in the morning. They're probably wondering if you're a state trooper or an inspector with the Department of Agriculture. It's the uniform."

"Fish and Wildlife," I said. "I work at the Hart Antelope Refuge."

"My husband Rollie goes hunting there every fall. That's right. Sorry to disappoint you sweetie, but I'm married." She stuck out her hand to show off a gold band sporting a solitaire diamond. "Breakfast will be right up. Eggs, bacon, hash browns, the works." She eyed my hair. "You look like a wheat toast sort, am I right?"

The coffee was hot and strong, but one cup wouldn't be enough. I looked out the window and could still see the girl wedged in the side of the gully. I pictured a truck unloading a horse on a seldom-used road and watering it in the shade of the junipers under the watchful eye of a bobcat.

The waitress slid a platter with three eggs sunny-side up, six strips of thick bacon, and a mound of shredded potatoes fried to a golden crisp. "Jam with your toast? We got blueberry, blackberry, and raspberry. All are homemade and for sale by the jar. What's that?" She pointed at the rubbing.

"It's a brand. I collect them."

"That's a funny sort of thing to collect. My daddy collected baseball cards, but Rollie?" She lowered her voice. "*Playboy* pinups. He plasters them all over the garage. Don't tell nobody, okay?" She winked.

"Do you recognize it?"

"Can't say that I do." She held it up for the men at the nearest table. "Hey, you know which ranch this belongs to?"

The oldest of the four men looked up from his biscuits and gravy. Silver bristled between jug handle ears and the brim of a sweat-stained straw cowboy hat. "Bring it on over, hon, and let's have a gander." He studied it and then said to me, "Where you from, son?"

"No Mountain."

"Harney County, huh? Well, then you ought to know this yourself seeing it's up in your neck of the woods."

"I'm new to the area."

"It's the Rocking H spread owned by the Harneys. And didn't they go and name the whole damn county after them. You're in Lake County here. You think Lake is named for some fellow named Lake? Hell no. It's because of all the lakes we got, most of 'em being of the dry variety."

His tablemates laughed.

"The Rocking H. Up by..." I let it drift.

"Just northwest of that damn refuge is where," he said. "What a waste of good land and government dollars. Setting aside all that for a bunch of antelope that's best off dressed, barbecued, and on my table for Sunday dinner."

That earned another round of guffaws.

THE ROCKING H was on the opposite end of the refuge from Joe

Moon's dusty spread, but bordering a wildlife sanctuary was all the two ranches had in common. I drove through a sea of grass that stretched for miles before reaching the ranch house. The pastures were irrigated by wheel lines, sprinklers screwed into water pipes attached to metal wheels. The spray created fan shaped rainbows. The sprawling home was set among shade trees, fruit orchards, and flowerbeds. A two-story bunkhouse rose next to an enormous barn. The corrals boasted new fence posts and rails. Everything was neat, orderly, and bespoke of hard work and financial success.

A pair of barking border collies ran alongside as I turned into the circular drive. The canines split up when I stopped in front of the house and stationed themselves on either side of my pickup. They maintained a steady growl.

"Charge," a loud voice commanded from the porch.

Instead of launching themselves at the truck's windows, the dogs dropped to the ground with their front paws tucked beneath their muzzles.

A man who looked around my age strolled across the gravel. He crouched by the first dog, scratched behind its ears, and then said, "Home." The dog raced toward the barn. He circled the truck and did the same with the second dog. It obeyed instantly. The man circled back around to my side.

I leaned out the window. "What's with charge? That some kind of joke?"

He squinted before speaking. "Herders are real smart. While they understand a hundred words or more, which is a lot more than most people living around here do, they respond best to one-word commands. Lay down is two words and down means don't jump up."

"If charge doesn't mean charge, how do you say sic 'em?"

"Kill," he said without batting an eye. "I'm Blaine Harney and you are?"

I got out of the truck. "Nick Drake. I'm with Fish and Wildlife."

"Is this a howdy neighbor visit or something else?"

"Have you heard about the special no grazing study area in the Hart Refuge?"

The rancher squinted. "I read the notice they mailed us. Why?"

"I spotted several cows with your brand on it."

"Are they still there?"

"No, I tracked them to Bluejoint Lake. They were still there as of a couple of hours ago."

"I'll send some boys down to bring them back. We're running twenty thousand head, so if one or two go astray, it's easy to miss."

"How big is your spread?"

"We own sixty thousand acres outright, but have grazing rights to another two hundred fifty thousand."

"It must be hard managing land that isn't contiguous."

"We know what we're doing. It's how we got to be the largest ranch in the county. Oldest too. When property comes up for sale with the right ingredients for supporting cow-calf pairs, we buy it. What we can't buy, like government land, we make a deal for the grazing rights. Rocking H cattle provides the economic lifeblood for this county. Always has, always will. Jobs, taxes, you name it."

"But you didn't buy the Crossed Bars Ranch."

Blaine Harney made a face. "We tried, but those religious nuts outbid us. It still sticks in our craw."

"It must be some consolation knowing they overpaid for it."

"They don't know the first lick about modern ranching techniques. They don't belong here, and they won't last long either. We'll wait them out, and then we'll see who pays what." He paused. "You're new here too, right? Well, enjoy summer while it lasts. You haven't experienced one of our winters yet. The high desert gets mighty cold. Snows too. Two or three feet easy."

"I'll welcome it," I said. "I've had enough hot weather to last a life time."

Blaine was a big man and his biceps stretched his denim snap button shirt. He sized me up. "I'm guessing you mean overseas. You in the war over there?"

"I was, but now I'm here. About those cows of yours."

"We'll try to keep them out, but you know those rules are new and there's still no fences. There's a lot of ranchers around here who don't pay attention to imaginary lines drawn up by some Washington bureaucrat. Harney County was free-range country before it was a county and before Oregon was even a state. No one used to say squat about grazing at Hart or the Malheur Refuge until a couple of scientists wrangled some tax payer dollars to do some kind of bullshit study. It's hard enough making a living without a bunch of handcuffs being slapped on you."

"You need to observe the restricted zone," I said. "I don't want to be spending my time writing up violations, but my job's my job and I won't turn a blind eye."

"No one's asking you to. You say you tracked our cattle to Bluejoint Lake? Where was it you first saw them?"

"East of Poker Jim Ridge."

Blaine thought for a moment. "Is that where all the sheriff action was taking place yesterday?"

"What do you mean?"

"What everybody is talking about. First, Pudge Warbler goes speeding down there. And then Sheriff Burton and his boys with lights and sirens blaring. They brought in a helicopter too. The word is they pulled a body out of there. Is that right?"

"I'm not with the sheriff's department."

"But whatever was going on was on Fish and Wildlife land, right? So, you must know something."

I shrugged.

The rancher grimaced. "Typical government bullshit. Never get a straight answer, only more red tape."

I took that as my cue to leave, but then two men came out of the ranch house and headed toward us. The pair moved slowly because the older of the pair was using two canes. Each step looked painful. The young man walking alongside him looked prepared to catch him should he stumble.

"Who is he and what's he selling?" the old man said in a slurred growl.

"He's with Fish and Wildlife." Blaine turned to me. "This is my father, Zachariah, and my little brother, Jesse."

The old man had fierce blue eyes and a shock of white hair that swept back over his collar. Jesse had his father's eyes, but his moved like tropical fish in an aquarium as they shifted from his big brother to me and back again.

"What's he want?" the senior Harney demanded.

"He was letting me know some of our stock wandered down to Bluejoint Lake."

"Lake County." The old man spat. "Those cows are as good as stolen by now. Nothing but goddamn thieves down there. Steal the breath right out of your mouth." He spit again.

"I'll hook up a trailer and run down and fetch them myself." Blaine turned to me. "How many did you say there were?"

"Six."

Zachariah Harney continued to glower. "Better take a lasso. Find the stealing bastards who rustled them and string them up."

"You load up cows and your horse in the same trailer?" I asked

The younger brother poked his finger at me. "What's it to you?"

"Just curious. I'm not from a ranching background."

"Then mind your own goddamn business," he said.

Blaine shot his little brother a look and then turned to me. "The horse goes in the back of a stakebed truck and the cows go in the trailer behind."

Jesse sneered. "Consider yourself educated, dumb shit."

"What do you know," I said. "You learn something new every day."

The sky was dusking when I arrived at Pudge Warbler's ranch. An older woman answered the door. She had high cheekbones and wore her hair in a long braid. The black strands had gray streaks as fine as cobwebs.

"I'm Nick Drake. The sheriff asked me to stop by." I used his former title to show respect.

"Not here," she said and made to slam the door.

"Do you know when he'll be back?"

She shook her head and then wrinkled her nose. "*Pongica kwedatse.*"

Pudge's daughter, Gemma, appeared behind her. "She says she doesn't know."

"That and then some," I said, recalling the deputy's warning about the Paiute woman's ready supply of insults.

Gemma's grin confirmed it. "Pudge is on his way. You can wait in his office."

November kept a firm grip on the door. "Wipe your boots. I don't want no *madukanna kwedapu* tracked in here." She watched me carefully as I used the doormat.

"What does that mean?" I asked her.

Gemma answered for her. "Dirt."

"I bet," I said.

The women exchanged sly looks before waving me inside. The house was modest and the mismatched furniture a mix of family heirlooms and items from the bargain basement. Paintings of high desert landscapes hung on either side of a stone fireplace.

Gemma pointed toward a closed door. "The office is in there."

"Don't touch nothing," the Paiute woman said before leaving.

"She really didn't mean dirt, did she?" I said.

"No. *Madukanna* is white man. *Kwedapu* is, well, shit."

"And what did she call me before that?"

"*Pongica kwedatse*? You sure you want to know?"

"I was in the army. I've heard them all."

"Okay, you asked for it. Anus of skunk."

"Well, that is a new one."

The office doubled as a sheriff's substation for the area. The large desk was heaped with papers. A shortwave radio and police scanner were on and humming. Floor-to-ceiling bookshelves lined one wall. The titles were organized by subject matter: Oregon history, the Old West, the Civil War, the Indian Wars, World War II, and anthropological studies of the Northern Paiute. The classics were also well represented, everything from Homer to Plato to Euripides. A brown leather couch looked like it had gotten plenty of use for reading and napping. A glass-fronted gun cabinet showed off a half dozen rifles along with two shotguns—one a pump, the other a double-barreled 10 gauge.

I caught my reflection in the cabinet's glass. I'd been away from the lineman's shack for two days and it showed. As soon as I sat on the couch, Pudge arrived. He slapped down a manila folder and eased into the desk's swivel chair.

"I'm getting too old for this shit, but damn if I'm gonna ride off into the sunset before I find the son of a bitch who murdered a girl in my own backyard," he said.

"I'm guessing Sheriff Burton laid out a different strategy than you had in mind," I said.

"It's the governor's strategy. We're supposed to concentrate on finding the missing Jenkins girl and not bother about the dead one. Aubrey Jenkins carries a lot of weight. I didn't know how much til I got up to Burns and got the lowdown. He's got his fingers in all sorts of pies. Timber, banking, real estate, you name it. But mostly he's got his fingers around Governor Lane's balls."

"Doesn't the sheriff think there could be a connection between the dead girl and Jenkins's daughter's disappearance?"

"The only thing he's thinking about is how to keep his job, just like the governor's doing. They're both hoping we'll find her shacked up with a boyfriend somewhere. Bust'em ordered us to go door to door. Motels, cabins, campsites. He said we got to focus on finding the living because the dead's dead and nothing's gonna change that."

I'd heard that before. A common story passed among enlisted men was about a lieutenant who'd ordered his platoon to leave their fallen comrades in the field after a firefight and pursue the enemy into the jungle. When they came back, the bodies of their buddies had been stripped and skewered on sharpened bamboo poles staked into the ground. The next time the lieutenant gave the same order, the men refused to obey. He vowed to bring them up on charges. That night someone tossed a frag grenade in his tent.

"Were you able to take a look at the map?" I asked.

"I did. It doesn't show a road leading to that playa you and me hiked to, but I know for a fact for every one marked down there's a bunch more carved by four-wheel drives."

I told him about the one I came across on my way to the lake, right down to the horseshit and oil stain.

"It could be something, but it could also be nothing," Pudge said. "Maybe a poacher, maybe a rancher looking for strays." The chair squeaked as he swiveled to reach for the map I'd given him. "Mark the spot and I'll give a looksee when I get a chance."

I told him about finding the cows at Bluejoint Lake and tracing them to the Rocking H.

He rubbed his jaw. "So, you met the Harneys. Well, sooner or later everyone in this county crosses paths with them. More often than not it turns into crossing horns. Since they own a big chunk of the county, they think that gives them the right to do whatever they please."

"Do you get along with them?"

"Zachariah and I haven't seen eye to eye since elementary school. I arrested his youngest for being particularly stupid one night not too long ago. He got drunk and drove his truck into a house. Keeping Jesse locked up til morning didn't help improve his old man's opinion of me any."

"The oldest son, Blaine, he seemed straightforward enough."

That set the desk chair swiveling again. "There's a lot I could say about him, but won't."

"How come?"

The swivel chair groaned. "Well, you'll find out soon enough. Blaine and Gemma were married for a spell. It didn't work out so good."

"Blaine asked about the body."

"How did he know about her?"

"He said everybody's talking about the sheriff's vehicles going back and forth, the helicopter too. Blaine may have been fishing about who it was, but I didn't say anything."

Pudge groaned louder than his chair. "Gossip and rumor spread faster around here than a range fire when the Cohos blow. A newshound from the *Burns Herald* came knocking on Bust'em's door first thing this morning. And not just any newshound either. The editor and publisher."

"Who's he?"

"Not a he, a she. Bonnie LaRue. Not much gets past her. Her husband ran the paper and when he died, she took over. She prides herself in knowing stuff a person is thinking about doing before they even do it. She's got a string of people feeding her info all the time, from hairdressers at the beauty parlors to the barkeeps at the taverns. When I was sheriff, Bonnie and me had our share of run-ins, that's for sure."

"So much for trying to keep this quiet."

"Bust'em's trying to buy time while we hunt for Kathy Jenkins, so he told Bonnie some yarn about the body being a missing motorist whose car broke down and got lost looking for help. He led her to believe the person has been there for a while. She'll run a little news item in the paper tomorrow, but knowing Bonnie, she's gonna sniff out the real story sooner or later."

I asked him if the coroner had issued his findings on the dead girl yet.

He patted the manila folder on his desk and kept his hand on it. "I guess I got no one to blame but myself for you thinking you're more than an animal cop now. Though we've been ordered to focus on finding little Kathy Jenkins, sooner or later we'll be investigating that girl's murder. I can't tell you anything because we got to do it by the book. You understand?"

"Of course."

"I mean, it's not like the department couldn't use some help, us being only seven men for the entire county, and me being the one living next door to where the poor girl was killed."

"I get it," I said.

"I mean, if I knew something, like she fit the description from a missing persons report about some young gal who went off to visit her draft dodging boyfriend up in Canada but never showed up, I couldn't tell you about it, much less show it to you even if it was in this folder, much less ask you to poke around while Bust'em has me going around like a damn vacuum salesman. You understand, don't you, son?"

"I was only asking."

"Okay then. I'm glad we got that straight." Pudge stood and stretched. "Well, it's almost supper time. I'm gonna go wash up. I'll meet you in the dining room in a little bit. If you want, help yourself to the reading material."

"You have quite a library."

"I got a fascination with military history, but November is the real bookworm."

He closed the door behind him, leaving me alone in the office with the thick books on the shelves and the coroner's report on his desk.

PUDGE WAS SITTING at the head of the table when I came out to the dining room. "Go ahead, sit down. November will bring the food in. She doesn't like people in the kitchen. Ever. And word of advice, don't leave so much as a bean on your plate."

I stood up again when Gemma joined us.

"Lookee here, Daddy. A real gentleman." She said it in a fake southern accent and fluttered her eyelashes.

Pudge groaned. "It's gonna be a long supper."

Gemma flashed a self-satisfied smile. November ferried in a platter of breaded pork chops, a pot of beans, and a bowlful of steamed broccoli. She sat and we passed the food family style.

Pudge doused everything on his plate with hot sauce, including the vegetables.

November stared at me. "You are a soldier."

"Was," I said.

"You still act like one. You eat hunched over, always looking around like you don't got time to swallow."

I realized the deputy and his daughter were staring too. "Some habits are hard to shake."

"Let's hope not all of them," Pudge muttered.

"Lot of Paiute went off to fight too," November said. "The ones who didn't die eat like you."

"She means WW Two," Pudge said. "She was living on the Paiute Rez in Burns then."

November crossed her arms. "Paiute have a long warrior tradition. You heard of the Paiute War? One hundred years ago. *Nemooaka madukanna* took our land at Pyramid Lake, so Paiute fought to take it back."

"*Nemooaka* means to cheat," Gemma said.

"You meet any Paiute in your war?" November asked me.

"There were Indians in my battalion, but I don't know which tribes."

"Which *people*," she corrected. "A Paiute person is *neme*. Many different Paiute people. I am *Wadadökadö*."

"Wada Root and Grass-Seed Eater," Gemma translated.

I went back to eating, but November kept staring at me as she rocked back and forth. "A spirit visits you."

I looked up from my plate. Her hair briefly turned into black feathers. I tried to blink it away.

Pudge said, "All right, November. You've taught him enough about Paiute for one evening."

November's pronouncement took away my appetite. I had a tough time swallowing the pork chop. I monitored everyone's plate. I planned to make my excuses and leave as soon as they were finished.

"How do you spend your days?" Gemma asked.

"Behind the wheel, mostly," I said. "I have a lot of ground to cover and I haven't even been to the Sheldon Refuge yet."

"That's where the wild mustangs are," she said.

November chimed right in. "Those are Paiute ponies. *Nemooaka madukanna* stole them from us."

"So, your job is to keep cows out of the refuges?" Gemma asked.

"That's taking most of my time."

"I can't imagine it makes you any friends among the ranchers."

"It runs the gamut. When I told Joe Moon, he didn't seem to care. Others let me know their opinion, all right."

"Joe is among the last of his kind," Pudge said. "Harney County used to have hundreds of small ranches like the Crescent Moon. People came from all over to claim free land under the Homestead Act. They scratched out a living growing feed for their stock and food for the family. Not a whole lot of them left."

"Because the soil isn't right for farming and the way of life is too hard?" I said.

"Both, plus take-overs from the big ranchers who have the political and financial muscle to bend the rules their way and control the prices. They squeeze out the little guys."

I knew he was talking about the Harneys at the Rocking H.

"Joe Moon has some Paiute blood," November said. "Many grandfathers ago one of his married a *Tsösö'ödö tuviwarai* woman."

"Was she a root and grass seed eater too?" I asked.

"No. Her people were Those Who Live in the Cold. They lived up in the mountain the white men named after an Indian killer, Major Enoch Steens. He warred with the *Tsösö'ödö tuvi-*

warai and drove them from their home." She made a dry spitting noise.

"Joe told me his family has owned the ranch a long time."

"Yes, a long time," November said. "Though he ranches like a white man, he still follows some of the *neme* ways. He goes to sweat lodge and I've seen him at round dance."

"It looks like he lives there all alone."

"It's true," she said. "His parents passed. He never married."

"That's not unusual out here," Pudge said. "It's a hard life Joe and the rest of his kind are living. Not many women want any part of it. Or men, for that matter. Family ranches go belly up all the time because the sons and daughters all want to live in cities now where the jobs are nine-to-five and the TV reception good."

Gemma was holding a forkful of broccoli. "Have you visited all the ranches that border the refuges?"

"I don't know about all," I said.

"What about the Rocking H?"

"Here it comes," her father muttered.

"Today as a matter of fact."

November's face furrowed with contempt. "General William Selby Harney was the biggest Indian killer of all. He slaughtered Indian people wherever he went. Creeks and Seminoles in Florida. Sioux at Ash Hollow. This county is named after a butcher." She made the dry spitting noise again.

"That's all true," Gemma said to her, "but you know the Rocking H Harneys aren't related to the General at all. They only took his name because they didn't have one of their own." She turned to me. "The family's founding father was an orphan who came here on a cattle drive and wound up a homesteader. He couldn't read or write, only make an *X*. Who did you talk to there?"

"I let them know some of theirs cows had crossed through the restricted area," I dodged. I took the napkin off my lap and made a point of folding it neatly before placing it next to my plate. "Thank you for dinner. It was delicious, but it's been a long day and going to be an even longer tomorrow."

Gemma held up her fork like it was a crossing guard's stop sign. "When you say you let *them* know, do you mean everyone who lives on the ranch, or was there someone in particular?"

"Now, Gemma," Pudge said.

"*Now* what? I'm only making conversation with our guest. It's what polite company does." She turned her sights back on me. "So, who was it?"

I held her gaze for a ten count. The room fell silent as everyone waited.

"It was Mr. Harney," I said and pushed away from the table as Pudge chuckled.

I woke with a start and sat up fast, banging my head on the underside of the bunk. It wasn't the first time I had dived for cover while dreaming. I lay back on the floor and wiped my forehead. Either blood or night sweat moistened my fingertips. The glow-in-the-dark numbers on the black face of the field watch I'd worn since boot read 0350. I knew there was no going back to sleep and so I shimmied out, put the water on to boil, and waited for sunup.

It wasn't a single nightmare that replayed like a diamond stylus stuck in a scratched groove on a Doors album, rather a kaleidoscope of memories, sometimes fully played out, other times only fractured images. Green leaves turning red as blood sprayed. The wild eyes of a guerrilla wielding an AK-47. A brown helmet knocked off a PAVN soldier's head as I swung my empty M16 like a baseball bat. And then there were the sounds. The squish of mud beneath sandaled feet running toward me. The gurgle in the throat of a GI shot in the lung. A grown man crying *Mother*, then *Mom*, and finally *Mommy*.

This nightmare was different. It had been triggered by reading the folder Pudge had left on his desk. I sat at the kitchen table and held a mug of coffee under my chin, inhaling the steam to try to forget the image of a laughing young girl's face turning into a dried leathery mask, her mouth agape in a permanent scream.

The missing persons report included a wire photo of a smiling and shiny-eyed girl wearing a flowered headband and a cascade of long blond hair haloed by sunlight. The picture had been taken a month ago in a suburban backyard near Los Angeles. Her name was Vicky Wells, and she had freckles on her nose. She told her parents she was taking a semester off from college to visit her boyfriend who'd fled to Canada to avoid the draft. She would travel by Greyhound and pledged she would call them the moment she arrived. The report said she loved folk music, hanging out on the beach with friends, and walking the family golden retriever.

The contrast between the sunny, carefree photograph and my memory of Vicky Wells's naked body wedged in the undercut of a gully at Hart Mountain was bad enough, but not nearly as haunting as the words scrawled on a single sheet of blue-lined notebook paper clipped to the report. It was the notes Pudge had jotted while listening to the coroner. *Thorns and rock cuts on feet. Scraped knees. Forced to walk or tried to escape? Bruises on face. Hands tied. Ligature marks on wrists. Rope, maybe cord. Raped. Strangled. Inch wide ligature. Maybe a belt? Lock of hair missing. Souvenir? Bite marks by wild animals.*

The more I thought about it, the more Vicky's face morphed into Kathy's, the missing girl from Salem. They shared many of the same features. Sheriff Burton and Governor Lane were hoping Kathy had run off with a secret boyfriend, but after three years in Vietnam and a stint in the rubber room at Walter Reed, I didn't think so. I could still hear the words my DI barked as he shaped new recruits at Fort Hood. He was a lifer who had a portrait of Jesus tattooed on his chest and a crucifix inked on his back. "Hope is not a strategy. Killing the enemy is."

Dawn seeped through the window. My stomach churned from too much caffeine and too many memories. It was times like this only one thing would help me outrun my craving for a spoonful of horse to silence the demons. I wolfed down a slice of bread and pulled on boots, jeans, and a leather jacket.

The Triumph was parked next to the Ford pickup. I straddled it and stomped the kick starter. The instrument dials sprang to life as the powerful 650cc engine throbbed. I was watching the oil pressure gauge and listening to the roar, so I didn't hear the Rolls Royce Silver Cloud pull up. I still didn't notice until someone tapped me on the shoulder.

It was Sister Star from the ashram.

I killed the engine. "What are you doing here?"

"You're not with the sheriff's department," she said.

"I never said I was."

"But Sheriff Warbler did, only he's not really sheriff anymore. He's only a deputy."

"All he said was my name, but I can see how you might have been mistaken because of my uniform."

"I'm here because I learned what you really do. We need you to come to the ranch and do your job."

"What's going on?"

"Something is killing our cattle. We lost a cow and her baby last night. Brother Michael thinks it might be a wolf."

"It can't be. The state paid bounties to kill them all. The last one was turned in twenty years ago."

"Then maybe it's a bear. Could you come and see?"

"Later. I've got something I need to do first."

"Please. We're afraid."

Sister Star was not alone. Damian, the young man with the

tattoo of the serpent-entwined dagger who'd been fixing the ashram's fence, was sitting behind the wheel of the Rolls Royce.

"Okay," I said.

Her voice turned plaintive. "When?"

"I'll be right behind you."

I pulled my goggles down and pointed the Triumph north. The Silver Cloud had a five-minute head start, but I knew I could make that up easily. I shifted through the gears, and the bike hit its stride at ninety. I left it wide open until I caught up with the Rolls as it turned into the ashram.

Brother Michael met us. The sun reflected off his bald head as he bowed. "Thank you for coming. I read in the paper this morning the sheriff's department found a body. Was it the girl you and the deputy who called himself a sheriff inquired about?"

"No."

"Whoever it is, they have achieved another stage. Death is not the end of life, merely the end of the body we presently inhabit. It is to be celebrated rather than grieved."

"From what I've seen, death and sorrow go hand in hand," I said. "Sister Star tells me you have a problem with predators."

"That is correct," Brother Michael said. "While we respect all forms of life, we must also protect those creatures who cannot fend for themselves."

"Show me the kill site."

He frowned. "It is in the far field, but I must warn you, it is quite gruesome. Many in our family are very upset. Vasudeva is at temple chanting for the animals, so their spirits may be released and reincarnated."

We headed for the field. Damian followed behind like a soldier walking sweep. Sister Star tried looping her arm through mine. Again, I shrugged away.

"You shrink from human touch because you are still at war. I can sense it in your aura," she said.

"I left the army a while ago."

"I mean the war you still fight within yourself. It's all the more reason you should undertake the journey of spiritual awakening. Open your heart. Open your mind. It will release you from what you saw and did. Vasudeva will serve as your guide."

"Let's see what's eating your cows first."

The remains lay in a heap near the barbed wire fence. A pair of turkey vultures were dining on strings of guts. I shooed the undertaker birds away before circling the carcass. Her hindquarters had been raked by claws and her throat ripped by teeth. The belly had been sliced open as neatly as if by a butcher knife. The ground was trampled by paw prints as big as my hand.

"A cougar killed the cow and dragged off the calf." I looked at the fence. "Is it still upright all the way around? Any digging under the bottom strand anywhere?"

Brother Michael beckoned Damian. "Tell him," he said to the young man.

"The fence hasn't been disturbed since I fixed it." He clasped his hands as he spoke. The knuckles on his right hand bore scabs.

"Did you see any cougar tracks when you were working on it, either on this side of the fence or the other?"

"No, not like the ones that are here now."

"It looks like the cougar jumped the fence with the calf between its jaws. He's probably dragged it off somewhere to eat. Or she has. It could be a female with a den full of hungry kits."

"The creature is that powerful?" Sister Star said.

"A big one, sure. They go two hundred pounds. Is this the only cow-calf pair that's been attacked?"

Brother Michael hesitated. "We cannot be certain. We were not as thorough as we should have been accounting for the herd when we first took possession. The cows were delivered by tractor trailers and they all seemed to arrive at once. It was very hectic. Some of the livestock may have wandered away before the fence was repaired. It is possible they may have been attacked beyond our property line."

A yellow plastic tag was still affixed to the dead cow's ear. It was a new branding technique. "There should be a list to go along with the ID numbers on your herd's ear tags. You can match them up and do a head count."

"We could if all the numbers had been properly entered into a logbook. We fell behind on the paper work when the cattle arrived." Brother Michael sighed and held up his palms as if in supplication. "Alas, we are relatively new to ranching, but with Vasudeva's guidance we shall learn and prosper."

I realized Gemma Warbler might have an inventory list. She'd told me she'd been out to Crossed Bars checking cattle registrations as part of her moonlighting job with the Department of Agriculture.

"There's a few things you can do to prevent it from happening again." I looked at Damian. "Beef up your defenses by raising your fence. Get a couple of guard dogs. Patrol the perimeter at night. Weapons should be locked and loaded. You know what I'm talking about."

The young man turned his head away. Brother Michael said, "We do not own guns. Our beliefs forbid it. Nor would we hurt a living creature."

"You don't slaughter your own cows?"

"Certainly not. We hire a local man who is skilled as a meat dresser. Joe Moon transports them to his place of business, prepares them in accordance to our spiritual beliefs and dietary specifications, and returns the sustenance to us."

Sister Star interrupted. "Isn't one of the duties of the Fish and Wildlife Service to dispatch predators?"

"Another branch does that. Wildlife Services," I said.

"But you're the only ranger in the region, and this is an emergency. Our livelihood is at stake. Maybe our lives too. What if the cougar was to catch one of us walking to the outhouse at night?"

"You must protect us," Brother Michael implored. "It is your sworn duty."

A mountain lion attacking a human was extremely unlikely, but I realized that agreeing to find the cougar could give me an opening for talking to Damian alone. He seemed to have recognized Kathy Jenkins when Pudge showed him her picture.

"Okay, but I'll need some help. How about it, Damian? Want to lend a hand? Cougars perch up high and if there's a den, it'll be hidden in the rocks. The big cats sleep during the day, so we'll need to hunt for them at night when they're active."

He looked at Brother Michael before answering. The bald-headed man nodded his assent.

"All right" he said. "I'll go with you."

"Roger that. I need to fetch some gear. I'll be back at sunset. Wear boots and bring a jacket. You don't want to get cold feet."

I returned home, donned my work uniform, and switched to the pickup for the thirty-minute drive south to the Malheur Refuge. I was overdue for a patrol there. As I pulled away from the lineman's shack, the ends of white envelopes sticking between the visor and headliner caught my eye. Joe Moon's letters. I'd forgotten all about them. I glanced at them before dropping them in the blue box in front of the post office. One was addressed to a bank in Burns, the other to a feed and grain store. I wondered if they contained checks or notes begging for extension on overdue bills. I wondered how long it would be until they foreclosed on his ranch, and when they took it away, what would a man who knew nothing other than cowboying do for a job.

The Malheur Refuge was flatter, wetter, and greener than Hart. Two rivers with the improbable names Donnen and Blitzen ran through it. They fed a good-sized lake ringed by marshes and grassy fields that was a key stopover for waterfowl migrating up and down the Pacific Flyway. The birds attracted poachers and my job was to keep that from happening.

The main entrance was right off the highway. There was an

unmanned information kiosk that overlooked the lake. A Volkswagen bus was the only vehicle in the parking lot. "Further" was painted in dayglow letters on the front of the bus and "Later" on the rear. Drawn curtains made from Indian bedspreads covered the windows and hung behind the front seat to black out the passenger compartment. I parked next to it and got out to tell the occupants that no overnight parking was allowed.

"Hello," I called before knocking on a neon rainbow painted on the double passenger doors. "I need to talk to you about camping rules."

No one answered. I knocked again. "Open up. It's the ranger."

A woman screamed down by the lake. The noise startled the rafts of ducks. They lifted off the water all at once in an explosion of wingbeats. She screamed again. I yanked the .357 magnum from the glove box and ran toward it.

A man's yell followed another scream. It pushed me faster. I gulped air. My throat burned. My heart raced. White skin flashed. A naked woman dashed out from behind a thick clump of cattails at the shoreline. She cried out again. Another naked figure sprinted right behind her. This one hairier. A lot hairier. A beard. Chest hair. Pubic hair. I crouched and gripped the heavy Smith & Wesson with both hands.

"*Dung lai!*" I shouted. "*Dung lai!*"

The naked woman skidded to a stop near water's edge and screamed again. Only she was screaming at me. The naked man stopped too. He turned, his face registering shock.

"Whoa, man. Cool out," he said. "Cool out."

Another figure was splashing a few yards offshore. It was a young girl frantically trying to reach land.

The man didn't bother to hide his penis. "Hey man, like, we're just skinny-dipping."

The woman who'd been about to jump into the water was shaking. "Can you put that gun away? It's really freaking me out."

I lowered the heavy revolver and held it at my side since I didn't have a holster. The young girl scrambled to shore and flopped onto the bank. She was skinny, her breasts small and pointed. She shook.

The woman went over and hugged her. "It's okay, Jenny. It's okay. He's just a cop. Just a big, dumb cop."

"Okay if I grab my shorts?" the man asked. I nodded. He pulled on a pair of cutoffs. "You, like, scared the shit out of us, man. How we supposed to know what you're saying when you shout it in, what, Chinese?"

"I heard screaming," I said.

"That was Jenny hitting the water. It's cold enough to freeze the tits off a witch. Linda was psyching herself up before she jumped in. Me too."

Jenny and Linda got dressed. Jenny looked to be in her teens, Linda in her midtwenties. The man was at least thirty-five.

The trio walked up to me. "What's your name?" I asked him.

"Barry," he said. "Like Barry McGuire. You know, the dude who sings 'Eve of Destruction.' Righteous tune."

"Swimming's not allowed in the lake," I said. "It's protected for the birds."

Barry grinned. "The Byrds. Hey man, 'Eight Miles High.' Like, my favorite song." He hummed the opening riff while playing air guitar. He was stoned.

"There's no overnight parking or camping either."

"Wow, don't be such a bummer," Linda said with a lot of attitude.

"Cool it," Barry told her. "He's the man."

She made an oinking noise. "He's only a Ranger Rick or something."

The Fish & Wildlife badge pinned to my breast pocket felt as heavy as the two-pound gun in my hand.

"I see your bus has Washington State license plates. Are you on your way home or on your way from?"

Barry wore a necklace made of colorful beads. He combed his beard with his fingertips. "From, man. We're headed to Frisco. That's where it's all happening. The Dead. Airplane. Hendrix. You name it. They say Dylan's going to play the Fillmore."

"And Barry says maybe we'll see The Beatles too," Jenny said. "I love Paul McCartney. He's so cute." Her giggle was a schoolgirl's.

"Ob-la-di ob-la-da," Barry sang. "It's from their new album, *The White Album*. Far out. You've heard it, right?"

"Are you planning on driving straight through to San Francisco?"

"Depends. You know, on what we find along the way. We're not into straight lines."

"We follow the sun," Linda said.

"Maybe all the way to South America," Jenny added with more giggles.

She was stoned too. They all were. "How old are you?" I asked her.

"Why do you care?" she said.

"How old?"

"Old enough. I'm eighteen."

"She is," Barry said quickly, pumping his head up and down. "Linda here is my old lady. Jenny is her little cousin. Tell him, babe."

"Her mom and mine are sisters," Linda said.

Jenny stuck her tongue out at me.

"If you're looking to camp, the nearest spot south is a forest service campground. It's about ten miles down the road."

"So, you're not going to bust us or anything?" Barry said.

"Just a warning this time. The refuges have different rules than national forests."

"Far out. Well, since we can't swim, we might as well split." Barry flashed the peace sign. "Later, dude."

"Like our magic bus says. Later." Jenny giggled and stuck out her tongue again.

The bus sputtered and then backfired a few times as they pulled out of the parking lot and headed south. My hand was shaking. I sat down and placed the .357 on the ground. I tried rubbing my hands together, but the shaking wouldn't stop, and so I shoved them under my armpits.

The shakes were not from the weight of the gun. It was the aftereffects of adrenaline. My body had always produced too much of it. A medic told me I had hyperadrenalism. The shrink at Walter Reed said it was one of the reasons why I craved heroin. It was the only thing strong enough to stanch the flow. Adrenaline is a two-headed beast, he told me. On the creative side, it can cause you to have visions and enhanced clairvoyance. On the physical side, it pushes you to do superhuman things, like lift a blown-up jeep off a buddy or run into a burning hooch to save a family of rice farmers. He also said if you can't figure out a way to control it, it can trigger a mental breakdown and send you jumping off a bridge.

I started humming The Beatles song. I didn't sing the words aloud, nor did I look up for the black-feathered creature. I just kept humming it. It took all five verses, but finally my pulse slowed and my hands stopped shaking. When they did, I got up and walked down to the lake.

Linda had struck a nerve when she called me a dumb cop. Barry had too by calling me the man. I could still feel the sting of a woman spitting on me at the airport when I stepped off the flight home from Saigon. I knew the bands Barry mentioned, knew most of their songs by heart. They were anthems in Vietnam, blasted on cheap stereo sets at every camp. If I wanted, I could go hear them in person right now. Just jump in my truck and follow the VW bus down to San Francisco. I'd be able to score smack in the Haight no problem. Trip to rock 'n' roll at the Fillmore. Nod off at a crash pad overlooking the Panhandle. And when I awoke, I could do it all over again.

The ducks returning to the lake broke the moment. They were as noisy with their splashdown as they had been with their takeoff. Green headed mallards here, cinnamon teal there. A pair of red-winged blackbirds perched on cattails and trilled at one another. A butterfly spotted like a leopard fluttered by. The water had cleared. I could see tadpoles hiding in the shallows between stalks of water sedge. A great blue heron waded silently toward them on graceful legs without making a ripple. The bird froze, allowing me time to admire its white striped crown and rusty thighs.

And then in a flash the tableau shattered as the bird stabbed its daggerlike bill into the water and gulped down tadpoles by the dozen.

Halfway back to No Mountain I recognized a bright red Jeep Wagoneer parked in front of a ramshackle ranch house. It was Gemma's mobile animal surgery. I pulled in behind it. Gemma was inside a sagging corral standing behind a cow that was sandwiched between the barred walls of a head gate. Her arm was shoved inside the cow's vagina.

"Just don't stand there," she hollered. "Grab the tail. We don't have much time."

I hustled over and pulled the cow's tail to the side.

"Not hers. The calf's. It's a breech birth. There, below my arm. You got it?"

A limp, rope-like thing was hanging. I grabbed it.

"Keep hold," Gemma instructed.

My shirt was soon slick with blood and amniotic fluid. "What now?"

"I'm trying to check her cervix." She maneuvered herself to get a longer reach. "Okay, it's fully dilated but the calf's hips are stuck on the other side. We're going to have to pull it through. I'll grab the legs, you pull on the tail."

I ground my boots into the soil to set myself.

"On my count," Gemma said. "Don't yank. Pull firm but steady. Ready, set, go."

We pulled together. The cow bellowed and tried to shuffle, but couldn't move because of the head gate holding her fast.

"It's coming. Don't stop. Steady. Steady. Steady. Here come the legs. Drop the tail and grab them above the hooves. Now pull. Good. There, the hips are through. Don't stop. There, now the shoulders are through. Here he comes. Look out!"

I stumbled backward and landed on my rear with the newborn in my lap as a whoosh of liquid came gushing out.

Gemma whooped. "All right! Hold him."

Towels were piled on a tarp. She grabbed some and rubbed the calf's face and head, clearing his nostrils and mouth. The mother bawled. Gemma dried the calf's body as well as she could and slid him onto the tarp.

"Here, keep rubbing his sides. It'll help with his breathing. I need to make sure the placenta separated."

The calf's eyes were rolled back, but his flanks were heaving as he gasped. I rubbed the bony body briskly as if working bellows to breathe life into a dying fire. Gemma knelt beside me and shoved a tube into one of the calf's nostrils. She gave it a hearty suck as if siphoning gas and then repeated the trick on the other nostril. The calf shivered and sneezed loudly. Snot blew everywhere. The newborn bleated.

"That's a good sign," Gemma said. "I'll give him a dose of colostrum. If he can get on his feet within two hours and nurse, he'll make it."

She retrieved a plastic basin from the back of her Jeep and filled it from a five-gallon jerrican of water. "Here, for washing up." She tossed me a towel.

"Why isn't the rancher helping you?"

"He died this winter. This is a mom and pop outfit, and the

widow is in a wheelchair. I was called out to a neighboring ranch to see about a lame horse and stopped by to check on her. She told me she thought one of her dairy cows was due. She was right."

"How often does a breech happen?"

"One in thirty births. That's about the same rate as twins. And breeched twins? Getting eight legs all jumbled up out of the mama is something you never forget."

I held the calf while Gemma mixed powdered colostrum with water in a baby bottle and shoved the rubber nipple in the calf's mouth.

"You act like you're no stranger to emergency medicine," she said.

I didn't answer, but I wasn't the only soldier who'd held up a field IV for a medic during the middle of a firefight or compressed a sucking wound with the palm of a hand and shoved wadding into a bullet hole.

Gemma seemed to sense it, so she didn't press. "I could've done it on my own. I've done it plenty of times, but I appreciate your help. What brings you out here?"

"I saw your Jeep. I was at Crossed Bars earlier this morning. They've lost some stock to a cougar. They don't know how many because they don't have a head count. I thought maybe you did from when you were there checking on their herd."

Gemma continued nursing the calf with the bottle. "I probably have a carbon copy somewhere. You know government forms. Everything is in triplicate. Would you let the mama out? There's a couple of latches."

I opened the head gate. The cow ambled out and went straight for a pile of fresh hay. She started grazing, none the worse for wear.

"So, what do you think now that you've been out there?" Gemma asked. "The religious folks."

"Reminds me of a monastery I visited once. Rules and discipline and monks that didn't question them."

"Where was that?"

"Outside of Hue. That's in Vietnam."

Gemma was rubbing the calf's head as it sucked on the bottle. "I remember reading about the Tet Offensive in the newspaper. It sounded awful." She grimaced. "What's it called, the monastery over there?"

"Thien Mu. It's the oldest Buddhist temple in-country."

I didn't add that my inside look of it came after our garrison was overrun and we holed up inside waiting for reinforcements that never came. We ran out of rations and our canteens ran dry. We were reduced to eating the offerings the monks had left on the altar and drinking holy water. By the time we fought our way out, we were hallucinating from dehydration and hunger.

The calf finished the bottle. Gemma clapped it on the back as if burping a baby. "The religious people asked you to take care of the cougar, didn't they?"

"I'm going back this evening and take a look around. See what I find."

"Does Pudge know that?"

"It's Fish and Wildlife business."

"Sure it is."

"Why do you say it like that?"

"Because something about you tells me you're going to be poking around for something more than a big hungry cat."

Damian wore a green field jacket and had swapped his Jesus sandals for a pair of scuffed combat boots. He stared out the windshield as we drove along a dirt road beyond the ashram's fence line.

"Where were you stationed in-country?" I asked.

"We don't live in the past. We exist in the present while we strive for enlightenment. The future is already ordained." The young sect member said it as if reciting from a note card.

"It's your jacket. I had one like it, but I never wore it. Too hot and didn't keep the rain out. A boonie was best for blocking the sun." I steered around a large rock. "Of course, it wasn't as good as a helmet when there was incoming. What AO were you in?"

"What do you mean by this?"

"You don't remember AO? Area of Operation."

"I meant, what do you mean by asking me these questions? What are you hoping to learn?"

"I recognized your tattoo. There were at least three parlors on Tu Do that did them. I hope you didn't pay more than a pack of Marlboros for it. Who knows, we could've been in the same paddy at the same time, watching each other's back. That makes us brothers."

"We do not look back, only forward."

"So, you said. There was this guy in my unit. He could've gotten out of going. You know, college deferment. We called him the Professor. He was always quoting somebody. And not rock 'n' roll songs either. One of his favorites was a Spanish guy named Santayana. 'Those who do not remember the past are condemned to repeat it.' Santayana had another that made even more sense to me. 'Only the dead have seen the end of war.' "

"There is no war on the true path. There is only peace and enlightenment."

"Tell that to the guys in the Pentagon. Or in Hanoi, for that matter. Is that why you joined up with this religious group? Because of 'Nam?"

"Everyone has their own reason, but it is of no consequence. What is important is the willingness to give oneself over to the true path."

I tried to dodge a large pothole, but the back wheel hit it and the truck bounced hard. "I haven't met your Vasudeva yet, but Sister Star is, well, far out."

"She is very devout," Damian said.

"She acts like she can see both the past and the future. You know, when she does that thing when she closes her eyes."

"Everything becomes clear when you're on the true path."

"Is that what your religion is called, the true path?"

"Names aren't important. Enlightenment is."

"Okay, so how long have you been at it, being on this path?"

"We do not look back, only forward."

"So, you keep saying." I downshifted. "I had an LT that believed that too. He ordered the platoon to keep moving out no matter what. Problem was, he wouldn't believe me when I told him Charlie had a way of circling around. They flanked us and shot us front and back. My LT learned the hard way."

I braked harder than I needed to, hoping it would be like slapping a buddy across the face to keep him from losing consciousness after he'd been hit. The abrupt stop didn't seem to faze Damian at all. We'd reached the crest of a low hill. The sky was turning from ash to charcoal. Outcroppings were melting into the penumbra. I scanned the tops with binoculars looking for silhouettes.

"How do you plan to find a cougar in the dark?" he asked.

"The same as on any patrol. Look for where it's most likely to hole up or ambush you." I lowered the binoculars. "Are you able to forget that part too or were you rear guard? Humping a clipboard in a supply depot or maybe on permanent shit burning detail. Those guys, you could smell them walking back to camp from a mile away."

That hit him harder than a slap. His cheeks flushed. He started breathing deeply "I follow the true path," he said as he exhaled. "It is my guide, my salvation. The true path leads me to peace and understanding." He closed his eyes and began chanting. "Om. Omm. Ommm."

I recognized all the familiar signs of a grunt just trying to keep his shit together during and after a firefight.

"So, you were in the tall grass," I said.

Damian kept chanting.

"You know, I envy you," I said.

He opened his eyes. "How so?"

"You've found a way to make sense of it all or at least put it behind you. Me? The only thing that helped was dope. A lot of it. But that was swapping one war for another. Either way you wind up a casualty."

He reached over and touched my wrist. "It took courage for you to tell me that. Vasudeva teaches us that having the courage to face your weaknesses and stop lying to yourself are the first steps on the true path."

"That or having nothing else to try or nothing else to lose."

We resumed our zigzag sweep. With luck, the headlights would pick up the yellow eyes of the cougar. With even more luck, the lights would make the big cat freeze. The route turned sandy. The wheels spun. Loose sand spit. I tried rocking us back and forth to gain traction. Damian was looking out the side window as the moon rose and its pale light began to soften the darkness.

"Khe Sanh," he said abruptly in a faraway voice. "They hit us from all sides. They threw everything at us and didn't care if they died. It was like that every day for eleven weeks. By the time we finally got relieved, we were down to using the last bullets in our dead's weapons. When I got back to camp, I found out my CO had put me in for a Section Eight. Three days later I was on a Pan Am Freedom Bird flying home."

He turned away from the window. "Of course, I couldn't go home because it is true. Was, I mean. I only enlisted in the marines because my father thought it would make a man out of me. So, I wandered. I was lost and then I was found by Vasudeva. And now I am on the true path." He sighed. "You don't have to say anything. I understand why you wouldn't want me sitting next to you. I'm used to it. I've been called every name in the book. I'll get out here and walk back."

The wheels finally bit hard surface and the pickup lurched forward. I gave it gas and got us rolling again.

"Like I said, we could've been in the same paddy. That makes us brothers no matter what anybody says. Here's what we're going to do. Same as on any patrol. You take right, I'll take left. Look for anything that moves."

We drove on without speaking. Most of the time, we weren't even on a road, but I wanted to get close to a distant outcrop. If

I were a cougar, that's where I'd be. Always take the high ground.

"I've been meaning to ask you," I said. "When I was out at the ranch last time and you looked at the picture of that missing girl, you acted like you recognized her, maybe had seen or talked to her."

"No, I never met her," Damian said quickly.

"So, you said, but so did everyone else on the ranch. It was like they'd all been told not to say anything." I let it hang, remembering that when we used to capture VC scouts, we often learned more by saying nothing. Fear, like matter, always expanded to occupy the available space.

"She made me think of someone else is all," Damian said.

"Who? Another girl who visited the ranch?"

"From my former life. I used to have a sister."

"Used to?"

"There is no room on the true path for anyone but fellow seekers of enlightenment. Vasudeva is my father now. Sister Star is my sister."

I pictured Damian's real father, a beer can crusher who beat the shit out of him every day and called him a pussy, a sissy, a coward, a faggot.

"What was your real sister's name?"

He hesitated. "Lizzie. Her name was Lizzie."

"And what about you? Damian's a pretty unusual name for an American kid. It's from the Herman Hesse novel, right? The German writer. He wrote 'Siddhartha.' Lots of guys were reading him in 'Nam. All the self-realization stuff."

"I don't know what you're talking about," Damian said.

I pretended to focus on the road, but I was studying my passenger out of the corner of my eye.

"I have a kid sister too," I lied. "She looks a lot like the girl in the picture the deputy showed you, only she's a few years older. I haven't seen her for a while. She left home to go to Canada to visit her boyfriend. Who knows, she may have even stopped off at the ashram for a night, so she wouldn't have to pay for a motel."

Damian shifted in his seat. "What's her name?"

"Vicky," I said.

"I don't remember a Vicky. A lot of girls stop by."

"Vicky would've stood out. She has this smile. Always laughing."

The truck shook hard as we bounced over a rocky patch.

"I'm sure she was especially happy when she heard you'd come home from the war," he said.

THE COUGAR HAD TAKEN the high ground like I thought he would. We left the truck and started hiking toward an outcropping separated from the cougar's perch by a gully. I had the .30-30 slung over my shoulder as we scrambled over boulders in the moonlight. Damian had refused to take the shotgun, and that was fine with me. The man brimmed with conflict and contradiction no matter how hard he tried to project peace and calm.

He reminded me of a lance corporal at Walter Reed who'd been a Saigon junkie too. The soldier had cracked up after a case of friendly fire. He'd machine-gunned three men in his own platoon during a night patrol. The corporal always waved a Bible in group therapy and proclaimed, "I used to be hooked on heroin, now I'm hooked on Jesus." One morning he didn't show up at group. The nurse said he'd been transferred in the night, but I later learned he'd hung himself with a bed sheet.

We reached the bottom of the outcropping. "You can wait here if you want," I said.

"No, the cattle were in my care. Vasudeva ordained that taking responsibility for one's actions helps purify the spirit."

We started climbing. I led. An overhang blocked our route to the top. I would need both hands to pull myself up.

"Here, take the rifle. It's likely to slip off. When I'm on top, you can hand it up."

The glow of the moon made Damian's face pale. "I told you, weapons are against our beliefs. I can't touch one."

"We don't have a choice here. Besides, the chamber's empty. It might as well be a stick."

I gripped the Winchester by the tip of the barrel and lowered it to him. When I felt Damian take the butt, I let go. Then I reached high and grabbed the lip of the overhang and hoisted myself up and over. I scooted around and peered down. Damian had flattened himself against the face of the rock clutching the rifle with both hands.

"Om. Omm. Ommm," he chanted.

I gritted my teeth and hoped the cougar couldn't hear the chant. "Come on," I whispered. "Hand me the rifle."

Damian repositioned himself and the gun. He held it against his shoulder and sighted through the scope. The barrel was aimed right at my face. I hadn't heard a round being chambered, but my heart beat could have drowned it out.

"Hand it up," I said.

He kept aiming it at me.

"Come on," I said. "Hand me the gun."

He could see my every expression magnified through the scope, whether my lip twitched or if fear crossed my eyes. I stilled myself the same way I did when hiding behind a tree next to a trail while a company of PAVN regulars trooped by.

"Hand it up," I said.

Finally, the tip of the rifle barrel inched toward me. I snatched it and yanked it up.

"Okay, grab hold of the ledge," I said. "It's like doing pull-ups back at boot."

The cougar was still perched one hundred yards away. It was a challenging distance to cover with a hunting caliber like the .30-30, especially at night, and though I'd scored high in marksmanship during training, long-range shooting was a skill I seldom had to use. Most of the firefights I'd been in were on battlegrounds the size of a small backyard.

I levered a round and braced my elbows against the rock to steady the barrel. The rising moon turned the cougar's perch into a milk bath. The cat came into sharp focus as I twisted the dial on the scope. Damian crouched next to me.

"Do you think it's the one that killed our cows?" he whispered.

"Probably. It's male, and male cougars don't share a territory."

I could see the big cat's powerful haunches and long tail. It twitched. I finished making the adjustments until I had the crosshairs right between the cougar's shoulder blades. They rippled as the animal moved his head from side to side surveying his domain.

A lot of soldiers had grown up hunting, but not me. The army had turned me into one. When I got to Vietnam, the war was not being waged for defense. It was one operation after another to draw the enemy out, so we could engage them. Our generals took a while to learn that's exactly what Ho Chi Minh was banking on. The first time I fired a gun at a man, I didn't have time to sight it, much less think about it. It was point and shoot and keep doing it until the enemy was either dead or had melted back into the jungle.

But now I did have time to think about it. How was the big cat any different than a rice farmer whose village had been torched and his paddies overrun? A farmer who still had a family to feed with whatever he could find? A farmer so desperate he would sneak into an invading army's camp in the dark of night to try to steal food?

"Go on, fire," Damian said. "What are you waiting for?"

The cougar turned his head without rotating his body to search for the source of the voice. The yellow eyes trained on our position and filled the scope. I pulled the trigger. The rifle punched my shoulder as it recoiled. The blast of the shot echoed. A spark flashed across the gully as the bullet ricocheted off a boulder. The cougar leapt and was gone.

"You missed," Damian said angrily. "I can't believe you didn't kill the damn thing. You blew it."

I didn't lever the spent shell but left the brass cooling in the chamber. "Did I?"

Blackpowder Smith's was the only tavern in No Mountain. It also did double duty as a dry goods store. Beer signs promoting Blitz-Weinhard and Olympia shared wall space with flyers for soap, cereal, and jeans. The proprietor had a billy-goat beard that reached his sternum, and he wore a black cowboy hat with a band made of rattlesnake skin. He was sitting across a chessboard from Pudge Warbler.

"Knight takes pawn, queen takes knight, bishop takes queen, and check," the deputy said as his fingers hovered over the board.

"You think you pinned me? I castle, I'll get your bishop and it's mate in three." Blackpowder Smith's voice sounded as if he'd swallowed lye. He saw me approach. "Don't give him any advice, young fella. It only confuses him."

Pudge put his hand back in his lap and concentrated on the board. "Thought I had you this time. Don't know how I missed your rook."

"Because you're always looking at the trees and miss the damn forest." Blackpowder leaned back with a self-congratulatory smile.

"Sheriff, you got a moment?" I said.

Blackpowder winked at me, acknowledging my use of Pudge's former title.

"I'm busy here," Pudge said.

"Busy losing," Blackpowder said.

Pudge threw up his hands. "Ah, hell. I've been thinking on this game so hard my skull aches. What do you say, Black, how 'bout we take a break?"

"It won't change the outcome. Your goose is already plucked, buttered, and cooked." The barkeep ambled away. "Don't try and move any pieces. I got 'em all memorized." He tapped the side of his hat without turning around.

Pudge gestured for me to take the newly vacated chair. "What's so important?"

"It's about last night. I spent it with a member of the ashram."

"Word of advice? No Mountain's a small town. There are some things you don't want to be bragging about. And as for your taste in—"

"Not that. I got called out to Crossed Bars to hunt a cougar and took Damian with me. He's the young guy working on the fence that took his time looking at the photo of Kathy Jenkins." I filled him in, right down to the point where the ex-GI lost his cool.

"Did he seem jittery to you like he had something to hide or because he went from shooting at the enemy to banging a tambourine?" Pudge asked.

"He did tell me he got section-eighted out of the marines. He was at Khe Sanh. The siege was the longest and bloodiest of the war."

"A fellow leatherneck? Well I'll be. Sounds like maybe he isn't right in the head."

"I think he saw both girls, Vicky and Kathy. Or other girls that look like them."

"What do you mean other girls?"

"He said lots of girls stop by."

Pudge started bobbing.

"Why, what have you found out?" I asked.

"Who said I found out anything?"

"Your manner."

"You sound like Sister Star. What was it she called it, my oral?"

"Aura. It's an energy field your body gives off."

"You learn that along with all that other hippie dippy religious stuff you know about?"

"What did you find out?"

It took him a while to convince himself trading information could help catch the killer.

"Remember those two from Crossed Bars who we couldn't question because they were shopping in Burns? Well, Bust'em talked to them. A man and a woman. The woman said she didn't recognize Kathy Jenkins from the facsimile he showed her, but she let on that another girl who looked like her had passed through earlier. She couldn't remember her name."

"Vicky Wells?"

"Maybe, or maybe someone else. Anyway, her fellow monk told her to shut up. And then he told Bust'em she was mistaken."

"What did Sheriff Burton do?"

"Not much he could do. They hadn't broken the law or anything. But there's a college boy who hangs around the sheriff's office. He's set his hat to join the FBI, but he isn't twenty-three yet so he's too young to apply. Until then, he's trying to get law enforcement experience. Bust'em has him filing reports and fetching coffee. Anyway, the college boy takes it upon himself to collect a bunch of missing persons reports from all over the country with links to Oregon—girls who live in the state, parents who thought their daughter might be headed this way, and so on. Turns out there's quite a few."

"He sounds pretty smart."

"He's the only college boy I've seen that hasn't grown a beard and forgotten to get a haircut regularly."

"What did Sheriff Burton say when he saw the reports all laid out?"

"What he's been saying since Aubrey Jenkins flew off in his helicopter. We got to focus on little Kathy. She's real, the other missing girls are, quote, unquote, 'theoretical.' "

I looked at the chessboard. I'd played my share. It was more than a way to pass the time between patrols. It was a reminder that war was as old as life itself and kings could fall the same as pawns.

"Since Sheriff Burton has you tied up knocking on doors, how about if I go back to Hart Mountain tomorrow and search the gully and others near it? Whoever put Vicky Wells there was no stranger to the area. He was careful to choose it because he could get in and get out without being seen. Maybe he's used the refuge more than once."

"That's my job, and I'll be the one doing the looking," Pudge said sharply.

"And the Hart Refuge is my beat," I said right back.

We had a stare down, but he broke it off. "Ah, screw Bust'em. He gave me a mess of paper work to fill out, but if I get it done in the morning, I can get down to Hart at noon. If you're there when I get there, well, it's still a free country, and we can look around together."

I took another look at the chessboard. "Queen to king two. Blackpowder will still castle. You move rook to queen one without castling and you'll have mate in three."

He made the moves in his head. "Damned if you're not right."

Loud voices came from the bar. Jesse Harney was standing chin to chin with Blackpowder Smith.

"I ordered a damn beer. My money is as good as anyone's, if not better," the younger of the two brothers who lived on the Rocking H Ranch shouted.

"And I say you're still eighty-sixed. You want me to lift it, pay for the tray of glasses you broke last time." Blackpowder let it hang before sticking in the knife. "Ask your daddy. Maybe he'll give you an advance on your allowance."

The bar thudded as Jesse kicked its base. "Maybe I will. And maybe I'll buy this dump and burn it to the ground."

"Ah, hell," Pudge said. "The stork carrying that kid dropped him one too many times." He pushed himself out of his chair and started for the bar. The approaching footsteps caused Jesse to whirl around. His eyes widened when he saw who it was.

"This doesn't concern you. I'm not doing anything more than ordering a beer like anyone else has a right to."

"Most people ask more politely," Pudge said. "But then again most people have more sense than to pick a fight with the only barkeep in town."

Jesse looked at me. Recognition flashed in his eyes. "What are you looking at, dog catcher?"

Pudge groaned. "Don't make this bigger than it needs to be, son. Blackpowder says he doesn't want your business and that's his right. Go on home and have a beer on your front porch swing. Save me the trouble of having to arrest you again for driving under the influence."

"That was a bullshit charge and you know it. You were only hassling me because my brother dumped your slutty daughter."

The deputy's bulky frame was a blur as he rushed at Jesse. Pudge had him by the shirtfront and hoisted him off the ground.

"I'm gonna finish what the stork started," he said through clenched teeth.

I recalled Gemma's warning about getting between her dad and his quarry. "Jesse Harney," I said. "I'm placing you under arrest for violating Section 5, Code 132 of the 1966 US Fish and Wildlife Refuge Act."

Both men swiveled toward me. "What are you talking about?" Pudge said.

"Yeah, what the fuck?" Jesse said.

"As a sworn law enforcement officer of the US Government, it is my duty to inform you that you are entitled to a lawyer. If you cannot afford a lawyer, the government will provide you with one."

"This is bullshit," Jesse whined. "What did I do?"

"You were served notice that your cattle had violated a restricted zone at the Hart Mountain National Antelope Refuge."

"So?"

"You are the responsible party."

"No, I'm not. Those cows are my old man's. I've never wanted anything to do with them or his stinking ranch. Besides, my brother brought them back. So there."

"No one has provided any evidence of that."

Pudge let go of Jesse. The flush was disappearing from the deputy's jowls.

"Take it up with Blaine, not me," Jesse said.

"I'll tell you what. If you go home and have Blaine call it in that the cows are all back on Rocking H property, I'll see what I can do about having the charges dropped."

"What did I ever do to you?" Jesse said.

"Your choice. Your brother makes the call, or I'll remand you over to Sheriff Warbler for holding."

"He's not Sheriff Anything anymore. Wait until my father hears about this." He wheeled and stomped out.

Blackpowder Smith cackled from behind the bar. "Check and mate. Nice move, young fella. Maybe you and me should be the ones playing chess."

A beat-up pickup stacked with hay bales was pulled to the side of the road on my route home. I pulled in behind. Joe Moon was draped over the front fender with his head beneath the raised hood. His flat brim cowboy hat with the eagle feather rested on the fender beside him. Grease streaked his hands and wrists.

"Need some help?" I asked.

He glanced over his shoulder. "The ranger, yeah?"

"Nick Drake. What seems to be the problem?"

"Fifteen years of bad roads. Alternator has a short."

"Did the Alt-Gen light come on?"

"It's been flickering forever. You know engines?"

"I've worked on my share, mostly motorcycles. Did the headlights flicker before it quit?"

He nodded. "I find the short, she'll restart with a jump."

"But if the alternator's shot, the battery won't hold a charge."

"Why I'm hoping for a short. Be a whole lot cheaper to fix."

"I got a flashlight in my truck. It'll make it easier to see the wires."

I went to get it and noticed a dream catcher hanging from his rearview mirror. The webbed hoop had strings of feathers. The white and brown ones were from an owl, the black ones from a raven. I recognized it as an Indian talisman. The last time I'd seen one was in-country. A GI in another squad wore one hanging from a leather necklace. I don't know what tribe, or people, he was, but he said it was a powerful charm that mimicked a spider's web and would catch evil spirits and protect him. I hoped for his sake it worked better than a dagger and python tattoo for stopping bullets.

I held the flashlight while Joe Moon traced wires with his fingertips. "I mailed those letters for you," I said. "I noticed one was to a feed store up in Burns. Is that where you buy your hay?" I nodded toward the truck bed.

"I trade labor for it with a farmer. I used to buy grain from the feed store til it got too expensive. Still paying it off."

"Must be hard keeping a ranch going," I said.

"It was hard for my pa and his before him. I do whatever it takes."

A spark flashed as he moved the wires. With so much oil staining the engine, I figured it was leaking from the head gasket. I hoped for our sakes it didn't have a fuel leak too.

"That should do it," he said. "You push me with your rig, I can jump start it."

We started off slow, but when we got rolling, I eased off and he popped the clutch. The engine caught. He revved it a few times and then pulled away. I followed the weak taillights and considered staying behind him all the way to his ranch in case it died on him, but then thought better. Every man has his pride and for someone on the verge of losing his ranch, it was probably the only thing Joe Moon had left.

∽

I'D FINISHED DINNER, washed the dishes, and was tipping back in the ladder-back chair on the front porch watching the stars gather when a red Wagoneer pulled in front. The driver doused the headlights and got out.

"Do you always nurse bourbon from a mug?" Gemma Warbler said.

"I never got the hang of drinking hot tea out of a glass without burning my fingers," I said.

"Tea?" Gemma made a face. "Are you Mormon?"

"A junkie. There's no such thing as leaving a drop behind in a spike. I'd treat a bottle of booze the same way."

"You certainly don't mince words. I see why Pudge has taken a shine to you." The veterinarian stepped onto the porch. "Me? I like bourbon and a touch of honey for a nightcap, but if tea is all you have, I'll take mine with a little sugar, please."

I went inside and reemerged with a mug in one hand and a chair in the other.

"Doesn't taste like Lipton's," she said after taking a sip.

"It's herbal. I have enough trouble falling asleep as it is."

"Again with the true confessions." Her smile was a sliver over the rim of the mug. "Sage with a pinch of lavender. Am I right?"

"I picked them at Hart. I have wild spearmint from Malheur drying on a shelf in the back."

"You know if I tell November about this, she's going to stop calling you names and start treating you like a son. She is *Wadadökadö*, after all. Her people got their name for eating seep-weed and dandelions."

"Please do. She scares the hell out of me."

Gemma smiled. "Said with a straight face. There is a sense of humor in there."

We sat and drank our tea and looked at the night sky. An annual meteor shower was in its early stages and the shooting stars blazed brighter with each passing night.

"That was a good one," she said as a particularly long streak arced overhead. "I brought you the herd list for Crossed Bars."

"Thanks. I'll drop it off next time I'm out that way. It should help them figure out how many cows they still have."

"Did you find the cougar?"

"He got away."

She gave me a wry look. "He did, did he?"

I sipped some tea.

"I also stopped by to tell you thanks," she said.

"You already did that when we delivered the calf."

"I mean for what you did at Blackpowder Smith's to stop Pudge from doing something that could've cost him his job."

"There really are no secrets in this town."

"The more you try to keep them, the more they get out." Her voice was tinged with lament.

I figured she meant what Jesse had said about her marriage to his brother, but I wasn't about to go near that.

"It isn't true," she said as if reading my thoughts. "I left Blaine. We fashioned ourselves as Romeo and Juliet when we were kids in school. You know, because our fathers hated each other."

Gemma's laugh was self-deprecating. "I moved to Corvallis for college and vet school, and when I came home, Blaine had grown up too. He was, I don't know, so familiar. We got married, but it didn't take long before I realized it was a mistake. We wanted different things. I love working with large animals and being my own boss. Blaine kept saying I'd have all the patients I'd ever need living on the Rocking H."

She blew on her tea to give herself time. "Let's just say corrals aren't only for horses."

Her direct way of speaking about herself threw me. I was never comfortable listening to men bare their souls before and after combat or in group therapy at Walter Reed. I never did. I knew if I pulled the cork, I might never be able to put it back in again.

"What about you?" Gemma said. "Ever been married?"

"No."

"What about being in love? Surely, you've been in love before." She laughed. "Did something stupid because of it."

"No," I said again.

"Never? I can't believe that. A man like you. Don't go getting a big head, but you know what I mean."

My thoughts immediately went to the nurse at Walter Reed who played The Beatles on her 8-track. For some reason my recovery became her personal mission. She had short brown hair and eyes to match and wore a gold cross on a thin gold chain around her neck. She would rub my shoulders and talk in a soothing voice when I had the shakes during cold turkey. One night, when I was having a really bad time of it, she came in and slipped into bed with me and held me in her arms. Afterward, in the bright light of the morning when the shadows had burned away and took most of the demons with them, I wasn't sure if the memory of us making love hadn't been a dream.

Carla. Her name was Carla. And she never stopped believing her fiancée who was listed as MIA after being shot down on a bombing run over Hanoi would come home.

"You seem as far away as those shooting stars," Gemma said.

"Sorry. Must be the tea. Makes me sleepy."

"I didn't come here to pry into your private life. Since it sounds like you're going to be spending even more time with Pudge, I thought it best if we're on the same side. He told me what you have planned for tomorrow."

"He did, huh?"

"He's been a lawman my whole life. My mom died young. He needed someone to talk to about work and I was it."

"When he was busy telling you about why we're going to

search the gullies, did he happen to mention maybe you should be careful driving around the county until he catches whoever killed that girl?"

Gemma stiffened. "Were you listening when I said corrals aren't built only for horses? Pudge understands that. Don't you?"

I waved my mug in surrender. "Point taken."

We sipped tea and watched the stars shoot.

"How come your dad never remarried?" I asked.

"Pudge is set in his ways. He had a girlfriend in Burns for a little while when he was spending most of his time there being sheriff. I thought she might be the one, but then they broke it off."

"How come?"

"Conflict of interest," she said.

"Why, who was she?"

"She runs the paper in Burns. Bonnie LaRue. She's a formidable woman."

"They had a professional conflict, you mean. The sheriff being an elected position and her newspaper covering him."

"If you ask Pudge, he'll tell you the conflicts were more of a personal nature. It seems they sparred over everything from women's lib to the Vietnam War to Richard Nixon. I think he still carries a torch for her, but don't tell him I told you that."

"Do you mind if I ask about the Harneys?"

"Ask away."

"Jesse showed he has a quick temper both times I've met him. He strikes me as someone pissed off at the world. I was told by someone who deals with that sort of thing that it means the person is really angry with himself." I didn't add it was my shrink at Walter Reed.

"Jesse's a little brother. He's always been trying to get out of Blaine's shadow."

"Blaine's the golden child, huh?"

"Zachariah clearly favors him. And not only because he's the oldest. Blaine loves ranching. Jesse hates it. Blaine's never thought of doing anything else. The ranch goes to him when their father dies."

"Where does that leave Jesse?"

"Blaine will always provide for him. He's been Jesse's protector since they were little kids. Zachariah is very strict. He had a stroke that's slowed him down some, but before then he definitely didn't spare the rod."

"How so?" I asked.

"When Blaine was twelve and Jesse nine, they lost some cows while moving the herd back to the ranch ahead of a blizzard. Zachariah was furious. He made them saddle back up and go find them and not come home until they did. It snowed all night. The wind chill factor reached twenty below. Both boys got frostbite. Jesse lost some toes."

"I bet he still blames his father for that. Some men in the war couldn't stop blaming theirs too. Either their dad forced them to enlist or they forced themselves to in order to prove something to him."

"I suppose, but Jesse did come back to take care of Zachariah after his stroke."

"Come back from where?"

"Portland. He'd gone there for college, but only stayed a year because his dad got sick."

"Well, at least he had one year away from home."

Gemma shook her head. It made her ponytail swish. "He went to boarding school his last two years of high school. He'd gotten in some kind of trouble."

"What happened to their mother?"

"It's your typical No Mountain secret. Everyone knows it. When the boys were little, she ran off with a rancher who has a big spread down in Lake County. They say it was to get away from Zachariah. He didn't spare the rod on her either."

Gemma mimed clamping her hand over her mouth. "That came out wrong. I didn't mean *that* rod."

She started laughing and so did I. It had been a long time, and it felt pretty damn good.

I stopped off at Blackpowder Smith's to buy a package of lunch meat and a loaf of bread on my way to meet Pudge Warbler. The billy-goat-bearded barkeep and store owner was manning the cash register as I put the items down and reached for my wallet.

"Going on a picnic?" he said as he rang me up.

"Packing a lunch for work," I said.

"Which is where?"

"The Hart Mountain Refuge."

"Don't suppose I could trouble you into taking a little detour north and drop something off?"

"What is it?"

"It's not an it, it's a him. One of those yogi types from Crossed Bars came in last night and got pissed and passed out. Now, I know monks invented ale and brandy. And growing up in an Irish Catholic family, I saw how much the fathers like their sacramental wine, wake or no wake. But this sad sack? I couldn't tap the keg fast enough. They don't call it drowning your sorrows for nothing."

"Where's he at now?"

"He's not the first man in here whose face hit the plank. I got a storeroom in the back with a couple of army surplus cots. I usually let them sleep it off and then they drive themselves home in the morning, but he didn't come by car. Said he walked. And with no boots either."

Blackpowder led me to his version of a drunk tank. "I lend an arm getting them in here, but damned if I'm going undress and tuck them in," he said.

Damian was curled in the fetal position. He still had on his Jesus sandals. I shook his shoulder, and he awoke with a start. He scrambled to the corner and cowered against the wall. I'd seen plenty of men do the same waking up after combat. Some retreated while others went for the sidearm they kept under their pillow. Either way, it was always best not to get too close.

"Rise and shine. I'll give you a lift back to the ashram."

"The what?" A look of confusion competed with the sleep wrinkles etching his groggy face.

"Crossed Bars. Brother Michael, Sister Star. Vasudeva. They're waiting on you. Come on. Roll out."

Blackpowder and I quick marched him to my pickup before he could object. I made sure to roll the passenger window down before closing the door in case he needed to throw up.

"I would've made him ride in the back," the barkeep said.

Damian's eyes were half-closed as I headed north. "I don't want to go back," he mumbled. "Don't take me there. Let me out right here."

Clouds were starting to fill the sky. The sun dodged in and out.

"What are you talking about?" I said.

"I'm no longer on the true path."

"Looks like you took a little stumble. Everybody trips one time or another. Why don't you give it some time?"

"I don't need any time. I need to leave."

"To where?"

"Anywhere but here."

"You see the sky? The weather looks like it could be changing. Go back, grab a shower, get some grub. Pray, work, whatever. You'll feel better tomorrow."

"No, I won't. I can't do it anymore. I've been trying so hard to keep my shit together, but it's no use."

He rubbed his forehead. It was beaded with sweat. I could smell his funk, his fear.

"What happened?"

"I'm done trying to be something I'm not."

"You mean, spiritual? A seeker of enlightenment?"

"I mean everything." His voice rose. "I tried so hard, but I can't move on. I can't. I can't forget."

"We're not talking about the ashram anymore, are we?"

He turned toward me, his face tightening. "You were over there. You know what it was like. You said you shot junk to forget. Well, I can't forget either. I'll never forget. Never."

"Maybe not, but you can't let the past dictate the future."

"You sound like Vasudeva. That's what he says. But it wasn't anything like they told me it would be. At school, my dad, the recruiter, in boot, training. Nothing like what they said. Nothing at all."

"If you were at Khe Sanh, you were in the tall grass, for sure. It, Ia Drang, Hue, they were all bad. No one could describe what it would be like. You got through it. You survived."

"It wasn't only the fighting. Everything. The food, camp, the officers, Saigon, the whores. The brass were out to make a name for themselves no matter who got hurt, and the gooks were out to kill us or rip us off. I hated it."

"What happened at Khe Sanh that got you section-eighted?"

He spanked his knee. "I did my job, goddammit. I did what I was told. I fought, I killed, I stayed alive, and they still called me a coward. I did things I can't get out of my mind no matter how hard I chant or how long I meditate."

"Flashbacks. A lot of soldiers have them."

"The dead. That's who I can't get rid of. All I want is some goddamn peace. Some mercy. Do you hear? Do you understand? Is forgiveness so much to ask for?"

"I'm sure your parents forgive you."

"Not my old man."

"Your mother then. What about your sister?"

"What sister?"

"You told me about her. Your real one. You said that picture I showed you made you think of her. What's her name?"

He stared out the windshield as if looking into space. "Lizzie," he finally said. "But she didn't forgive me. She can't. Let me out. Come on. Let me out or I swear I'll jump."

We were getting close to the timbered entrance to Crossed Bars. I slowed down. "I'll tell you what someone told me once."

"What?"

"It's about forgiveness." I could hear Carla. Feel the nurse's gentling touch. "You have to learn how to forgive yourself first."

"And you, have you forgiven yourself?" Damian asked.

I pulled over in front of the entrance, but did not turn up the drive, thinking it would be better if he walked the last part himself.

"I'm working on it," I said.

DARK CLOUDS WERE BUNCHING up like cattle ready to stampede at the first clap of thunder as I waited at the refuge for Pudge. I tried calling him on the radio, but all I got was static. Too much electricity was already in the air.

Assuming he'd been ordered to report to Burns, I decided to

get a move on before the rains hit. I followed the road back to the pond that had been guarded by the bobcat and stopped to check for signs of new tire tracks and fresh horse droppings. There were none. I drove on and reached the end of the track at the edge of the playa that Pudge and I'd surveyed from the other side after finding Vicky Wells.

I parked and set out. I carried the 12 gauge for rattlesnakes as usual, but I'd also strapped on the Smith & Wesson. There was a killer out there somewhere, exactly where was anybody's guess, and walking point in-country taught me expecting the unexpected could make all the difference.

As I walked in a zigzag search pattern, I looked for footprints, horseshoe prints, and dried blood. The coroner's report had listed cuts and thorns in the soles of Vicky Wells's feet as well as scrapes on her knees.

I spotted nothing.

I entered the gully where I found her and retraced my steps to the now empty tomb. The chalk lines left by one of Sheriff Burton's deputies were still visible on either side of the opening. I crouched and looked inside. The exposed slab where the girl had been placed was darker than the walls and ceiling. The coroner had said the high desert air had slowed decomposition, but not enough to prevent a stain caused by leaking body fluids.

Had the killer meant to leave the front side open? If he'd walled it in with rocks and grouted it with sand and dirt, the body would never have been discovered. Maybe the killer hadn't worried about hiding his victim. Maybe he wanted her found. Or maybe he left it open so he could come back and view her. The coroner's report had mentioned a lock of Vicky's hair had been snipped. Was it some kind of trophy?

I hiked back to the playa. It was wide and sloping and bordered on one side by a stretch of corrugated hills. Other gullies ran between the folds. All spilled onto the playa, a dry lake bed that dated back long before the Paiute settled here. I picked the closest one.

It was narrower and not as deep. The sun dodged behind the clouds, and the tight chasm grew dark. I crouched and studied the ground. No cows had used it as a passageway. That meant it was probably boxed. Flat rocks lay atop a bed of coarse sand the same way lily pads floated on ponds. I could make out the *S* track of a snake that had slithered between them and the tiny prints from a kangaroo rat. And then I spotted it, a depression made by a boot heel. Whoever left it had been using the flat rocks as stepping stones.

I heard a tap. I thumbed the shotgun's safety off. Another faint tap. And then another. Silence. And then a tap. And another. And then silence. I crept forward. The gully grew even tighter as it bottlenecked. I shimmied through the narrow gap.

The gully widened on the other side of the short, narrow gap. Twenty yards farther it looked like it dead-ended, but it was only a fresh rockfall. As I approached it, a shadow from a bird flying overhead started circling on the ground. I kept my eyes down and scrambled over the rocks. The tapping grew louder. The beats closer together. Who was making it? Was it Kathy Jenkins? Was she still alive and trapped inside a cave destined to become her tomb? Or was it the killer waiting for me?

I shouldered the 12 gauge and inched forward. The tapping was coming from all sides. The staccato beat grew louder and louder. It was as if the pounding was trapped inside my head. And then I felt it on my skin. I raised my eyes to the heavens and let the heavy drops of rain tap on my face and splatter all around.

Gullies and gulches at the Hart Antelope Refuge were as plentiful as the raindrops. It would take a miracle to stumble upon one used by the killer. My shoulders slumped and I fell to my knees and let the rain drum on my back.

Time slipped sideways as I silently mourned Vicky Wells and any others who might have been murdered and buried by the faceless killer. I mourned the dead soldiers I'd served with, brothers and commanders alike. I mourned the villagers who were too scared to flee when their hooches were torched, the rice farmers caught out in their paddies during a bombing run. I even considered mourning the enemies I'd killed, but I wasn't ready to do that yet.

The rain grew heavier. Sheets of water washed into the gully and began to pool around my knees. The district supervisor had warned me about flash floods that could turn a dry wash into a torrent in minutes. If you get caught in a gully during a rainstorm, he'd told me, whatever is falling on you is falling ten times harder higher up. A flash flood is like a sinner. It gets faster and meaner as it goes downhill.

I started to hike out. Water swirled around my boots and lapped at the tops of the stepping stones. The rain was picking up pace and so I picked up mine. I reached the rockfall, gripped the shotgun in one hand, and began to climb. The dirt between the stones turned to mud and I had to grab for a hold with my free hand. The rock came loose. I pushed it aside and grabbed for another. It gave way too. I threw it behind me and grabbed for another. The pitch-black bird was back. *Look out! Look out!* it screeched. The rocks on top began to slide off in all directions. I made a grab to keep from sliding down with them, but instead of a rock, I grabbed a hand cold to the touch.

A waterfall created by the sudden storm gushed over the lip of the gully wall. It splashed down and quickly exposed pale skin. I dropped the shotgun and began digging. I pulled away rock after rock and tossed them aside. Little by little the hand became an arm and then a shoulder and then a torso. The waterfall washed away the last layer of grime that covered a face.

Kathy Jenkins, her eyes were wide open, stared up at me unseeing.

I sucked in a wet gulp of air and let it out in a long, loud cry of sorrow and anger. It rolled down the gully like thunder's echo. There was no time to search for evidence the killer might have left behind or my 12 gauge that had sunk beneath deepening brown water. I lifted the young girl's body and slung her over my shoulder. Then I scrambled down the other side of the pile of rocks and ran, chased by the roar of a surging wave growing bigger and stronger as it churned.

I reached the bottleneck. I couldn't squeeze though carrying her. *Leave her*, the black bird screeched. *She's already gone! Save yourself!* I couldn't. The floodwaters would bury her beneath a river of mud and rock, never to be found again. She deserved better than that.

I slid her off my shoulder and stood her at the entrance to the tight bottleneck. "I'm sorry," I said. And then I pushed her so she toppled onto her side inside the narrow gap. And then I turned sideways and walked over her, cursing the killer out loud so I couldn't hear the crunch of her bones beneath my boots.

When I passed through, I reached back in, grabbed her wrists and yanked her out. I hoisted her up and ran. The roar of the floodwaters was deafening. The big wave smashed into the bottleneck. Like the cars of a runaway freight train, wave after wave behind it kept coming. The collision created a powerful jet of water that shot through the opening and struck me square in the back with the force of a firehose, knocking me down and bowling me over.

My ears rang. Lights flashed. Blood gushed from my nose. A phalanx of North Vietnamese regulars were pummeling my platoon with mortars. The first shells fell short, but not the next round. The blasts threw bits and pieces of men and weapons into the air with all the discretion of a handful of confetti tossed into the wind. I sat in a heap, dazed and deaf, blindly firing my M16 in the direction of the big guns.

Something was weighing against my legs. Another GI. "You're going to be okay," I told him. "They called in the Skyhawks, the Phantoms too. They'll be here any second and light 'em up. Hang on, brother. I'll get you out of here."

I looked down at his face, but it was not a him. I looked down at the rifle in my hands, but saw a six-shooter instead. And then I remembered where I was. I picked up the girl, tucked her under my arm, and ran as fast as I could.

I stumbled out of the gully and stepped aside of its mouth just as a ten-foot-high wall of angry water thick with mud and rocks rushed out. It poured onto the dry lakebed along with the floodwaters from all the other gullies that ran between the folds of the corrugated hills. The torrents proved no match for the ancient playa. It guzzled them down as thirstily as if it were made of sponge.

The rain was still falling hard when I reached my pickup, and the sky was veined with lightning as bright as the bits of comet that Gemma and I had watched. Little Kathy Jenkins was not something to be put in the truck bed like trash to be hauled away. I wrapped her in a blanket and positioned her on the front seat. Only after fastening the seatbelt around her waist and making sure the passenger door was locked did I get in beside her and begin the long, lonesome drive home to No Mountain.

N o Mountain's City Limits sign was a lie. It wasn't officially a city, but an unincorporated community. Still, a green rectangle mounted on a silver metal pole greeted motorists on the outskirts of town. It listed the population as 177 and the elevation at 4,111. The second was accurate, the first did not include the people who now lived at Crossed Bars. The sign was perforated by bullet holes as were most of the road signs in Harney County. I tried radioing Pudge Warbler again as I passed it, hoping that proximity to civilization would finally lead to a connection.

The radio crackled with static as it had every other time, but then a deep voice boomed. "Where the hell you been, son? I tried raising you at oh dark thirty to tell you I wasn't gonna be able to meet you."

"We got to meet right away. Are you home?"

"I wish. I'm in Burns. Have been all day."

"I'll come there then."

"You'd be wasting your time. They got me going six ways from Sunday. It's a goddamn goat rodeo up here."

"What happened?"

"Looks like we caught the killer. He's sitting in county lockup as I speak."

"Who? How?"

"It's a long story and I got to run. I'll tell you tomorrow."

"I found Kathy Jenkins. She's dead."

Pudge took a deep breath. "Oh Lord. Are you sure it's her?"

"I'm sure."

He exhaled loudly. "Did you mark the site good?"

"I got her with me."

"You're breaking up. I don't think I caught that."

"She's in the front seat next to me. I couldn't leave her. The storm."

"Oh Lord," he said again. "As if this day wasn't already one for the books. Aubrey Jenkins is on his way here. We're told he's flying in with the governor. That means the governor's tallyman Richard Travers will be with them too. I got to think this one through."

I passed by Blackpowder Smith's and the collection of storefronts that made up downtown No Mountain.

Pudge came back on. "Okay, here's what you do. Go straight to the coroner's office. It's on North Fairview. Whatever you do, don't go near the sheriff's office on Court Avenue. It and the jail are painted pink. You can't miss 'em but you got to miss 'em because that's where Jenkins and the governor are headed. Watch out for newshounds. Travers is sure to have called them to grab a headline for his boss about catching the killer. Stay in your truck. I'll meet you out front."

"Who's the killer?"

"I'll tell you when I see you."

"I'll be there in thirty minutes."

"Don't speed. The last thing we need is for you to get pulled over by some eager beaver state trooper."

"What are you going to tell Sheriff Burton?"

"Nothing for now, and then as little as possible til we know what we got."

The radio went silent. I hunched over the steering wheel and peered into the gloaming. The rain had stopped, and it was a relief not to have to listen to the *slap-slap-slap* of the wipers anymore. My clothes were still soaked with cold rain. I hadn't turned on the pickup's heater to help dry them. Vietnam taught me what heat could do to a corpse.

Occasionally I would glance over at my passenger. I'd ridden with the dead before, in the belly of Hueys during evacs and in the back of a Deuce and a Half, transporting casualties from the field. Chaplains and corpsmen always talked to the dead. Not me. There was nothing much to say at that point. This time was different. I wanted to tell the girl I hoped she hadn't been terrified or suffered. I wanted to say that they had caught her killer and he was going to pay for what he'd done. But the only words I could muster aloud was an apology.

"I'm sorry," I said. "I should've hunted those gullies sooner. I might've been able to save you."

Burns City Limit sign was the same size as No Mountain's. Its population was 2,788 and the elevation thirty-six feet higher. The sign was perforated by bullet holes too. I kept my eyes straight ahead when I stopped at the first traffic signal. If any of the drivers at the intersection thought it strange that my passenger was cloaked in a blanket, they didn't honk or roll down their window and point and shout.

I found North Fairview and circled a squat brick building that housed the county's morgue and medical examiner's office. The parking lot was nearly empty. I circled again. On the second pass Pudge's truck was idling at the curb. I pulled alongside so we were window to window.

The deputy's small brim Stetson shaded his eyes, but I knew they were aimed at my passenger.

"You're positive she's the Jenkins girl?"

"No doubt about it. He took the time to place her atop a rockfall he created in the gully next to where he put Vicky Wells. They're not tombs, they're monuments. It feels like some kind of ritual. I couldn't leave her there. It was flooding. We'd never have found her again."

"I called the coroner. He's gonna meet us inside. I didn't tell him who it was I was bringing in."

"There's something I got to tell you."

"What?"

"She's pretty banged up. And not just from what he did to her."

"What are you trying to say, son?"

"The gully was flooding. I had to make a run for it. It was rough going."

"I've lived in Harney County all my life. I've seen my share of flash floods. Sounds to me like you should get a medal outrunning one while carrying her. Go along with that Purple Heart and Bronze Star they told me you earned in Vietnam."

"I had to step on her." I sucked my teeth. "I had to step on her a lot."

"Doc's waiting. Let's get her inside," is all he said.

"I'm sorry."

"Don't blame yourself. You found her and brought her home."

"But I was too late. I could've done more. A lot more."

"We all could've. We all should've."

THE HALLWAY WAS LIT by flickering fluorescent lights and reeked of floor wax and formaldehyde. I sat on a metal chair. The white sheet draped over my shoulders did little to stop the shaking. It was all they had. There was no need for warm blankets in a morgue. A puddle had formed on the linoleum beneath me, fed by drips from my clothes.

I wanted a cigarette even though I'd quit. I wanted a fix even though I'd quit shooting junk and was focused on reaching my goal. The staff at Walter Reed was big on making them. Get through the first week and you're home free, they told me when I was admitted. Six hours later I felt the first wave of withdrawal. It started with the shakes. Two days in I would've given anything to stop them, that and the vomiting, the shits, my heart beating so fast I grew convinced some jungle creature was living inside me and pounding on my chest to get out.

"It's because you're so bighearted," Carla had told me, placing a calming palm against my bare skin. "Get yourself straight, and you'll make someone very happy someday."

I made it through the first week because no one would give me a fix no matter how hard I begged, how much money I said I'd pay, how vicious my threats got if they didn't. The heroin was finally out of my bloodstream, but not out of my mind. Thirty days, the shrink told me. Make it thirty days and you got a chance. I reminded him that's what he said about the first seven days. His smile was as noncommittal as the Jell-O they served for breakfast, lunch, and dinner. Every day of that first month was a 24-hour fight, but I got through the thirty. Now what, I asked? Ninety days, the shrink responded. You have to get past ninety, and you'll be on your way to your new life. New hopes. New dreams.

Every single day of the ninety I went to meetings. Every day I made the pledge. At the end of ninety, the shrink said I'd done a good job, but now I had to get through six months, and then a year, and then five, and then ten. Ten, he said, after ten years I'll pronounce you cured.

They let me out on the condition I go to a place where the

odds of finding a dealer were slim to none. The middle of nowhere. Harney County. I was working hard to reach a year clean and sober. Every morning I took a pebble and placed it in a tin can on the kitchen shelf in the lineman's shack. Every night before going to bed I put in another pebble. I had a row of cans filled with pebbles. When temptation got too strong, I'd take the cans down and rattle them one by one.

"You look like you caught a cold," Pudge said, plopping down on the metal chair next to me. "You ought to see a real doc after we're done here. One that works on the living and not the kind our friend in there sees."

I knew my shakes were not from a cold or the flu. It was the aftereffects of the adrenaline that made it possible to outrun a flash flood carrying a dead girl.

"Who's the killer?" I said, trying to keep my tongue from getting between my teeth.

"I'll get to that in a moment," Pudge said, "but first we got some business needs doing before any more time goes by."

"What kind of business?"

"The official statement kind. I need to take yours. You need to tell me everything that happened, start to finish. Don't leave anything out. Details matter. If we're gonna pin it on this asshole, we can't give him another kind of hole to wiggle through."

"Okay, but a cup of coffee would help. Or tea. Anything hot."

"It's coming. I asked the gal that runs the office if there was some. She said she needed to make a fresh pot."

I started talking. Despite the shakes and the itch from wet jeans chafing my skin that reminded me of the pain of jungle rot, I spoke as clearly as I could, citing landmarks, routes, and times. I told him how I believed there could be other girls entombed in the gullies. I told him how I spotted the heel print and sensed I was not alone. I even said how I mistook the splatter of raindrops for someone tapping on the rocks. I described the rockfall and how I blamed myself for not recognizing it as a monument built by a killer who seemed bent on glorifying his deeds rather than hiding them. I told Pudge everything except about the black bird.

The former sheriff jotted notes as he listened. He didn't interrupt until I reached the part where we'd loaded the dead girl onto a gurney and wheeled her down the hallway and through swinging double doors that led to a cold white room with a shallow sink big enough to hold a body.

"You had yourself one helluva day, son. One helluva day."

"What now?" I asked.

"I'm gonna wait for Doc to come out and give me confirmation of who he's got in there. Then I'm gonna go tell Bust'em and watch a shit storm more powerful than the one outside. This one's not gonna go pretty. No way it will and no way it should."

"Because her father will be here. The governor too."

"The whole shebang," he said.

"What do you want me to do?"

"Go home. I got your statement. You not being here will be one less person Bust'em will try to smack down to make himself look good in the eyes of the governor."

"Yourself included?"

"I've been around too long to worry about some pissant like Bust'em. Or the governor for that matter. What are they gonna do, fire me? And Aubrey Jenkins? Well, I got nothing but sorry for that poor man. If taking a poke at me helps ease the living hell he's about to enter, it'd be my pleasure to offer him my nose. Go on, now. Git."

"Okay, but you never answered me. Who do you have locked up?"

Pudge pushed his Stetson back on his bulldog head. "Someone from not around here. A drifter. A hippie sort. A state trooper pulled him over on Highway 205 right before it crosses the state line."

"South of the Malheur Refuge?"

"That's right."

"Why did he stop him?"

"A busted taillight. He ran his license. That's SOP. Especially when the driver's got long hair and a beard. Turns out the driver had a record. Did some time for possession. He also had an older charge on his record for a domestic assault and battery beef, but it got dropped when the girlfriend declined to press charges. The trooper looks in the vehicle and sees a woman and a girl in there. Oregon State Police had been alerted about Kathy Jenkins since they're the ones who patrol the highways. He calls it in, and wham, bam, the driver's in the slam."

"Where he's from, the suspect?"

"Washington State."

"Was he driving a VW bus?"

Pudge straightened. "Tell me you didn't go and drive by the county jail like I told you not to and saw it parked in the impound lot."

"Is his name Barry? The young girl, Jenny?"

Pudge leapt out of his chair. "What in the Sam Hill is going on here?"

"I nearly shot him at Malheur the other day. I thought he was the killer when I saw him chasing a naked woman. That's the one named Linda. Turns out they were skinny-dipping. They told me they were on their way to San Francisco."

"Oh Lord," he groaned. "As if this day wasn't already one for the books, now it's gone from shit storm to honest-to-god holy hell. Forget about going home anytime soon. You're coming to the sheriff's office with me. We're about to face the equivalent of the Four Horsemen of the Apocalypse."

T he rain started again. It drummed against a blocky two-story pink building that housed the Harney County Sheriff's Office and Jail. A covered walkway connected it to the Harney County Courthouse, a statelier brick building fronted by a parklike lawn. Sheriff Burton, his back to Pudge and me, stared out the only window in his office.

"I didn't expect so much rain in June," he said. "It's the first day of summer and it's raining cats and dogs."

"I thought you grew up in Klamath County," Pudge said. "You should know June's monsoon season in the high desert."

"Grants Pass, actually. On the other side of the Cascades. We moved to K Falls my sophomore year. Dad got a job at the Modoc Lumber Company mill. I spent my summer vacations working there pulling green chain. Minimum wage and glad to get it. Two-by-fours, mostly. Those and two-by-sixes."

"But the weather in Klamath isn't that much different, is it?" Pudge said.

"It's not as cold in winter."

"This June's wetter than most. Next month it'll be hot enough to crack rocks and you'll be praying for rain."

The way the two lawmen were talking was the same as when army brass analyzed what went wrong with yesterday's battle plan. They'd talk about home, what the cook whipped up in the officer's mess last night, whether they'd be able to score tickets for the Bob Hope Christmas Show. Anything to lend a sense of normalcy to the dark side of the killing business.

Burton finally turned around. "So, Doc is certain it's the Jenkins girl?"

"No doubt about it," Pudge said. "Poor little thing."

"And he's certain she was killed the same way as the other girl?"

"He's still got to run some tests to confirm cause, but, yeah, she had the same sorts of things done to her. Wrists tied. Raped. A hank of hair cut off. She had scrapes and bruises too." Pudge glanced at me. "It's like some kind of ritual. The killing, the burying part."

Burton's face tightened. "We can't tell any of that to her father. Governor Lane either. They're on their way from the airport. I'm meeting them next door. The courthouse is more fitting for men like them." He waved at his battered furniture and walls in need of fresh paint.

"They read the report, they're gonna find out."

"Yes, but they're not going to hear it from me. Or you either. Understood?"

Pudge didn't answer.

"You either," the sheriff said to me. "You don't breathe a word of it. Not a word. You shouldn't even be here."

"Drake's name is gonna come up. He's in my notes, and it'll go into the report. He found her and brought her in. This goes to trial, he'll be in the witness box."

"He shouldn't have been looking," Sheriff Burton said.

"That little girl would've been buried beneath rock and mud and lost forever if not for him. Either that or the flood would've jammed her in a crack so small even the buzzards wouldn't've found her."

The sheriff socked his fist into his palm. "He shouldn't have been looking, period. I thought I made myself perfectly clear when we found the first girl. He is not, I repeat, not one of my deputies. Period. He is not, I repeat, not part of this investigation. Period."

"The Hart Refuge is in my jurisdiction," I said. "You don't have the authority to keep me from patrolling it. As long as the killer's doing his killing there, I'll keep looking. Don't try and stop me."

The sheriff started to argue, but turned on his deputy instead. "Do you know how this looks? How it could be made to look? Make me look? He's only been in Harney County a little while and all of a sudden he's the only one able to find dead girls? And now you tell me he met our suspect too. Do you know what Governor Lane is going to do when he finds that out? What Bonnie LaRue will do if she ever gets hold of it? They're going to have a field day with me."

"Well, you wanted to be sheriff," Pudge said. "Campaigned pretty darn hard for it too. This goes with the territory."

"That's right. I am sheriff. And as sheriff, I could fire you right now for dereliction of duty. That's your territory down there and you let two girls get killed and left to rot in a gully. What kind of lawman are you? And as for your friend here..." He jabbed an accusing finger at me. "Now that I think of it, who's to say he's not in on it? Awfully damn coincidental him knowing our suspect and letting him go free and finding bodies all over the place."

Pudge sighed loudly. "I knew you'd be looking for someone to blame. That's a load of horse pucky and you know it. You try spreading that around, and the governor really will put your ass in a sling. Listen, Bust'em, word of advice. No charge. I been where you are. There's only one way to play this. Be a man, face the father, break the news, comfort him, and then pledge you won't quit working the case so another father doesn't have to go through what he's going through."

He reached for the door. "Come on, Drake, let's give the sheriff a few minutes to work on his speech."

~

THE KITCHEN at the sheriff's office was in need of a scouring pad and mop. The trashcan overflowed with fast-food wrappers and Styrofoam coffee cups. A poster with a bucking bronco advertising the Pendleton Roundup shared wall space with Polaroids of deputies dressed in hunting camo crouched next to trophy bucks. The last name and date on a clipboard holding a sign-up sheet for kitchen duty was a year old.

"If I had a dollar for every donut I ate in here when I was sheriff, I'd be retired," Pudge said. "I can't count the number of nights I slept in that chair where Bust'em now parks himself."

He opened the refrigerator and poked around inside. He lifted a take-out container with Chinese writing on it and gave a sniff. He put it back and closed the door.

"Barry and those two girls, Jenny and Linda, they gave me no reason to think they were anything but hippies heading to San Francisco," I said. "The young one said she was eighteen and the older one's cousin. All a big happy family having a picnic and going swimming."

"Buck naked. How come you remember their names?"

"Hard to forget. I drew on them."

"We don't get many longhairs here. They do over on the west side of the mountains. Especially in Eugene because of the university."

"Has Barry said anything yet?"

"Only that he hasn't done anything. He wasn't told why he was brought in, and we didn't mention any killings when we questioned him."

"What about Linda?"

"That gal. She's got quite a mouth on her, calling everyone *pigs*. She even went after the state trooper. Like to scratch his eyes out."

"She's in jail too?"

He pointed toward the ceiling. "There's two floors of cells here, men's and women's, though we don't get many female inmates. We got both of them on 48-hour holds. Then we either book them as suspects or accessories, we haven't decided which yet."

"What about Jenny?"

"If that's her real name. She's got no ID. Since she can't prove who she is or how old, we sent her over to Child Services to be on the safe side. She says she's from Tacoma and doesn't really know Barry and Linda. Says they picked her up hitchhiking. CS is trying to get a bead on her parents, but the girl's not being much help. She says her mom moves around a lot and doesn't leave a forwarding address, probably because she's skipping out on past rent."

"If Linda really is her cousin, she should know how to reach them."

"It's like those people down at Crossed Bars. You're wearing a uniform and ask the three of them a simple question and they all get amnesia."

"If Barry is really the killer, why is Jenny still alive? Linda, for that matter."

"Who knows? Right now, we're going on the theory that Linda's in on it and they abducted Jenny. Barry swears he never touched her, but we need a rape test to rule it out. Child Services has to get the mother's permission for that since we can't prove her age, but there's that no way to contact her thing standing in the way."

"Why would Jenny cover for them if they kidnapped her?"

"Maybe she's in shock or something. CS is gonna have a psychologist talk to her first thing in the morning."

"And Barry's sticking with the story that she's Linda's cousin and has permission to travel with them."

"That's the size of it, but if Jenny turns out to be underage and they do a medical on her and he had sex with her, we'll tack statutory rape to the murder rap. Doesn't matter if it was all peace and free love. He'll go down for the Mann Act too for bringing a minor across the line from Washington State."

"Barry's not the killer," I said.

"What makes you so sure?"

"He's a stoner. So is Linda. They were high on pot when I chased them out of Malheur."

"I guess you'd know." Pudge paused. "What about Jenny? Was she on drugs too?"

I shrugged.

"Child Services will ask her," Pudge said. "The troopers found a bag of the stuff in the Volkswagen bus. Barry already took a twelve-month bounce for possession so this will be his second offense. He was only released from lockup in Pierce County, Washington a little while ago. Maybe little Jenny wasn't the first girl Barry picked up hitchhiking and gave Mary Jane to. Maybe when Doc gets the results back from the autopsies on Vicky Wells and Kathy Jenkins, he'll find it in their blood work. If that happens, case closed."

"I still don't think Barry's the killer. He doesn't have the look."

"What look?"

"The look that stays in a man's eye after he's taken a life. It never goes away."

Pudge looked down at his boots. There were creases in the leather from age and use, like those in his face. "Even in war. Even when justified."

"And then there's Vicky Wells," I said. "The coroner told us she'd been in the gully two weeks or so when we pulled her out. Where was Barry then?"

"We're running down a time line. Barry's no help. He says he doesn't even know what day it is. He says calendars are for squares. Bust'em is still working out how long until we got to call in a public defender. That new law, the Miranda one the courts decided after an arrest down in Arizona a couple years back? Well, up here it's still all a gray area of what we can and can't do with a suspect."

I took a closer look at the Pendleton Roundup poster. The artist had painted the bronc with all four hooves off the ground, the rider holding the reins with one hand, the other high over his head, his hat flying off behind. The words "Let 'er buck" and "Since 1910" were spelled out in old-timey lettering.

Pudge said, "Gemma works the Roundup every season. She tends to the animals that get hurt, but it's mostly the cowboys who come away with busted bones. If you've never been to a rodeo, Pendleton's is the best there is. It's a couple hundred miles north of here, but worth the drive. What do you say? You want to have a little chat with your old pal Barry?"

"Why would I want to do that?"

"See for yourself if you still think he's not guilty. He's clammed up and maybe seeing a familiar face might get him to unclam."

"He won't admit anything to me. He doesn't know me."

"You never know unless you try. I've been in this business a long time and seen it all. We had a gal in here whose husband wound up dead in his own barn. She said he tripped and fell on a pitchfork. We didn't buy it, so we locked her up. She wouldn't talk to anybody. Lawyer, priest, not even her own mother. Not a word. Then one day a guard's walking by her cell and hears her. She's drawn a likeness of her husband's face on the wall with lipstick. She's talking to it, telling it she loves him and she's sorry she ran him through with the pitchfork and hopes he'll forgive her."

Pudge pointed toward the door. "I can set you up in a room and bring Barry to you."

"A room you can listen in on."

"Of course."

"Are you hoping to learn something about Barry or something about me?"

"I don't follow."

"What Sheriff Burton said, about the girls getting killed not long after I moved here. That it's coincidental I found them."

"Did you kill them?" he asked without blinking.

"No."

"Well, then, there you go. I'll show you the room we use for talking to suspects. And, yeah, it's outfitted with some recording equipment. We probably won't be able to use it in a trial or anything, what with all these new laws protecting the bad guys more than their victims, but it could help. I'll get the college boy to make sure it's working proper."

W e met up in a square gray room. The only furnishings were a metal table with a chair on either side. A two-way mirror adorned one wall. The others were bare. The college boy's name was Orville Nelson. He wore his hair boot-camp short and a narrow black tie was snugly knotted beneath the button-down collar of his white shirt.

"Orville is biding his time until he's eligible to apply to Quantico," Pudge said by way of introduction. "I keep telling him he'd better grow some whiskers and change his last name. The Feds have a long memory. Baby Face Nelson killed more agents than any other gangster."

Orville pumped my hand vigorously. "Pleased to meet you, Mr. Drake."

"I understand you'll be manning the tape recorder," I said.

"Affirmative. It's a TEAC reel to reel. I'll be operating it remotely from a room on the other side of the mirror."

Pudge headed toward the door. "Make yourself comfortable. I'll go round up Barry."

"Do you carry a radio?" Orville asked.

"Not on me. It's in my truck."

"Good. The frequency can interfere with recording. The microphones in the room are in the ceiling. They're multidirectional."

"You're the expert."

"You know, it won't be long before law enforcement personnel no longer have to rely on shortwave radio transmission for communications."

"How's that?"

"We'll use wireless telephones. A network of antennas will transmit the signal from your phone to a satellite and then beam it down to the phone you're calling. All in the blink of an eye."

"No more wires, no more poles?"

"Do you watch *Star Trek*? It's a new TV show. Space, the final frontier."

"I haven't been anywhere where I could watch TV for a while."

"Intergalactic travel, teleportation, phasers, robotics, handheld computers." Orville ticked off the list on his fingers. "It's not all science fiction. It's only a matter of time."

"I'll take your word for it. Anything else I need to know about the set up in this room?"

"Speak in your normal voice is all. While we've been talking, I've had the recorder running. When I go back to the observation room, I'll be able to fine tune the audio levels."

"Mind if I ask you something before the suspect gets here?"

"Not at all."

"I was told you've been collecting missing persons reports and connecting some dots."

"Affirmative. I could do a lot more if we had data analysis resources like the FBI uses. Have you heard of the program they started last year?" His voice kicked up a notch. "It's called the National Crime Information Center. They turned thousands of handwritten and typewritten records of wanted criminals into computerized files. That means the data can be transmitted, cross referenced, and analyzed. You can have all that information at your—" Orville snapped his fingers. "That's the department where I want to work. Computerized police work is the future."

If Orville had served in Vietnam, his squad would've called him Crystal Ball. Everyone had a nickname. They served to strengthen the bond between brothers. They also helped buffer the pain when it was a Froggy or a Cowboy or a Jumbo who got killed rather than a John or a José or a Calvin.

"Could you walk me through the dots after we're done here? I'd like to hear your take on the missing girls," I said.

Orville brightened. "Yes, sir. I can point out the similarities I found. Age, physical characteristics, last whereabouts, time and place in Oregon. Things like that. Of course, I'll have to ask Sheriff Burton for permission."

"Ask Deputy Warbler instead," I said.

The door opened and Pudge steered Barry to a chair and handcuffed him to it. "You got ten minutes." Orville followed him out.

Barry was dressed in jailhouse denims and rubber sandals. His beard was matted, and his hair greasy. The beaded necklace was gone.

"Are you the public defender? It's about time you got here. They've had me locked up since last night. Whatever they think I did, I didn't do. I haven't done shit."

I realized Barry didn't recognize me because I wasn't wearing my uniform. Pudge had dug out a pair of jeans and a plaid flannel shirt from the lost and found for me.

"I'm not a lawyer," I said. "I'm with Fish and Wildlife. We met at the Malheur Refuge. You were about to go swimming when I stopped you."

"Oh right. Ranger Rick. That's what my old lady called you. You scared the shit out of us, pulling your gun and screaming Chinese. Is that what this is all about? Hey, you're the one who let us go, man. You didn't write us a ticket or nothing."

"Where did you go after you left the refuge?"

"To a campground. That's right, now I remember. You told us about it. The one in the national forest. Don't tell me we broke some kind of rule down there? You're the one who told us about it."

"You said you were on your way to San Francisco, but that was a few days ago."

"We are. Well, we were until this yahoo with the Oregon State Police red-lighted us. No way I was speeding. In a VW bus? Give me a break. And now all this gestapo shit. Interrogating me without a lawyer. I know my rights."

"Because you were arrested once before, served time."

"More gestapo shit. I wasn't pushing, just sharing a joint with some friends in a park. I didn't know it was next to a school."

"And the assault and battery charge?"

"It got dropped and it was a big misunderstanding anyway." Barry tried raising his hands for emphasis, but the handcuffs held him fast. "Ouch, goddammit."

He grimaced. "I was shacking up with a real head case. Don't get me wrong, the chick was a stone fox, but upstairs? A total paranoid. Always accusing me of cheating on her. One night I get home late, and she comes after me with a wine bottle. I grab her wrists to protect myself and the next thing you know she's screaming bloody murder and the neighbor calls the cops. It was as good a time as any to break up, so I split. The cops catch up to me, but little Miss Head Case decides not to press charges. Turns out she'd been balling the neighbor who called the cops the whole time we'd been living together."

"Did you stay in the campground the entire time after you left Malheur?"

"Right on, man. Out of necessity. That little sewing machine of an engine was really crapping out. I had to pull all the plugs and clean them. Fix the timing too."

"The backfiring. I heard it when you pulled out of the parking lot." I said it more for the recording than for Barry.

"I got it working good enough to get us down to Frisco and we would've gotten there too except for that cop. Come on, man. Why are they going bat shit? They won't tell me nothing. And where's my old lady and her cousin? They must be freaking out. The cops better not have left them standing out in the rain. And they also better not have wrecked my VW either. Towing can really screw up a bus if you don't do it right. Those rednecks probably don't even know the engine's in the rear. This is such a bummer. A total bummer."

"Is Jenny really Linda's little cousin?"

"More or less. It's distant like, third or fourth twice removed. I don't know how all that stuff works. But Linda's and Jenny's moms know each other from back when they were kids. I never met her, Jenny's mom, but Linda says she got into the heavy stuff. You know, coke, junk. And she was with one loser after another. Pimping her and stuff."

"Pimping Jenny too?"

"I don't know about that. I mean, maybe. You saw her coming out of the lake. She's not bashful. Maybe some guy's been in her pants."

"You?"

"Whoa!" Again he tried to raise his hands and, again, the cuffs kept them down. "No way. Not me. Linda would kill me. I already told that to the cops."

"Jenny says you picked her up hitchhiking."

"That's a lie. She does that a lot. Jenny showed up at our pad the day we were leaving for Frisco. She gave Linda some sob story about how she had to get away from her mom's latest boyfriend. Some scary biker dude. Linda's got a soft spot for her, so instead of sending her home, she brought her with us. You know, liberating her."

"Why would she lie to the cops about that?"

"If I had to guess, it's to buy time to keep from getting sent back. Linda told me Jenny's pad isn't exactly Ozzie and Harriet. More like Peyton Place. And now with that Hells Angels dude living there."

"When you left the campground, were you headed straight to San Francisco?"

"More or less. It's not like we travel in straight lines, man. Linda and me, we go where the mood takes us."

"Any place in particular?"

"The Alvord Desert. It's supposed to be really far out. Heavy. You know, spiritual and stuff. Some people even think aliens use it for a landing site. We were going to camp there and drop some..." He grinned. "You know, see what we saw."

"Alvord is east of here, on the other side of Steens Mountain," I said.

"I don't know. I never heard of it until a few days ago."

"How's that?"

"Some folks told us about it."

"Where was that?"

"This place run by a bunch of religious freaks. Not Jesus freaks, they're into the Eastern shit. Buddha. Zen. Yoga. Hindu. Whatever. I'm cool with that. To each his own, you know what I mean?"

"What was the place called?"

"An ashram. It used to be an old cattle ranch. Two Bars. Crossed X's. Something like that. You can crash there and get a free meal."

"How long did you stay?"

"Only a couple of nights. There were too many rules. You know, going to their temple and having to work. They had this field set aside for people on the road, and we parked there and crashed."

"Who told you about the Alvord Desert?"

"What do you mean?"

"Was it another traveler or a member of the group living there?"

"It was one of the monk dudes. He said the desert was, like, a holy place, that people do their pilgrimage there. Wait a sec, he didn't call it pilgrimage. It was something else. I don't remember the word. Whatever. He said you go out into the middle of this huge flat desert with nothing growing in it, not even a weed, without any food or blankets and sit out there until you see God or whatever it is their religion calls the big man upstairs. I mean, you don't even get to take a piece of jerky with you."

"Do you remember the monk's name?"

Barry scrunched his face. "He was American, but his name wasn't a common one like mine or, what's yours again?"

"Nick."

"Right. It wasn't like that. It wasn't completely Oriental either even though he dressed that way. Like Gandhi or Ravi Shankar or something like that. I would've remembered."

The door opened before I could ask him if it was Damian. Pudge and another deputy rushed in.

"He's gonna take the prisoner back to his cell," Pudge said. "And we're needed next door. Pronto."

The lights in the courthouse meeting room were dimmed and the venetian blinds drawn. The men on one side of a conference table were arranged as if a tableau of Da Vinci's *The Last Supper*. Governor Lane sat in the middle with Aubrey Jenkins to his left and Richard Travers to his right. Sheriff Burton, the coroner, and a handful of men I didn't recognize flanked the trio. The sole woman in the room sat in the corner behind a stenotype machine. She wore tortoiseshell cat eye glasses and a blank expression.

Pudge and I took our seats across from them.

The governor cleared his throat. "Deputy Warbler, Ranger Drake, I called you in here because your names have come up repeatedly in the past half hour. I am about to make a proclamation that includes you. Before I do that, I want to say for the record how I wish I had the power to roll back the hands of time so there would not be a need for this meeting. It is a sad and solemn occasion. Tragic. Heartbreaking. My first inclination upon landing and receiving word that my goddaughter had been found was to fly home immediately so my good friend Aubrey Jenkins could be with her mother. But he vowed to remain here, so he could provide whatever assistance he can to bring the perpetrator to justice."

Governor Lane placed his palm on Jenkins's shoulder. "That is the kind of man Aubrey is. Strong, courageous, selfless. A true Oregonian. We can all take strength in his resolve."

The others nodded. I half expected to hear an "amen."

"While I cannot change what happened," the governor continued, "I can take steps to make sure the person responsible pays for what he did. To that end, I am placing every resource at my disposal to bring the killer to justice as swiftly as possible. I will not rest until he is proven guilty without a shadow of a doubt. And my sincerest hope is that this unspeakable crime will convince Oregon voters to reverse the decision they made four years ago to outlaw capital punishment so that the death penalty can be reinstated in time to apply it to Kathy's killer."

Travers slid him a note and then signaled the stenographer to be ready.

Governor Lane stood and spread his arms as if commanding the sea to part. "In the power vested in me, I hereby constitute a special task force to oversee the investigation of the murders of Kathy Jenkins and Vicky Wells. It will be comprised of men of my choosing and will report directly to me. It shall be granted power to use whatever lawful means necessary to investigate and bring forth a trial and conviction." He gaveled the table with his fist. "The good people of Oregon demand justice, they deserve justice, and by God, justice will be served!"

Jenkins looked straight ahead with the same glacial stare he had when we found Vicky Wells. Travers was the opposite. He beamed as if his boss had won a landslide vote. He knew what a successful conviction could do come next election.

His beaming dulled when Pudge raised his hand. "Governor, a point of clarification?"

"Go ahead, Deputy Warbler."

"This task force, well, the way you put it, it sounds like it's limited to the deaths of little Kathy and Vicky Wells. We—"

Travers interrupted him. "Your point?"

"We have reason to believe they're not the only victims."

"It's *Deputy* Warbler now, isn't it?" Travers said. "Ever since the county voted to replace you with Sheriff Burton."

"*Your* point?" Pudge said.

The governor put his palm up. "Deputy Warbler, do you have evidence the suspect committed additional murders?"

"No."

"Then it is mere speculation on your part."

"No, meaning there's no direct evidence linking him to any killing. All we know for sure is he and two females were in the general vicinity of the area where the two bodies were discovered. What we do have is a stack of missing persons reports of girls about the same age as the victims. A smart young fella working for the Harney County sheriff went through them and came up with lots of similarities. It appears they fit a pattern."

"You're basing your belief on reports of runaways?" Travers scoffed. "The country is filled with young people—boys and girls—running off to dodge the draft or follow some rock music group or play hooky and take drugs."

"Governor, sir," Pudge said. "I'm basing my belief on twenty-five years in law enforcement. Now, most killings are done by people who know the person they're killing. Couples, families, neighbors, drinking buddies down at the tavern. But then there are the killings done by folks who are pure and simply evil. They get a taste for it. Like that man in Chicago a couple of years ago who stabbed all those nurses or this so-called Zodiac Killer running loose in San Francisco. Once they do, they don't stop—they can't stop—until they *are* stopped. That's what I believe we may have here."

"But I was told we have the killer locked up." Governor Lane scanned the table. Sheriff Burton ducked.

"We have a suspect locked up," Pudge said. "Maybe he did it, maybe he didn't. But that still doesn't mean there aren't more bodies out there. If you limit your task force to the two we do know about, we could miss finding some important evidence that would make a guilty verdict rock solid. That's what you want, isn't it? Rock solid."

Jenkins had been sitting quietly with his hands on his lap staring straight ahead. He placed one hand on the table. The governor saw it and quickly leaned over. Jenkins whispered in his ear. The governor nodded.

"You make a valid point, Deputy. And since you and the ranger have already been able to locate victims, I hereby order you two to continue the search. Sheriff Burton will continue questioning the suspect and his passengers, and the district attorney and his team will start building the prosecution."

"Does this mean you're not calling in the FBI?" Sheriff Burton blurted.

The governor started to respond, but Travers waved him off and called to the stenographer. "Betty, would you strike that last question and turn off your machine. Thank you." When she stopped typing, he said, "It's off the record now, sir."

Governor Lane aimed his jaw at the sheriff. "These crimes happened here in Oregon. My state. Your state. And they are going to be solved by me and you and everyone in this room. The last thing I am going to do is rely on the federal government's help. Hell, do you think they would give us the time of day after the year they have had? Look around. They are still busy looking into King's murder down in Memphis, Kennedy's in Los Angeles. There have been riots in Detroit, DC, New York City, and Chicago. Men are burning draft cards and women burning bras. Drug pushers and addicts are running rampant. I would say the feds are pretty damn busy trying to keep their own house in order."

He harrumphed and then thumped the table. "Oregon is our house, and we will clean it ourselves. Any questions?"

No one moved.

"One other thing," Governor Lane said. "The last thing we need right now is to have the newspapers and TV scare the good citizens of Harney County needlessly or provoke someone into taking matters into their own hands. We are going to keep a lid on information about the crimes and their investigation, so nothing tarnishes the case that could make it even harder to take it to trial and get a verdict."

The governor hooked his thumb at Travers. "Richard has arranged a meeting with the local editor and publisher of the *Burns Herald* to ask for her assistance, and he will be working with her directly as my representative. I am confident Mrs. LaRue will understand there is a greater good to be achieved by delaying any more stories like the one that ran the other day."

"Good luck trying to keep Bonnie quiet," Pudge muttered.

Travers jumped to his feet. "I'll be serving as Governor Lane's point person. Your first assignment, gentlemen, is to provide me with all your contact information. That means your home telephone number in addition to the number to your office. Consider yourself on 24-hour notice from here on out. I'll send around a schedule for regular report outs. That'll be all. Get to work."

⁓

ORVILLE NELSON WAS HUNCHED over a folding table set up in a file room.

"It's after midnight, son. Don't you got a home to go to?" Pudge said.

"Ranger Drake asked to see the missing persons reports." He pointed to a stack of file folders. "And home is in Redmond."

"Meaning you sleep in here because Bust'em is too cheap to pay you a decent wage to afford a room." Pudge fished two twenties from his wallet and slapped them on the table. "Any man worth his salt deserves to get paid. What do you got for us?"

"I've organized the reports and created a spreadsheet of the details."

"A spreadsheet?"

"It's a computing term. The original concept was BCL, that's Business Computer Language. It's used by IBM. The program was written in Fortran and it—"

"In English," Pudge said.

Orville hesitated as he struggled to find nontechnical words. "BCL is a computerized business and accounting system. It's used to compute numbers. A spreadsheet is the form the computer generates. It's based on the bound ledgers accountants used for keeping track of revenue and expenses, employees' hours, and so on."

"What's bookkeeping have to do with murder?"

"Here, take a look at the one I made. I've created different categories on the x-axis. That's the row that goes across the top. Age, date reported missing, physical characteristics, last known location, destination if known, mode of transportation if known, and so on. And then on the y-axis, the column that goes top to bottom, I've listed the names of missing persons."

"You got pretty good handwriting," Pudge said.

"I would've typed it if I had had the time. Of course, if we had access to a computer like they do at the FBI."

"You're lucky they give you a pencil around here."

"This spreadsheet will help us keep track of details and also see any similarities or patterns."

Pudge winked at me. "Hear how he says 'us?' Looks like we got ourselves a partner."

Orville exchanged the spreadsheet for a map. "I've also plotted information from the reports on this highway map. I drew a transect from point A, that being the last known location of the missing person, to B, their destination if known."

The lines crisscrossed the country. Most ended up in California. Dubuque to Hollywood. Omaha to Hollywood. New York City to San Francisco. Macon to San Francisco.

Orville traced a north south line with his finger. "This one is for Vicky Wells. According to the report filed by her parents, they last saw her at their home in Santa Monica. I marked it on the map as A. They reported she was going to Vancouver, Canada by bus. I marked that as B. Now, the Santa Monica Police Department made some phone calls after her parents reported her missing. They confirmed that her last known sighting before her body was found was at the Greyhound station in Weed, California." He pointed to it on the map. "The bus broke down and the passengers were reissued tickets for later departures. However, Greyhound has no record of Miss Wells ever using her new ticket. The Santa Monica police believe she grew impatient and hitchhiked."

"Well, we know she wound up over here." Pudge pointed to the Hart Refuge. "That means she didn't go up the new interstate the bus would've taken to get to Vancouver via Portland. Weed is at the Highway 97 junction. A lot of big rigs use it instead so they don't have to drive over the Siskiyou Mountains. Maybe a trucker picked her up. That gives us something to go on."

Orville went back to the pile of folders. "Not all of the missing persons reports contain information about destination or mode of travel. And some of them are not very recent. This one is two years old. A Miss Sharon Spirelli was living in Portland and attending nursing school. Her roommate reported that she never returned from spring break. The roommate didn't know where Miss Spirelli was going, so we don't have a destination, only the last known location. Portland."

"What about personal information on the missing girls? Like, if they had a boyfriend. Whether or not they'd ever been in trouble with the law for running away. Drugs. Prostitution. Things like that," Pudge said.

"If there was anything, I listed it in the category I call Personal." Orville winced. "I can't wait until everything gets put on computers. We'll be able to see birth certificates, fingerprints, driver's license, and whether or not they paid their bills."

"Sounds like what they do over in the Soviet Union," Pudge said.

I picked up a pencil and drew a series of concentric rings around Hart Mountain, stopping when the outermost ring reached the state line.

"Looks like a target and your antelope refuge is the bull's-eye," Pudge said. He counted the lines that transected my circles. "That makes, what, six, seven missing girls that more than likely entered Harney County."

I tapped the map. "We should concentrate on those reports."

Orville thumbed through the stack of folders. "I color coded them all by area." He removed the ones with red labels stuck on them and counted them out. "That makes eight."

"Read them out loud for us, one by one," Pudge said. "Sometimes hearing is better than seeing."

We spent the next two hours going through them. When we finished the last, Pudge pushed his hat up and wiped his brow with the back of his thick hand. "People file missing persons reports, but they don't always cancel them when the person shows up. We need to get updates."

He motioned to Orville. "You need investigative experience

for your FBI application? Well, here's your chance. First thing in the morning, start working the phones. See if we can rule out any of these eight girls. Call their folks, the local police, whoever, and whatever. Get any information you can. And don't ignore the ones in the reports that may be a couple of years old or more. Who knows how long this bastard's been at it."

I asked Orville to search for information on Damian too. "The Department of Veterans Affairs will have records for everyone who got a dishonorable discharge the year he did because they have to record when to cut off their paychecks. You'll be able to narrow down the ones who served in combat because their record will show they were getting an extra sixty-five dollars a month."

Orville gathered up the folders. "Anything I turn up, I'll put in the spreadsheet."

"Even better, call me on the radio," Pudge said.

"You're not going to be here in the office?"

"Hell no. Drake and me are heading home to No Mountain."

"To look for more bodies?"

"And the killer."

The rain left ankle-high puddles in the parking lot. I was running on fumes and the thought of my narrow bunk was the only thing keeping me going. My time asleep would be brief since Pudge asked me to pay a visit to Crossed Bars first thing in the morning to confirm if and when Barry had stayed there. I had my hand on the pickup's door handle when a dark Mercedes-Benz eased alongside. The rear passenger window rolled down.

"A moment of your time?" Aubrey Jenkins said.

The last thing I wanted was to endure his thank-yous for finding his dead daughter, knowing that eventually he'd learn I'd walked across her like she was a gangplank. A chauffeur slid out of the front seat, nodded curtly to me, and opened the rear door. He closed it behind me but remained standing an arm's length away. Jenkins pushed a button and the window silently rolled up.

"You have my condolences," I said.

Jenkins didn't acknowledge me. He stared straight ahead as if looking at oncoming traffic.

"You are not married. You do not have children," the rich man began. "If you did, you would know that when you lose a child, you not only lose a part of yourself—your own flesh and blood— but you lose your future, your dignity, and your standing. Your wife will never be the same, never treat you the same. She will blame you for the loss, hold you responsible for not being able to protect her child. It makes no difference if she is right or wrong. It is the way it is. Your friends, your business partners, your employees, they will see you differently, treat you differently. Always in the back of their mind, they will wonder how a good girl from a good family could be involved in a murder. Murder involves criminality. They will wonder what you did to bring it upon yourself."

It would have been easier if Jenkins had broken down and started crying or punched the back of the seat or kicked, screamed, and ripped his clothes, but he continued to speak as if he were discussing the weather, a book he'd read, a play he'd seen.

"Their pity turns to suspicion and then to self-protection," Jenkins said. "If it happened to you, they tell themselves, it must be because you were weak, defenseless. If it happened to you, to let your daughter be stolen, tortured, raped, and murdered, it could also happen to them unless they prove that they are not weak and defenseless. And so, they set out to do so at your expense. They shun you to strip you of your standing in the community. They tarnish your name, your reputation, with rumors and gossip. They cheat you in business to take away your wealth, your power. And when they are finished, after they have used you to prove they are strong and not defenseless, they leave you as dead as the daughter they are convinced you allowed to die."

He turned to face me. His eyes burned cold, and I could feel their iciness. "All that will happen unless I do something to prevent it, Mr. Drake. You are going to help me make sure it does not."

"Deputy Warbler and I are already working on it like the governor ordered. We went over some things, and now we're heading back to Hart Mountain to resume a search for evidence."

"That is not the kind of help I mean."

"I don't follow you," I said, even though I knew where the conversation was going.

Sitting in the back seat of the Mercedes felt the same as it did when I accompanied my lieutenant to a colonel's tent in Da Nang. The colonel was the regiment commander and ordered our squad to carry out a classified assignment. His words were 'special order.' When my LT asked him where the order originated, the colonel bristled and bits of saliva fluffed at the corners of his lips. "That is not your concern," he fumed. "What is your concern is following my order to the letter and making sure when your men reach the objective, they do their job." He turned to me. I was the squad's fire team leader and had more in-country experience than my LT. "Educate your lieutenant it's guerrilla warfare we're fighting here, Sergeant. Remind him there are no civilians. If they have hands, they can fire a gun. If all they have is feet, they can still kick the shit out of you. Everyone is a combatant, and you will take no prisoners."

"I have friends in high places," Aubrey Jenkins said. "I have seen your military file. You were decorated."

"As I said before, you have my condolences."

"You were a long-range patrol scout with the 1st Cavalry and served back-to-back tours in Vietnam starting in 1965. Your job was to be the eyes and ears of the battlefield commander. You excelled in reconnaissance, intelligence gathering, and tracking. You fought, you led, you killed."

"And I took drugs and ended up in the looney bin." I

grabbed the door handle. "I did things I'm not proud of. I cost my soldiers their lives. I cost old men and women and children their lives too."

"I spoke to your doctor at Walter Reed Hospital. He said your case is not unique. He called it a new kind of shell shock brought on by trauma and stress. He said your drug addiction was the field hospital's fault. They did not know about your addictive personality. They did not know that the reason you always volunteered to walk point and go on search and destroy missions was because you were addicted to combat. They did not know any of that when the medic gave you morphine after you were wounded."

"You seem to have spent a lot of time asking about me," I said, more edgy than wary.

"I have built a successful business empire because I learn about everyone I am associated with, from a sawyer at one of my mills to the bank president at one of my savings and loans. I need to know the kind of man you are."

"I know what kind I am. I know it every morning I wake up and every night before I go to bed. I have a shelf full of tin cans with pebbles in them to remind me. I rattle them and rattle them until they drown out the screams of the people I let down that still rattle around in my head. We're done here."

"That is precisely why I need you. You know what happens when people are abandoned, left to die on a battlefield or in a gully. You have seen it. You saw my daughter. Help me, Mr. Drake. I will make it worth your while. Sheriff Burton is a lawman, a politician, but not a soldier. He has not seen the pure evil in men. More importantly, he has not done something about it."

Jenkins paused. "I want you to find the man responsible for my daughter's death. And then I want you to hold him until I can get there. I want to see him, to tell him to his face what he can expect. I need everyone—my wife, my friends, my business partners—to know that I am not weak and defenseless, so they will never try to protect themselves at my expense."

"What makes you think the man they have in custody isn't the killer?"

"Because you do not. I saw it in your eyes."

"And suppose you got a chance to face the real killer. What is it you will tell him?"

"You were in war. You know what happens to the enemy."

Aubrey Jenkins pushed the button and the window rolled down as quietly as it had rolled up. It was the signal for the chauffeur to open the door. As I got out, I looked back at Kathy's father, but he had resumed staring straight ahead at a vision I wanted no part of.

The chauffeur closed the door and put a slip of paper in my shirt pocket. "Call the number, day or night. Anytime."

"You know what he asked me to do?"

"I've been with Mr. Jenkins a few years now. I drove straight over from Salem because I knew he wasn't about to fly home with the governor. I knew he would stay here until this is finished the way he wants it to finish. You should know Mr. Jenkins always gets what he wants. It doesn't pay to disappoint him."

The chauffeur's nose had been flattened and a thin scar ran through his right eyebrow. He was wearing a suit, but it was too tight. His shoulders and biceps strained the fabric. The shoulder holster holding the gun tucked beneath his left armpit did too.

"What did you do before you became his driver?" I asked.

"Many things," he said.

"And now?"

"Anything."

〜

THE SHAKES TURNED into jitters as I drove away. The memory of the mission after the colonel issued his special order was the one I had tried to bury the deepest, but Aubrey Jenkins brought it roaring right back. A coppery taste of panic filled my mouth. My adrenaline kicked back on. It set my legs jiggling, my heart racing. I'd never be able to fall asleep. I'd run and run and run until all my springs snapped like a watch wound too tight. I needed something to slow the race. I needed something, anything.

A neon sign flickered on the side of the road leading out of Burns. It was on a pole next to a mini-mart. "Open 24 Hrs." I whipped into the parking lot and rushed inside. The glass-fronted refrigerator holding cold drinks beckoned at the rear. I yanked out a quart bottle of beer. Only one, I told myself. Only one. Take it home and drink it and go to sleep.

I felt proud of myself carrying only the one bottle and not a case to the counter.

The clerk had pimples and a sparse moustache. He pointed to the wall clock that joyously promised 'Things Go Better With Coke.'

"No can do," he said in a whiny voice. "Not for another three hours."

"What do you mean?"

"No alcohol sales between 2:30 and 7:00 am. It's the law."

"I've been on the job two days straight. I'm so tired I can't fall asleep. I got to get up early and go back to work. Come on."

"Sorry, I don't make the rules, the government does. They're the ones decided only they can sell the hard stuff in their own stores. Goddamn monopoly, you ask me. No way I'm going risk losing my job and my boss's beer and wine permit. He'd skin me alive and then he'd kill me."

"I am the law." I slapped my breast where my badge usually

hung. I was still wearing the flannel shirt from the sheriff's department lost and found.

"I've heard every story in the book. Now get out of here." The clerk reached for something behind the counter.

"I'll pay double. Triple. Whatever you want. I need this beer. It's just one bottle."

"And I said, forget it. Either haul your ass outside and wait til seven, or I'll call the cops and you can wait in the tank."

I could feel the jitters taking over, sense my shirt bulging from where my heart was fighting to leap out.

"One beer, please? I need to sleep. Please?"

He grabbed the bottle. "You need to sleep, go over to that aisle and buy yourself some sleeping pills. You don't even need a prescription."

My hands were shaking so hard I toppled the first box of pills. The ones behind it fell like dominoes. I quickly read the ingredients. Methapyrilene. Scopolamine. That was the juice the black hats gave to VC officers to make them talk. I'd seen what it did. I dropped the box. Next to the sleeping pills was a row of cough syrup bottles. The print on the label was tiny, but I spotted an old friend. Dextromethorphan. I'd resorted to it before when I couldn't score. I held the bottle in my hand and could all but hear its siren call, feel its warm embrace. I tucked two bottles under my arm and rifled through a rack of cold medicine looking for one with pseudoephedrine as its main ingredient. Just in case, I told myself. I didn't have to look far to find it.

The clerk didn't offer an opinion as he rang up the meds along with a quart of 7Up. He placed them in a brown paper bag and took my money. I didn't wait for the change, but hustled straight out to the parking lot, opened the soda pop, emptied half on the ground, and then poured in both bottles of cough syrup.

The now purple brew started bubbling over the top of the green bottle like magma. I leaned over, put my lips around the mouth, tilted my head back, and gulped. Fizz scorched my nostrils and throat. My eyes watered and my stomach somersaulted. I got half of it down before I gagged. Some of it came rushing back out in a dark wave that splashed the cracked asphalt and the wheels of my pickup. I gulped some more and kept it down.

I climbed into the cab, tucked the open bottle between my legs, and steered south with the window wide open. When I got the cramps, I stuck my head out and sucked in air and then chased it with another swig of the vile home brew.

Halfway to No Mountain the opioids in the dextromethorphan kicked in. My old friend was back. Everything would be just fine. I'd get home and tuck into bed and drift off to a place where all the dreams were good and the only thing to worry about was morning and finding another fix. I could see it all play out. I'd wake up with a headache from hell, the sweats, and the shits. I'd jump on the Triumph and wind the engine up past the red line and wouldn't stop until I hit Eugene or Portland or anywhere in between where I could score. I'd need the works too, but that would be easy. A candle. A spoon. A safety pin. An eyedropper. Light, cook, stab, squeeze. Sweet dreams and sweet relief.

The truck veered off the road and onto the shoulder. It bounced over gravel making everything rattle, rattle like a can full of pebbles stored on a kitchen shelf. I swerved back onto the blacktop. "No!" I shouted. I reached for the box of cold pills, ripped it open, and choked down a dozen dry.

The jolt from their amphetamine hit hard as it collided with the opioid. Bursts of color engulfed the cab. I looked over and saw Kathy Jenkins bathed in neon light. She smiled and started to speak, but when she opened her mouth a rattler's tongue flicked out. I reached to yank her away from the snake. The truck swerved again and nearly rolled over. I slowed down and straightened the wheel. "Sorry," I cried. When I looked over, her father had taken her place.

"The killer," he said in an eerily calm voice. "Bring him to me."

More neon lights flashed, and a bottleneck guitar began to keen as Jim Morrison moaned about swimming to the moon and climbing through the tide. Jenkins became the chauffeur who aimed his gun at me. I ducked before he could fire. When I looked back, his face melted into the snaky front man of the Doors, writhing in black leather plants as he gripped a microphone and screamed we were on a moonlight drive with no time to decide. And then as the guitar caterwauled and the piano pounded, Morrison became the colonel who wailed, "Kill, kill, kill! No one gets out of here alive!"

I chucked the bottle out the window and all the cold pills too. And then I hunched over the steering wheel and held on tight as the wind blew through the cab and tried to rip the skin from my face. I stomped the gas pedal and prayed I could hold the devil at bay long enough to get home and rattle my cans for as long as it took.

S omeone was pounding, pounding on my head. They could've been using their fists, but it felt like a ball-peen hammer. I tried opening my eyes. All I saw were the blue stripes of a pillow's ticking. The white pillow case was wrapped around my neck and the sheets were wrapped around my legs. The blanket had been kicked to the floor. I was still wearing the clothes from the lost and found. The pounding didn't let up. It wasn't coming from inside my head, but outside the lineman's shack. I stumbled to the door and yanked it open. Jesse Harney stood in the bright light of day.

"That was total bullshit you said about arresting me for our cows being on the refuge." Spittle sprayed as he shouted. "I told my brother and he said it was bullshit, that you couldn't do any such thing, and we're going to sue you for lying."

I tried pushing the door shut, but he grabbed the knob and pushed back.

"You chickenshit," he shouted. "You're no better than that old fat fuck who isn't good enough to be sheriff."

Instead of pushing the door, I yanked it open. It pulled Jesse right inside. He stumbled toward me, and I kneed him in the crotch, grabbed his arm when he bent over, and threw him face down on the floor. I landed on him with my knee in his back and put him in a choke hold. He gasped for air and kicked the floor. I locked my fingers around my wrist and tightened. The kicking grew more frantic and then started to slow.

I could feel tangled vines and rubbery leaves, see the black pajama shirt crisscrossed with bandoliers, hear the crack of the neck, and the explosion of gas exhaled from the body. And then I shouted at myself and let go.

Jesse coughed and gasped while he tried to crawl away. When he finally caught his breath, he cried, "I'm going to tell my brother on you!"

"Get out of here," I said.

He pulled himself to his knees, wheezed, and then held his hands to his sides as he stood. "You're going to pay for this."

"Just go," I said.

He stumbled out of the shack. Before he got to his truck, he grabbed a rock and threw it. I closed the door as it hit. I went into the kitchen and made coffee while rock after rock banged against the side of the shack.

Jesse was gone by the time I showered, dressed in my own clothes, and left to go to Crossed Bars. I expected Brother Michael and Sister Star to appear when I arrived, but they were nowhere to be seen. The ranch was eerily quiet except for chickens scratching in the yard and a loose shutter banging. The breeze that blew it was the last gasp of the once powerful storm.

No one answered when I knocked on the front door. I peered through a window. The kitchen was empty. Stacks of clean dishes towered next to the sink. Two pots were on the stove, but I couldn't see the blue flames of the burners. I tried another window. It looked into the dining hall. A man was sitting alone at one of the tables with his back to me. I went around to the front door and entered.

The man was short and round and had a long gray beard. He wore a sheepskin skullcap and his hair matched the color and length of his beard. He was spooning soup from a large bowl.

"Excuse me," I said. "Are you Vasudeva?"

He looked up. "I am known by many names." His voice was soft and tinged with an accent that spoke of both London and Delhi.

"I'm Nick Drake. I'm with the Fish and Wildlife Service."

"Ah, yes. The ranger who chose to deal with our predation problem by saying 'Shoo, kitty. Scat cat.' " Smile lines creased his face.

"Has he come back?"

"I do not believe so. Perhaps your solution worked after all."

"Perhaps," I said.

"You do not look well, my son. Not well at all."

"It must have been something I ate."

"The body is a temple and must be treated as such. Would you care for some soup? It is quite healthy and delicious too."

"No thanks."

He shrugged and spooned some more from his bowl.

"Is Brother Michael or Sister Star here? I need to talk to them."

"They are here, but they are not talking. Everyone is at temple in silent meditation."

"For how long?"

"Time is relative. As long as it takes or as short."

"But you're not there."

"Oh, but I am. I am everywhere and nowhere." The smile lines appeared again. Soup stained his beard, but he was either unaware of it or uncaring.

"Perhaps you can help me," I said.

"I help many people. What is your wish? Peace? Enlightenment? Or perhaps you need help with a woman." His eyes twinkled. "Do not be bashful, my son. The body is a temple. It needs every kind of nourishment. Tell me. I can help."

"I am looking for some people who may have spent the night here during the last week or so. A man, a woman, and a teenage girl. They drove a Volkswagen bus with Washington State tags. It had a rainbow painted on the side and the words 'Further' on the front and 'Later' on the back. They were heading to San Francisco."

"Why do you seek them?"

"I was asked to find them. Do you remember seeing them spend the night in your field?"

"A Volkswagen bus, you say?"

"Yes. It has curtains in the windows."

"I do not recall it. The vehicle is too light and the motor too noisy for my taste. I prefer more substantial automobiles where you can ride in absolute silence." He smiled. "As if borne by a silver cloud."

"Your Rolls Royce."

"You know of it?"

"I have seen it. Damian drove Sister Star to my house to tell me about the cougar."

"An exquisite automobile. My favorite."

"You have others?"

"Oh, but of course. I am a bit of a motorist. An aficionado, if you will." He pointed the spoon toward the heavens and proclaimed, "Partaking in an earthly delight helps to distinguish the transcendental from the tangible and thus teaches one what is truly important."

"I have a Triumph motorcycle. A Trophy TR6," I said, seizing the opening.

"You do?" The spoon clattered to the table. "You must give me a ride."

"It's no cloud, more like riding a bolt of lightning."

He squealed with delight. "Ah, a motorcycle. When I was a boy, I rode one everywhere. My father had a Bajaj. It was a two-stroke 90cc, but it was a limousine for us. He would carry my mother, my sister, and me on it, and the four of us would fly over the streets of our village. My greatest day was when he let me drive it myself. Oh, the joy, the freedom." He looked around before saying, "When I joined the Sri Amrita Ashram to study, I carried the feeling with me. I still do."

"We'll have to do it another time. I drove my truck today."

He sighed. "Yes, another time."

"So, you don't remember seeing the VW here?"

"Many vehicles pass through bringing pilgrims and the curious. I usually confine myself to temple. I do not pay attention to those who do not pay mind to their spirit."

"And the pilgrims and curious who are girls, young women. Do you pay attention to them?"

"As does Buddha, Shiva, Vishnu, Krishna, Mahavira, Allah, and Jesus Christ. All sexes can follow the true path. Why do you ask?"

"I have also been asked to find some girls whose families have reported them missing."

"No one is ever lost, my son. All one needs do is accept the true path and one will find one's true self. Would you like to see my automobiles?"

He led me to what was once a horse stable. He pulled aside the sliding doors and flicked on the lights. Five luxury automobiles gleamed. The 1968 Rolls Royce Silver Cloud was flanked by a red Cadillac Seville with sharklike fins, a green Bentley S3 Continental Flying Spur, a gold Jaguar Mark 2, and a black Lincoln Continental convertible with suicide doors.

Yasudeva slipped on white cotton gloves and walked from car to car rubbing their hoods and checking his fingertips for dust.

"Quite a fleet," I said.

"Are they not beautiful? They embody creativity, art, and spirit. Think of all that it takes to bring one to life. The concept, the design, the teamwork to build it. All of the natural elements —Earth, wind, fire, and water—go into the manufacturing and driving of one."

"You're lucky to have them."

"The people I guide on the true path wish me to have them."

"How's that?"

"They bestow these as a symbol of their trust, faith, and gratitude."

"You mean they bought them."

He held up two fingers as if about to make the sign of the cross. "The journey on the true path does not require worldly possessions. Many choose to leave their encumbrances behind or redirect them for other use."

"They sell their stuff and give it to you."

Vasudeva's hand fell to his side. "Not to me. To the ashram. It is the gateway to the true path."

The sliding doors opened wider. Brother Michael entered. He steepled his palms and bowed. "Enlightened Father, Mr. Drake, I see you have met."

Vasudeva raised two fingers again and traced the shape of a triangle over Brother Michael's head. "Blessings."

"May I be of assistance?" Brother Michael asked.

"Our friend the ranger owns a motorcycle. I hope to ride it soon," Vasudeva said and then walked out without saying another word.

"Which one was yours?" I said.

Brother Michael looked confused. "Which one what?"

I swept my hand along the row of expensive cars. "You used to be a lawyer. You probably made a lot of money. When you gave it all to Vasudeva, did you write him a check or buy him a car?"

His lips tightened. "You lack enlightenment, so I will assume your rudeness is because of it. Why did you come here today?"

I handed him the copy of the Crossed Bar's herd inventory that Gemma had given me. "You'll need to check each cow's ear tag with the list. Any that don't get checked off may be wandering around on the other side of your fence line."

"Oh. Thank you very much."

"You should organize a roundup and bring them back. The cougar is still alive."

"Yes, so Damian said."

I caught something in his tone. "We could go back out and try again."

"I do not think that will be necessary."

"I'd like to talk to Damian," I said. "Is he around?"

"No, he has left the ashram."

"Why?

"He is on a journey."

"What kind of journey?"

"A spiritual one. It is to be expected among those seeking the true path. They journey beyond the ashram to discover that the ashram is wherever they go."

"Did he say where he was going?"

"No. Nor did I ask. It is part of the journey."

"Will he come back?"

"That is up to him."

"Do you know the Alvord Desert?"

"Why do you ask?"

"I heard it's a spiritual place. Maybe he went there."

"Perhaps it is. I have not been there myself."

"Can I ask you something else? Do you remember if a group driving a VW bus camped in your field recently? It was painted in Day-Glo and had a Washington license plate. A man, a woman, and a teenage girl."

"Yes, I recall them. They only stayed one or two nights. Are they friends of yours?"

"Not really. Did you happen to speak to them?"

"I did, but it was not a constructive conversation, nor very polite. They ate some meals with us, and when I asked the man to help repair the roof and the women to help in the kitchen, they made unenlightened remarks and packed up and left. It happens sometimes. There are takers in life and there are givers."

"It appears there are plenty of givers around here," I said, taking a last look at Vasudeva's fleet of earthly delights.

I pulled into the Warbler ranch and found Gemma loading her red Wagoneer. She set a wooden crate on the tailgate and put her hands on her hips.

"Pudge would say you look rode hard and put away wet. What happened?"

"Since he tells you everything, I'm sure you already know about yesterday."

"He didn't say anything about what you did after you left Burns in the wee hours."

"It was a long drive home," I said.

"And you went straight there and drank your green tea and went to bed." Her ponytail swished. "Uh-huh."

"Something like that."

"My patients may have four legs, but I am a doctor."

"What's that supposed to mean?"

"It means I know the signs when a body is trying to rid itself of something that's not good for it. Twitching, sniffling, rapid eye movement."

"I caught a chill is all." I grabbed a box from the pile and shoved it in the back of the Jeep. "What's this stuff?"

"I got an SOS about a large herd of sick cows. Sounds like they got into a field full of *Halogeton glomeratus*. Better known as goosefoot. Cows are usually smart enough to avoid it, but if they don't get enough salt in their diet, they'll eat it."

"Is it deadly?"

"Very if you don't treat it right away. They fall into a coma and die. Luckily, Blaine is an old hand when it comes to sick cows and spotted the warning signs, namely cattle stumbling around like they're drunk and about to pass out."

"Will you be seeing him?"

"I divorced Blaine, not his cattle." She paused as she reached for a box. "Why do you care if I do?"

"I don't, but his little brother paid me a visit this morning. It didn't go well for him. I expect Blaine will tell you about it."

"Why did Jesse come see you?"

"Mainly to complain about me threatening to arrest him at Blackpowder Smith's. He told me Blaine is going to sue me over it."

Gemma stuck out her bottom lip and blew the strands of hair that had gotten loose from her ponytail. "If Blaine has a beef with you, he wouldn't send his little brother. He doesn't hide behind anyone."

"Neither do I."

Gemma slammed the tailgate shut. "Stay away from things like goosefoot, okay?"

"I'll try."

"Try harder." She got in and leaned out the window. "Maybe I'll swing by your place after I'm done and check on that tea to make sure you didn't mix up your herbs."

She sped off before I could think of something to say. Her Jeep blazed like a fireball as soon as it hit the blacktop.

November already had the front door open when I climbed the porch steps. "You look like you drank bad firewater."

"I thought they only called it that in Hollywood Westerns."

"Maybe one day somebody will make one where an Indian is the hero."

"Maybe. Didn't Gemma tell you I make my own tea? She said you'd appreciate that."

"She says a lot of things, like it's no big deal when her no-good ex calls for help." The Paiute woman's spit arced all the way across the porch and hit the ground.

"I take it you think he smells like a *pongica kwedatse* too."

She wrinkled her nose. "Big time."

I found Pudge in his office. He was on the phone and jotting down notes. When he hung up, I told him I'd come from Crossed Bars.

"You spoke with the little swami? What's he like?"

"Everything he says sounds like he memorized something somebody else said. But he's smart enough to get people to give him money. A lot of it." I described his fleet of cars.

"Those and the ranch they bought him. He wouldn't be the first to figure out there's plenty of profit in religion. Back in the day, circuit riders made more than cowpunchers. There's a church up in Portland that spent more on stained glass windows than the annual budget for the Harney County Sheriff's Department."

"Vasudeva didn't remember Barry, but Brother Michael did. He confirmed the trio stayed there and then dined and dashed."

"Like Barry told you they did, huh? You've had yourself a busy morning. I take it you didn't get any sleep. You look like roadkill."

"Brother Michael told me something else. Damian is gone. He said he went on a spiritual quest."

"You don't say? Well, take a look at this." The deputy passed over a sheet of shiny facsimile paper. "The college boy sent this over a little bit ago. Talk about your eager beavers. He didn't get any sleep either."

"What is it?"

"It's a list from the Veterans Administration. He took advantage of the time difference and called Washington DC. I swear that boy doesn't sleep. He sweet talked some fella into providing him the names of all the soldiers who got less than honorable discharges following the dates of the Khe Sanh battle. Did you know they provide that information to employers? Man applies for a job, and his boss can see what he did to get tossed out of the military."

The list was in alphabetical order by last name. It included, age and rank at time of discharge plus a Separation Program Number. The SPNs included "41E Obesity" and "461 Inadequate Personality."

"We can rule out some of these based on age and cause," I said. "Damian is no older than early twenties, tops, and he's certainly not fat. Unless he was lying about being in Vietnam, we can narrow it down even further because some of these guys got thrown out before they made it through boot. It looks like there's a half dozen or so possibilities."

"Orville's already working on tracking them down. That and making phone calls to the families of the eight girls from the missing persons reports. I told Bust'em he's gonna have to start giving him a paycheck."

"Was that the sheriff on the phone?"

"He got Doc's preliminary report. Pretty much confirms what we already knew. Same things were done to Kathy as Vicky Wells, right down to snipping a lock of her hair. He's still waiting on some tests, but as far he can figure, she's been dead about four days. Rigor had already set in and gone by the time you found her, why you could sling her over your shoulder."

I winced. The sound of her bones snapping under my boots

still echoed. It always would. "What did he say about the injuries after she died?"

"Post mortem. That's the term he used. As far as he can tell, and this is what goes into his report, any post mortem cuts and broken bones were caused by the no-good son of a bitch piling rocks on top of her after he strangled her."

The report would not be easy reading for Aubrey Jenkins no matter how the words were parsed.

Pudge said, "Bust'em also told me the young girl picked up with Barry is talking right now with a psychologist from Child Services."

"Jenny."

"Yup. Jenny. Bust'em was in the room for the first part of the interview, but then she got skittish and the psychologist said it would be best all-around if he left. He's gonna fill me in after he talks with the psychologist when they're done."

"What did she say before he left?"

"He said she lies like she's taking a breath. She mixes them in with real stuff. Bust'em is sure she's doing it on purpose. Like Barry told you, she doesn't want to get sent back home."

"Any luck finding her mom's address?"

"They're still working on it. We sent Jenny's picture to Tacoma PD and the Washington State Patrol too."

"What about Linda?"

"Nothing's changed. All she does is call us names. Clock's ticking on both her and Barry's 48-hour hold. I'll give Bust'em a call back and let him know Brother Mike confirmed they stayed at Crossed Bars. Even so, that doesn't clear them. It only confirms they've been in the area for the past several days."

"Did you tell him I don't think Barry did it?"

"He's not in a listening mood. He's got the governor's tallyman camped out in his office. Bust'em wants it to be Barry more than anyone. It would make his life a whole lot easier."

"Then we have to find the real killer."

"I've been thinking on it. We know Vicky Wells got stuck in Weed, waiting for a bus. Maybe she goes to get a cup of coffee, and our guy overhears her and offers her a ride. Or she goes outside and sticks out her thumb. Maybe he's a trucker and been picking up hitchhikers all along. It sure would explain how she got over here from the interstate."

"That's going to be hard to nail down without a witness or a confession. There must be hundreds of big rigs on the road every day."

"That's true. It's gonna take a lot of legwork to sort them all out, but I was thinking maybe we put our college boy to work on that too. See, the long-haul truckers all got to stop at the scales. The State Department of Transportation operates them. They keep records. One call from Governor Lane and all that paper work gets handed over to Orville, and he goes does his spreadsheet thing."

"That may account for Vicky Wells, but what about Kathy Jenkins? We don't know if she was hitchhiking or not."

"We don't. But her father keeps talking about her diary, how he read something in it that made him think she'd run off to join a religious group over here. Maybe there's something in it about her hitchhiking before. Maybe she's not the sweet innocent thing he believes. Or says."

"Jenkins is still in Burns," I said. "He didn't go home with the governor."

"How do you know that?"

"I spoke to him in the parking lot after I left the sheriff's office."

"What was he doing there?"

"Waiting for me. His chauffeur drove up from Salem and was with him."

"What did he want to talk to you about?"

"Finding the killer and telling him first."

Pudge sucked air through his teeth so hard it put indents in his jowls. "He doesn't believe Barry did it either. Hell, he doesn't want it to be Barry. He wants it to be someone else, so he can dish out his own punishment."

"That's about the size of it."

"Oh Lord, just what I need. A vigilante. And a rich and powerful daddy one too." Pudge hitched his belt. "You can bet more than the ranch that's not about to happen, governor's friend or no governor. Not by a long shot."

"One other thing."

"Aren't you a bundle of good news. What is it?"

"The chauffeur? He does a lot more than drive."

"Figures. The only thing this changes is putting a little more giddyap in our step and using the eyes in the back of our head more. While I wanted to get down to search the gullies today, we got to wait for them to dry out or the mud will suck our boots clean off."

"What are you going to do until then?"

"I'm gonna call Bust'em and then the college boy. Why don't you go talk to Aubrey Jenkins and ask if he has Kathy's diary with him? Make him believe you're taking him up on his offer. He did offer you something, didn't he?"

"He did."

"Good. It'll make him trust you. And, Drake?"

"Yes?"

"Whatever you do, don't trust him. And not his gunman either."

Operation Rolling Thunder was getting underway when I arrived in-country as a cherry. The campaign to bomb Vietnam back to the Stone Age went on for three years. Firecrackers, Walleyes, Rockeyes, Paveways, pineapples, daisy cutters, clusters, dumb bombs, fuel bombs and guided bombs, I saw them all fall and felt them all explode. My head ached now like it did when B-52s and their fighter escorts rained hell and transformed air into fire and jungles into ash. My mind was gauzy, disconnected, and dull from pain. I stopped off at Blackpowder Smith's to buy aspirin. He asked if I wanted to wash them down with a beer.

"On the house," he said. "For what you did for Pudge the other day."

"A glass of water is fine," I said

He watched as I ground up three aspirin, dumped the powder into the glass, and drained it without taking a breath.

"Gets into the blood stream faster," I explained.

"So does whiskey." He placed a bottle on the bar between us.

I waved it off. "Not for me."

"AA? Not that I judge."

"NA," I said. "Same twelve steps, but key tags instead of poker chips. Though anything will do in a pinch, even pebbles from the yard."

The bottle disappeared. "I hear you served," Blackpowder said.

"I did."

"Me too. Had two ships sunk on me. I didn't blame the navy or myself, only the U-boats firing the torpedoes. I'm proud of what we did over there, but your lot? I don't understand why they're giving you boys shit and some of you are giving yourself shit. Your country calls, you answer. The same as when you stepped up when that spoiled brat tried provoking Pudge to take a swing. I'll tell you, I'm no member of the Zachariah Harney booster club, but that man may as well as put a match to his fortune what he spent trying to straighten his youngest out."

"Sending Jesse to a fancy boarding school and all, you mean."

Blackpowder's laugh was as rough as the hand-sawn timber on the tavern's false front. "It may have cost him plenty, but from what I heard it was anything but fancy. It was a military school in Portland that's one step away from being juvenile hall. Uniforms, cold showers, plenty of discipline, and hard-asses for teachers."

I waited for the aspirin to kick in. "Why did he go there?"

The tavern owner put his elbows on the bar. "Because he's a big-time screwup. School in No Mountain only goes up to junior high, so when the kids go to high school they got to go up to Burns. Some have a hard time fitting in. Jesse, thinking he could ride on Blaine's coattails, waltzed in and tried to throw his big brother's rep around. Beginning of junior year, some senior girl invites him to be her date for homecoming. Only Jesse's so dumb he doesn't get she's only doing it to get back at her all-star boyfriend."

The bartender shrugged. "Jesse gets fresh with her, he gets slapped, he calls her an unladylike name, and a fight breaks out. Zachariah gets a call from the principal to come pick him up. Zachariah being Zachariah no doubt gives him the belt when they get back to the Rocking H. Wasn't a whole lot later when Zachariah's prized bull winds up mysteriously sick, so sick that all Zachariah could do is put one between his eyes. Next thing you know, Jesse is on the bus to Mount Hood Military Academy."

"It didn't seem to have taught him any manners." I glanced at my watch. "Can I get change for a buck? I need to use the pay phone."

"If you won't let me buy you a beer, the least I can do is save you a dime. Use the house phone."

He brought me a heavy black rotary dial telephone from its perch next to the cash register. "I'm no fan of those new push-button phones," he said. "Too easy to push the wrong one and get slapped with a big bill for calling China."

I dialed the number on the slip of paper the chauffeur gave me.

"Mr. Jenkins's office," a woman answered. I gave her my name. "Hold, please, while I connect you."

A few clicks and a minute later, the chauffeur came on. "What do you have for us?"

"I need to meet with Mr. Jenkins," I said.

"Good work. Where do we come?"

"No, it's not that. There's something I need to ask him first. It could prove helpful. I'll come to you." He gave me an address.

SOUTHFIELDS WAS a large ranch outside of Burns. The two-story main house was constructed from stone and timber and resembled a lodge. Puffy cumulus clouds riding the thermals over the volcanic peaks of the Cascades provided an oil painting backdrop.

The chauffeur led me to a lush pasture enclosed by a white post and rail fence where a dozen horses grazed. Their coats were shiny, their manes and tails brushed. Aubrey Jenkins stood with a polished boot tip perched on the bottom fence rail. He was wearing the hunting jacket with the leather recoil patch.

"I understand you seek information," he said without preamble. "I presume that means you have accepted my request. If not and you are acting out of pity, leave immediately. I abhor pity. There is no room for such in my world."

"There wasn't much room for it where I come from either," I said.

His gray eyes searched mine. "Then my judgment of you is correct. I am glad we have an understanding. What is it that you need?"

I glanced at the chauffeur. "It could be of a delicate nature."

"Like pity, I have neither the time nor tolerance for delicacy. What is it?"

"We're running down a couple of theories. One is Vicky Wells was picked up hitchhiking. It explains how she got to Harney County. Do you know if your daughter ever hitchhiked?"

"I would never permit nor condone such behavior." His knuckles turned the same color as the top rail of the fence he was gripping.

"Nor would any father," I said. "But that's not what I asked. Sheriff Burton said you had reason to believe your daughter came to Harney County in search of a religious group. He thinks either you or your wife read that in her diary. Kathy didn't drive. If she had come by bus, there'd be a record of a ticket, but the sheriff's department asked, and the bus company couldn't produce one. A friend could have given her a ride, but I'm going to assume they've all been questioned." The sneer on the chauffeur's face confirmed who'd administered the interrogations. "That leaves hitchhiking."

Jenkins didn't relax his grip. "Were you a perfect son, Mr. Drake? Did you always obey your parents, always act to please them, never disappointed them?"

"I may have tried when I was young, but part of growing up is doing things to separate yourself. You can't help but disappoint them. All you can do is try not to disappoint yourself, but that's impossible too."

He stared at the pasture full of horses. The mares had their heads down as they grazed. A pair of frisky colts played an equine version of tag. A stallion held his head high as he kept watch.

"Magnificent creatures," Jenkins said. "Blood, bone, and muscle, like any other horse, but quarter horses are very different. This ranch belongs to a business acquaintance. His stock is considered to be among the best horseflesh in Oregon, perhaps the best anywhere. Quarter horses excel at sprinting. No other breed is faster over short distances. They are carefully trained in reining and cutting. That makes them ideal for herding, calf roping, even rodeo events such as barrel racing. Breeding and training, Mr. Drake. That makes all the difference."

"In horses, yes."

"In people too."

He let go of the fence. "My daughter had breeding, but she had not yet completed training. She was like one of those young colts out there. Innocent, carefree, even a little mischievous."

"What did Kathy do, Mr. Jenkins? What did you read in her diary?"

"My daughter was very pretty and very smart. She liked to play and laugh and do all the things little girls do, but she was also very impressionable. When she went to high school, she fell in with the wrong crowd. We tried to educate her about the price that comes with making poor choices. We discovered she was going up to Portland to attend parties and rock concerts. Her grades fell. She quit piano and French lessons."

Jenkins hesitated. "I had a decision to make. Earn my daughter's ire, perhaps even lose her love, or save her. I chose the latter. I arranged for her to be admitted to a top all-girls college-preparatory academy in Massachusetts starting in the fall. When I told her, she grew furious and said she would run away and join a religious cult. I thought it was an idle threat, and, soon enough, she calmed down. The situation seemed to have righted itself. However, when she failed to come home from a slumber party at a friend's, we called the parents and learned she had never arrived. Her mother found her diary. Kathy wrote about meeting undesirables and smoking marijuana. She had a clipping from some filthy underground newspaper about a San Francisco guru and his colony of freaks and fanatics. She told none of her friends of her plans to run away."

He breathed deeply. I could see his jaw tremble slightly as he exhaled. "Did she hitchhike to Harney County? It is likely. But only her killer knows for sure. And that is one of the questions I plan to ask him when you find him and turn him over to me. Good day, Mr. Drake."

I was entering the sheriff's office when a tall woman dressed in a trim navy-blue suit came out.

"You're the new wildlife ranger," she said. "I'm Bonnie LaRue. I publish the *Herald*. I've heard a lot about you."

"Afternoon," I said as I stepped aside to let her pass.

"I understand you're a war hero. There's so much bad news about Vietnam these days, I believe Harney County could stand a dose of good. Why don't we walk over to my office right now and chat? I can see a feature profile. Harney County Hero: From Defending Freedom to Defending Wildlife."

"Maybe some other time."

"Why not now?"

"Sorry, I'm busy."

"You don't want to talk about what you did in the war that earned your nation's gratitude?"

I slipped my hand from her grasp. "Mrs. LaRue, I don't have anything to say about my time in Vietnam, but we both know that's not what you want to question me about."

She laughed. "How is dear Pudge? Is he working you too hard?"

"My boss is in Portland. He's the district supervisor of Fish and Wildlife."

"My, my. You are new in town. When you see that wily old lawman, remind him I'm still waiting for that trip to San Francisco he promised me. We were going to stay at the Palace Hotel and see the opera." She took a few steps toward the street and then glanced over her shoulder. "You should know that after speaking with Governor Lane's flack and Bust'em, I have the whole story anyway. If you change your mind and want to be quoted, you know where to find me. I'll be sure to spell your name correctly."

The door to Sheriff Burton's office was closed. So was the door to the office Richard Travers had commandeered. I walked down the hall to the file room. A pyramid of Shasta Cola cans rose atop the folding table that Orville Nelson was using as a desk. Crushed empties and balled up paper filled the waste basket next to it. The baby-faced FBI-hopeful had a telephone handset tucked under his chin while he pounded the keys on a green Hermes typewriter.

"Affirmative, Deputy. I'll finish the report and fax it right over." He paused. "Yes, sir, *fax.* You don't need to say the whole word. Ranger Drake? He just arrived. Okay, I'll fill him in."

"Fill me in on what?" I said when he hung up.

"There is a lot going on, sir. A very lot." Orville's words ran together.

I pointed to the cans. "You might want to slow down on your caffeine and sugar intake."

"Oh, these? They're like water. Coffee is too strong for me."

"What did Pudge want you to tell me?"

"I have a status report on my two assignments. I'm typing them up now. I don't have any results on my third assignment yet."

"The truck scales," I said.

His head bounced like an old car with shot springs. "I spoke with Mr. Travers. He's the governor's right-hand man. He set up an office here. He put someone at the Department of Transportation on it to help coalesce the data. DOT is moving heaven and earth to get it to us. Mr. Travers's exact words: heaven and earth." Orville beamed and took a swig from a can, no doubt tasting access to power along with the cola.

"Were you able to narrow down the missing girls any?"

"Affirmative, by three. Two returned home and their reports were never canceled. One was a runaway, the other a wife who'd secretly moved to Nevada for six weeks so she could be eligible to file for divorce. The third has also been accounted for. She's in a correctional facility in Kansas. She'd been arrested along with her boyfriend for holding up a gas station."

"That leaves five."

"Technically speaking, but we don't know for certain if those are all valid missing persons. We also can't rule out additional ones. Remember, we based our supposition on the likelihood they traveled through Harney County and were reported missing relatively recently. There could be victims that were never reported missing or ones with older reports, like that student nurse in Portland, Miss Sharon Spirelli."

"At this point, all we can go on is *likely*. What about your second assignment, finding out about Damian?"

"That turned out to be much easier. I succeeded in obtaining a list from the Department of Veterans Affairs and—"

"Deputy Warbler told me. Who is he?"

Orville ignored my impatience. "The data was very complete on the majority of entries on the list, right down to last known addresses and phone numbers. Six seemed to be the most likely given our parameters. I spoke to three on the phone. They'd returned to their last knowns and have never left since their discharge. I spoke to the mother of a fourth. She lives in

Tennessee. She said the recruiter should never have signed her son up, that he's simple. I think by that she means mentally retarded. The recruiter may have overlooked that on purpose in order to meet his quota. He should be reported to the FBI, by the way. Anyway, the mother said her son was at work. He's a janitor at a grocery store called the Piggly Wiggly."

"And the other two?"

Orville crushed his can of Shasta and opened another. A look of triumph flashed across his whiskerless face. "Now those are what I call possibilities turned likelies. One of them, at least according to his father, said his son never returned home after being discharged. He said that he wasn't surprised by that. The son had enlisted under duress because he had impregnated his high school girlfriend and wanted to flee his responsibilities rather than face a shotgun wedding. The father's words: shotgun wedding. His whereabouts are unknown."

"He could be Damian. Did the VA provide you with any photos? Did you ask the father if he could send you one?"

"No and yes. No, the VA didn't, and yes, I did ask him for a picture. He said he would look around and mail it."

"Not send it by facsimile?"

"Negative. He didn't know what it was. But it doesn't matter."

"Why not?"

"He described his son. He doesn't match your physical description. I'm now convinced the second man is your Damian."

"What makes you so sure?"

"The evidence I gathered may be circumstantial at present, but it won't be once we corroborate it."

"Now you sound more like a lawyer. What did you find out?"

"I spoke to a Mrs. James Edward Gallagher. When I asked if her son, a Daniel William Gallagher, was there, she became quite emotional. She peppered me with questions about why I was calling. I told her I was doing routine administrative work about veterans. I, well, I allowed her to believe I was with Veterans Affairs. I didn't say that straight out, but she got that impression. FBI agents train in undercover work and are often called upon to adopt a persona, so I am still within policy and protocol bounds."

"Take it from me. There are times when following the rules can get you killed."

He took a gulp of cola. "Mrs. Gallagher maintains that her son was falsely accused of cowardice and drummed out of the military by an officer who was trying to cover his own incompetence."

"Wouldn't be the first time."

"It's her contention that Danny—that's what she calls him—should have received a commendation. When I asked if she knew his whereabouts, she said they hadn't heard from him for some time and were very worried. She said her husband was especially distraught as he felt ashamed by his son's dishonorable discharge."

"Do you think she really knows where Danny is and didn't want to tell you?"

"It seemed to be the other way around. She thought I might be able to locate him, and that's why she agreed to speak so candidly. The last communication she received was a postcard from California."

"What did it say?"

"She read it to me. I got the feeling she carries it around with her. 'Don't worry about me. I found a new path. Things are getting better.' "

I felt a jolt as if I had chugged a can of Shasta. "Where does the mother live?"

Orville couldn't contain a grin. "Beaverton, Oregon."

"Did she describe him?"

"Yes, and he fits your description of Damian."

"What about a picture?"

"She says she has plenty and offered to mail me one."

"Beaverton is next door to Portland, right? That's a six hour drive each way, under five and a half if you push it."

"Are you thinking of going there?"

"I was thinking you would. I'm heading home. Deputy Warbler and I are going to search the gullies at Hart tomorrow."

Orville all but saluted. "Willing and able, sir. This qualifies as field investigative work and will help with my Quantico application. I'll leave before daylight and return by dark."

"When you're there, find out if Damian has a sister. He called her Lizzie. He said she couldn't forgive him for what he did in the war. Find out why."

"Roger. And while I'm there, I can stop by his high school and gather more intelligence."

"It's June. It'll be closed for summer vacation."

"Not this one. It goes year-round."

"What kind of school is it?"

"A military academy."

I felt another jolt. "Mount Hood?"

"Affirmative. Mrs. Gallagher said Danny's father wanted him to be a soldier and so he enrolled him there. Do you think they'll let me use a sheriff's car? I could get there and back faster with lights and siren."

Before I could say anything, Sheriff Burton burst in. "I heard you were here, Drake. I need you to come with me right now. We're launching a raid on Crossed Bars. You've been there. You know the people. You can help sort them out."

"Why a raid?"

"The girl who got picked up along with our suspects says they're running a sex ring. She swears they tried to molest her, and other girls are being held captive in the barn. Let's go. The team is rolling out right now."

SHERIFF BURTON SHOWED some restraint as we drove out of Burns. He kept his lights and siren off as he led a convoy of sheriff's vehicles. I brought up the rear until Aubrey Jenkins's black Mercedes-Benz slipped in behind my pickup. I radioed Pudge. He answered as he was speeding toward Crossed Bars from the opposite direction.

"Bust'em should know by now Jenny is blowing smoke," he said. "For a young thing, she certainly knows how to get somebody by the short and curlies. She just bought herself another two, three days enjoying Harney County hospitality at taxpayer's expense."

"How do you think the sheriff will play it when we get there?" I said.

"I'll bet you he's going in without a plan, only a warrant. That might slow down Brother Mike some, but storming into that barn turned into a church will be another matter. I'm hoping the swami and his flock are peaceniks like they say."

"He thinks I can help him sort things out."

"That was my idea. I told Bust'em you were there talking to the college boy. You have more of a connection to these folks than anyone else."

"Any goodwill is about to turn into bad will," I said. "We're coming up on the ranch now, and they've all turned on their lights and sirens."

"I see them. They're following Bust'em like ducklings paddling after their momma."

The strings of marigolds hanging from the crossed timbers entranceway swung in a cloud of dust as we drove up to the ashram. By the time I got out, Sheriff Burton was waving a warrant in Brother Michael's face. Two deputies took up positions on either side of the barn door. A third was heading for the rear to make sure no one rabbited out the back while a fourth was creeping around the other buildings.

"This is a complete violation of our rights!" Brother Michael shouted, his face turning crimson. "We are a church and recognized as such. We are protected by the First Amendment of the United States Constitution. I repeat, the First Amendment. It also protects our right to assemble peacefully, as does the Fourteenth Amendment that extends our rights under state law. The Fourth Amendment protects our right from unreasonable searches and seizures, of which, this travesty of justice most certainly is. Did you know the Fifth Amendment of the US Constitution also states categorically that a person may not be deprived of property by the government? Most believe it only has to do with self-incrimination protection. Shall I go on?"

Sister Star was standing so close to him, their saffron robes looked like one. "Persecution. Pogrom. Inquisition," she chanted.

Sheriff Burton wasn't backing down. "And my right to search this place and arrest anybody trying to interfere is guaranteed by this piece of paper duly issued, signed, and authorized by a justice of the Oregon Superior Court."

"We have the right to know what we are being accused of, or are you going to trample that too?" Brother Michael countered.

I answered first. "The search has nothing to do with your religious beliefs or your place of worship. Accusations have been made, and the sheriff has no choice in the matter. Let him search the ashram. If you have nothing to hide, you have nothing to fear."

"What sort of accusations?" Brother Michael asked.

"Sheriff?" I said.

The sheriff's aviator sunglasses had slipped down. He put a

finger to their bridge and pushed them back up. "I have an underaged female in protective custody who recently stayed here. She says a person or persons living on the premises attempted to molest her. She also says other females are being held against their will for sexual purposes."

"That is preposterous!" Brother Michael shouted. "We are a place of spiritual awakening. This is police harassment and a gross miscarriage of justice. Our constitutional rights are being violated, and we will take the necessary legal steps to protect them."

The other members of the ashram had stopped whatever work they were doing and were gathered behind Brother Michael and Sister Star. Some men held tools. A shovel, a hoe, a pitchfork. A couple of women carried commercial-sized cooking utensils. A ladle. A fork. A cast iron frying pan.

"Oh Lord," Pudge muttered. He elbowed the sheriff out of the way. "Brother Mike, Sister Star, what Drake said are wise words. Right now, what that little girl said is only an accusation, not a verdict. We may be the law, but we do believe in innocent until proven otherwise. Stand your people down before someone gets hurt and turns this into something everybody's gonna be sorry for. How 'bout it?"

Instead of defiant grumbles and angry shouts, the ashram's members started chanting. "Om. Omm. Ommm."

All steepled their hands beneath their chins and bowed. The crowd parted as Vasudeva made his way through. He had his hands steepled too, and he wore a splotch of white paint daubed between his eyebrows.

"Children," he said. "Are you not travelers on the true path? Do you forget my teachings?" He broke the steeple and raised two fingers. "Peace, joy, enlightenment only come to those who are free of anger and hate."

He directed his gaze at Pudge and me. "You are welcome to

look inside all buildings, talk to all people. But you must not carry weapons when you enter our temple, for it is sacred. You must also not wear shoes. Only bare feet must touch the temple ground, for it is holy."

"Fair enough," Pudge said. He marched to the barn, handed his .45 to one of the deputies, pulled off his boots and socks, and disappeared inside. I followed suit.

The barn was lit by candles and the air was choked with smoke from sticks of incense as big around as broomsticks. Prayer rugs were scattered across the packed dirt floor, and some were piled with colorful pillows covered in bold prints. Pudge took the flashlight from his utility belt and shined it around. The barn was empty. He raised the beam to illuminate a hay loft. A rickety wooden ladder provided the only access.

"I try to climb that barefoot, I'll either get a splinter or slip and break my hip. That's a job for a younger man." He shined the beam on me and then reversed his grip and handed the flashlight over. "Take it. I'll grab a candle and make like a stick."

The smoke from the incense got thicker the higher I climbed. It made me think of the Thien Mu temple during Tet where gun smoke and the smell of death replaced that of sandalwood after a few days being holed up inside.

A few old bales of straw remained in the loft. Cobwebs clung to the eaves and scurrying mice were the only sounds of life. I climbed back down.

"Nothing," I said.

"That girl's a pathological liar. Let's go outside and see what kind of trouble Bust'em has gotten himself into," Pudge said.

Vasudeva was sitting in a white wicker rocker eating an orange. One of his followers held a red umbrella over the gnomish guru to shade him. The rest of the flock stood in an orderly line and took turns speaking with Sheriff Burton. Brother Michael and Sister Star stood to the side watching over their charges, but made no attempt to interfere or coach their responses.

"Nothing in the barn," Pudge said to the sheriff.

"We're missing two people according to your count," he replied. "One is supposedly out in the fields tending sheep. I sent a deputy to fetch her." He hooked a thumb at Brother Michael and Sister Star. "They say they don't know where the other one is."

"Damian," I said. "He's on a spiritual quest."

The sheriff scowled. "A what? Well, as long as he's not a girl and underage, that's one less I have to worry about." He went back to questioning the next in line. Name, age, last address, and whether or not they were there on their own free will.

The chauffeur hailed me. He'd rolled down the window of

the black Mercedes but didn't get out. Jenkins was sitting in the back seat. The engine was idling and cool air escaped through the open window.

"What's the deal?" the chauffeur asked.

"Not what the sheriff expected."

"That being?"

"No draftees here, only volunteers."

The chauffeur rotated his head as if his shirt collar was too tight and then rolled his shoulders. I could hear his thick neck crack. "What kind of answer is that?"

"It means there's not going to be a riot, a chase, or an arrest."

"We are wasting our time here," Jenkins said. "They are zealots and fools, not killers."

The automatic window rolled up in my face. The chauffeur gave me a death stare from the other side before putting the big car into gear and driving away.

A trio of deputies started elbowing each other and snickering. The object of their oohs and aahs was a beautiful young woman accompanied by the deputy who'd been sent to find her. Lustrous hair cascaded over her shoulders, and she wore a headband made of braided wild flowers. Her skin was as smooth as porcelain and her lips full and pink. She was barefoot and wore the same robe as the other women, but it looked neither drab nor baggy as the late afternoon sun turned it diaphanous. She cradled a lamb and was humming a tune that sounded as if she'd learned it while tending a flock in the verdant hills of a country across the sea from long ago.

The deputy escorting her was struggling to maintain his composure, but blush marks bloomed on his cheeks and his voice cracked when he spoke. "I found her out in the fields, Sheriff. She was singing to the sheep. And dancing too. Dancing with that baby one."

One of the snickering deputies started humming "Mary Had a Little Lamb." Another started in with "Wooly Bully." Sheriff Burton wheeled around and shot them a look sharp enough to draw blood. The snickering and humming stopped immediately.

The young woman carried the lamb to Vasudeva and crouched next to him. She bowed.

He raised two fingers and said, "All creatures, including this newborn, are sentient beings and thus possess potential for enlightenment." He patted the lamb. "Thank you, my child." And then he patted her head.

"Our shepherdess has a gift with animals," Brother Michael said. "She can speak to them. When she sings, they never stray."

"That a fact," Pudge said.

After the interviews were completed, Sheriff Burton and his deputies departed. Vasudeva ambled toward the dining hall. I stopped Brother Michael before he could follow.

"I need to get a message to Damian," I said.

"As you told the sheriff, he is on a spiritual journey."

"To the Alvord Desert?"

"That is where some who seek the true path go, but I do not know for certain. His journey is his own now."

"I spoke to Danny's mother. She's worried sick about him."

"Danny? Who is Danny?"

"You know who. Danny Gallagher. Private First Class Daniel William Gallagher, US Marines. Dishonorably discharged following the battle of Khe Sanh."

"We do not live in the past. We live in the present and strive for the future. We do not look backward. We only look forward as we seek enlightenment." Brother Michael bowed his head. "Om. Omm. Ommm."

I grabbed his elbow. "She only wants to speak to him, to

know he's well and to tell him she loves him. Surely, that will be good for his spirit."

"I do not know a Danny. All I know is a Damian." He started chanting again.

Bile rose and my pulse quickened. I tightened my grip. "Tell me where he is, or I'll radio the sheriff and tell him you're the one who molested the girl."

Brother Michael tried to shrink away. "That is a lie. That is blaspheme."

"Then you have nothing to fear."

He hesitated. "Damian's journey on the true path has been a difficult one. His past is a burden that he needs to unshoulder. He can only do that by reckoning with his old self to find his new self."

"Will he return to the ashram?"

"Only if it is willed."

I let go of his arm. "If you hear from Danny, have him call me. It's important I speak to him."

Brother Michael sighed with relief when I got in my pickup. I was halfway to the timbered entranceway when another truck drove toward me. It was Joe Moon. I pulled to the right so he could pass, but he stopped too.

"What's the ruckus?" he asked.

"The sheriff was acting on a bad tip."

"About what was in the newspaper, the dead driver they found?"

"Something else. It was nothing. What are you doing here?"

"Work. I butcher their stock. They don't have the stomach for it."

"That's right. I remember Brother Michael telling me they hire a local man to dress their meat according to their religious beliefs."

"I got meat for them all wrapped up and ready for the freezer."

"That reminds me how long it's been since I ate. I'm going home and cook dinner right now. Take it easy."

"There's no time for easy, only work," he said.

I did KP at boot, but never when I was in-country. Forward operating bases had dedicated cooks and potato peelers. Meals on patrol consisted of candy bars or, if we were bivouacking, MCIs, the Meal, Combat, Individual cans of wet food that were the army's latest version of C-rations. Even so, I could make a meal without burning down the lineman's shack.

I put on a pot of spaghetti noodles to boil and stirred a frying pan full of ground beef, garlic, onions, and tomato sauce while I listened to the radio. The night had turned clear and the college station from Eugene was coming in pure. The DJ was in a mellow mood and spinning hits like "Hey Jude" and "Mrs. Robinson" and "Sittin' On the Dock of the Bay" with the occasional outburst from Cream to punch it up, "Strange Brew" and "Sunshine of Your Love."

The music wasn't on that loud, but loud enough to cover the sound of the door opening and closing and the footsteps that came with it.

"Guess what my favorite song is," Gemma Warbler said while I was tasting the sauce.

I whirled around. She eyed the spoon. I was brandishing it

as if it were a KA-BAR. I whisked it behind my back. "Sorry. Didn't hear you knock."

"That's because I didn't. You told me what happened to Jesse when he did."

I started to say something, but then caught her smile. "Funny," I said.

"You didn't answer me. Guess what my favorite song is."

"Young Girl" by Gary Puckett & The Union Gap was playing. "This one?"

Gemma frowned. "No way. Guess." She started making dance moves.

I took the hint. "Something by The Temptations. Maybe The Supremes."

"Close. Marvin Gaye and Tammi Terrell sing it. Come on, it's easy. Think about it." She watched me struggle. "Okay, where are we?"

"Got it. 'Ain't No Mountain High Enough.' "

"Bingo." She held an imaginary mike up to her lips and sang, alternating between the two voices.

I couldn't clap while clutching the spoon so I banged it on the edge of the pan. It spattered tomato sauce on the stove top. "You sound like them."

"I wish. I told you I was going to come by and check your tea. Did you forget?"

"No," I lied. "Look, I made plenty of dinner. Hungry?"

"I could eat a horse."

"And you a veterinarian."

"Careful, you're letting that sense of humor show again." She slipped off her jeans jacket. "Need any help?"

"It's about ready. There might be some Parmesan in the fridge."

Gemma opened the door and poked around. She held up a

cellophane sleeve and wrinkled her nose. "Left over from the pizza parlor in Burns?"

"I'm used to eating ready meals."

"So it would appear." She went to the shelf and looked at the tin cans of pebbles, but didn't comment on them, assuming they were homemade bookends for my collection of field guides. She read the spines.

"Birds, plants, mammals, reptiles, and even stars. Have you always been into nature?"

"I've been studying up since I got here," I said. "I need to know who my customers are."

She laughed and took a couple of plates out of the rack next to the sink and inspected a pair of forks. "Should we eat on the porch or in here?"

"Inside. The mosquitoes came out after all that rain."

"I see you have a field guide for them too." She folded paper towels into napkins, laid the forks on them, and placed two glasses of ice water at the corners. "We can make believe it's Chianti."

I brought over two full plates, and Gemma wasted no time twirling noodles and licking sauce from her lips.

"I've been meaning to ask," I said. "November is an unusual name. How did her parents come by it?"

"They didn't. At the time, the Bureau of Indian Affairs sent Paiute children away to schools where the kids were given new names."

"They could do that?"

Gemma swallowed a forkful. "They wanted the kids to speak English, so they anglicized their names. November's real name is Girl Born in Snow."

"I'm guessing there's a story behind that."

"And you'd be right."

The way Gemma told it, when November's mother was seven months pregnant with her, she went to visit a sick relative who lived a hundred miles away. She had to walk because there were no cars in Harney County at the time, only horses and buckboards. On the way back, she went into premature labor. It was late fall, the time of year the county usually saw its first snow. Sure enough, it started to come down. Her mother kept walking, but the weather turned worse. She was out in the middle of the high desert with no shelter and only the clothes on her back and a blanket. So, she hunkered down to wait it out. She gave birth as the storm howled and the snowdrifts piled around her. When the winds died down and the snow stopped blowing, she wrapped her newborn in the blanket and continued her journey.

"When she arrived home," Gemma said, "her husband asked what she was holding. Her answer became a beautiful name."

"Her mother was tough. I can see where November gets her strength," I said.

Gemma pointed with her fork. "You have no idea how strong she really is. She's a medicine woman."

"Like some kind of doctor?"

"She heals using the old ways, sure. Tinctures made from herbs and minerals. Songs and chants. But her real medicine is more about healing up here and in here." Gemma tapped her head and then patted her heart. "It's how she came to live with us."

"How's that?"

"When my mother got her cancer diagnosis, the doctor told her there was nothing anybody could do. She was only given a few weeks to live. As she was leaving the hospital, an orderly told her about a medicine woman who lived on the Burns Paiute Reservation."

"November."

"Yes, Girl Born in Snow. My mother was desperate. She didn't want to die and leave a young child behind."

"You mean, you."

She nodded. "My mother put herself in her care. November built a wiki-up. That's a traditional shelter made of sticks laying on each other and covered with grass and branches. She and my mother lived inside it for a week while November tried to heal her using all the medicines she knew. But it was no use. The cancer had spread everywhere. Finally, November told her she could only keep her spirit alive, not her body, but by doing so, she could heal that which pained my mother the most. Namely, worrying that I would grow up without her. November moved in with us to make sure I would always know my mother, feel her spirit. Pudge might not admit it, but November helped heal him too."

"I'm surprised she agreed to live with *madukanna*," I said. "She doesn't seem to hold us in high regard."

"She's able to see the good in good people and the bad in bad people regardless of race." Gemma sipped some water. "November says she knows the spirit that visits you."

"What spirit?" I said.

"She said she saw it the first time you had dinner with us."

"I don't know what she's talking about."

"Don't freak out. November believes everyone has a spirit that visits. All they have to do is be open to seeing them. And they aren't necessarily bad spirits either. They can be good and helpful."

"You sound as if you know all about Paiute beliefs."

"Not all, but a lot. November taught me. The Paiute believe that power, or *puha*, can reside in any natural object. It exists in the sun and moon and wind and rain for sure. Then there are supernatural beings. Not all animals are necessarily supernatural, but those that have songs and legends about them are. She says you are visited by a spirit that is caught between two super-natural beings."

"And what would those be?"

"One is a raven. Ravens symbolize transformation and bring about change. The other is an eagle. Eagles are powerful hunters."

"That's also what my field guide says about eagles. Were you able to save the Rocking H's cows?" I said.

Gemma's expression told me she knew she'd hit a nerve, but didn't press it. "We were lucky. We only lost two."

"I doubt luck had anything to do with it."

"Oh, and he makes compliments too. Why Mr. Drake, you do surprise me." She gave it her *Gone with the Wind* accent.

"I meant Blaine spotting it early and you knowing the right antidote."

"Getting toxic weeds out of a cow's four stomachs and multiply that by a hundred head?" She shuddered.

"I don't think I need to hear how you do that."

"You don't." She twisted another forkful of noodles. "Blaine didn't know you'd punched out his little brother."

"I didn't punch him. Wait, you told him?"

"Uh-huh. Blaine may act the protective big brother, but it's not like he doesn't know who Jesse is. He's been covering for him forever. Did Pudge tell you Blaine called to apologize for Jesse after what happened at Blackpowder's?"

"No, but maybe that explains why Jesse got pissed off and directed it at me."

"Probably."

We finished eating, and I cleared the table and put the kettle on. "I finally met Bonnie LaRue."

"What did you think of her?"

"What did you call her, formidable? That and then some."

"What did you two talk about?"

"She did most of the talking. She wanted me to confirm what was going on with the murders. Bonnie let me know that the governor's man Travers and the sheriff had told her about them. How much they said, I don't know. Maybe Travers was able to get her to hold off running a story in exchange for earning the governor's favor."

"Maybe, but Bonnie is used to getting her way. I understand where that comes from. It's not easy being a woman in what's always been a man's profession, especially out here. Burns is still the Wild West and there are plenty of people who think women should be seen and not heard. After Bonnie's husband died, she had to fight hard to keep control of the paper."

"Do you run into that with the ranchers too?"

"In the beginning, people told me I shouldn't even try to become a big animal vet. And then I had to win over their trust. But when you're the only horse doctor in a hundred thousand horse town, the ranchers learn pretty quick to keep their lips as well as their flies buttoned if they want me to save their stock."

"Formidable," I said.

She laughed. "Are you going to pour us tea or what?"

We sat at the table and drank mugs of wild spearmint.

"Blackpowder told me a story about Zachariah Harney's prized bull getting poisoned," I said. "Did he eat goosefoot too?"

"I don't know. I was in Corvallis finishing veterinarian school then. It would take a lot of goosefoot to bring a big bull down, though there are other plants I suppose he could've gotten into at the same time. Lupine, camas, locoweed."

"Blackpowder said it happened after Jesse got into trouble in high school. Right after Zachariah had to put the bull down, he packed Jesse off to military school."

"If you're asking did Jesse poison the bull, I don't know."

"Blaine never said anything about it?"

"It was one of those things that didn't get talked about at the

Rocking H. Zachariah is like that. No one is allowed to talk about his wife running off or mistakes and accidents."

"What do you mean by that?"

"All sorts of things happen at a working ranch. A farmer gets his hand caught in the combine. A kid forgets to latch a gate and the stock wanders onto the highway. In Zachariah's world, there is no room for accidents and no tolerance for those who make mistakes."

"Even if they're his own flesh and blood?"

"Especially them."

"Everyone makes mistakes," I said.

"Is that what happened to you in Vietnam? You blame yourself for something, and you started taking drugs to try and forget?"

I hid behind the mug of tea and blew on it even though it was no longer too hot to drink.

"You don't like to talk about it, do you?" Gemma said it softly. "That's okay. I didn't mean to pick a scab. I've never taken drugs, never had any interest to, but I do know what it's like to let something into your life that takes you over, or at least tries."

She was talking about being married to Blaine, and I felt like I owed her some kind of explanation.

"I don't try to hide the fact that I'm a junkie," I said. "Admitting it out loud is one of the twelve steps because, while I don't shoot dope anymore, I can't say I wouldn't if there was a nickel bag sitting here on the table right now."

I waited for her to say something, but she didn't. She was using the same tactic I used when interrogating prisoners. I rushed to fill the silence.

"I screwed up in Vietnam. The shrinks told me it's impossible not to screw up in war. And maybe they're right. But knowing that doesn't bring back the dead, and it doesn't do much to bring back your faith in mankind."

"Why heroin?" she said.

I exhaled. "The truth? It put me on a razor's edge between death and pleasure. It was the only place I could go where I could try to be with those whose deaths I caused, to hear their blame, to tell them I was sorry, but not feel any pain doing it."

Gemma put her mug down and started skating it on the table without saying a word.

"Well, that was a downer," I said. "Guess I'm not much of a dinner companion. Look, it's getting late."

"It has been a long day." She kept her eyes on the mug she was pushing in circles.

"Will I see you for breakfast?"

Her head jerked. "What kind of woman do you take me for?"

"What?"

"Do you really think that kind of line works? I don't know whether to laugh at how lame it sounds or be insulted."

"I don't know what—"

"Has it worked for you in the past? *Hey baby, let's get naked and then I'll make you pancakes.*"

"You got it all wrong."

"No, I got it right. You think cooking me dinner and playing the radio is all it takes for me to jump in the sack?" Her cheeks puffed as she exhaled loudly. "Listen, hot shot. Just because I'm divorced doesn't mean I'm easy. It takes a lot more than a plate of spaghetti and a cup of tea. A helluva lot more."

"All I meant was—"

"For starters, there has to be some chemistry. A mutual attraction. And then there's knowing who the other person really is." She snorted. "And don't get me started on a romantic setting. Here?"

Gemma waved her hand around the room and then stopped when she reached the single bunk in the far corner. "You got to be kidding me. Who knows when the last time those sheets were changed. And then there are the clothes that have to come off. I'm still wearing the jeans and shirt I spent all day in forcing cows to puke and shit. Some turn on."

"Can I get a word in here?"

"No." She got up from the table.

"Gemma, please. I meant, will I see you at the ranch in the morning? I'm coming over at first light. Pudge and I are going out to the gullies to search for evidence, and he wants to plan it out over breakfast."

She hesitated and then said, "Well, that doesn't mean all that other stuff isn't important."

Gemma grabbed her jeans jacket and headed for the door. I followed her out to her red Wagoneer. As she opened its door, she turned.

"You're wrong, anyway. You're not a bad dinner companion, though your sauce could use more spices."

"I'm pretty out of practice," I said. "The talking part."

"How come?"

"Well, you know."

"No, I don't know," she said quickly. "What I said about having to really know someone? Tell me the real reason."

I could've walked away. I probably should've walked away. "Because I've caused enough hurt to last a lifetime."

Gemma slid behind the wheel and shut the door. She stuck her hand out and grabbed my chin before I could shirk her touch. "You can't be in this life and not get hurt at least once. But that's a good thing because knowing what hurt feels like makes the opposite feel all the better."

P udge was wringing the morning paper like it was the neck of a chicken destined for Sunday dinner. He hurled the twisted remains to the floor and kicked them beneath the dining table.

"There's no putting that cat back in the bag," he said. "Bonnie got it all, from the girls' names to their causes of death to yesterday's raid at Crossed Bars."

I had barely started in on my first cup of coffee. "Who did she quote?"

"It sure wasn't the governor or Travers, though that weasel is my bet for having spilled the beans. I'll bet Bust'em gave it up too."

"She talked with them both."

"How do you know that?"

"She told me."

"You spoke to Bonnie LaRue?"

"Yesterday. She was coming out of the sheriff's office as I was going in to see Orville."

"What did she say?"

"That you owe her a trip to San Francisco and she's still waiting."

He groaned. "Hope the killer doesn't read or he's likely to go to ground. Her front-page story makes everything a whole lot harder now."

"Maybe it will get someone to call in with a tip. Someone might have seen something."

"That's exactly what Bonnie would say. It's one of the things we locked horns over when I was sheriff."

"But it might get someone to call."

"It'll do that all right. Wives mad at their husbands, neighbors wanting to settle a grudge, drunks who think Blackpowder is watering down their beer. They'll all swear the person is acting suspicious. Probably get calls about Martians landing too."

"I forgot to tell you I spoke with Aubrey Jenkins yesterday. He said his daughter Kathy wasn't such a choir girl after all. She'd been hanging out with the wrong crowd and ran away when he told her he was shipping her off to boarding school back East."

"What I figured, but it's always good to get the parents to admit it to themselves as much as to us." Pudge poured himself more coffee from a blue enamel pot November had left on the table. "Jenkins must think he's got you in his pocket to tell you that."

"But it doesn't make him trust me. His chauffeur drove by my place last night, checking on me. I could see him trailing me this morning when I drove out here."

"Maybe he put a tracker on your pickup." Pudge's chuckle meant he didn't believe it, but it made me wonder.

I told the lawman about my talk with Brother Michael and the Alvord Desert. "It could be where Damian went. I mean Danny Gallagher. That's what his parents call him. Danny."

"Only if you buy he's really a would-be monk and went out to that godforsaken salt flat to twiddle his navel. He could be in Mexico by now." He shook his head. "It's too damn coincidental that him and Jesse went to the same military academy in Portland."

"Damian—Danny—may be hard to find, but Jesse won't."

"Nope. That's what I plan to do on our way to Hart Mountain this morning," he said as November brought in a large frying pan.

"That's not its true name," the Paiute woman said. "A white rancher had a brand the shape of a heart and called the mountain that, but he didn't learn to spell so good."

Pudge dished himself some *huevos ranchero* and applied a liberal dose of hot sauce. "Before then it was called Warner Peak."

"Another white man name," November said. "They steal our names like our land. It is *tenna tanoho tabi*. Antelope run on hillside. It is a sacred place."

"Now, November," Pudge said around a mouthful of eggs. "There's not a place in Oregon that isn't sacred to one Indian people or another. You got the Tillamook up on the north coast, the Coos and Umpqua down the coast, Umatilla and Warm Springs people on the plateau, and Klamath over the hill. I don't have enough fingers and toes to count all the tribes."

"And not enough to count how many are no more." She slammed the pan down and stalked back to the kitchen.

Pudge watched her go and then said, "We better get a move on before she comes back and lays that pan upside my head."

I cleaned my plate and swallowed the rest of my coffee. "Where's Gemma this morning?"

"She got out of here when it was still dark. Another emergency call about sick cows eating something they shouldn't've. You'd think how fast the plants grow right after a heavy rain, there'd be plenty of good graze, so they don't go looking for bad."

"Blaine Harney's cows again?"

"Probably. She was gone by the time I got up. November told me she sent her off with a bag of fry bread and a thermos of joe."

"You're not worried about her going to a remote corner of the county alone with a killer on the loose?"

"Of course I am, but Gemma's Gemma. Her patients always come first. When she started her practice, she had to teach me not to fret, but not until I taught her how to handle a gun. She keeps one in her vet bag. I told her it's not only sick livestock that sometimes got to be put down."

THE WHEEL LINES weren't spraying when we drove through the Rocking H's fields. They'd turned even more verdant from the recent rain. The two border collies gave the same yapping greeting as we pulled up to the house, although this time I didn't wait for someone else to order them to charge. They obeyed instantly and dropped to the ground when I issued the command from the front seat of Pudge's pickup and raced to the barn when I stepped out and added, "Home."

"Prepare for an earful," Pudge said as we climbed the porch steps.

Before we had time to knock, the door swung open. Zachariah Harney tottered on the other side, fumbling to raise a shotgun to his shoulder. Pudge and I rushed him at the same time, banging into each other as we squeezed through the doorway. The deputy got his hand on the barrel and yanked it away as I bear-hugged the old man, pushing him backward. I steered for the couch and sat him down.

"That's a helluva way to say howdy," Pudge said.

Harney wheezed while he tried to catch his breath. When he had it, venom spit. "You son of a bitch! You're lucky I had the safety on or you'd be wearing buckshot. You're going to pay. When I'm done, you won't have a clod to kick, much less any dirt to call your own." He started wheezing again.

"You sound like you need a glass of water, Zachariah," Pudge said. "Is Jesse around or should Drake get you one?"

"Get out of my house," the old man sputtered.

"I'll find it," I said.

The house was rambling. The walls were paneled wood, and the furniture dark and manly. Despite the flowerbeds outside, there were no vases of cut flowers, no soft throw blankets draped over the arms of the easy chairs, no smell of perfume in the air. The kitchen was big, but no cookbook was in sight. No apron hung from a hook either.

The plates stacked inside the cupboard were heavy, the glassware thick. I grabbed the nearest tumbler and held it under the faucet. The sink was empty of dirty dishes, but the bottom in need of steel wool. I filled the glass and returned to the living room. Pudge had pulled up a chair and was sitting across from the senior Harney. The lawman's face was a mix of pity and concern. He was shocked by how old and weak his schoolmate looked and no doubt thought it could be him sitting there.

"Here's some water," I said.

I held the glass out, but Zachariah had trouble lifting his arm and his hand trembled. Pudge took the glass and held it to the man's chalky lips. As he drank, his eyes burned with anger and shame.

"Where's Jesse?" Pudge asked.

The old man gagged after swallowing. It sounded as if he were drowning. "Work. Ranch doesn't run itself."

"Is he here or out in the fields?"

"What's it to you?"

"I need to talk to him about a friend of his. Where is he?"

"You deaf? I told you he's not lazing around like he's wont to."

"I understand Gemma and Blaine had their hands full yesterday dealing with cows that got into goosefoot. She's back at it today. Is that where Blaine's at too?"

"She shouldn't've run off after he married her, but that's a woman for you. She made my son the fool."

Anger flashed in Pudge's eyes, but he didn't take the bait. "Go see if you can find Jesse," he said to me.

The first room I checked was the master bedroom. It had a trapeze rigged over the bed to aid Zachariah pulling himself up. A bedpan was shoved under a nightstand crowded with pill bottles. No framed family photographs stood on the dresser. The only ornament on the walls was the mounted head of a pronghorn.

Matching the next bedroom to Blaine was easy. A shirt left hanging on the back of a chair was extra-large. A wedding photo of Gemma and him was propped on the nightstand. It sported a sterling silver frame. Gemma wore a long white dress and was hiking up the hem to show off red cowgirl boots. Her eyes sparkled with laughter. Blaine had on a western-cut suit complete with a bolo tie. The clasp was engraved with the Rocking H brand. His grin was the kind I remembered from *Field & Stream* articles where anglers posed with trophy rainbow trout held as far away from their body as their arms could stretch to make them look bigger.

Jesse's room was down the hall. Jane Fonda wearing a low-cut white space suit and holding a ray gun gave a come-hither look from a *Barbarella* movie poster. Marlon Brando, Richard Burton, and Ringo Starr leered at a naked blonde whose long tresses covered her nipples in a poster promoting *Candy*. Raquel Welch spilled out of yellow bikini in an advertisement for

Biggest Bundle of Them All, a movie billed as the world's sexiest robbery.

Out in the yard, the sound of metal pounding on metal led me to the other side of the barn. A burly man wearing a heavy leather apron was shaping a horseshoe on an anvil.

"Have you seen Jesse?" I asked.

"Who wants to know?" He held aloft a hammer with a head the size of a ten-pound sledge.

"It's about a friend of his."

"Jesse don't have friends." He went back to hammering.

The door to the tack room was ajar. I looked inside.

"Who's there?" a man called from the shadows. He had a thick accent.

"Nick Drake," I said.

My eyes grew accustomed to the gloom. A white-haired man was hunched over a workbench. He wore thimbles on one hand and was stitching a leather strap with a thick, curved needle. His eyes were the color of milk.

"What's your name?" I asked.

"The saddler," he replied and clacked his thimbles. "I make new *latigo*." He held up the wide leather strap and then put it down and held up another strip of leather with buckles. "And this *manello* too, for hobbling horses. Beautiful, no?" He felt around the workbench, his fingers his eyes until he found a handful of leather strings. "These *tientos*? No reason saddle ties can't be pretty. You need something? Tell me, I make it."

"Thanks anyway," I said and left him to his work.

I headed back to the house. When I came around the barn, a stakebed truck sped straight at me. I jumped out of the way as the driver slammed on the brakes. The truck fishtailed to a stop. Jesse Harney got out.

"What the hell are you doing here?" he said.

"Looking for you."

Jesse's head swiveled between me and the pickup with the gold star on the door. "Where's my father? You better not have disturbed him."

"He's inside having a drink with Deputy Warbler."

Jesse ran for the house. Pudge and Zachariah hadn't moved. Neither showed surprise when the youngest Harney burst in and accused the deputy of harassing his father.

"Don't wet yourself, boy," Zachariah said. "He's not here about me or you. It's about a friend of yours."

"What friend?" Jesse balled his fists but held them at his side.

"A classmate of yours from Mount Hood Military," Pudge said.

"Who?"

"Daniel Gallagher."

"Never heard of him."

Jesse said it too fast. Pudge noticed too but didn't let on. "Maybe you knew him as Danny."

"I don't know any Danny."

"You sure?" Pudge let it sit before adding, "It's a small school."

"I told you, I don't know him." Jesse crossed his arms, but kept his fists balled.

"Don't you want to know why I'm asking?"

"I don't care, but, okay, how come?"

"For starters, he's been living up the road at the old Crossed Bars Ranch. Only he doesn't go by Danny anymore. He's Damian now. He's part of that religious outfit living there."

Zachariah sputtered. "Crossed Bars should've been mine. They stole it from me. I hope they choke on it, what they paid."

"I don't talk to those people," Jesse said. "They're not my type."

"Who are your type?" Pudge asked.

"Not them, that's for sure."

"Okay. Well, since Drake and me were passing by, I thought I'd stop in and ask. We'll be off."

"Passing by to where?" the old man asked.

"You don't read the *Herald*? It's in the paper this morning. We found two dead girls at Hart Mountain. We're going to take another looksee."

I kept my eyes on Jesse. The young man kept his arms crossed but didn't say anything.

Zachariah struggled to clear his throat. "Dead girls? Dead from what?"

"That's what we aim to find out." The lawman pushed out of his chair. "Hope you're feeling better. Sorry if we gave you a start arriving like we did. Next time I'll call first.

"Make sure you do," the old rancher said.

Jesse was watching them carefully. Finally, he said, "You never said why you were looking for this Danny guy. What did he do?"

"Why do you think he did anything?"

"You're a deputy. Why else would you be looking for someone? Does it have to do with the dead girls?"

Pudge's shrug was noncommittal. "The folks he's been living with at that church are worried about him. Well, they don't call it a church. They call it a temple. And they don't call a ranch a ranch either. They call it an ashram."

"What the hell's that?" Zachariah said.

"I'm not sure I know. Never heard of one before they moved here."

Jesse started rocking on his feet. "Who cares what it means. Why are they worried about him?"

"Sorry, lost my train of thought there. Seems Danny, or Damian as he goes by now, left without so much as a by-your-leave."

"So? It's a free country."

"True, but it seems Damian, well, when he was still Danny Gallagher, served in the Marine Corps and fought over in Vietnam like Drake here. One of the reasons he joined up with the Crossed Bars outfit and got religion is because he has a case of shell shock. At least that's what the monks living there say. He left and everyone's concerned about him. Just want to make sure he's doing all right."

Jesse clamped his lips.

Pudge took a couple of steps toward the door and then stopped. "Don't most boys who go to military school go into the service after they graduate like Danny did?"

"Some. Not all," Jesse said.

"But you didn't. How come?"

Jesse shook a fist at his father. "Because of him. My toes froze off when he made me go look for his stupid cows in a blizzard. I was only nine. He made me into a fucking 4-F."

W ith the cooling effect of the rains gone, the temperature climbed. The playa served as a griddle and triggered rising columns of super-heated air. A half dozen turkey vultures soared on the thermals, dipping and circling without needing to flap their B-52-like wings. One of the birds was smaller than the rest, and its silhouette against the bright blue sky was way too familiar. I watched and waited for it to call to me while standing beside Pudge's truck.

"Ready to go?" the deputy said as he adjusted his holstered .45 and squared his small brim Stetson.

I was strapped too. I hadn't replaced the shotgun I'd dropped during the flash flood, and so I wore the heavy Smith & Wesson. A handgun wasn't as good as a 12 gauge when it came to stopping a striking rattler, but if it came to that, it'd still be better than shouting "charge."

I pointed to the circling vultures. "Over there."

"I thought we were gonna check the gullies starting with the one next in line to where you found the Jenkins girl?"

"Looks like they've spotted something."

"Could be an antelope got stuck trying to cross when the playa was muddy," Pudge said. "Or maybe a cow."

"Maybe," I said.

I raised my binoculars and found a dark bird that wasn't the size of a vulture, and then I dropped my gaze straight down to the ground. The lenses filled with a heap of mud. It was drying out and turning pale in the sun. I started walking toward it. I walked fast.

"Wait up," Pudge called as he broke into a trot.

Heat waves bent the light and curved the playa's floor between me and the muddy heap. I was walking through a mirage that made the ground ahead as shiny as a mirror. A trio of turkey vultures landed. One of the birds with naked red heads stood atop the lump while the other two poked at it with their curved, bone-colored beaks.

"Oh Lord," Pudge said as he joined me.

He drew his .45 and fired off a couple of warning shots. The big birds had to get a running start to achieve lift-off. They flew away reluctantly.

Limbs stuck out from a cocoon of dried mud. A crusted eye, a plugged nostril showed too. The hair resembled a root ball from a newly fallen tree. Pudge crouched but didn't touch the body.

"The first one made me upset. The second got me good and mad. I'm running out of how to describe myself right now," he said, his words coming in short, choppy bursts. "Vengeful comes to mind."

I walked around in widening circles. "There's no other tracks but ours and the vultures. I think he put her in one of the gullies like the other two, and the flash flood washed her out."

"You're probably right. And for the waters to sweep her all the way out here, it surely swept away any evidence in there, even if we did know which one."

"What do you want to do, call Sheriff Burton and the coroner?"

"We might as well take her in ourselves seeing that he didn't leave her out here, and we don't know where and when he killed her." He grimaced. "Given her condition, I think she's been dead longer than the others. I can bring my rig in close and we can wrap her up so any evidence that may still be on her, doesn't fall off."

"While you get the truck, I'll walk up that nearest gully and see if there are any signs."

"Good hunting," he said.

A thick layer of silt covered the gully floor. The walls were slick as if scrubbed clean and smoothed by sandpaper. I could tell the boulders that were newly deposited from the ones that had remained unmoved. Their dark tops had once been bottoms unbleached by the sun. I expected to see the shadow of the coal-black bird on the ground ahead, but it was nowhere to be seen. I checked the walls for undercuts that could've been used as a sarcophagus like the one that held Vicky Wells, but if there had been any openings before the flood, the silt had filled them up.

The gully wasn't that long and I reached the end without seeing anything but rock and sand and the occasional broken branch that had been trapped on the upstream side of a boulder. I turned around and closed my eyes. It was deadly quiet compared to the last time I'd been in the gullies. There was no tapping of raindrops, no gush of waterfalls pouring over the gully's lips, no thunder from a rushing wall of floodwater. All I could hear was silence, all I could sense was emptiness. Any terror or pain the dead girl had felt had either been washed out with the flood or had already been absorbed by the mute stone walls around me. I recalled what Gemma had said about the Paiute's belief that natural objects had power. Why hadn't the stones exerted their *puha* to stop the killer? Where was her guardian spirit to warn her?

Pudge honked the horn. I started making my way down the gully. Halfway there something caught my eye. A glimmer, a flash. I looked around, expecting to see a vein of quartz in a rock or a large flake of mica that had caught a sunray. I squatted and put my forearms on my knees and refused to blink despite the glare.

There. Again. A glimmer. I didn't take my eyes off it as I walked toward it. The shine came from a crevice between two boulders that had come to rest atop each other as the waters from the flash flood receded.

It was neither quartz nor mica nor feldspar nor any of the other dozen shiny minerals trapped in Oregon rocks. It was a buckle attached to a leather strap the width of a *manello* used for hobbling horses.

PUDGE STRUGGLED to control his anger as we rolled the mud-caked body in a tarp, carried it to the truck, and laid her in the bed. He'd angled the rearview mirror so he could keep an eye on his precious cargo and checked it every so often on the drive to Burns.

"That strap doesn't prove Jesse Harney is our killer even if it is the same width of whatever was used to strangle Vicky and Kathy and left bruises around their necks," the lawman said after I showed it to him. "There's lots of ranchers in Harney County and lots of cowboys who hobble their horses. It could've been sitting there since cavalry times. An antelope hunter might've dropped it twenty years ago."

"But it could be from the Harney ranch," I said. "And *tientos* like those new ones the blind saddler made could have been used to bind their wrists and left those rope burns around them."

"It's my experience it's the guilty man who runs away, not the innocent."

"All we know about Damian, or Danny, is he got kicked out of the marines and got religion. Maybe he is on a spiritual quest. Who knows? But Jesse, he's got a temper. He killed his old man's bull. He's still angry at him. He also lied about knowing Danny. How come?"

"What I'd give to get those two fellas in a room together and see who points the finger first."

"You think they killed those girls together?"

The question hung in the air like a stink that needs the windows rolled down fast. Pudge glanced in the rearview mirror before answering. "That's a helluva thing for anyone to think, son. What I was getting at was maybe one of them knows what the other's been doing and not saying anything. Maybe one has something on the other."

We pulled into the morgue's parking lot. "Wait here," Pudge said. "I'll go round up Doc. Once we get her inside, we can go over to the office and tell Bust'em what we found."

Loading a body onto a gurney and rolling it into the cold white room with its long shallow sink didn't get any easier the second time around. Nor was there any satisfaction in seeing Sheriff Burton's discomfort when Pudge gave him the news that another murder victim had turned up in his county. The sheriff's chances for reelection were mirrored in his eyes as he realized how voters would react when they discovered he was powerless to stop a homicidal maniac. Burton was surely hearing the echoes of doors being locked and men demanding protection for their wives and daughters.

"I'm going to have to tell Travers and he's going to tell the governor." Sheriff Burton's voice had a whine to it. "Bonnie LaRue will have the story before the night's out."

"You should've kept it to yourself the last time she was here," Pudge said.

"You heard about that?"

"Don't forget, I used to sit where you're at now."

"We have to get a handle on this. Come on. I need your help."

Pudge smacked the desk. "It's not you who needs our help, it's these girls' families. Don't ever forget that if you want to stay sheriff."

Sheriff Burton flinched. "What should I do?"

"For starters, stop thinking the hippies you got in jail are the killers. Doc unrolled the tarp and could see right away the newest victim isn't so new. He said she's been dead at least a month. Barry and Linda were still in Washington then."

"Maybe they drove back and forth."

"Barry has an airtight alibi. Remember? He was doing a yearlong stretch in a county lockup for holding marijuana. Days after he got released, he and Linda loaded up their bus and were heading for San Francisco with Jenny. By the way, how's that little liar doing?"

"She's not my problem anymore. We tracked her mother down. She was lying about her age. She's sixteen. We put her on the Greyhound to Tacoma this morning escorted by a staffer with Child Services. They're probably arriving right about now."

"Jenny will take off running as soon as she hits the ground," Pudge said.

"I don't care. She's one less thing I have to deal with."

"You can get rid of two more by cutting the pair upstairs loose."

"I can't do that. Even if they had nothing to do with the murders, they brought a minor across state lines."

"Jenny's mother and Linda related?"

"Yes, the mother confirmed it. Cousins of some sort."

"There you go. You'll never make the Mann Act stick."

"But all that marijuana in their bus."

Pudge snorted. "You got an unsolved triple homicide on your hands with one of the victims being the governor's goddaughter, a budget that doesn't even cover new snow tires for your deputies' vehicles, and a newspaper publisher who is out to have you for lunch. You sure you want to devote all your resources to busting a couple of hippies holding a sandwich bag of pot?"

"Well, when you put it that way—"

"Do what any other sheriff would do. Release them, have a state trooper escort them to the state line, and as soon as they cross over, send a fax to the California Highway Patrol and let them deal with it."

"A fax?"

"That's right, a fax. You don't need to say the whole word." Pudge sighed. "Come on, Drake. Let's go see what our college boy's been up to."

The pyramid of cola cans had grown taller. Orville Nelson's white shirt was still wrinkle-free despite his 12-hour round trip to Portland.

"You don't have an apartment, but you own an iron, don't you?" Pudge said by way of greeting.

"I wish I hadn't missed the raid on the religious cult," Orville said. "It would've given me civil disturbance experience. The FBI is very focused on the cause of urban rioting."

"Calling Crossed Bars a disturbance would be a stretch," Pudge said. "And what's with cult?"

"It's from a new book I've been reading about religious groups that follow charismatic leaders who use extreme methods for gaining converts. The author calls them doomsday cults."

"When do you have time to read?"

"I make time," the G-man hopeful said. "Take a look at this. It's a yearbook from Mount Hood Military Academy. His mother lent it to me. You can see Danny Gallagher's class photo on this page."

"It's Damian," I said. "No question about it. Was his father there?"

"Negative. I got the impression that Mrs. Gallagher didn't tell him I was going to pay a visit. I can profile him though. Mid to late forties, working class, drinks Rainier, an Elks member, bowls, and hunts. There's a gun cabinet in the living room."

"Sounds like most men I know," Pudge said.

"What did you find out about the sister? Lizzie," I said.

Orville's head dipped. "There's a memorial to her atop the mantle. All these framed photos of her. She drowned when she was a little girl. Mrs. Gallagher really choked up talking about it."

"What happened?"

"She insisted it was an accident. Danny was older. The children walked down to a pond to feed the ducks. Danny turned his back to talk to some friends, and Lizzie slipped and fell in. By the time Danny got her out, she was gone."

"That's why she couldn't tell him how she felt about him being in the war. She'd been dead ten years," I said. "I bet his dad never stopped blaming him for her death. What did they say about Danny at the military school?"

"I spoke to the dean of students. He said Cadet Gallagher didn't stand out in scholastics or athletics. The school favors wrestling, boxing, and obstacle course. The curriculum is weighted toward mathematics and history. There isn't much in the way of a literature and social studies department and nothing in arts and drama. Music classes are devoted to marching band."

"It's an all-boys school, right?" Pudge said, looking up from the yearbook. He was dog-earing pages.

"Correct."

"Well, they do mingle with the fairer sex according to this."

He held up the yearbook. A page of photos showed cadets

wearing dress blues at a formal dance. The girls wore long dresses and white gloves.

"Those are co-eds from St. Anne's," Orville said. "The two schools hold joint dances. Junior and senior prom. The military academy doesn't do homecoming."

Pudge lowered the yearbook and turned the page. "Remind me, what was the name of that missing nursing school student a couple of years back. We didn't include her in our list because there was no reason to believe she'd ever traveled through Harney County."

"Sharon Spirelli," Orville said.

"You sure?"

"Positive. I have the missing persons report in one of these folders. Do you want to see it?"

"I'm looking at her right now." The deputy held up the yearbook again and read the caption below a photo of a couple dancing. "Cadet Daniel Gallagher and Miss Sharon Spirelli waltzed to Strauss's "Blue Danube" at the Senior Prom."

"Holy shit," I said.

"Couldn't say it better myself. And, look." Pudge turned to another page. "Here's a class picture of Jesse Harney." He turned to another. "And here he is again marching past a reviewing stand. Look who's marching right beside him."

"Danny Gallagher," I said.

Pudge slammed the yearbook shut. "Orville, get on the horn to Portland PD. Confirm when Miss Spirelli graduated from St. Anne's and when she enrolled in nursing school. I need those dates and the date she went missing. And then I need the dates Gallagher enlisted in the marines, where he went to boot—my bet it was Camp Pendleton—and if he ever came home on leave before shipping out to Vietnam."

"I'll get right on it, sir."

I took the yearbook and examined each photo in the senior prom spread.

"What are you looking for?" Pudge asked.

"Jesse. I wanted to see if he was at that prom too, and if so, with who. Look."

Pudge eyed the picture. Jesse was standing along a wall with a row of other cadets. "That's the stag line. They don't have a date to the dance. They're waiting for one of the bucks to break a leg doing the fox-trot so they can swoop in and sweep up the doe."

"Maybe Jesse had to wait a year."

"What do you mean?"

"Gemma told me he returned to Portland to go to college, but then moved home to take care of his dad when he had a stroke. Maybe he looked up Sharon Spirelli the year he was there."

"While Danny was away fighting for his country." Pudge rubbed his jaw. "He wouldn't be the first GI to get a Dear John letter. Okay, Orville. Add it to your list. See if you can find anything that puts Jesse and Miss Spirelli together the year she was in nursing school and he was in college."

Sheriff Burton insisted on issuing an all-points bulletin on Daniel William Gallagher, aka Damian. Pudge tried to talk him out of it, explaining that all we had was circumstantial evidence, but the sheriff wouldn't hear of it.

"I'm releasing the two upstairs, and I need to have something to show Governor Lane and Aubrey Jenkins I'm making progress," he said.

I was waiting in the lobby for Pudge to finish the paper work on the APB so I could get a lift back to No Mountain when loud voices erupted on the stairway leading down from the second floor. Barry and Linda were giving the deputy escorting them an earful.

"Power to the people," Barry chanted, a clenched fist raised in a power salute. "No justice, no peace."

Linda was singing a tune from The Beatle's new album about lots of piggies living piggy lives.

The deputy breathed a sigh of relief when he spotted me. "Here, you show them where their bus is. I've had enough."

Barry grinned through his greasy beard. He raised both fists like a boxer after landing a knockout punch. "Free at last. Free at last. Thank God almighty, we're free at last."

"Well, if it isn't Ranger Rick," Linda said.

I walked them out to the impound lot where their brightly painted VW was waiting. The keys were already in the ignition.

"I can't wait to put this place in the rearview mirror," Barry said. "What a shithole."

Linda waggled her finger in my face. "You're no better than the rest of the pigs here. They were trying to pin a murder on us." She shrieked with righteous indignation.

Barry said, "Sorry, dude, but you can dig where she's coming from. We're all about peace and love, but these rednecks see longhair and a chick with free-range boobs, and they think the commies have landed."

"You haven't asked about Jenny," I said.

"They already told us. They shipped her back home. You know she'll beat feet first chance she gets."

"She should if she's got any brains," Linda said. "Her mother's a skag and her old man's a speed freak."

"You should come with us, man," Barry said. "This scene sucks. Frisco's where it's all happening."

"Word of advice?" I said. "If you got a stash in the bus, even if it's only a roach, eat it or chuck it out the window before you cross the state line."

Barry looked at me openmouthed for a few moments before the lights went on. "Hey, man, thanks. You're cool."

The bus sputtered to life, backfired, and exited the parking lot. Pudge joined me as the taillights disappeared around the corner.

"Let's go," the deputy said. "I want to get home, have three fingers of rye, and sleep in my own bed before tomorrow's shit storm hits."

"It's going to be that bad?"

"This has already shaped up to be one of those cases where each day is worse than the one before. No reason for it to change now."

We got in his truck. "Did Sheriff Burton issue the APB?"

"Yeah, though I call it a CYA. While I was trying to talk him out of it, Bonnie LaRue called for a comment on the latest victim. I got to hand it to her even if I don't like it. She's good at what she does."

"Is she running a story tomorrow."

"Front page above the fold is how she described it. She hadn't gotten word on Damian Gallagher yet. I mean, Danny. Ah hell, listen to me. I got our marine turned monk all mixed up now. Anyway, knowing Bonnie, she will. Tomorrow's story will drive him even further underground."

"What about Jesse Harney? Did you talk to Burton about him?"

"No, because I got to take that road careful. Gemma was married to Blaine, even if it was only for a short while. It won't stop me from doing my job, mind you, but I need to be sure before I hang Jesse out to dry. He was Gemma's brother-in-law, and I'd hate to see her name dragged into it for no reason."

We were on the final stretch of road to No Mountain. "What's the plan for tomorrow?" I asked.

"OSP will try to locate Damian. The state troopers can field a much wider net. I told Bust'em you and me would take another look in the gullies. If we find something, well, that'll write our next move."

My truck was still at his place, but I told him to let me off at the lineman's shack, and I'd ride my motorcycle over in the morning.

"You're not worried Jesse might take off like Danny?" I said as he let me out.

"Honestly? I don't think that boy's got the smarts to know how to run, much less when."

I tilted in the ladder-back chair and listened to the crickets saw their hind legs against their wings. The night music wasn't loud enough to drown out my thoughts of Jesse and Damian. Was the unnamed girl we'd found Sharon Spirelli? It didn't seem likely given how long ago the student nurse went missing. So, who was she? Another runaway? Another traveler who decided to hitchhike instead of riding the bus? A daughter snatched from a bedroom? A waitress walking home alone late at night?

The black Mercedes pulled in front and the chauffeur got out.

"Your phone broken? You forget your way to where Mr. Jenkins is staying?" His footsteps were heavy as he climbed the steps. The porch boards creaked under his weight.

"It's late," I said.

"Tell me something I don't know." He came closer in a cloud of aftershave and stale cigarette smoke. "Like the reason why you didn't tell us about this punk who now has an all-points on his ass. Every trooper in the state is looking for him. How is Mr. Jenkins supposed to get to him first? Tell me why you didn't share his name when we were all together at that ranch full of spoiled brats spending their trust funds on a man who walks around with ice cream in his beard. Come on. I want to understand."

"Mr. Jenkins doesn't need a call from me. I'm sure the governor's man Travers is doing a fine job keeping him in the know."

The chauffeur stepped closer. "I told you Mr. Jenkins pays when people do what he asks. What he doesn't pay for is a smart mouth."

He kicked at my chair's back leg, but I saw the move coming before he thought of it and was already springing to my feet by the time his shoe connected.

"I'm going to let that go out of respect of the poor girl whose body I found today. Tell Mr. Jenkins I have nothing to say but condolences for his loss."

The chauffeur drew a black automatic. "We'll see how smart you are when I shoot your ear off. Left or right, you decide."

"Do you think your gun scares me? I've faced shoulder-fired grenade launchers made from hollowed bamboo."

"Left or right?"

"I'm afraid of a lot of things. Like how good heroin feels. Like a woman at my door wanting to know why I let her husband die or a Vietnamese kid asking if I killed his daddy. The scariest of all, what really makes me afraid?"

"I don't care. Left or right. Choose."

"Looking in the mirror and knowing what happens if I lose control."

The chauffeur's nostrils flared. He moved the gun as if pointing to something on a chalkboard. "I'm going with the left."

"Have you ever been shot?"

His upper lip tightened.

"That's what I thought."

He hesitated as he tried to think up a lie. I backhanded his gun wrist with my left and straight-armed him in the throat with my right while stomping on his foot. It was how I'd been trained, how I'd done it in-country. He instinctively grabbed for his throat to keep from choking on his Adam's apple. It made wrenching the gun away easy. I turned it on him.

"Now, I am afraid," I said. "I'm afraid I can't stop myself."

He staggered backward, his eyes bulging, his fingers ripping at his collar as he struggled for air.

"Go," I said. "Drive away. But next time I see you following me like you've been doing, I won't try to stop."

They taught me how to disassemble and assemble an M16 blindfolded. I could do it in thirty-four seconds. I had the chauffeur's automatic apart and the pieces hurled into the front yard in six.

The adrenalin pulsed through me with the power of a flash flood. I went to the sink and drank glass after glass of water, hoping it would wash out what was as poisonous as goosefoot. The chambers of my heart were making a racket. My willpower was running in full retreat. I thought of firing up the Triumph and chasing after it, to push the bike past the redline and speed across the desert into the light of the dark black night.

I sat on the edge of my bed, unbuckled my belt, and cinched it around my bicep. The veins in the crook of my arm swelled immediately as I made a fist. The dull scars of old needle tracks turned from the color of old liver to bright purple. I told myself I had a vein full of smack and fell backward as the remembered rush of pleasure quickly overtook the adrenaline. A sense of peace with the world enveloped me. My eyes closed, my heart slowed, my breathing became the sound of gentle waves lapping on a white sand beach. The mattress opened the same as a trapdoor, and I fell through and went down and down and down.

～

I CAME to lying on a bed of soft grass. Wispy clouds the color of dove breasts floated across the blue sky. A breeze sent the tall, green blades whistling, and so I listened to their song. I didn't know how long I'd been lying there, but my thigh burned from a cramp, so I reached down to rub it. My fingers came away wet and sticky with blood. My blood.

And then the beat of my heart amplified and the whistling was not made by the wind, but by rounds fired by machine guns swishing through the tall grass like a scythe calling "hush" with each deadly slice.

I rolled to my belly. "LT," I whispered. "LT, where are you?"

A groan answered above the din of automatic weapons. I crawled to it. Corporal Rodriguez was clutching a small bible his mother had given him. It was open, but the pages were splattered with blood.

"I'm shot to shit, Sarge," he moaned. "It's God's punishment for what we did."

"Hold on," I said. "We'll get out of here."

He coughed and a gout of dark blood pelted the pages and he died. I crawled down the column. Two privates were dead, another was dying. "Where's LT?" I asked him. "Where's the DJ?" I asked, using the universal nickname for a radio man. He could not answer, so I kept crawling.

Maybe Rodriguez was right. Maybe the ambush was the work of God, retribution for the colonel's "special order" for the village he'd ordered us to hit. We rode in on helicopters the way 1st Cavalry soldiers used to on horseback. The LZ was hot coming in, and we took fire immediately. A Cobra provided cover as we scrambled out of the Huey and fanned out.

Our target was two klicks away because we wanted surprise on our side. But it was us who got surprised when we marched in, surprised by the colonel. He must have read reluctance in my LT's eyes when he explained that special order meant no prisoners because he had ordered another squad to launch a raid from the other side of the village without telling us.

Their LZ was closer. By the time we reached the objective, half the village was in flames. Teams of two were going from hooch to hooch, shooting through walls made of dried palm leaves and throwing torches on thatched roofs. We hurled a color smoke bomb to show we were friendlies before rushing in.

"What the fuck?" my LT yelled at his counterpart. "This is our mission! And there are women and children inside!"

"Was yours," the other LT drawled. "First come, first served. And the colonel was clear. Special order."

A deadly standoff was brewing. The other LT was flanked by his noncoms who clutched their M16s against their chests. My LT glanced at me. I'd been in-country a lot longer, and he'd never let officer's school or ego blind him.

I approached the other sergeant. "Stand down," I said.

"Fuck you," he said.

"Stand down or I'll cap your LT."

"You'll what?" his LT said incredulously.

I jammed the barrel of my M16 into the sergeant's chest when he looked at his LT for orders. "You're closer," I said.

Every man in my squad instantly pointed his gun at the other side before they could raise theirs.

The other LT fumed. "Wait til the colonel sees my report."

"Wait til the battalion commander sees mine," my LT countered.

THEIR EXCHANGE WAS CUT off by a couple of single rounds fired at us from the jungle. They were poorly aimed, and from the sound of them, shot from an ancient hunting rifle by an old rice farmer trying to protect his home. But then a bomb went off. Chunks of burning thatch and shrapnel hurled toward us. The standoff buckled as both squads wheeled around and responded instinctively. We didn't quit firing until the village was cinders. It was only after the shooting stopped that we discovered the explosion was caused by a metal vat filled with rendered water buffalo fat inside a burning hooch. On the way back to the LZ, my squad marched straight into perdition.

I kept crawling as the withering cross fire continued to rake our column and finally reached my LT. Despite a sucking chest wound, he was trying to call in our position and request air cover. The DJ was dead. So was the radio.

I shoved a wad of packing into his chest, hit him with a morphine syrette, and grabbed his wrist. I crawled back the way I'd come, ignoring that I'd been hit too, past the dead privates, past Corporal Rodriguez and his splattered bible, past any beliefs I once had that the war was just and my actions pure.

The black bird was screeching at me. It wouldn't shut up. The noise was piercing, a siren, a wail. Louder and louder it grew as if the bird was now a huge flock. My ears rang. I tried to cover my head from the din, but my arm was a concrete block. I yanked it hard, so hard the pain woke me up.

My arm below the belt was pale blue, my fingers numb. I unbuckled myself and threw open the front door to see a convoy of Oregon State Police cars speeding past with their lights flashing and sirens blaring. They were headed to Burns.

29

T he governor was flying in for a press conference. Richard Travers had gone to the airport to meet him. Sheriff Burton was busy preparing a statement. The coroner was going over his notes from the quickie examination he'd made. A pair of state troopers were in the kitchen drinking coffee and admiring the snapshots of the sheriff's deputies dressed in hunting gear kneeling next to their trophies. Orville Nelson and Deputy Warbler were in the file room the FBI-hopeful used as his office. I'd chased the convoy on my motorcycle and found them there.

Pudge took off his hat and ran his meaty palm across the top of his head. "Sometimes things have a way of sorting themselves out," he said. "Lord knows this doesn't answer all the questions. That's the hard part you got to swallow along with the good part."

"I don't buy it," I said. "Tell it to me again."

"The story's not gonna change," he said. "OSP's been using airplanes to monitor speeding truckers on the highways. The governor ordered one to fly over the Alvord Desert. The pilot spotted a man lying way out in the middle of the flats. He set his plane down and got out to take a looksee. It was Danny Gallagher or Damian or whatever you want to call him. He'd slit his wrists with a kitchen knife he took from Crossed Bars."

"And the note he left?"

"Like I told you the first time. He said he was sorry for all the lives he took, that he couldn't live with the guilt anymore, that he'd fallen off the true path and was lost for good, that he couldn't forgive himself."

"And it was in his handwriting."

"Whose else would it be? He was all alone out in the middle of all that that big empty nowhere. One set of footprints going in, none coming out."

My initial thought that Aubrey Jenkins and the chauffeur had tracked him down evaporated. It wouldn't have made any sense anyway. Jenkins had told me the whole point of wanting to get Kathy's killer alone was to let everyone know he was not weak, not defenseless. He wouldn't have made it look like a suicide.

"Damian was talking about Vietnam, not the murdered girls," I said. "He's been trying to get his head straight about the war ever since Khe Sanh. It's why he joined the ashram. He wanted to leave his old self behind."

Pudge sighed. "There's too much that stacks up against him. The bodies were all killed since he started living at Crossed Bars. Damian Gallagher. Ah, hell, there I go again. Danny Gallagher. Anyway, according to Brother Mike and Sister Star, one of his jobs was to keep the tanks in Vasudeva's fleet topped off. The swami doesn't like them even a quarter empty. Driving those cars to the gas station is opportunity. Damian picked up his victims hitchhiking either to or from the ashram."

I remembered him driving Sister Star in the Silver Cloud when they came to the lineman's shack to ask for my help with the cougar.

"But why would he do it?" I said.

"You mean a motive? Take your pick. Crazy. Pervert. Rapist. Psychopath. He was ashamed at being tossed out of the army for being a coward. He was ashamed for letting his little sister drown. Maybe he's been holding a grudge against women since Sharon Spirelli sent him a Dear John. There could be all sorts of reasons."

"It's too convenient and you know it. Sheriff Burton, Governor Lane, the district attorney, they all want this solved and Private First Class Daniel Gallagher, US Marines, just handed it to them."

"I don't deal in convenient. I deal in justice," Pudge snapped.

"But this isn't it," I snapped back. "What about Jesse Harney? Talk about having opportunity and motive. He has a history of being humiliated by a girl in high school. He killed a prized bull. He blames his dad for being 4-F. And then there is means. The leather straps made right there at the Rocking H."

The deputy placed his hat back on, squared it, and jutted his chin. "You're a criminal psychiatrist now?"

"I spent months in a ward talking to shrinks every day and sharing meals with crazies. You're damn right I picked up a thing or two."

"Listen, son. I don't like this a whole bunch either. I wanted to catch the killer myself and get a confession out of him. And I wouldn't have minded one bit if after he told it to me, he pulled a gun and tried to shoot it out. But this is what we got."

"Tell me you don't believe Jesse could be the real killer."

The lawman hesitated. "What I believe and what I can prove are two different things."

~

I DIDN'T STICK AROUND for the press conference. Governor Lane would appear solemn and talk gravely about the victims, but he'd leave little doubt among the citizenry that a rabid killer was no longer on the loose because he'd directed the investigation himself. Richard Travers would make sure Bonnie LaRue quoted his boss word for word and the picture she ran of him was suitable for use as a reelection campaign poster. Sheriff Burton would stumble through his statement while Pudge and the rest of the deputies stood stoically at attention, not even rolling their eyes when he neglected to thank them. The *Burns Herald* would run the story on the front page with a headline in as big a type as would fit.

As I rode home I considered fetching my pickup. It was still at Pudge's. Instead, I sped past No Mountain to the Malheur Refuge and parked in the spot where I'd first seen the Volkswagen bus with the rainbow on the door. I wondered if Barry and Linda had made it to San Francisco without getting busted. I wondered if I had made a mistake not going there too.

The waters of the lake were calm and mirrored the reflections of clouds. The great blue heron was still there, wading among the shallows as it hunted tadpoles and smolts. A trio of ungainly white pelicans glided overhead. A chipping sparrow trilled nearby, the song the same as the whir of a sewing machine.

I thought of Danny Gallagher. I no longer saw him as Damian, but as a fellow soldier thrust into a world few could imagine, a world turned upside down where the lines between courage and fear blur until they become one and can drive a man to fight as well as run away. I'd met a lot of Dannys in Vietnam, met a lot of them at Walter Reed. I knew what it was like to be a Danny. I had been forced to reconcile the savagery both around me and within me and try not to let it destroy me too. Danny hadn't murdered Kathy and Vicky and the girl still to be named. I was sure of it. He was troubled enough by the burden of having been encouraged to kill fellow human beings in war. Killing wasn't something he ever wanted to experience again.

The water started to turn from blue to rose to purple as the sun continued its daily path to drown itself in a sea far beyond Oregon's high desert. I returned to the parking lot, straddled the Triumph, and rode back to No Mountain promising myself that I wouldn't read the morning paper, that I'd go back being a protector of wildlife rather than a hunter of men.

I almost believed myself.

30

The phone rang as soon as I got home. The only person whoever called me was the district supervisor in Portland, but he'd only done so a couple of times since I took the job. It kept ringing as I tracked it down by following the cord from the wall plug to where it disappeared beneath my bunk. I reeled it in.

"You didn't go away mad or anything, did you?" Pudge asked.

"Would it change anything?"

"Not for them. They've closed the book. They all said their piece, and the governor and his tallyman Travers flew off."

I didn't reply and the phone line hummed while Pudge took his time getting around to saying why he really called.

"Listen, what I wanted to ask you is, well... by any chance is Gemma there?"

"What makes you think she'd be here?"

"She told me you two had dinner the other night. Not that it's my business. Gemma's a grown woman and comes and goes as she pleases. The thing is, November says she hasn't been home since she drove off yesterday morning. I only got back a little while ago myself."

"She's not here, Pudge."

I could hear him click the roof of his mouth. "I hoped she might be."

"You sound concerned."

"I'm not fretting about it, only wishing she was around so I could talk to her about what happened with Danny Damian and all. I'm used to her being my ear about work."

"Did you try calling Blaine Harney? It was his herd she was going to see again, wasn't it?"

"No, I didn't call him. Blaine and her, well, that'd be their business. My guess is she's still trying to save those sick cows or sacked out in the back of her Jeep. She does that when she's way out in the county somewhere and too busy or too tired to drive home. I told her to get a shortwave radio, but she put in one of those tape deck machines instead. She says she'd rather listen to music than truck drivers telling each other dirty jokes."

"I have to swing by your place in the morning to pick up my truck," I said. "I'm overdue for a visit to the Sheldon Refuge. If she's not back, I can take a look for her on my way down there."

"Okay, but I'm sure she'll show up sooner or later."

Pudge hung up, but the dial tone wasn't the only worried tone still echoing.

THE NIGHT PASSED about how I expected it would. Long, restless, and filled with bad thoughts about bad people doing bad things. I spent most of it staring at the glow-in-the-dark hands of my field watch, urging them to sweep faster. As soon as dawn broke, I was dressed and making coffee. It felt like months rather than hours since Pudge said this was one of those cases where each day was worse than the one before. There was no reason to believe that was going to change any time soon.

When fists started pounding on my door, I knew he'd been right.

Brother Michael and Sister Star pushed inside as soon I twisted the knob. They both started speaking at once. Gone were the measured voices, the tranquility, the projection of enlightenment and the divine.

"Help us," they cried. "You have to help us."

"What's wrong?"

Sister Star was suddenly rendered mute. She started pulling at her long, dark hair, her face as pale as a death mask.

"It is our shepherdess," Brother Michael said. "She has been taken."

"You mean by the cougar?"

"No, by a man. Tell him, Sister Star. Tell him what you saw."

She let out a low moan and then closed her eyes. "Something woke me, and so I rose and went to temple early. That's when I saw a man running across the field with our shepherdess hanging over his shoulder. I could tell it was her by her hair. It nearly touched the ground."

"Does she have a name?"

"She asks to be only known as a shepherdess."

"Okay, what about the man. Is he someone from the ashram?"

"I couldn't see who it was."

"Sister Star woke me, and I woke everyone else," Brother Michael said. "All are accounted for except the shepherdess. She prefers to sleep in the stable with the baby animals. That is where he found her."

"Was he running toward a vehicle?"

"I don't know," Sister Star said. "I saw him pass our fence line and disappear into the dark."

"Did you call the sheriff's department?"

Brother Michael shook his hairless head. "No. We do not

trust them since they desecrated our ashram with guns and now with their accusation that Damian is a murderer. He may have chosen to leave this world behind to reach another level of consciousness, but Damian did not do what Sheriff Burton said."

"Can you see the shepherdess now?" I asked Sister Star.

She closed her eyes and started making a low, throated noise. It was either a mantra or a moan of pain.

"I can see her. She's still alive." Her eyes blinked open. "Save her. You must save her."

"Go back to the ashram," I said. "Go back and gather everybody together and start praying. Pray hard and don't stop."

I called Pudge. He sounded half-asleep when he answered but woke up quickly when I told him what had happened.

"This time is different than the others," I said. "He had to know he could be seen. It's as if he wants people to know it's him."

The lawman swore. "Sick bastard. He must've heard the news about Danny Damian and didn't want him getting the credit."

"This is no truck driver picking up hitchhikers. It has to be somebody local, somebody who knows there are girls coming and going from Crossed Bars."

"Then it must be Jesse," Pudge said. "As soon as I'm dressed, I'm going straight to the Rocking H."

"You need to call Sheriff Burton and the state police in case he's fled. He could be on the highway right now."

"I'll radio him, but I got to tell you, I'm not sure Bust'em is gonna be in a hurry to help. This is gonna blow up everything he and the governor said."

I reached for my holster. "Then wait for me."

31

Pudge's pickup wasn't parked out front, but he'd left the snowmobile plank leaning against the open tailgate of mine, so I rode the Triumph right into the truck bed and tethered it. November opened the front door before I could knock.

"He went to the Rocking H," she said. "His anger is like a cold rock."

One way or the other we'd end up back in the gullies, either chasing Jesse or looking for the body of the shepherdess.

"I gave Pudge a map," I said. "Maybe it's still in his office."

The Paiute woman followed me. The map was folded on the desk and I spread it out to see if there were any shortcuts. November looked at it too. She leaned forward. Her long braid slipped over her shoulder and swished the paper. She quickly flicked it back over her shoulder and mumbled in her native tongue.

"What did you say?" I asked.

"That's a sacred place."

"Yes, you told me the Paiute don't call it Hart Mountain."

"I mean this place." She pointed at the playa. "It is filled with sorrow."

"I know. It's where we've found three dead girls."

"No, from long ago. *Neme* call it 'The Hand That Holds The Sorrow.' See, this is the palm and those are the five fingers." She traced the playa and the gullies that emptied into it. They extended from the palm left to right, from the pinky to the thumb.

"Why is it called that?"

"The old ones tell the story. They heard it from their old ones. And theirs before them."

I was in a hurry to join up with Pudge, but something made me stay and listen as November told the legend.

There was once a great warrior named *Nana Nadakwinai.* Man Who Jumps. He was the son of a chief and grandson of a chief. He could jump over flames during the fire dance without getting burned. He could jump and pluck a bird out of the sky. He could jump over gullies when chasing antelope. He could jump on the back of his enemy's pony and count coup. He could do all these things, but he needed a son because he couldn't become chief if he didn't have any one to follow him.

Man Who Jumps fell in love with a beautiful maiden. They married and tried to make a baby, but it didn't work. The warrior grew convinced his wife was cursed. After one year and a day, he took her to the middle of the playa and told her she was as barren as it was and killed her. He returned and remarried. But after another year and a day when there was still no baby, he took the new wife to the playa and killed her too. He returned and started again. After he killed his fifth wife, an old medicine woman told him he was the one who was cursed. To break the spell, he would need to return to the playa and give the five women proper burials to free their spirits. Only then would he finally be rid of the curse.

He returned to the playa to bury them in the gullies, but all the *neme*—the fathers and mothers, the brothers and sisters of the women he killed—were waiting there with their bows. He laughed and told them they could not hit him, and he would take a new wife and become their chief. They let fly their arrows. Man Who Jumps leapt high to dodge them. He jumped higher than the birds who fly, higher than the clouds in the sky. He jumped right into the heavens.

"And if you look up into the night sky," November said, "you can see the constellation of five stars *neme* call Great Mother. Those are the wives of Man Who Jumps and the rest of the stars are their children. And on a winter's full moon you can see the shadow of Man Who Jumps, for only that cold, distant place would have him as chief."

A sick feeling washed over me like it did when I finally admitted I'd been wrong about the war. I grabbed the map and ran to my truck. The wheels shot gravel as I jammed it into gear and stomped the gas pedal. The motorcycle in the back groaned as it tested the ties that bound it. I picked up the mike and radioed Pudge.

"Pick up!" I shouted. "Pudge, pick up. Pick up, dammit."

The speaker to the radio clicked and hummed, and finally the deputy's deep voice rose above all the snippets of dissonant voices chattering on the same channel.

"Where the hell are you?" he said. "I got tired of waiting."

"I just left your place. Jesse isn't the killer. I repeat, Jesse's not the killer."

A loud burst of static made me wince before Pudge came back on. "What makes you say that?"

"He hates the Rocking H. He's sick of being Blaine's little brother. He'll move back to the big city as soon as Zachariah dies."

"What's that have to do with anything?"

"November told me a legend, and it all makes sense. The killer wants to be chief but can't because he doesn't have any children and what's the point of being chief of something if you don't have someone to become chief after you."

"That doesn't make any sense at all, son. I'm closing in on the Rocking H. Where are you?"

"I'm driving a hundred miles an hour. Listen. Our killer is killing these girls because he doesn't have a wife or kids and all that's left for him is some ranch in the sky. Or at least that's what he's convinced himself. It's not Jesse."

"Are you saying it's Blaine? He's shooting blanks and Gemma left him, and so he went on a raping and killing spree?"

I swerved around a pothole. The front wheel of the Triumph banged against the rear of the cab and nearly knocked the Winchester out of the gun rack.

"It's not Blaine either."

"Then who the hell are you talking about?"

"Joe Moon. His whole life is his ranch, but he's losing it. And Pudge? The legend is about a would-be chief who killed five wives. There are five gullies at the playa. The gullies are the fingers. He killed Vicky Wells and put her in the pinky, Kathy Jenkins in the ring finger, and the third girl in the middle. He's got two gullies left he needs to fill to get his ranch. The shepherdess makes one." I took a deep breath. "And Gemma makes two."

The radio went silent. Even the static cleared. I tore through No Mountain on my race south. Pudge came back on.

"I'm not gonna let that happen," he said, his voice frighteningly calm.

"I'm driving to Joe Moon's right now to check, but my guess is he's already on his way to the gullies. He knows he's running out of time, and so he probably has both women. I'll come at the playa from the east and you come from the west. We'll block all his moves and pin him in the open. He'll have nowhere to go."

"Like chess," the deputy said. "And this is one game I'm not gonna lose."

FOR MONTHS, we'd targeted sections of the Ho Chi Minh trail. We intercepted bicycles loaded with Chinese carbines, old women with baskets filled with North Korean machine guns strapped to their backs, and a boy no older than eight who'd been cradling a Soviet rocket for two hundred miles. We blew up footbridges and blocked the trail with downed trees only to find them rebuilt and cleared within a few days. We knew we were stopping a trickle when we caught a cart pulled by a water buffalo tended by two Buddhist monks. It was piled with straw that covered dozens of crates of new AK-47s and hundreds of boxes of ammo. I was sure the bales of hay stacked in the back of Joe Moon's pickup had a hollowed-out spot to conceal the girls he'd picked up hitchhiking as he drove them to their deaths.

My adrenaline started to course as I turned off the blacktop and followed the road that turned from gravel to dirt that would lead me to the rusty metal sign with a crescent moon cut from the center and on to Joe Moon's windblown ranch. I slowed as I approached a dip caused by a partially collapsed culvert that ran beneath the road. As I bumped over it, I caught movement out of the corner of my eye. I slammed on the brakes and drew the .357.

Gemma crawled out of the culvert and stumbled toward me. I was out of the cab with one arm around her and turning us in a circle as I swept my gun in all directions by the time she could say a word.

"It was Joe Moon," she gasped.

I helped her into the front seat and handed her my canteen.

She gulped desperately. Rope burns reddened her wrists. Her lips were cracked, her face smudged, and a bruise the size of fist purpled her cheek. The knees of her jeans were torn.

"What happened?"

Gemma wiped her mouth with the back of her hand. "I got a flat and was fixing it, and he stopped to help. He hit me from behind, and when I came to, I was tied up in the root cellar beneath his house." She shuddered.

"It's okay. You don't have to say anything more. You're safe now."

"No, I want to tell you. I need to tell you. He has another girl. We have to help her." She shuddered again.

"You saw her?"

"I heard her after I escaped. He bound my wrists with leather straps. I worked and worked all night to loosen them. I can make my hand get really small after all the times I've needed to reach inside a cow and feel for the calf. I was finally able to pull my hand through and untie myself."

"Where was Joe Moon?"

"Upstairs most of the time. I could hear him walking around and talking to himself. But then he left and drove away. I assumed he was going to get my Jeep and hide it." She swallowed more water.

"How did you get out of the cellar?"

"I pounded on the door. I hit it with my shoulder. The wood was so dry it splintered. It was still dark outside, and so I ran. At first, I ran down the road, but then I was afraid he'd come back and see me, so I ran alongside it. And then he did come back. I could see his headlights coming. That's when I saw the culvert and hid inside."

Gemma drank again. "As he drove over me, I heard a woman's voice pleading with him to let her go. I knew he was taking her to his ranch, and he'd discover I was gone. I'd finally worked up the nerve to make a run for it when he came back. He honked his horn and yelled out the window that I was cursed. And then he drove away again. I thought he might be trying to trick me, so I stayed put until I heard another truck drive over. Thank God it was you."

Her face twisted as she looked at me. "He's crazy, isn't he? I mean, really crazy."

"He thinks he's Man Who Jumps. The girl he took is from the ashram. They saw him do it. Your dad and I are going after them."

"Does Pudge know Joe Moon took me?"

"We only figured it out a little bit ago. Let's get him on the radio."

Pudge didn't say anything as Gemma told him how she got away. Finally, in the same eerily calm voice, he said, "Did he force himself on you?"

"No. He said he was going to take me somewhere to become his wife. He was going to rape me there and kill me like the others, wasn't he?"

Pudge didn't answer. Gemma looked at me. I nodded.

"Then why are we sitting here?" she said angrily. "That's what he's going to do to the other girl. Come on. Let's go."

I put the truck in gear and pointed it toward the playa. Gemma was still holding the radio mike.

"Tell your dad we're on our way," I said. "And tell him you'll be driving."

"I can hear you," the deputy said. "Where the hell are you gonna be?"

"I'll be on my bike. I can ride up over the hills and get in front of him. If we're too late and he gets into the gullies, I'll be able to get the drop on him."

"There's five. Which of the two do you think he'll choose?"

"The one that points to the moon."

32

The Triumph was designed as a road bike, but as I took off with the rifle slung across my back and the pistol on my hip, I was counting on its engineers not to have forgotten that the English pioneered motocross forty years before. I weaved between boulders and thorny bushes, plunged down a gulch and roared up the other side. I jumped trenches and raced along the razor edge of a deep ravine. Rocks pinged off the underside of the fenders, and grit sandblasted my face and shins. The clutch screamed in protest at my assault on the steep backside of the corrugated hills. The engine wheezed from choking on filthy air and grimy oil as I crested the summit.

The playa fanned out below. Pudge's truck was angling in from the west side and mine sped in from the east. I knew father and daughter were coordinating their arrival over the radio.

Something shimmered from a stand of twisted juniper trees on the north side. I put the Winchester's scope on it. Sun was reflecting off the windshield of an old beat-up pickup parked in a wide spot on a seldom used track near a water hole that quenched the thirst of bobcats. The oil stain I'd seen next to the pond wasn't the only thing I failed to match to Joe Moon when I helped him jump start his leaky truck. The lumpy pile of road apples wasn't a horse length from the water hole. It was the length of a swaybacked mule.

The shoeless beast was now plodding trackless toward the mouth of the index finger gully. It had no saddle, only a halter fitted with reins. Joe Moon's gray flat brim cowboy hat with a rounded crown and an eagle feather stuck in the band shaded him as he rode. He held the reins loosely in his hands, his arms around the shepherdess's waist. I zeroed the scope on him but couldn't risk a shot because of her. He wore a loose, untucked shirt that could easily conceal a handgun tucked in his waistband. I had to assume it did. I didn't have to guess about the leather scabbard strapped to his thigh. It was long enough to hold one of the knives he used for butchering the ashram's livestock.

Pudge must have been doing some calculations of his own when he saw the mule and rider nearing the gully. He rolled the dice and hit the lights and siren. Gemma sped up too. Joe Moon glanced over his shoulder at the vectoring pickup trucks, but instead of reining to a stop, he kicked the mule with his heels and disappeared into the gully. I dropped the motorcycle and scrambled down the hill. It was steep going and the ground cover loose. I slipped on a patch of scree and fell. That triggered a slide that swept me toward the edge of the gully and a five-story drop to a boulder field below.

I dug in my bootheels, jammed the rifle butt down, and came to a stop on the lip. I got up and ran along the edge looking for a place that would give me the high ground and put Joe Moon back in my sights. A bottleneck lay up ahead. The wide spot on my side would give the killer little cover when he emerged from the narrows. I waited for him with the sun at my back.

The shepherdess was the first to come through. A *manello*

was buckled around her neck. Her hands were bound at the wrist by *tientos*. Her ashram robe had been hacked off above the knees. She was as barefoot as she was when I last saw her at the ashram. Joe Moon emerged right behind her. He'd tied a short rope to the *manello* and held it like a dog leash. His face was expressionless, his gait unhurried.

I shouldered the Winchester. "Don't move," I called down. "It's over. Let her go."

Joe Moon jerked the leash to bring the shepherdess closer. He bent at the knees to keep his head behind hers.

"Who's there?" he said.

"Nick Drake."

"The ranger, yeah?"

"Drop the rope. Let her walk toward me."

He pinpointed the direction of my voice. His wide hat blocked the glare that was my only shield.

"She's my wife," he said.

"Let her go."

Sunlight flashed off the blade of the butcher knife he pulled from the scabbard and held at her throat.

"You don't belong here. This place is sacred."

"There will be no sorrow in the hand today," I said.

He stiffened at that, but his surprise was short-lived. "That is for me to decide. Not you."

"Your position is hopeless. Let her go."

Joe Moon must've heard Pudge approaching because he maneuvered the girl sideways, so he'd have his back to the gully wall opposite me. The lawman squeezed through the bottleneck. His gun was drawn.

"You know who I am. You know what I'll do," Pudge said. "Now hand over the girl."

"Your bullets can't hit me," Joe Moon said. "No one's can."

The gully darkened from a passing shadow, and like thunder

follows lightning, noise soon ripped the air. It wasn't the screech of the black bird, but a familiar *thwap-thwap-thwap* of a chopper. Aubrey Jenkins and the chauffeur had never left Burns. They'd been monitoring the shortwave.

The helicopter banked right over me. The chauffeur was pointing his automatic out the open side of the bubble cockpit. The rotor's wash sent a blackening curtain of sand and grit down into the gully. Joe Moon shoved the girl toward Pudge. When the lawman made a grab for her, the killer followed right behind and plunged the butcher knife into his belly. Then Joe Moon wrested the .45 away and started shooting at me. The chauffeur reacted by shooting blindly into the gully.

My line of sight was clouded by flying grit kicked up by the circling chopper's whirling blades. A miss and a ricochet could strike the shepherdess or the slumping deputy. The only thing I could do to stop some of the flying lead was to turn the rifle on the helicopter. Aim, fire, lever a shell, and aim and fire again and again. The first round went wide, the second struck the tail rotor, the third hit the chauffeur. The chopper's engine screamed as oily black smoke belched from the tail. The pilot knew his stricken bird was doomed, and so he steered for the playa in hopes of setting it down on the flats before it crashed.

I didn't wait to see if he made it. I looked down into the gully and could see two people as the dust settled. Joe Moon and the shepherdess were gone, but Gemma had followed her dad through the bottleneck and was now kneeling over him as he lay on his back. She ripped off her shirt and wadded it. Then she grabbed the handle of the knife stuck in Pudge's belly and pulled it straight up and out. She pressed her shirt hard against the wound to stop the bleeding.

I scrambled down. "I have first aid in my truck. I'll go get it."

Gemma jerked her head toward the other edge of the gully. "No, get them. Bust'em is on his way. He radioed us."

Joe Moon had dragged the shepherdess up the side and was pulling her behind him as he ran.

"Are you sure?" I asked.

"I am," Pudge said through clenched teeth. "Gemma's a damn doctor. Now, git."

"In case he doubles back," I said and propped my rifle next to them.

The side of the gully was steep, and I climbed it hand over hand. Once on top I could see Joe Moon. He was following a deer trail, but the barefoot shepherdess was slowing him down. I could catch him as long as there was enough trail before he reached where he was going. It could only be in one place. The fifth gully. The thumb. It was shorter than the other four, but deeper, a lot deeper.

The sun was straight overhead now, and no shadows showed ahead of me as I ran. I ignored the holster flopping against my hip. I ignored the burning in my chest as my lungs sucked in hot air. I ignored the words yelling in my head that I was planning to kill a man again. Two hundred yards. One hundred yards. Fifty yards. I was closing in, but Joe Moon was closing in on the edge of the gully. I couldn't let him reach it.

At thirty yards, I drew the heavy revolver and fired into the air while running. Joe Moon slowed down as he looked over his shoulder. I fired again, this time aiming right over his head. He skidded to a stop at the edge of the gully and turned around with the shepherdess held as a shield. He still had Pudge's .45 and aimed it at me.

We were ten yards apart, but I could see down into the gully and the rocky spires that poked up from the bottom far below. The gun designed to stop grizzlies weighed no less than it ever had, but I held it rock steady on him.

"I know what you're going through," I said. "The letter to the bank I mailed for you? They foreclosed. Your cows need grain and vaccines, but the feed store won't extend you any more credit. The odd jobs you work aren't enough."

"You don't know nothing," he said.

"I know plenty about being on the losing end. I've been on it a long time."

"You got a job, a new truck. What have you ever lost?"

I could've said my squad, my beliefs, my self-respect, but all I said was, "Me."

"I lost more," he said. "The future."

"Killing this girl isn't going to help you get your ranch back or get you a son either. All it will do is make your ancestors ashamed. Your pa, your grandpa, all the others, all the way back to the old woman who was Those Who Live in the Cold."

"How do you know about her?"

"It doesn't matter. What does is what you do now. You can shoot me, you can kill the girl, but it won't bring you a ranch. It'll only bring you shame."

The shepherdess had been standing as if paralyzed, her breathing rapid, her pupils enlarged. I recognized the symptoms, had seen plenty of soldiers in shock after a firefight and villagers after a bombing run. But then she started swaying and began to hum.

Joe Moon took a step back as if moving away from someone contagious. I stepped to the side to give myself an open line of fire. He still held the leash, so I couldn't risk a shot. He'd tumble backward and drag the shepherdess into the gully with him.

The shepherdess's voice started to grow louder, the hum turned into words, her sway became a dance. Her lilting song swirled around the three of us, and as it did, Joe Moon's shoulders began to droop, and his gun hand wavered.

Sirens wailed in the distance. I didn't need to turn around to know that he was watching a half dozen Harney County Sheriff's Department vehicles speeding across the playa, one stopping at a helicopter that had crash-landed in the middle, another veering off to the mouth of the fourth gully, the others heading toward us.

"It's over," I said.

His eyes went from looking at the hand that holds the sorrow back to me. "I will be Joe Moon no more forever," he said. "I am *Nana Nadakwinai*."

And then he pushed the shepherdess toward me and jumped for the moon.

33

The flames of the campfire flickered and so did the stars overhead. Pudge Warbler had called the Alvord Desert the big empty nowhere, but as I sat cross-legged on the dry, cracked ground that resembled jigsaw pieces, I felt maybe I was finally somewhere. Earlier that day, Brother Michael and Sister Star showed up at the lineman's shack to tell me the shepherdess had been discharged from the hospital in Burns and was back tending her baby lambs. They handed me a bundle wrapped in brown paper and told me I would know what to do with it. I assumed it was a thank-you gift and waited until they left to open it.

Inside was a green field jacket and a pair of combat boots. Danny was wearing them the night we hunted the cougar. The regimental emblem had been torn from the jacket's left shoulder, the name patch ripped from above the right breast pocket, but I knew what they'd been: "US Marines, 1st Battalion, 26th Regiment" and "Gallagher, D." I placed the boots near the fire with the green coat folded on top and stuck my Winchester behind. The only thing missing was a helmet to perch on it. Danny may have taken his own life, but as far as I was concerned, he'd fallen in combat as sure as if he'd taken a bullet. He deserved a battlefield tribute.

I blew his name into the flames and told myself the war couldn't go on much longer, that there would be an end to the Dannys, that all wounds would heal, and the world would finally choose to wage peace instead.

Sheriff Burton had ordered his deputies to search the gullies for more victims, but none were found and no more were expected after a search of Joe Moon's house turned up a trio of figurines he'd made from the hair he'd snipped from his three victims. Jesse Harney swore he never knew Sharon Spirelli, and there was no evidence to ever link them together. The student nurse had disappeared without a trace, one of the thousands of females reported as missing persons each year.

I blew her name into the flames along with those of Kathy Jenkins, Vicky Wells, and Joe Moon's third victim. I told myself someday there would be an end to missing persons and the rape and murder of girls and women would end.

I was coming to peace with the spirit bird too. It still came and went, and whether someday it would choose to become a raven or an eagle, or always be both, no longer mattered. What did was what I chose to do. I could stay in No Mountain and work on the wildlife refuges until I reached my goal of one year clean and sober, and then aim for three years and then five and then ten, taking each day one at a time, or I could go back on the needle and die.

I blew my name into the flames and the "Blackbird" song lyrics too. I told myself someday there would be an end to guilt, that forgiveness was always possible, and one day I'd be able to mourn my enemies too.

A pair of headlights stabbed the darkness. The vehicle stopped on the other side of the campfire, and the door opened and closed.

"What are you doing way out here all alone, roasting marsh-mallows?"

"Stargazing," I said.

Gemma Warbler walked around the circle of burning sticks. She looked at Danny's boots and jacket but made no comment as she spread a blanket next to me and sat down.

"How's your father?" I asked.

"Being Pudge. He's bored of bed rest and tired of November cussing him out for getting in the way of Joe Moon's knife. She says he owes her his life."

"How's that?"

"She says it's all the Indian fry bread with powdered sugar she's been feeding him all these years. It gave him an extra couple of inches around the middle to absorb the blade. I told you, people always underestimate Pudge."

"Well, the shepherdess certainly owes her life to November. If she hadn't told me the legend about Man Who Jumps, who knows how much time Pudge and I would've wasted questioning Jesse."

"I suppose that's true for me too," she said.

"Not really. You freed yourself. You got away. What's that word again, formidable?"

Gemma lay back on the blanket and pointed straight up. "Do you know that constellation?"

The flat expanse of the Alvord Desert brought the stars right down to the ground. There were more twinkling lights above me than grains of sand beneath. Five stars making a *W* shined the brightest.

"That's Cassiopeia."

"I see you've been studying your astronomy field guide along with all the ones on plants and animals. Does this mean you're going to stick around?"

"For a little while, at least," I said.

"Cassiopeia is the name white men gave it," she said.

"I know. *Neme* call it Great Mother."

"Do you know what I think the *W* stands for?"

"Women," I said. "Wise and powerful."

She smiled. "And when you see the *W*, what do you think?"

"Why," I said.

"Why am I asking?"

"No, I see it and I think why. Why are there stars up there and people down here. Why is this a desert and why a jungle over there. Why are we fighting over it. Why do people kill each other, kill themselves. Why anything, I suppose." I shrugged. "I ask why, but the stars don't answer."

Gemma patted a spot on the blanket next to her. "Keep asking. You might be surprised."

A NOTE FROM THE AUTHOR

Thank you so much for reading *The Sorrow Hand*. I'd truly appreciate it if you would please leave a review on Amazon. Your feedback not only helps me become a better storyteller, but you help other readers by blazing a trail and leaving markers for them to follow as they search for new stories.

To leave a review, go to *The Sorrow Hand* product page on Amazon, click "customer reviews" next to the stars beneath the title, click the "Write a customer review" button, and share your thoughts with other readers.

To quote John Cheever, "I can't write without a reader. It's precisely like a kiss—you can't do it alone."

Thanks,

Dwight Holing

ACKNOWLEDGMENTS

Writing, like soldiering and sleuthing, takes team work, and the creation of this novel is no exception. I relied heavily on the help of others and I gratefully acknowledge them for their contributions.

Many thanks to Ben Colodzin, PhD, author and mental health warrior, who shared his extensive knowledge and insights gained from 30 years of experience working with combat veterans afflicted by Post Traumatic Stress Disorder (PTSD).

I owe a tremendous debt of gratitude to my reader team who plowed through drafts, provided invaluable feedback, and were unafraid to point out my missteps. Your fingerprints are all over this novel. Thank you, one and all, including Gene Ammerman, Jill Arnold, George Becker, Ron Fox, Gino Cox, Mark DiRienzo, Kevin R. LaRose, Marcia Lilley, Jeffrey Miller, Kenneth Mitchell, Dee Nordaby, Annie Notthoff, John Onoda, Haris Orkin, Rhonda Sarver, and Carol Surine.

Thank you Rick Parchen for your spectacular photograph of the Alvord Desert, and kudos to designer Rob Williams for turning it into such a stunning cover. You are both true artists.

Thank you Janine Savage for your eagle eye and incredible grasp of English grammar and all its peculiarities.

All novels are the product of research, some more than others, especially ones dealing with history. This novel falls into the "more" category. A special shout out to the Northern Paiute Language Project at University of California, Santa Cruz and the Burns Paiute Tribe of the Burns Paiute Indian Colony of Oregon, a federally recognized tribe of Northern Paiute in Harney County, Oregon. Any mistakes, regrettably, are my own.

And, finally, to my parents. Thank you for making a home for us along the shore of Klamath Lake, Oregon, the perfect base for discovering the natural wonders of the great outdoors.

GET A FREE BOOK

Dwight Holing's genre-spanning work includes novels, short fiction, and nonfiction. His mystery and suspense thriller series include The Nick Drake Novels and The Jack McCoul Capers. The stories in his collections of literary short fiction have won awards, including the Arts & Letters Prize for Fiction. He has written and edited numerous nonfiction books on nature travel and conservation. He is married to a kick-ass environmental advocate; they have a daughter and son, and two dogs who'd rather swim than walk.

Sign up for his newsletter to get a free book and for information about the next Nick Drake Novel and news about crime fiction and special deals.

Visit **dwightholing.com/free-book**. You can unsubscribe at any time.

ALSO BY DWIGHT HOLING

The Nick Drake Novels

The Sorrow Hand (Book 1)

The Pity Heart (Book 2)

The Jack McCoul Capers

A Boatload (Book 1)

Bad Karma (Book 2)

Baby Blue (Book 3)

Shake City (Book 4)

Short Story Collections

California Works

Over Our Heads Under Our Feet

Made in the USA
San Bernardino, CA
28 February 2019